# RIVERMONT ROYALS: BECKETT

# REIGN

# REIGN

ELIZABETH STEVENS WRITING AS

## E.J. KNOX

Kinky Siren
an imprint of Sleeping Dragon Books

Reign
by E.J. Knox

Paperback ISBN: 978- 1925928273
Digital ISBN: 978- 1925928266

Cover art by: Izzie Duffield

*To a new year,*
*May you not continue in the way you started.*
*Please. My immune system couldn't take it.*

# CONTENTS

# AUTHOR'S NOTE

This is a dark, angsty, contemporary high school bully/enemies-to-lovers romance with enough steam to melt your screen. Do not engage in public consumption unless your poker face is impenetrable.

Do not read if you don't like bossy alpha males claiming what's theirs, a nerdy but feisty heroine determined to keep what independence she can, unlikely friendships, snarky love-to-hate-them side characters, or bad boys with secret hearts of gold.

This story is set in a fictional boarding school in an unspecified South Australian location. Please be aware that I've taken some creative liberties in terms of combining some aspects of Aussie schooling with how I wanted the school to work for plotting purposes. I have also taken slight liberties with the geographical settings because I wanted some snow in April in South Australia.

This book is written using Australian English. This will affect the spelling, grammar and syntax you may be used to. It might come across as typos, awkward sentences, poor grammar, or missed/wrong words. In the majority of cases (I won't claim it's infallible, despite all best efforts), this is intentional and just an Aussie way of speaking (it took my US beta readers a bit to get used to). I can't say 'the' Aussie way, since we seem to differ even within the same state. Just think of us as a weird mix of British and US vernacular and colloquialisms, but with our own randomness thrown in. I still hope you enjoy it, though!

# RIVERMONT ACADEMY HEIRARCHY

## THE ROYALS

### Inner Sanctum

Beckett Maxwell (the King/Money)
Preston Worthington-Smythe (the Brains)
Jaeger Richards (the Weapon – King's left-hand/assassin)
Rowan Finch[-Michaels] (the Cleaner)

### Second Generation

Fox Maddox (the Heir)
Gunner Kennedy (the Fists – Heir's left-hand/assassin)
Regina Maxwell (the Princess)
Phoenix Maddox (the Handmaid – princess' right-hand)

## COURTERS

Sienna Jason (the Duchess)
Clint Baker (Fox's cleaner)
Alexander Newman-Wright (Fox's brains)
Locksley Brownlow (Fox's crony)
Joel Arnold – called Forgmartin by Jaeger
Tyler Rogers – called Rockefeller by Jaeger

# HAREM

Isabella Ramirez (thinks she'll end up with Beckett)
Mariana Barrett (Isabella's right-hand)
Gwen Cameron

# EVERYONE ELSE

Jude Beahan (the Joker)
Sadie Whelan (the Revenge)
Dylan Gray (the Dork)

# THE QUINTET

Abby Rhodes (the Endgame)
Sam Kaplan (the Master)
Eden Quin (the Un-Queen)
Hunter Gibson
Bianca [Finch-]Michaels (the Other)

# CHAPTER ONE

One arm. Then the other. Repeat. Remember to breathe.

As my body sheared through the water, I felt all the familiar anxiety start to drain away. My heart rate slowed. My brain settled. The restless energy in my limbs found a purpose.

The pool was my safe place. Where I could come and drown out the rest of the world, like some dollar store Percy Jackson. And the start of the school year needed a lot of drowning out, or I risked being the one drowned.

My hand hit the wall and I floated to a stop, revelling in the free feeling being in water always gave me.

"You actually trying out for the team again this year, Harlequin?" I heard the condescendingly humoured voice, and I froze.

My hand gripped the side of the pool to stop me sinking while I tried to remember how to stay buoyant.

"No. That would be too humiliating," he said. "Even for someone with as much practise as you."

As much as sinking to the bottom of the pool would have been a much more pleasant experience, I forced myself to tread water and look up at the loyal left-hand of Rivermont Academy's king. And it was a *long* way up to look.

Jaeger Richards stood at something like six foot and a million, he was built – for nefarious purposes, no doubt – and his platinum silver hair was always impeccably coiffed. He towered above me in his red, grey and black Rivermont tracksuit, white sneakers and a duffel bag slung over one shoulder.

We were the only two people in the pool, the rest of the large room was empty. His words echoed on the open tile and glass, making it sound like he was everywhere. He may as well have been.

"I'm not trying out," I told him, my voice embarrassingly small.

"What was that, Quinjet?" he asked, cocking his head to the side.

I cleared my throat, feeling my cheeks heat. "I said I'm not trying out," I told him more clearly.

He nodded. "Good. I'm not used to *saving* lives." He dropped to a crouch and looked down at me. "And I'm not sure you're worth the breath it took the first time."

Oh, Jaeger did so love reminding me of that one time, three years previously, when he'd 'saved' my life. I'd felt so much pressure to succeed but concurrently wanted to bomb out so badly that I'd given myself a cramp mid-lap. Jaeger had pulled me out of the pool and given me mouth to mouth. While I was still most definitely breathing. Had he not sported an unexplained shiner to his right eye later that day, I might have considered giving him one myself.

It was made all the worse because, had he not acted so quickly that day, I may well have actually needed the CPR. There was nothing worse than feeling like you owed your life to a Royal.

So, I had nothing to say to that. It was well known where my place was on the hierarchy compared to his. He and his fellows lorded it at the top, while I kept my nose down at the bottom. I'd learned, over the last four years, that it was better not to engage them. They usually got bored and went to torment someone who'd give them the response they were looking for.

But, Jaeger didn't move on. He straightened but kept right on standing there. Like he knew I'd have to get out of the pool in front of him now if I didn't want to do it in front of everyone who would be arriving soon for the swim team tryouts.

I sucked in a breath and hauled myself out of the pool. Dreading what he was going to say about my two-piece bikini, I didn't look at him. So, I almost missed when he threw my towel at me.

"Cover that shit up," he growled.

I did, but not because he told me to. I had half a mind to tell him that 'that shit' was perfectly acceptable, thank you very much, when there was a commotion at the main doors. Once again, my bravery would have to wait. The ill-timed interruption most likely saving my bacon from a hiding courtesy of Jaeger Richards.

"Leave the water to the real swimmers, Mannequin," Jaeger snarled.

Without looking back, I hurried to the girls' locker room as fast as the water dripping down my legs would allow.

Once in there, I nearly careened into a new body.

"Oh, crap," she laughed, self-consciously. "Sorry."

I shook my head. "No. You're fine. My bad."

I looked up into warm brown eyes and watched as she wrangled her long brown hair into a swimming cap.

"I'm Abby," she said.

I smiled. "Eden."

"Nice to meet you." She looked at my bathers and towel combo. "Are you on the team?"

The question alone proved just how new she was to Rivermont's infamous halls. The accent suggested a recent overseas import.

I practically snorted. "No. Uh, no. I'm barely even a recreational swimmer."

She looked at me like she thought I was a little odd but hoped it was in an endearing way. I gave her a smile that I hoped reassured her it was, in fact, in an enduring way.

"Cool. I'll – uh – let you get on with…it, then," she said.

"Cool." I nodded. "Yep."

She grabbed a towel and headed for the pool.

"Good luck," I called.

She threw me a smile over her shoulder. "Thanks. I'll see you around, I guess."

The locker room was full of other students getting changed into bathers for the tryouts. But none of them thought it odd that I was changing out of mine.

By the time I headed back out to the pool, the bleachers were filling up and there were bunches of kids in their bathers hanging around. Some were warming up in the pool, others were talking with their friends or sitting and mentally preparing.

I found the curly mop of hair that belonged to my best friend.

But between him and me, Jaeger was standing in the middle of the current swim team.

He'd stripped down to his budgie smugglers. Not that there was much room in them for smuggling anything the way he filled them out so…impressively.

There was nothing for it but to walk by him and hope he ignored me as heavily as I wanted to ignore him. I almost managed it, too. I thought I was clear free when I heard someone mention the coach and Jaeger getting on the team.

Here, Jaeger threw me a knowing smirk, just to check I was listening. I rolled my eyes, told myself I wasn't blushing, and looked away quickly.

"You mean I *won't* have to sleep with the coach for my place on the team this year?" Jaeger asked, his eyes still on me, which I knew as mine were still surreptitiously on him.

"Because that would stop you," came the posh drawl of Preston, heralding *Their* arrival.

The rest of the inner sanctum of the Royals of Rivermont Academy.

Not literal royals, as far as anyone knew, but they may as well have been given the way they ruled the school. It was an inherited admission. One didn't just become a Royal by being popular. The only way to do it was by birth. Or possibly marriage. Although, I didn't see any of the current court marrying for anything less than financial gain.

"It's not lack of necessity that stops him," came His harder voice – the voice of their king – and I blushed hotter.

"No," Jaeger agreed. "I bow to my liege," he said cryptically.

Then he sniggered and bumped shoulders with Rowan, another of the inner sanctum. Rowan returned Jaeger's snigger with a glare.

Rowan kept his hair short – almost shaved – and his temper shorter. He was constantly sporting bruises somewhere on his body and numerous girls had offered to go looking to find the most recent. He wore dark jeans and a grey wife-beater tank that showed off the tattoo on his left shoulder. His look was completed with sneakers, and a perpetual scowl on his face.

At this point, the fact I was still close enough to hear their conversation was worrisome. So, I determined to hurry away. Except my hurrying away coincided with the Royals heading for their own seats. So, I crashed into the Royal princess and her right-hand.

Regina Maxwell was literal perfection. From her luscious thick curly brown hair to her pristine manicure and designer clothes, she looked like she'd stepped out of some luxurious magazine I was too ignorant to even know about. She towered over me, even as she stood in front of me in nothing but the Rivermont issue racerback one-piece.

Her right-hand was giving me equal the stink eye.

Phoenix Maddox was an enigma and no mistake. Her hair was dyed blue, making her grey eyes dazzle. Had some pleb like me attempted to come to school with blue hair, I'd have detention with a side of 'be lucky you're not expelled'. But Phoenix Maddox could do whatever she damn well pleased and never be expelled. And, even being in the year below me, she'd tried pretty much everything at that point.

"Move along, then," Regina said, waving her hand in a definite dismissive motion.

Flabbergasted and with my tongue tripping over itself in a vain attempt to get the witty quips in my head to come out coherently, I nodded and hurried off for the safety of Sam's side.

Sam grinned when he saw me. His mop of brown curls bounced and he pushed his glasses up. As usual for the end of January, he was in knee-length shorts and a geeky t-shirt, with high-top Chucks. We'd bonded on our first day in Year Eight over a love of all things Rick Riordan. Ever since, he'd been my best friend.

He cocked an eyebrow as I got closer. "Why is your hair wet?"

I pointed at the pool. "There's this magical stuff called water."

Sam smirked at me. "You funny. Good swim?"

I nodded. "Until the left-hand of *God* got here early."

Sam looked over to where Jaeger was flexing his muscles for the other Royals.

"Has he got even more ink?" Sam asked, cocking his head to the side like that gave him a better vantage point.

"Isn't that what they do?" I replied loftily, like I had any idea.

But there did seem to maybe be a little less bare skin on Jaeger's body than there had been at the end of the previous year. There was definitely something different about his mostly-naked body, and that was the only thing I could come up with.

Our heads swivelled to the middle section of the bleachers, not that far below us, where the younger Royals and courters were saving the best seats in the house for the inner sanctum. Between the heads of various other students, we saw them. Oblivious to those around them unless forced to interact, they glided through life on the assumption that the rest of us cared they thought they were above us all. The only reason they were at the pool was in support of Jaeger and, to a much lesser extent, Regina as the king's sister.

It was the first day of term one but, with the Australia Day holiday the next day, it was an admin day. And admin day meant sports' tryouts. And sports' tryouts meant swimming tryouts, the only tryouts I was remotely vaguely interested in. Which made it unfortunate that sport was compulsory at Rivermont Academy and the only team I could successfully tryout for was the Softball team; just because I was good at whacking balls did not mean I enjoyed it.

It was then I realised there was no one on the other side of Sam.

"Where's Hunter?"

Sam flicked a curl out of his eye. "Oh, didn't he tell you?"

I shrugged. "I guess not. Tell me what?"

"He's trying out for the team this year."

"I didn't know he swam," I said, surprised.

Sam shrugged now. "Me either."

"Well, if he gets on the team, we all know what he did to get there," was heard from below.

I looked down the bleachers to see Gunner standing there with Fox, both of them looking our way. Two more Royals. In our year. Neither inner sanctum.

The Royals had two levels; the four in the inner sanctum were all in Year 12, and what we plebs liked to call the second generation were…well, younger. The second gen were in our year – Year 11 – and the year below. They were largely carbon copies of the inner sanctum and of less interest to anyone with eyes.

Gunner and Fox were as easy on the eyes as any Royal, but there was something ever so much…less about them. Compared to others that is.

Gunner was constantly living in the shadow of his cousin Jaeger. I often imagined that if Jaeger hadn't dyed his hair that platinum silver since before I'd met him, that it'd be the same dark brown as Gunner's.

"Or, should we say *who* he had to do to get there?" Fox asked, cocking an eyebrow at me.

He was a ball of compressed, blond anger. The king's unofficial heir, he was determined to be the next king of Rivermont Academy as soon as possible, even if he had to kill the current king to do it.

"If you have to explain it, you've failed," came that posh drawl again. The one that unmistakably belonged to Preston, third inner sanctum member. First Gen. Right hand of the king.

If they'd been a crew in one of those bank heist films, Preston Worthington-Smythe would be the brains. He was polished and refined, always wearing a long-sleeve button up and a vest, no matter the weather. In winter, he wore an overcoat around his shoulders without bothering with the sleeves, and a fedora was mandatory when not inside. He acted like everyone was beneath him, probably because they were. I didn't know what his family did, but they had a wing of the main school building named after them.

"Good luck, Jaeger!" was called from overlapping courters and current favoured members of the Harem, surrounding the Royals like yuppie groupies.

The coach's whistle blew. The remaining spectators found their seats and those trying out for the team hovered at the end of the pool. While the coach talked to the swimmers, I looked for Hunter.

I found him waving enthusiastically at me and Sam.

"Oh, Eden," I heard a false falsetto from below us "Pay attention to me, Eden. Watch me make a fool of myself for you, Eden."

Fox and Gunner chuckled as though they were hilarious.

"Ignore them," Sam whispered to me.

"Speak for yourself," I teased him.

He smirked, but just pushed his glasses up his nose and pretended he wasn't sneaking looks at the Royals.

Like anyone with eyes, he enjoyed looking at them. They were nice to look at. When they weren't sneering at everything and everyone around them. Which was never.

The first of the swimmers started their tryout, and I tried blocking out the Royals. But blocking out the Royals was like trying to block out the sun. Much like the sun that they all revolved around; their king.

Beckett Maxwell.

He of the hardest voice of them all.

He sat on the bottom bleacher between Rowan and Preston, his elbows on his knees as Preston whispered things in his ear.

From any angle, Beckett was a gorgeous specimen of masculinity. But, from the back, it was safe to ogle the lines of his person like a water-starved wanderer stuck in the desert.

He wore black jeans and a dark grey tee, both of which somehow looked expensive. His near-black hair was short at the sides and long enough on top to run your– his hand through. Even at not quite eighteen, he often sported a five o'clock shadow, even if he'd been clean shaven in the morning.

He was like an oasis. If an oasis were full of poison and murderousness. Because Beckett Maxwell was as likely to chew you up and spit you out as look at you. Everything he left in his wake was damaged beyond recognition, mere shells of former selves. Be it cars. Buildings. Bottles. People.

The shrill piercing of the whistle reverberated around the pool and was just the kick in the head I needed to pull my eyes off the back of Beckett's head.

One by one, the swimmers stopped where they were, treading water in their allotted lane. All except the one in lane four. Jaeger kept leisurely going until he reached the end, then turned to face the coach.

"Problem?" he asked, as though just realising that everyone else had stopped.

The coach crossed her arms and looked down at him. "We're doing time trials, Richards. Not pandering to your ego's current whim."

The swimming coach was about the only person in the school I knew who didn't let Jaeger do anything and everything he wanted. Which only made things worse for me.

"I thought we could do a little warm up, Coach Quin," Jaeger said in response.

"You thought you could flex your clout, more like," my mother said.

Because, yes, my mother was the swim coach. It was why all the Royals knew my name. It was one reason why they gave me so much shit – the other being because they enjoyed bullying other people. Particularly children of faculty with scholarships. It was why Jaeger called me any word with 'quin' in it except my actual name. Still, for all the negative attention it got me, I couldn't help but feel a little proud that my mum could get a Royal under some semblance of control.

"I want actual times, people," Mum called. "If Jaeger Richards decides to swim slower than my dead grandma, then that's his prerogative. That does not mean you need to swim slower than him. Am I understood?"

"Yes, coach!" came the hesitant cry from around the room.

There was a giggle from the Royal box like Jaeger's stunt was at all original.

Gag me.

Jaeger was the school's best swimmer in years. He held every single boys' record the school had. He could probably beat everyone trying out today blindfolded. But because he was Jaeger Richards, and because he knew no one dared beat him even when hand-delivered the rare opportunity, he'd been a dick just because.

Which, really, summed up the Royals in general.

# CHAPTER TWO

The rest of Admin day went the same as usual. I got a spot on the Softball team, much to my chagrin. Sam got captain of the Chess team (despite my continual jealousy-fuelled protestations it wasn't a *real* sport). And Hunter had somehow won a spot on the swim team.

The next day was the Australia Day holiday. Political issues aside, it was still a public holiday, which meant a holiday at school. Not that I didn't spend pretty much every holiday at school courtesy of being the daughter of faculty.

Mum had a residence in the teachers' 'village'. I lived there with her when it wasn't term time. During the term, we'd decided it would be good for my sense of normalcy to live in the dormitories with the other girls. And by 'we'd decided', I did mean it was managements' policy.

As the blazing January heat was still the height of summer, students could be seen lounging around on every available patch of grass surrounding the dorms. Come midday, the lawns would be empty, though.

"Are we going to the party this year?" Hunter asked. It was obvious by his tone that he was actually asking if we could go for once.

Sam and I exchanged glances.

"I'm not going to be seen dead at one of their parties," I said. "But knock yourself out."

Hunter tried covering his actual intentions with a scoff. "What? No. It'll be totally lame."

It wouldn't.

At least four times a year, the Royals hosted a huge party on campus in a clearing in the woods. Everyone was unofficially invited. The Royals were so rich, they didn't care who drank their copious amounts of procured booze, so long as it was drunk. And the teachers couldn't do a damned thing about it. Being mostly Rivermont alumni, they probably didn't want to. Twisted rights of passage, and all that.

The first year I was at Rivermont, there'd been a teacher who'd tried to put a stop to a party. They never taught at Rivermont or any other school again – so said my mum. That was the strength of the Royals' pull in this place. They were an institution probably as old as the Academy itself. Not that it mattered. Because even the plebs were of a certain calibre and that calibre was *way* higher than any paygrade I could ever hope for.

Sam and Hunter were considered losers at Rivermont, but their parents were still CEOs of huge corporations with a fleet of cars. Sam's dad actually had a helicopter.

Some families were into far less savoury things than legal business ventures. At least if the rumours were to be believed. School chatter said Jaeger's family were hired assassins and that their biggest clients were the Maxwells.

The three of us walked into the boys' dormitory only to find Gunner, Fox and a few of their cronies in the lobby.

"Got to get in a quickie before lunch?" Gunner asked me.

Me. It was always directed at me.

"Come on," I said, grabbing Hunter's arm to pull him away before he could even react.

I firmly believed that Hunter only got so aggro with the Royals because he knew I'd stop him from actually doing anything. If I was more sadistic, I might have let him go and watch him piss himself in fright.

"They're not worth it," I told Hunter.

"I'd have said the same about your little friends," Fox said.

"They're better than you!" I snapped, not meaning it at all the way it came out.

Fox smirked. "I'd wager you're wrong."

"You couldn't pay me to test your theory," I told him.

"Everyone has a price," Fox said.

"Even you couldn't afford mine."

Fox's smirk grew. "You really think *you're* worth that much? You?"

I'd meant that it was impossible for Fox to have enough morals, but I knew what it had come out sounding like. There was nothing I could do or say that would backtrack my ill spoken words.

"You walked into that one," Gunner said snidely.

"The amount of guys who've had her, you probably could," Fox sneered.

We all knew the rumours about us, about me: what kind of guys have a girl best friend and don't share her? Ergo, Hunter and Sam must have been giving it to me on the regular. Yeah, it was that kind of school.

Before I could roll my eyes at their originality, Beckett appeared out of nowhere, slamming Fox into the lift doors behind him.

"You've got a long way to come if you think that counts as wit and insult," he purred at Fox menacingly, like some giant, lethal cat flexing his dominance. He had one hand on the lift by Fox's head.

Everything about Beckett was menacing and predatory. Don't let the protective image fool anyone. He didn't care about me. He merely cared about the precious hierarchy he reigned over.

Even still, a familiar little thrill ran through me. It was impossible for it to not. Beckett Maxwell exuded this…presence and I was somewhat ashamed to say that – like every other androsexual at Rivermont – I fell for it for a moment. I couldn't *not* stop and stare. For a split-second, I admired him, my interest was piqued, and I took one step into flirtation-ready territory.

The next second, reality was righted and I regained my senses. It wasn't easy to forget for long just what kind of guy he really was. And it was even more glaring when he used something as irrelevant as me to belittle one of his own people. He was nothing if not a bully who liked to throw his authority around. And it worked. Because no one said no to Beckett.

Fox's smirk faltered but didn't fall. "It's not that long, Beckett. And I'm a fast learner."

Oh, the balls on Fox Maddox.

I doubted any king liked to be reminded their heir was just waiting until he was forced to step down…or died. And Beckett was no ordinary king.

I had to respect Fox. For about five seconds.

There was a blip in Beckett's boredom. The tiniest hint of exasperation, a 'fine, if I have to put you in your place, I suppose I can'. He sighed, then looked like he was about to run his hand through his hair but instead his elbow casually crashed into the side of Fox's head. It was such a natural movement that it easily could have been an accident. Had Fox not been whipped sideways by the force of it.

"You want my crown, Maddox?" Beckett hissed as he stood over Fox. "Then take it."

We all knew it for the empty goad it was. Fox wouldn't do

anything about it. Not now. He couldn't take Beckett in a fair fight. Beckett had Jaeger and Rowan to fight his battles for him not because he couldn't, but because powerful men delegated. They showed their status by having others do it for them. Unless it helped cement their power.

Beckett smirked knowingly at Fox, but his eyes were as dead as his heart. "I didn't think so." He patted Fox none too gently on the head, forcing the younger guy into a bow. "Wait your turn, little heir. One day, you might get to play at king. If I let you."

The problem with Beckett's voice was that it was damned sexy. There was something about his apathy and general disinterest, the fact that he knew he was above everything in his day to day life and did not care at all. That he was so secure in his supremacy, like it was an unshakable fact upon which the entire universe was founded.

Confidence was sexy. End of story.

But Beckett also had this way of threatening people with his already deep, guttural voice even lower, almost seductive in his taunting. It did things to my stomach – and lower down – that had no right feeling *anything* about the King of Rivermont Academy.

Fox glared at me like it was all my fault he'd dared to challenge the supreme arsehole that was his king. I knew I'd pay later.

"Now, be a good little boy and help Clint and Locksley with the booze," Beckett demanded.

Fox's glare for me turned murderous, but he knew better than to disagree with Beckett again.

"Yes, sir," Fox said sullenly.

"Good boy," Beckett said.

He passed a stern look over Gunner and their cronies, looked at Sam and Hunter like they were less that the dirt on the bottom of his ridiculously expensive trainers, and was very careful not to let his eyes light on me at all. I'd have been disappointed if he was any other stupidly sexy guy whose attention I was hoping to get even a moment of. As it was, it was Beckett Maxwell and I knew that even a moment of his attention would be instantly regretted.

Beckett walked into Hunter on his way out like it didn't bother him, like Hunter was so irrelevant that Beckett didn't even notice. But it bothered Hunter, who took an instant step towards Beckett's retreating back.

Fox scoffed. "You think *you're* going to stand up to Beckett?" he jeered.

Gunner laughed and Hunter took a step towards them. I didn't hold him back this time, I just headed for the stairs as Sam followed me. Fox snapped his teeth and lunged at Hunter, who scurried after me and Sam as Fox and Gunner guffawed to themselves like they hadn't just been scolded by their king.

"He bumped me!" Hunter said indignantly.

"Big whoop," I muttered as I trudged to Sam's room.

"One day, he's going to get what's coming to him," Hunter said.

"Yeah," Sam said sarcastically. "An international, multi-trillion-dollar company, an endless string of gorgeous women, infinity 'get out of gaol-free' cards, and everything he could ever want or need."

I looked at Sam and we shared a knowing smirk.

"It's so unfair," Hunter grumbled.

"Says the guy who is also going to inherit millions," said Sam.

"You can talk, Mr Helicopter," I laughed.

"You know you can borrow it whenever you want," Sam told me.

I nodded. "Yeah, I'll call that in when I have a super sexy date to woo and impress with my flashes of extravagance."

"Did you watch *Fifty Shades* again?" Sam laughed.

"No," I told him with an eye roll as Hunter asked me, "You watch

*Fifty Shades*?" like I did it all the time.

"*We*," I said pointedly as I looked at Sam, "wanted to know what all the fuss was about."

"And?" Hunter asked.

I shrugged. "I don't get it."

"She rewrote the pool table scene," Sam said happily. "Like she's out having kinky sex."

"Look, the sex I'm *actually* having might be kinda vanilla, but I know what I like the sound of."

"Well, we know what we need to do then, don't we?" Sam asked.

"And what's that?"

"Get you a man who likes a little more spice than vanilla."

"Tell you what," I told him. "We'll find yours first, then we'll work out who's gonna put his hand around my neck and plough me until I forget my own name."

Sam laughed as we walked into his dorm, and it made me smile. His laugh always made me smile. It was so open and carefree.

"Is that actually what you want?" Hunter asked. I didn't know if he was trying to hide his disapproval – or maybe just disappointment – or not.

I shrugged again. "I dunno. But I would like to try it at least once."

We didn't notice the school emptying as we were safely tucked away in Sam's room but, by the time we headed for dinner, very few students were around. None of the staff made a big deal about the fact that the dining hall looked like the Great Hall over Christmas break, but Hunter did.

"Do you think they serve dinner at these parties?" he asked.

"Why don't you go and find out?" I suggested.

"You obviously want to," Sam added.

Hunter rearranged in his seat. "Go into the woods in the middle of the night just to get pissed and no doubt beaten by the outer sanctum? No, thanks."

But he wasn't fooling anyone with the note of wistful longing in his voice. I didn't know why he was so desperate to go, and yet so desperate to make us think he didn't. He could both want to go and actually go for all Sam and I cared. It was a free country and he was his own person.

"Okay," Sam said as though that would be an end to it. "What are your plans tonight, Edie?" he asked me.

I shrugged. "Stay in my room and get started on the English book?" I guessed.

In reality, I knew I was going to try to get a swim in. Sam knew I was going to get a swim in. Hunter trusted me at face value. And a good thing too because he would have wanted to come with me – more so now that he was on the swim team, I assumed – and I preferred to be alone in the water. I preferred to be alone than with Hunter without Sam.

"Tekken championship?" Sam asked Hunter.

Hunter nodded. "Anything to not be doing homework already."

After dinner, we said our goodnights. The boys headed off to the boys' dorm and I headed off to the girls' dorm to get my swimming gear before heading to the pool.

Probably half my wardrobe was bathers and towels. I might not have been swim team material, but I spent just as much if not more time in the pool than any of them did. Especially when guys like Jaeger seemed to get along on sheer talent alone and didn't need to bother with boring shit like practising.

As I walked into to the pool change room, there was someone just getting out of their bathers.

"Abby, right?" I said as I pulled up to the locker my mum reserved for me.

She smiled at me. "Right. Eden?"

I nodded. "How are you finding everything?"

She blew out heavily. "It's madness. These people are so rich! I feel like I've walked onto the set of *Gossip Girl* or something."

I huffed a laugh. "Does your family only have one plane?" I teased and, thankfully, she took it the right way.

"My stepdad's the rich one. They married over Christmas after a legit whirlwind, moved Mum and me here to Australia, and I was promptly shipped off to boarding school. I knew he was crazy rich, but I didn't get to spend much time in this world before getting to Rivermont."

"Is it jetlag that has you swimming through dinner?" I asked.

She smiled. "Something like that. I also just kinda don't really know where to sit."

"Well, you're in luck. The Royals have their first big bash of the year today so the dining hall is basically empty."

"The Royals?"

It rarely occurred to me that outsiders didn't just automatically know everything about the hierarchy of Rivermont.

"The popular kids," I clarified. "Their king is kind of like the head prefect. Except he wouldn't lower himself to reading announcements or trying to make the school a better place for anyone else."

Abby clearly understood what I meant. "Sounds like a great guy."

I shrugged as I got changed. "He doesn't much bother with the plebs. It's Jaeger you have to watch out for."

"The tattooed, bleach blond idiot on the team?"

I grinned. "That's him."

She smiled. "Good to know, thanks."

"No worries. Oh, and if you need somewhere to sit, there's always a seat with us."

Her smile widened. "Thanks, Eden. I'll leave you to it. Have a good swim."

"Thanks." I waved as she left, then breathed deeply.

Abby seemed nice. Friendly. Sincere. Someone I could get along with. But social interaction outside Sam wore me out. Still, it might be a good thing to have more than two friends.

As I sheared somewhat lazily through the water, I mentally prepped myself to be a more functional human being and maybe keep myself open to making a friend in the new girl. If she wasn't into it, all good. I knew what my mum would say, and she'd remind me that I'd never get anywhere – that I might miss out on something epic – if I didn't put myself out there.

So, fine. Out there, I would put myself and we'd see what happened.

I was still towelling my hair dry as I headed back to my room. As usual, I avoided the lift and took the stairs instead. It wasn't so much health motivated as it was avoidance of small spaces motivated. I didn't have a real phobia of small spaces, but small spaces were often shared and, anytime I could not be locked away with someone not Mum or Sam, that was swell.

It was late – well past curfew and time even most party-goers were out of the elements after starting at midday – and I didn't expect to see anyone out of their room. As such, I wasn't paying all that close attention to where I was going or what I was doing, instead going by muscle memory and habit.

So, naturally, the one person who was in the vague vicinity happened to be in the same place as me at the same time.

As I came around the corner and pulled the towel away from my head, my eyes registered the other body too slowly for my body to react.

Beckett came around the corner at the same time as me, his arms swinging up as he threw his jacket back on.

I had enough time to take all that in, but apparently not enough time to avoid our arms bumping into each other. There was a slight pause in his step, and I used the chance to look him over.

His hair was suspiciously more dishevelled than usual. His long-sleeved tee was sitting awry against his neck and collar. The evidence of what he'd been doing in the girls' dorms was obvious. After all, there was only one reason why any of the royals crossed the boundaries between the girls' and boys' dorm buildings. Not that it always required crossing boundaries.

Sex.

Someone had been lucky enough to get Beckett back to their dorm room after the Royals' Australia Day party. Although, lucky was subjective.

I considered it lucky when I got through two hours without one of the Royals paying me any attention. I certainly had no interest in getting one in my dorm. The fact I was alone with the King of Rivermont Academy sent my heartbeat into overdrive and my tongue felt three-times bigger than it was supposed to.

Luck was apparently on my side, though.

After his slight pause, Beckett finished pulling on his jacket, straightened his collar, and continued walking as though nothing had happened. But then, I didn't know why that surprised me, because, of all the Royals, Beckett was the only one who never paid me any direct attention. Not unless he absolutely couldn't avoid it. As far as he was concerned, I may as well have not existed.

I wasn't going to call him out on it; no one with a brain wanted the attention of Beckett Maxwell. Also not one to squander an opportunity, I watched him walk away. He was a dick, but I could still appreciate he was a good-looking dick with a very fine arse.

He continued down the corridor, past the elevator and towards the stairs. He disappeared down them with a steady jog. I'd have said that my presence in the hallway had no bearing on his behaviour, but the way he did that little skip you do before you rush down stairs suggested he wanted out of there as quickly as possible.

Or, I could have been imagining I had any power whatsoever over the King of Rivermont.

With the both of us safely out of each other's direct vicinity, I continued on to my room like nothing had happened. After all, nothing may as well have happened. Beckett having sex with someone in the girls' dorms was such a regular occurrence that it didn't even qualify for a message to Sam. For all the novelty, I may as well have texted him and told him it was night-time.

I got ready for bed, and told myself that I wasn't thinking about a certain Royal in certain compromising situations as I fell asleep.

# CHAPTER THREE

The next day, the whole school was just plain ignoring and accepting that a significant portion of the students were hungover or just plain didn't turn up to class.

Lessons started for the year.

Sitting in the first lesson of the year was the time I felt the most normal. It was the time when I could pretend that I felt some hope and excitement about something – anything – and that it would last this time.

Sam sat on one side of me, but Hunter wasn't in our class. I'd looked for him and everything.

"Where's Hunter?" I asked Sam.

He looked around the room. "He's doing PE this year. I think it's in this stream."

I frowned at Sam. "First he tries out for the swim team, and now he's doing PE?"

Sam shrugged at me. "I got nothing. I don't know why either."

I nodded. "Fair enough."

Fox Maddox walked into the classroom, with Gunner Beck close behind him, and I grumbled to myself. I heard Sam sigh in solidarity.

I watched Fox's eyes alight onto me and prepared myself for the verbal onslaught. But honestly, anything that came out of his mouth on a good day was ten times better – read: less damaging – than what came out of Jaeger's mouth on a bad day.

My eyes stayed on Fox as he came towards us – keep your eye on your enemies and all that – so I saw when he got the slight tilt to the corner of his mouth. I watched the look in his eyes as he was clearly thinking up something he thought was terribly witty and clever.

And he winked at me.

That was it.

He winked at me.

A cheeky little wink with absolutely no sign of malice.

Fox had passed me, so my eyes turned to Gunner.

Nothing. Nothing out of Gunner either except a very small, knowing smirk as he followed Fox to their seats at the back.

I looked at Sam and saw him looking at me with equal surprise on his face.

"What was that?" I asked.

Sam's eyes darted to where Fox and Gunner were sitting, and back to me again. "Have we fallen into the multiverse?"

My eyes darted to Fox and Gunner, and back again. "First Hunter, now them…?"

"Are you still you?" Sam asked me.

"I don't know. Are you still you?"

"I think so…"

"Okay, everyone. Lesson One," Mr Erikson called as he walked into the room. "Who's already forgotten their books?"

It was only the first day proper of school and I was already distracted. Sam and I kept throwing looks over our shoulders at Fox and Gunner. Part of me knew Sam's solidarity on this one was just enjoying looking at Gunner. Sam looked at Gunner the same way I looked at Beckett; look, drool, fantasise, get a grip, never EVER touch.

But Fox and Gunner weren't overly suspicious. The times they were looking at us, they didn't look like they were plotting their next prank. They looked… I actually never though it would be possible for them to look pleasant. Like actual, real human beings with feelings and brains.

It was unnerving to say the least.

The unsettling behaviour continued through to the end of the lesson.

I joined the rest of the class as they stood up and turned to find I was about to run into Fox. I was prepared for the jibe. I was prepared for the snide comments. Physical contact wouldn't have been out of place for him.

He smiled, said, "Sorry, Eden," and indicated I go before him.

I snuck a look back to an equally confused Sam, and paused as I tried to work out if this was a scenario that was going to backfire on me. It probably was, but Fox's smile just grew even warmer.

"After you," he said to me encouragingly, with nothing but sincerity in his eyes.

My eyes darted to Gunner behind him and there was a little less sincerity on his face, but nothing that had me worried about what they were going to do next. Still, history suggested that they were lulling me into a false sense of security. The only thing for it was to get out of there faster than this could go bad.

I nodded. "Thanks," then high-tailed it out of there and hoped Sam was right behind me.

"What was that?" Sam asked when I finally slowed to a reasonable pace.

I finally let out a breath. "I don't know. Weirdness."

And the weirdness did not stop.

Fox opened a door for me at the beginning of Recess. He winked at me, then he and his cronies just walked away.

Fox wasn't the only weirdness of the day.

As I was dropping Sam off at his classroom after Recess before going to mine, a body fell against the wall beside me and Sam. We turned to see Jaeger looking down at me. I could smell the chlorine on him, that wasn't weird. What was weird was the look on his face.

Jaeger wore a bright smirk. It was cocky and cheeky and designed to elicit a smile – if not a blush – from me. Embarrassingly, it almost did both those things.

"Can we help you?" I asked him.

"Can anybody?" he replied wistfully, looking off into the middle distance dramatically.

I blinked, my eyes sliding to Sam and back again. "I…don't know…? Do you *need* help?"

He inched closer, and leant his head towards my face. "I need the kind of help only you can give, Quintet."

I tried not to laugh at the utter ridiculousness coming out of his mouth. "Uh huh…"

I saw Hunter up the hallway. All humour fell and I felt a sudden rush to the necessity of getting Jaeger out of there. The last thing I needed was Hunter's opinion on Jaeger dropping in on me in the hallway. It was just lucky that my normal exchanges with Jaeger usually occurred when we were alone.

"I'm serious. I'm ailing and you've got the cure." Jaeger sure looked serious. The kind of serious that added a pout to his gorgeous full lips but left a mischievous twinkle deep in his eyes.

The kind of guys I usually attracted weren't this suave. I liked that. I liked when they were a little awkward, not so sure of themselves. It was way less intimidating and made me feel less unsure of myself. But, when an objectively attractive guy looked at you and left you with absolutely zero doubts about what he wanted to do to you, it was hard not to pay attention.

"How do you know my cure isn't worse than what ails you?" I quipped, taking a step away from Jaeger.

Jaeger was the kind of guy who always had one eye on his surrounds. He knew people. He glided through life like he was shallow and paid attention to only the shiny things that got him laid, but he was the opposite. He walked into a room and immediately sussed it all out. He continued sussing it all out. Which is how he knew my reaction was to Hunter more than him. His green eyes grew knowing, and I felt it was for a variety of reasons. None of them good.

"I wouldn't want to stir the pot," he said.

"That's all you ever want to do," I reminded him, and he grinned.

"Until later, Harlequin." He tipped an imaginary hat and sauntered off.

He caught up to Beckett, further up the corridor. One of the Royal harem from our year, Isabella Ramirez, was in pride of place beside Beckett where she thought she belonged.

Isabella was ridiculously stunning, and I could already picture their wedding photos. The both of them with their dark hair, complimenting each other perfectly. Isabella was almost as tall as Beckett, though she did wear heeled shoes everywhere she went. Where Beckett's eyes were like molten dark chocolate, Isabella's were like caramel. It was another annoying way they seemed made for each other.

She looked back to Jaeger as she hung onto Beckett's shoulder, then further down to me like she knew Jaeger had come from talking to me. She smirked at me unpleasantly. I didn't know what game the Royals were playing, but Isabella's face was the first real indication I had to not like it. Especially when she turned that look on her henchwoman, Mariana and they both looked at me conspiratorially.

"What did he want?" Hunter asked, his eyebrows narrowed in suspicion.

Sam shrugged. "Same thing the Captain of the Rivermont Redcoats always wants. To annoy the coach's daughter."

On Hunter's face was written exactly what he thought of that: not much. I was never sure if Hunter was overly sensitive and had a massive chip on his shoulder or some kind of complex, or whether Sam and I were far too apathetic of the bullying we endured. Some days, it was clearly one and on others it was definitely the opposite.

"Is he usually that flirty?" Sam asked, knowing that Jaeger and I 'talked' more than anyone else in the school saw.

"I'm not sure Jaeger knows how *not* to flirt and insult at the same time," I answered honestly.

"Seriously, though," Sam said. "First Fox and now Jaeger?"

"It's odd," I agreed.

"Fox is hitting on you, too?" Hunter asked, his eyes darting between us as though there was some other meaning to our words.

"I guess?" I offered.

Sam nodded. "He's playing the proper gentleman. He opened a door for her."

"He also winked at me," I pointed out. "I don't think gentlemen wink."

"Ugh, they think they can have whoever they want," Hunter grumbled.

I shrugged. "It's some game. No one wants me."

"I don't get why you don't say anything."

"Because they'll be encouraged by a positive or negative response," Sam said, and I nodded to him; sometimes it was like we owned one brain between us.

"So?" Hunter shrugged. "They should know no means no."

"They should," I agreed. "But no response is the easiest way to make him bored and get him to stop."

"You should–" Hunter started, but Sam cut him off.

"I don't like it either. They could both do with a swift kick to the Royal jewels, but Eden's right. This is the best way to get them to stop."

"She really–"

"Arguing isn't going to help anything," Sam said, more forcefully than he usually was with anyone. "Telling her what she should or shouldn't do isn't going to help. We're her friends. It's our job to support her and her decisions."

Hunter opened his mouth to continue arguing, but Sam shut him up with a, "Bup, bup, bup. No."

I smirked to myself and nudged my best friend in thanks. I had nothing against Hunter, but he and I had never quite gelled in the same way as me and Sam. We just weren't on the same wavelength. Which was fine, because it takes all kinds to make the world go round, but I was also glad that Sam felt comfortable enough to stick up for me. It was a credit to Hunter that, even when Sam got that bit extra forceful, Hunter didn't get all huffy about it or get in a strop with Sam, but just took it in stride.

By the next day, I was actually getting kind of used to not just Fox but also Jaeger hitting on me. Not in the way that I was going to start reciprocating. But in the way that I could ignore it better because it didn't take me off guard anymore.

Fox was still playing gentleman, which was a very strange look on him. If I hadn't gone to school with him for three years, then I would have said it suited him. He continued opening doors for me. He was kind and polite and smiled at me warmly whenever he saw me.

If it weren't for the likes of Isabella and the occasional slip of Gunner's mask, I'd have thought maybe Fox had suffered an aneurism or something.

As we left the library after school, we ran into Gwen, another of the Royal harm.

Like most of the harem, Gwen was everything I would never be, and I wasn't sure I wanted to be. She was vapid and vain and had a serious superiority complex that had her firmly believing she was going to marry one of the inner sanctum before she graduated. She was also tall and curvy and blonde and beautiful. Her hair had notes of strawberry in it and her eyes were always sparkling blue to the extent I was sure she used some sort of eye drops. And her lips were always set in an 'everything's beneath me' kind of pout that I was certain would put her in good stead as a future Mrs Preston Worthington-Smythe.

"Eden," she said, like my name was a sour taste in her mouth, as she looked me over. "I heard Fox was going to take you to the formal." It felt like she was trying to be friendly, but she didn't have the required software.

I blinked. "Did you?"

She nodded. "The rest of us are having a party before, or whatever."

"Okay," I said slowly. "Uh… Well, I'm not–"

She shrugged. "Yet."

I frowned in confusion but she just waved to us in a very 'toodleoo, love' kind of way, and sashayed away.

"Are *you* going to the formal with Fox?" Hunter asked, more accusation than question.

"No!" I scoffed. "Gross. I wouldn't be seen dead at the formal with a Royal, let alone Fox Maddox. The guy is heinous."

"That face is honestly wasted on that personality," Sam said.

"Talk about the guy who gets a hotel room to steal your virginity on prom night," I laughed.

"Oh, no doubt," Sam agreed. "Although, I'd consider it."

"If that ship hadn't sailed," I added and Sam shrugged coyly.

"I wonder why she thought that?" Sam mused.

We were still puzzling out the interaction with Gwen when we walked into the boys' dorm. I saw Jaeger walking towards me down the hallway.

"What do you think he'll pull this time?" Sam asked, the amusement in his voice overriding the annoyance.

"He'd better not try anything," Hunter muttered.

Sam shrugged. "He'll get bored eventually."

"She should still do something about it."

"She does have a name," Sam told him.

I nudged him gently. "It's fine. If I ignore him, he'll go away."

I almost thought that this was the time Jaeger went away. But alas, not so much. As he passed us, he caught my hand softly, causing me to turn back towards him, and raised it to his lips. Damn, he was smooth. He winked before he kissed the back of my hand, and I furiously told the heat in my cheeks to knock it off.

"Quinlet," he said smoothly.

"That's not a word," I told him.

"Endearments don't have to be."

I could feel Hunter's ire rising hot behind me. Sam just snorted at the idiocy.

"Sure," I said as I extricated my hand and started to walk off.

"Richards," came a low, warning growl.

Jaeger turned. The open, easy charm on his face dropped, then Beckett was shoving him backwards and walking up to him, so the two men's chests were hard against each other.

Jaeger was taller than Beckett, but there was no question as to who was the more powerful in that situation. They were stark contrasts in everything. Jaeger's platinum hair versus Beckett's almost black. Jaeger's easy laziness versus Beckett's hard rigidity. Jaeger's warm, playful green eyes versus Beckett's hard, deep chocolate brown ones. Jaeger's questioning amusement versus Beckett's inexplicable fury.

Even the way they wore their uniforms was a stark contrast. Beckett's was worn perfectly, like the power suit he would no doubt don as soon as he graduated and would die in. His clothes were ironed, his trousers with a perfect crease down the centre of each leg and showing off the curve of his arse unnecessarily nicely. His tie with the impeccable triangle and at the exact right length. His blazer that was pressed and de-fluffed and tailored to fit him like a glove.

Meanwhile, Jaeger's uniform looked like it didn't know what even the concept of an iron was. His top button was undone, and his tie was loose. His trousers were just a little bit too tight – some would say, in all the right places – and his belt was silver. He wore the academy sweater vest and his shirt sleeves pushed up to his elbows, showing off the tattoos on his forearms in a very direct screw you to the establishment. But, much like their policies on parties on campus, the establishment didn't bat an eye to the presentation of its students so long as they adhered to the loosest of the uniform guidelines.

"What?" Jaeger chuckled at his irate king.

Whatever Beckett said was too low for me to hear the words, but I heard the deep hum of his strong voice like it was pulsing through my whole body, and I traitorously felt myself shiver. Jaeger's face dropped all amusement. Jaeger nodded and held his hands up.

"Yeah, all right," Jaeger said. "My bad, boss."

Beckett spoke again, still too low for me to hear. I didn't know what Beckett was getting so worked up over, but Jaeger was taking it dead seriously. To my knowledge, Beckett had never beaten on Jaeger, Rowan or Preston. The inner sanctum was sacred. There was something both incredibly sexy and utterly terrifying about a man who could elicit not just blind obedience but also unshakable loyalty from three powerful men in their own right with nothing more than words and the force of his personality.

"Fox started it," Jaeger told him, as though that was a decent explanation.

From the way Beckett reacted, it was a piss-poor explanation and Jaeger knew it. I still didn't hear the words, but it got through to Jaeger no question.

I was starting to form a hypothesis, but my brain seemed to refuse to want to acknowledge it. It was like I had an idea about why Beckett was so pissy, but couldn't quite bring myself to believe it could be true.

Did this have something to do with me? Why? What? The only thing that made sense was that I was so far down on the bottom of the Rivermont hierarchy that Beckett thought it was beneath the Royals to be flirting with me, even with whatever no doubt heinous prank they were pulling.

Well, screw you, sir.

Jaeger nodded again. "Scout's honour, man." Jaeger's eyes flickered to me. "Hands off."

I frowned at them seemingly making decisions on my behalf, but Jaeger's expression almost seemed to warn me against opening my mouth. I felt my frown deepen and there was a definite shake of Jaeger's head.

Beckett's head twitched as though he had to stop himself looking at me, then he said to Jaeger, only just loud enough for me to catch, "I will not tell you twice," in that velvety smooth voice that seemed determined to caress my body.

"You won't need to," Jaeger answered earnestly. As Beckett turned away, Jaeger asked him, "What about Fox?"

I just caught Beckett's reply, "Leave his treasonous arse to me," before he strode away.

"What was that?" I asked Jaeger, as though years of him insulting me and two days of him flirting with me had created some kind of intimacy between us where I could ask anything of him.

Jaeger watched Beckett retreat for a moment longer before looking at me. His whole demeanour had changed. There was no sign of the flirt I'd seen the last twenty-four hours. He wasn't even the guy who always insulted me and thought he was charming about it. He was a totally different Jaeger than I'd ever seen before.

"The king has spoken," Jaeger said quietly, almost like he hadn't really meant for me to hear him. Then he grinned at me. "All hail the king."

Hunter scoffed. "Your king can–"

I elbowed Hunter. It wasn't like him to make outbursts against a Royal, let alone one of the inner sanctum.

Jaeger noticed the elbow and smirked, back to his usual self. "You'd do well to keep your guard dog muzzled, Harlequin." He gnashed his teeth at Hunter playfully. "Our king comes from a long line of lions. Lions eat puppies like him for appetisers."

And, just like that, things were back to normal.

If normal was Beckett apparently having an issue with Jaeger flirting with me. I wasn't sure why a guy who'd never looked at me twice was suddenly so interested in who flirted with me. Probably just another example of him flexing his authority.

"Sure," I said to him before he flashed a grin, stuck his hands in his pockets and sauntered off after Beckett.

# CHAPTER FOUR

A Friday morning first lesson Free was the most useless Free lesson there was. Why couldn't it be last lesson? Last lesson on a Friday was technically Lesson five, not six, as Lesson six was already a write off for Assemblies or Teacher meetings. Had my Free stream given me Lesson five off, then I'd be done for the week at Lunch. Not that I had anywhere to go or anyone to see, considering I lived at the school, but it would have been nice, nevertheless.

The same thoughts occupied my brain every Friday morning as my body followed the familiar path to the Library, the same as it did every Friday morning. I was nothing if not a creature of habit. Most Friday mornings, I didn't see another soul about as I was always making my move after classes had started; most of the Friday morning Free crew were still in bed, the rest of the school were in lessons.

So, I noticed when my year-long routine was suddenly upended.

As I walked around the corner of the Franklin Armitage Library towards the doors, I ran into someone. My books fell and I dropped to pick them up without even noticing who I'd walked into. Naturally, one of my books had slid further than the rest and I was just reaching to get it when the someone dropped to a crouch and handed it to me.

"Thank–" My words died on my lips as I looked up, straight into the piercing dark brown eyes of the King of Rivermont, and panicked the fuck out.

Beckett Maxwell was looking directly at me. In fact, so far into my eyes that I was pretty sure my entire soul was on display for him to read at will. It wasn't like he hadn't looked in my general direction at least once in the four years I'd been on the Rivermont campus, but it was one hundred percent the first time he'd ever actually looked at *me*. I was sure of it.

His face was as hard as ever. That stony statuesque expressionless look. Even with it – which was pretty much the only face I'd really ever seen on him – he was gorgeous. His square jaw, strong nose, that stubborn stubble, those inscrutable eyes with a hint of something terrifyingly tantalising.

My body didn't know how to react as his eyes searched mine.

Flutters skittered through me. My heart pounded. My skin prickled. My mouth felt dry. My tongue darted out to lick my lips nervously and I watched his eyes follow the movement. He was so unreadable. I didn't know what he was thinking. He could just as easily kick me onto my arse as help me up.

We could only have been crouched on the ground together for the space of a couple of heartbeats at most, but it felt like hours as tension swirled around me. What was he thinking? What was *I* thinking? My head was a mess. I wasn't even going to get started on what was happening between my legs.

Beckett stood in one smooth motion, and I was definitely expecting the kick. Instead, he extended his hand to me. There was a very thick air of expectation simmering around him and I knew I had to take his hand. With neither of us saying anything, I gingerly put my hand in his – furiously ignoring the undoubtedly one-sided sparks that seemed to explode between us as I did – and let him pull me and my books to standing.

"Th…thanks," I stammered, not quite sure what was happening here.

He looked me over carefully once more, gave me a single nod, then headed on his way – smoothing his shirt further into the waistband of his trousers at his back – like he had a million more important places to be, and I'd just put him three hours behind in his day.

I watched him go because there would be very few times that Beckett walked away from me and I didn't take the chance to perve, especially when there was no one else around. So, I saw as he blew out heavily, acting for all the world like nothing had happened but having a vague vibe to him that felt just a little bit more off-kilter than usual.

I understood that. I was feeling just a little bit more off-kilter than usual as well.

Something felt…different as I made my way to my usual Friday morning table in the library. I couldn't put my finger on what it was, but it made my heart thud heavily in my chest, it had the hair on the back of my neck pricking, it gave me this sense of overwhelming destiny, and like something was coming that I would be powerless to stop.

Which was stupid, and I was glad when Sam interrupted the idiocy of my brain.

"Okay, I have news," he said as he bustled over to my seat in the library.

I blinked. "Shouldn't you be in class?"

He sat down across from me and fixed me a look that clearly told me that, whatever his news was, it had precedent over our futures. "There is dissent within the Royal court."

My heart stopped thudding and instead skipped a little, and I had no idea why. It all felt connected, but I didn't know the why of that either. First Beckett looks at me and now dissent in the Royal court. What was coming next?

"What? How?" I asked. Given that the Royal court were a bunch of bullying arseholes, I really shouldn't have cared. But I was a gossipy hag – and proud – at the best of times, and I totally cared.

Sam shrugged. "Don't know exactly. But I have it on good authority that Beckett's reign is getting wobbly."

I didn't need to ask where Sam got his info or on whose good authority he got it. What – or who – Sam got up to in his own time was his business. All I needed to know was that his intel had never been wrong.

I rubbed a finger over my chin. "We haven't had a sitting Year Twelve King toppled in…?" I tried to do the maths and failed.

Sam's maths was ten times better than mine and that's why he was going to study economics and accounting at uni. "Seventy-six years."

Which was not to say that every King of Rivermont was a Year Twelve or that there was always a King of Rivermont. It highly depended on who and which Royals were currently enrolled. Beckett had secured his reign the day he'd walked onto campus in Year Eight. He'd had a much bigger version (at the time) of Jaeger do all the heavy lifting for him, but he'd taken the crown from all of the heir assumptives very easily and he'd held it for four years.

"Shit," I whistled. "Fox?"

Sam shrugged again. "I would assume so. Everyone's prepped for him to take the crown next year after Beckett graduates. Makes sense that his followers are backing him if he's making a play now."

"And his followers are basically everyone if they think helping Fox will be good for them."

"All but the inner sanctum."

I huffed a laugh. "The inner sanctum could take the rest of the school easily," I pointed out.

Sam nodded. "True. But apparently there are some laws his majesty is laying down that are *not* being followed."

"Oh, juicy," I chuckled, wondering what rules they were. "But serves the arsehole right."

"Just because you like looking at his arse."

"Arseholes can have nice arses. They're not mutually exclusive concepts."

"Again, true."

I tapped my pen on my book. "I guess we'll have to wait and see what happens."

"Whatever it is, we'll be safe in the stands while we watch their whole world implode."

I smiled but didn't really feel it. I forced it wider to hide my inexplicable weirdness. "I'll bring the popcorn."

He nodded and reached over to squeeze my hand absently. "Brilliant. I'll see you next lesson?"

"Sure. See you, then."

He gave me another nod before pushing himself to his feet and heading off again.

I went back to my History essay, forgetting the juicy goss for the space of another half an hour until the bell rang for lesson two. I checked the time on my phone as though the bell for second lesson hadn't rung at nine-fifteen every morning for the last four years of my life, and gathered up my books.

My chosen Friday morning library desk was the desk I chose most other times I was in the library, too, to be honest. I'd come to Rivermont in Year Seven, even though the school only catered for

Year Eights to Twelves. That was how badly they wanted Mum as the Redcoats' coach. Mum and Dad had just split and Mum didn't have the money to send me to another boarding school while Dad was gallivanting around the world with only his mid-life crisis for company. For that first year, I was sort of semi-home schooled, setting myself up in the Rivermont library to do my work independently with just a couple of the teachers checking in on me a few times a day.

So, my desk had become my desk. Somehow the school had got the memo that you just didn't sit in that desk. I didn't know how or why, but I wasn't going to complain if it left me to my favourite spot. I didn't like change. I liked routine. And that desk had become my routine when Mum and I had moved. Even the year after when I'd found Sam, I still took comfort in my desk and the fact it was always there for me.

I took the familiar paths from my desk to get outside and head to the Ballentyne Building for Maths. I hated Maths as a rule and I wasn't that good at it, but Sam helped me through, and it left me with the most options for applying to uni the next year…when – if – I actually worked out what I wanted to do.

As I came towards the only entrance and exit to that section of the library, I felt another presence. It was the sort of hairs at the back of the head prickle, feeling eyes on you, skin tingling like the air wasn't completely empty of sentient beings. I looked around and paused mid-step as I saw the goddamn King of Rivermont leaning on a bookshelf like he was on some perverted sentry duty.

He was looking straight at me, and I couldn't help feeling – knowing – that he was there because he knew where I was. He was there for me. I just didn't know why, and I wasn't sure I wanted to believe what I felt to be true.

We just stared at each other for a few seconds, neither of us saying anything or doing anything. I felt unbelievably awkward and like I'd been caught out doing something I shouldn't. He looked like he was perfectly at home and waiting didn't bother him at all.

Was this what he'd had to run off to do after we bumped into each other outside? Top of his priorities list for that day included – what? – stalking me in the library? It seemed ridiculous to think it, but there the evidence was, literally staring me in the face.

My phone buzzed in my hand, and I looked down to see a message from Sam asking where I was. It was all the help I needed to break the spell Beckett had seemed to cast over me. I shook my head and hurried out, feeling his eyes on me until I'd turned out of view, but still somehow even then.

Adding Beckett to the list of weird shit that had gone down that week, I endeavoured to forget about it as I headed for next lesson. Seeing Gunner seemingly similarly waiting for me a little further on in the library distracted me momentarily from Beckett, but then I had double French with only Fox for company between Recess and Lunch.

And Fox wouldn't let me forget about Beckett's weirdness. Because every time Fox tried flirting with me, all I could do was remember my hand in Beckett's as he helped me up. Not that Fox didn't put up a very good effort.

He chose the seat next to me to sit, which was something he'd never done before. He had Alexander, one of his cronies in the class, and usually sat with him. Alexander was Fox's Preston. The unnaturally posh, uptight arsehole with a hyphenated name who always looked like there was a bad smell under his stupidly handsome face.

But that day, Fox sat next to me.

It wasn't difficult to notice because nobody sat with me in French. Or, more accurately, I didn't sit with anyone in any class unless it was Sam, and Hunter always sat with me/us if he was in the same class.

So, when Fox's body dropped next to mine and I registered the blond hair and brown eyes and cheeky little sexy smirk, my eyes flew up and looked around like I could work out what joke I was currently the butt of. But there seemed to be no joke. No one looked at me or Fox. Even Alexander was oddly un-nosy about the whole thing.

Fox said nothing to me directly as we got started on the lesson, but then we were tasked with practising our vocab with our partner. The partner being whoever was sitting next to us. I looked around again as though I was the kind of person who'd actually try to swap who I was sitting with.

I noticed Abby sitting on the other side of the classroom with an empty seat beside her and made a mental note for the future. She smiled at me warmly and I smiled back unhesitatingly.

"You know," Fox said as he leant into me, leaning his hand on the back of my chair so his arms were pretty much around me. "You're beautiful when you smile."

The corner of my lip tipped. I couldn't stop it. It was either that or just laugh out loud. It was utterly ridiculous that a Royal like Fox was paying me any attention at all. But I had to admit, I was a little flattered as well. Which was the stupidest part, because I was under no delusions that Fox believed any of the lies that he was spouting for whatever game he was playing.

"I'm serious," he said with a wide, questioning smile on his face as he searched my eyes. "You don't believe me?"

"You were just this week giving me shit about the number of guys who've had me, and now I'm supposed to believe you're interested?"

He shrugged. "The heart wants what the heart wants."

Now I did smile fully. The effect on Fox would have been encouragement, but I couldn't help it. It was hilarious. Not just that Fox was doing it in the first place, but because he wasn't going to let himself be called out on it.

I had to give him some kudos.

My smile faltered as I happened to look at the classroom door and saw Jaeger in the corridor, leaning on the wall opposite our classroom where I was in full view of him. He had his arms crossed and, when he saw me looking, he gave me a very 'amused but not in a good way' half-smirk and raised his eyebrow in question. Like he was asking me what in the hell I was doing and why was I doing it with Fox.

I gave him a look that I hoped told him that I wasn't doing anything, and I had no control over whether Fox tried it on with me. I could see Jaeger only partly believed me. I was gratified to see – hope – that he was more annoyed with Fox than he was with me. His face was dark as he watched Fox, and he kept an eye on Fox flirting with me all lesson, just shooting off what looked like the occasional message on his phone.

It reminded me starkly that for all Fox's playing at superiority, there was at least one someone who was more superior and, I suspected – for all the rumours of dissent – always would be.

Fox had all the technical clout of Beckett or any of the Royals. He was going to be the next Beckett, after all. The next King of Rivermont Academy. And he had presence. He affected people, mostly for ill. But his effect was oh-so less than certain other members of the Royal court. Compared to them, he seemed relatively harmless, more full of false bravado than posing any real threat.

And that was especially clear after what happened in the library in last lesson. At least as far as my body was concerned.

Our History teacher was all for independent study and student-led learning – I didn't know if the theory was genius in that it got us focussed on what interested us, or genius in that she didn't have to come up with lesson plans – so she'd sent us to the library to keep working on finding a topic for our major essays.

So I was in an aisle, looking over spines and trying to find some inspiration, or at least narrow down my inspiration, when a very different kind of inspiration found me.

Two hands planted on either side of me, boxing me against the library shelf, and I jumped. My jump had me stepping backwards and I felt a very hard front at my back. Then there was a nose against my neck and goosebumps were skittering down my arms. My eyes closed as my head titled to give them better access and I felt them smile against my jaw.

"Eden Quin," he murmured as his nose trailed firmly up my neck.

My nipples tightened and I was pretty close to forgetting the name he'd just purred into my ear as I practically, embarrassingly melted back against him. I took a deep breath and told myself to calm down. One of his hands dropped to my hip as he stepped up even closer behind me, and a thrill ran through me.

I didn't know why Beckett Maxwell was seducing me in the library stacks, but neither could I bring myself to do anything except enjoy it. It was horribly shallow and the worst possible idea, but holy shit was he turning me on. As though I could convince myself that we could walk away from this and pretend it had all been just a really good dream on my part, I leant into him and hoped he didn't stop.

As Beckett's lips brushed over my neck, his hand ran up my side, edging onto my stomach, and came to a stop just under my breast. I ached for him to keep going, to feel him caress me. My skin burned at the thought his hand could just as easily slide down to ease that ache.

"Turn around," he ordered.

Without thinking, I did it.

Beckett pressed me against the shelving at my back and every one of my senses was overwhelmed with him as he gently nudged a knee between my legs. It felt like a test. The fact I let him in, I couldn't be sure if I passed or failed the test.

He smelled like something similar to a musky wood, more pleasing than cedar, and something else smoky. But there was a crisp, clean note that elevated the whole scent pleasantly and left a tingle in my nose.

He felt like warmth and fire and potential passion.

One hand roamed my body freely, while the other reached down to find the bottom of my skirt. His nose trailed over my neck as his fingers gently played against the skin of my thigh. I felt his lips brush over me as his fingers more firmly found purchase against my leg. Then, as he dragged his fingers up my thigh, his teeth grazed my neck and my hand went to his chest, curling around his shirt like I was trying to get him even closer.

I didn't know what was about to happen between us in the library stacks, and I knew we could be found out at any moment, but I was very willing to find out exactly where this might go.

All rationality had left me. Were I a car, the only thing in my petrol tank would be pure carnal lust. I was firmly grounded in the present, with no thought about what came next or what it meant. I didn't care who he was or the heinous things he'd done.

I just wanted him, and I wanted him to keep wanting me.

If that's what this was.

If it wasn't, I couldn't say I cared just then anyway.

Beckett's hand slid up under my skirt and gripped my arse firmly. His face dropped towards mine. The way my heart thundered, one would have been forgiven for thinking that I was about to kiss Beckett-fucking-Maxwell.

That sobered me up.

My fist around his shirt loosened and I pressed my palm against his chest.

"What is this?" I asked him.

"Did you want me to stop?"

No, but he still should.

I took a deep breath and pushed against him. He took a step back and I knew I wasn't the only one regretting it.

"What do you want, Beckett?" I asked.

"Based on your reaction, the same thing you want."

If that was his idea of flirting, it very nearly worked on me. "You think you can ignore someone's existence for four years, then they'll just randomly hook up with you in the library?"

"Yes."

I blinked at his assurance. "Seriously?"

"I'm Beckett Maxwell, Eden. Everyone wants to try me once."

My experience suggested that was true. It didn't hurt him to think I disagreed, though. "No," I countered as I shook my head. "Just, no."

He took a step towards me, all predatory fury. It shouldn't have turned me on. It should have been a warning. But my body had no interest in whatever the warning was.

"No one says no to me," he said, his voice low.

I pulled up my big girl undies and squared my shoulders at him. "I do."

His lips quirked in a half-smirk. All condescension. "For now maybe."

I wasn't going to dignify that with an answer. I just went back to my desk and tried to pretend I wasn't certain he was hiding out in an aisle keeping an eye on me until the bell for the end of school rang.

# CHAPTER FIVE

Thanks to a swimmer for a mum, I was used to getting up well before the arsecrack of dawn and heading to a pool. And that first Saturday of the school year was no different. Summer Saturdays had a routine for the Quin ladies; swimming practice, breakfast, softball. As it was the first week back, softball wasn't a game but a practice so Mum was piking out for some extra training with the newbies to the Redcoats and I'd figured that was fair enough.

I plopped onto the bleachers next to the pool as students flowed in and out of the changerooms in various states of awake at six on a Saturday morning. Always chipper and always annoying, Jaeger bounced in and found me straight away. Because no matter what he'd been up to the night before, he was always at practice. Were he anyone else, I'd have said he actually cared about swimming.

"Good morning, Quinlet," he said as he stretched his arms, and I ignored the way his biceps bulged.

I sighed. "Good morning, Jaeger."

"Oh, Mannequin. I'm hurt. Anyone would think you weren't happy to see me!"

"Anyone would be right," I told him, wondering where this new sass of mine was coming from.

I suspected it came from the fact there was something different about the way Jaeger had taken to interacting with me the last few days. Since Beckett had put him in his place. It wasn't that he was any less annoying, but he was less…intimidating. He was less mean. It made those parts of me that were usually so good at self-preservation forget themselves and say exactly what was on my mind, instead of keeping it to myself like I usually did.

"Beckett sends his apologies, but he had a late night so he won't be making it this morning," Jaeger said, as though the person I really wanted to see was Beckett.

A thrill ran through me as I recalled the library incident from the previous afternoon. I crossed my legs and shifted in my seat as though that was going to stop my clit throbbing or me wishing I was back in those library stacks again.

"If I wanted to see Beckett at six in the morning, my first port of call would not be the pool," I told him.

Jaeger chuckled like he could read my mind. I had no doubt he knew all about the library incident. "For interest's sake, what would be your first port?"

"Probably his bed," I said as I looked around the pool, pretending that anything else in there was more interesting than him or the idea of Beckett in bed.

"He'll be pleased to hear it."

"I'm not going anywhere near his bed."

"You a washing machine kind of girl?" he teased, and I didn't dignify that with an answer, so he tried something else. "Don't you have softball after your breakfast with our illustrious coach?"

I frowned at him. "I haven't had nearly enough caffeine to deal with you this morning, Jaeger."

Mostly because I may have been kept up all night with fantasies of his king that I was desperately trying to forget. Fantasising about Beckett would lead to nothing good. Not in the least, it was a waste of time. A waste of time my mind seemed very keen on engaging in.

"Oh, feisty this morning, Quinjet. Me likey. Beckett does so like his woman with a bit of fire."

I rolled my eyes, even as I noted with feigned disinterest the singular form Jaeger chose to use there. "Good for Beckett."

Jaeger leant towards me, and it was quite unseemly with him in nothing but his budgie smugglers. I almost blushed, but I'd been around swimmers for years. "Do you like your men with a little bit of fire, Quinton?" he asked seductively.

I had a feeling where this line of questioning was going and I was putting a stop to it now. "I prefer them with morals and tighter trouser zips," I told him.

"You might reconsider once you've benefitted from the expertise gained thanks to those loose trouser zips..." Jaeger purred, and I looked at him dead on.

"If you're implying that Beckett will fuck me raw, ruin me for all other men, and I'll love every minute of it, then you can push on," I told him. "I don't care, and I will never care." I mean, it was all lies, but he needn't know that.

Jaeger blinked and, for a second, seemed to lose his normally easy composure in the face of my bluntness. "Beckett know about that mouth on you?" he asked, frowning like he was thinking. "He can't or he wouldn't be taking the slow and steady approach. He'd have *totally* lost his mind over you. And I'm implying nothing, I am telling you plain and simple."

I didn't doubt Beckett could be the best sex of my life, but I was not going to even think about that. Much. "Push right on, Jaeger."

He shrugged. "I'm just saying. Beckett's cock's a much better ride. And cleaner."

Now I frowned. "Than whose?"

"Fox."

I laughed out loud. "I care even less about Fox's cock than I do about Beckett's, but thanks."

Jaeger's eyes shone with mischief. "You're not as innocent as you look, are you, Quintet?"

I leant towards him and gave him a mischievous smirk of my own. "You're not as stupid as you look, are you, Jaeger?"

That mischief turned into pure glee. "Fuck, you're something." He shook his finger at me with a rough chuckle. "You are definitely something."

"Richards!" Mum yelled. "In the pool. Now!"

Jaeger bowed to me. "The sultry tones of a woman who thinks of me every night."

I nodded. "Sure. You tell yourself that."

He winked at me. "Just call me 'Daddy'."

I snorted and tried to cover it. "No."

"RICHARDS!" Mum yelled again.

"Remember. Fox, bad sex. Beckett, good sex," Jaeger said as he started walking backwards towards the pool.

"Fox, arsehole. Beckett, worse," I countered, my tone sarcastically suggesting it was a revelation.

He just grinned and jumped backwards into the pool, but from then on it felt like there was some joke we were in on together.

I was sure it was purely the fact that I found it amusing that Jaeger was talking up Beckett and talking down Fox as though there was any chance in hell that I was actually going to choose either of them. Like we were in the midst of some rom-com love triangle and I was in the enviable position of having two gorgeous men to choose from, and it was up to the best friends to 'help' me make the right decision.

The whole of my existence since school started back felt like one big joke and I was just waiting to see how it all imploded on me.

First Fox is flirting with me. Then Jaeger's flirting with me. Then Beckett tells Jaeger to knock it off. Then there's rumours of dissent in the Royal court and supposedly Beckett's laws aren't being followed. Then Beckett's flirting with me. If it could be called flirting. And, to top it all off, Jaeger Richards playing wingman.

I just didn't know…

Wait.

Shit.

Beckett laying down laws that weren't being followed?

Something was tugging on my brain insistently. Like it was just there, quite interested in being acknowledged. But I knew what it was, and I didn't want to acknowledge it. Because acknowledging it meant that I was considering the idea that Beckett had laid down the law that no one was allowed to flirt with me, and Fox was disobeying. Not just that, but Fox's disobedience about *me* of all people was risking Beckett's crown.

The idea wasn't just laughable, it was certifiable.

It was insane. Logic suggested it was a possibility. It was impossible not to jump to that conclusion. But I would refuse to believe that that conclusion was the right one. I'd just pretend that I hadn't even thought of it and try to go about my now up-ended life.

Swim practice ran late, all thanks to Jaeger of course, so Mum decided to make it just one long practice and finish earlier than they would have otherwise. So, I ducked out to get Mum and me a breakfast burrito from the café and we compromised on our Summer Saturday routine.

"I think I might kill him," Mum sighed as she watched another time trial.

"Who?" I asked. "Jaeger?"

She nodded. "I might just ruin my whole career by killing him."

I laughed. "I thought you had him under control."

Mum scoffed. "It's all about appearances, Edie," she said. "I act like I have control over Jaeger, so he thinks I have control over him, and therefore I do."

"So, mind games?" I clarified.

She threw me a smirk. "Mind games."

"Is that really all it takes?"

She sighed as she kept an eye on practice. "I've found it the only way to deal with men. Sure, we get a reputation for being manipulative and conniving and all-around terrible, but we also get somewhere. We don't get trodden on. Being a woman still sucks sometimes, Edie. And sometimes we have to compromise on who we want to be to get where we want to be."

I could see a sense in that. "That does suck."

She nodded. "It does. Especially with people like the Rivermont Royals. They are so up themselves that there's very little anyone can do to dent their facades. But these guys aren't their parents. Yet. There's still a bit off insecurity in them. Still a bit of uncertainty. Still a bit of moulding we can do to make them easier to get along with."

"Huh," I said. "You make it sound so easy."

"Easy it isn't. Remember Jaeger's first year? At fourteen he was defiant and cocky and so goddamned arrogant. Plus, he was already taller than me. It took every ounce of strength I had to secure and maintain my authority over him. He's better now, but he still pushes the boundaries every freaking day. The only thing that makes it easier is that I know he defers to me now. In the pool, at least."

I watched Jaeger shear through the water. He made it look so effortless. Like he was part-fish and was finally at home. He wasn't the only Royal on the swim team – Regina Maxwell was currently sitting on the bench waiting her turn in the pool – but he was the only

Royal who seemed to have something outside being a Royal that he cared about. Loved even.

Mum touched a hand to my back as she started yelling things at one of the other swimmers, and I watched Jaeger pull himself out of the pool. His eyes found mine and I saw the humour there. He nodded his head to me as he pulled off the red Rivermont swimming cap and stretched his shoulders.

Jaeger Richards knew he was a good-looking guy. He knew everyone else knew it too.

"Are all the hot guys at this school total jerks?" I heard a voice and turned to see Abby had appeared next to me.

I pretended to think about it. "Uh, yeah. Pretty much. Yeah. Sorry. Welcome to Rivermont, where all the eye-candy have the personalities of caustic soap."

She laughed. "Ah well. At least they're nice to look at."

"Are my ears burning?" Jaeger asked as he walked by us.

He winked at Abby and, out of the corner of my eye, I saw she fidgeted a little.

"Only along with the rest of your soul in Hell," I told him.

His face broke out in a shit-eating grin. "Touche, QT. Well played."

"I notice you didn't deny it," I told him.

He levelled a heated gaze on Abby and I, and I was almost affected by it for a second. "The things I've done, Harlequin, my soul belongs in Hell."

A shiver ran through me, even though I was fairly sure he was teasing. The only problem was, I might have believed he was teasing, but I was also quite convinced that it was the sort of teasing joke that was firmly grounded in – and all the funnier because it was the – truth.

Jaeger winked again, then headed off to sit next to Regina. She eyed me suspiciously, looking me down and up like I was found severely lacking. The likes of the princess of Rivermont finding me lacking wasn't a blip on my radar. I didn't need her to approve of me. But I did need her brother to leave me alone.

"Abby, you're up," Mum called as she walked back over to me.

She smiled. "Okay, Coach. Later, Eden."

I waved and Mum nudged me.

"You making a friend, Edie?" she teased and I rolled my eyes.

"Maybe," I told her.

"A friend that's not Sam?" she gasped sarcastically.

I nudged her back and fought a smile. "Yeah. I know. Unbelievable, right?"

"Nah. Good for you, sweetie. Abby's a real nice kid. Bright and an incredible swimmer."

I nodded. "Good to know you're approving my budding friendships."

She shrugged. "It's not about my approval, Edie," she reminded me. "You're old enough to make your own decisions, your own mistakes, your own way in the world. I trust you to make the right ones and learn from the wrong ones. You only learn by doing."

I smirked. "And some of the best times of your life were mistakes?" I finished for her, knowing where this conversation always went.

She grinned. "And some of the best times of your life will be mistakes. Have fun, Edie. Just be careful, too."

I nodded. "I will. I'll leave you to it, and go get ready for practice?"

Mum kissed the side of my head. "No worries, darling. I'll see you later?"

I nodded. "Will do."

"Have a good practice."

"Thanks, Mum. Love you."

"Love you, too."

"Softball, Quinjet?" Jaeger called, miming a softball swing.

I frowned. "What business is it of yours?"

He shrugged and I did not like how nonchalant he was being. "It's no business of mine."

"You watch yourself around my daughter, Richards," Mum warned.

Jaeger held up his hand in the Scout salute. "On my honour, I have zero intentions about your daughter, Coach."

Mum nodded. "I should think so." She gave me another smile, then headed off to get started back in with the newbies to the team.

"You have no honour," I said to Jaeger as I headed for the door.

He nodded, but it was half-hearted. "I live by a code. It's not the same as your code, but there's still honour in it."

I looked at him after that weirdly profound announcement.

"What?" he laughed.

"Have you got layers?" I accused.

He leant towards me as we walked, putting his finger to his lips. "Sh. I won't tell anyone if you won't."

I frowned as I tried to reconcile this Jaeger with the one that I'd known for the last four years. "Okay…" I said slowly.

He gave me a cheeky salute and veered off back to the pool as we got to the door.

I looked back to watch him mucking about with some of the other swimmers, and caught Regina watching me warily again. I didn't know what was up with her, but I was sure she knew more about the weird happenings of the Royals with me that week than I did. And she clearly didn't like something about it. The part of me who wanted to give her the benefit of the doubt liked to think she didn't like whatever game they were playing with me. A more cynical part of me felt like she didn't like either my reaction or the fact that there was something about the game that wasn't just a game.

I just didn't know what that might have been.

But I sure thought about it a lot as I got changed into my softball gear, rummaged around for the mitt I was sure I'd had only a couple of days before, and slung my cleats over my shoulder. And I still had no answers, and just more questions floating around my head.

"Hey, where you off to?" Sam asked with a warm smile as I walked out of the girl's dorm almost an hour later.

I smiled. "Practice in lieu of week one's lack of games. You?"

He shrugged as he fell into step with me. "Not all who wander are lost."

I smirked at his reference. "Fair."

"Shall I come to practice then we can hang?" he asked.

"If you like. Though, I warn you, we're full of Year Eights and have yet to break them in." Thursday's practice had been a total shambles.

He laughed. "That's all right. You know I don't know the rules anyway."

Sam took my bag for me as we navigated the awkward little path that led from the girls' dorm side of the campus to the softball pitch side of the campus.

My best friend was a proper gentleman. One day, he was going to sweep some unsuspecting guy off his feet with wit and charm and beauty and the most wonderful personality. If only he could see all those things in himself. And if I sounded a little bitter and jealous of my best friend's future boyfriend, I was a little, but only because I knew it would be very difficult to find a guy half as good as Sam while we were still at Rivermont. Especially when my traitorous body seemed only happy to respond to guys who were the total opposite.

"What are they doing at your practice?" Sam asked me as we walked out to the softball pitch, and my eyes swivelled to see who he was talking about.

It didn't take long. They stuck out like sore thumbs on the relatively empty bleachers of the softball pitch, not in the least because I was pretty sure it was the only time they'd ever been on that side of the campus.

Jaeger with his platinum blond hair glaring in the sunlight, all back to its perfect coif after swim practice.

And Beckett with his sunglasses on. I couldn't tell whether he was feeling a little seedy that morning, or if he was trying to be inconspicuous.

"I don't know but…" I started, then paused and I didn't know why I was hesitant to tell Sam about the library with Beckett the day before.

Usually, I would have told him already. For some reason, I hadn't.

"But, what?" he pressed.

Which was the push I needed to pull my finger out and tell him. There was no reason not to. I dropped to the ground to change my shoes like that was going to give me the courage to tell him. "But Beckett's been following me around the library. Yesterday, we were in there for History and he… Well, things happened, and I very nearly gave it up to him right in the middle of Greek Mythology."

Same snorted and I looked at him incredulously.

"No, sorry," he laughed, shaking his head and sneaking another look at Beckett and Jaeger. "Seriously?"

I nodded. "Yeah. Funny?"

He shrugged. "A little bit, to be honest."

"I've suddenly got three Royals hitting on me, and you think it's funny?"

"To be fair, it's only two now because Beckett had a problem with Jaeger hitting on you." He gasped. "Do you think that's why?"

"What's why?" I asked as he helped pull me back to standing.

"Do you think Beckett went all caveman on Jaeger because he wants you for himself."

I scoffed. "Like I told Hunter. No one wants me. It's just some sick game."

"Yet you still nearly had sex with Beckett in the stacks like a proper library gremlin."

I sighed. "Yeah. I very nearly did that."

"No regrets?" he teased, and I shoved him playfully.

"Sam! It's not funny," I said, but failed to completely hide my laugh.

He grinned at me coyly, like that was an apology. And for us, it was. "You can't say it's not a little bit funny."

I sighed and my eyes roved the pitch aimlessly. They fell on Beckett, and I saw he was watching me and Sam avidly. From that distance and with his jaw as hard as it was, I almost mistook his expression for jealousy. That was as ridiculous an idea as the fact that he and Jaeger were at my practice.

"Quin!" the Coach called, and I nodded to him.

"Not a word to Hunter," I warned him, and he mimed zipping his mouth shut.

He went to the bleachers, and I went to huddle with the rest of the team.

I caught the ball passed to me by Sienna, and nodded in thanks.

She was technically one of the Royals' courters. Higher on the pecking order than one of the harem, but not quite a Royal. As far as any of those arseholes went, Sienna was nice enough. She kept to herself and only maintained her place in the precious hierarchy because her dad was a rich enough arsehole to think about giving Preston's family a run for their money. Literally.

One good thing came from Beckett and Jaeger being at my practice. It took far less effort to imagine that every ball was their faces, and I managed to smack each one far more successfully than usual.

# CHAPTER SIX

The next week was absolutely no better.

Fox was sticking with the gentleman persona. His flirting technique was trying to be coy and cute and nice. Had any other guy turned around and tried it on, I might have fallen for it. But, by the middle of the next week, even I wasn't falling for Fox's bullshit anymore. It had gone way past flattery and just veered into broken record territory. Which, I think, went to show just how little practise Fox had ever had with being cute and nice, that he constantly fell back on all the same tactics. They got boring.

Jaeger was still talking up Beckett and talking down Fox at every opportunity. His efforts were slightly more welcome, only in that I found them worryingly endearing and very amusing.

And Beckett.

Jesus.

The King of Rivermont wasn't bothering with cute or coy or nice or endearing or amusing. He was going full sex appeal. And it was fucking working. Beckett's sex appeal had worked on me when he never looked at me. Now that he was looking at me and directing that sex appeal right at my body, I was a goner and I wanted him badly.

Just thinking about him had me throbbing and humming and breathing more heavily. I replayed the incident in the library far too often. It was the first time I'd really appreciated having a bedroom to myself, because I found myself lying in bed every night getting lost in fantasies of it being Beckett's hand between my legs instead of mine.

I'd worked myself up so much about him that I was on the precipice of actually giving into him, without caring one whit about what the game was or how it was going to eventually blow up in my face. I just needed to know if he felt as good as I thought he would. I needed him to sate this hollow ache he elicited in me. I needed him to use and discard me so I could get on with my damned life.

To make all the matters worse, every single person in the school noticed that there was some kind of competition running between Fox and Beckett. One that was different to the usual, and one that involved me. It was impossible for them not to notice that both Fox and Beckett were paying me more attention, and thus draw the most logical conclusion.

I wasn't the only one waiting for the punchline to finally be made clear.

Fox and I had three of seven classes together. Aside from sitting next to me and heavily flirting with me through the whole of French class, he'd used every opportunity to pay me a compliment or ask my seemingly innocent opinion on something, to hold doors open for me or bow to me.

Beckett, on the other hand, was a year ahead of me and so we didn't share any classes together except having a free at the same time. He had to fall back on annoying me in the corridors or in the library. He was there in my free on Tuesday and again on Wednesday. I saw him on the way in and the way out, and made sure I was sitting at my desk the whole time I was there to give him less opportunities to try to feel me up in the stacks.

I kicked myself for that one multiple times and even tried arguing that him trying to feel me up in the stacks was a good thing. But luckily, my head won the debate over my body, and I stayed firmly in my seat. Not that it stopped him from finding ways to crowd my space and turn me into a ball of compressed raging lustful hormones at least once a day.

At the end of Homegroup on Thursday, I was sitting with Sam when Beckett's self-appointed future missus approached me, followed closely by her harpy, Mariana.

Isabella leant on the table and sneered at me. "You will choose Fox," she threatened. "Beckett's mine."

I blinked, wondering why she thought it mattered to me all of a sudden. "You can have them both for all I care. Have them at the same time if you want."

Fox held his hand over his heart on his way out of the classroom. "Oh, Eden," he cried. "You wound me. Throwing my love back in my face like that."

I rolled my eyes. "Sure, Fox. My bad." Then turned back to Isabella. "I don't want Beckett. Go back to planning how your wedding can be more expensive than a real-life royal's."

Isabella's nostrils flared and Mariana crossed her arms.

"You do not want to cross me," Isabella told me, her voice all ice.

I nodded. "I have no intention of doing so. Please inform Lady Catherine that your inbreeding program is still perfectly safe."

Sam snorted beside me, but he recovered impressively quickly when Isabella turned her glare on him. Clearly, she didn't have any idea what to say to that. So, she just flicked her hair over her shoulder and swept out of the room dramatically.

"I don't think she knows who Lady Catherine is," Sam mused as we headed for Recess.

I snorted. "Probably too much to expect she knows anything about the classics."

"That, of course, implies that Beckett is playing the part of Darcy–"

I snorted, "Badly."

"– and you, his Elizabeth," he continued like I hadn't interrupted.

I frowned at him. "I will never be *his* anything."

"What if he offered one night, no strings, no consequences? One night in his bed and then he goes back to pretending you don't exist?"

I smirked at him. "There is no world where there wouldn't be consequences, but I would totally consider fucking Beckett if it meant my life could go back to normal, yes."

"Good to know," Beckett's voice slid over me.

Sam looked quite possibly more embarrassed than me as we turned to see Beckett leaning against a wall. I had no idea how I'd missed him, but my cheeks heating did nothing to wipe the cocky half-smile of victory off his face.

Whelp.

Now I was in trouble.

It was one thing for my body to traitorously scream at Beckett that I wanted him, but my voice had all-but now done it, too. Now he knew, in very not heat-of-the-moment moments, that I thought about him. Sexually. Like he needed any more leverage over me.

I *could* tell him exactly what I was thinking. I could just fire back and tell him that I'd consider it, but I wasn't so despondent for my normal life that I'd stoop that low. And, I would have. It was right on the tip of my tongue. But I was still labouring under the probably, by now, false assumption that I could make him lose interest by not reacting to him.

It was an assumption that had been working better for me than any other response for the last four years. I was loathe to just give up my tried-and-true method. What if I did fire back and that made him

– or Fox – more interested?

Despite knowing that my response, or lack thereof, had zero impact on Beckett's or Fox's interest levels, I was still hesitant. I didn't want to try something new and put myself in a worse position.

There was the smallest chance that little to no response would make Fox bored enough to make Beckett bored. That wasn't no chance. And I'd keep telling myself that until Beckett graduated, and Fox could just take the crown and let me get back to my life.

"Eat with me," Beckett said. It was an order. A demand. There was no expectation or belief I would do anything other than what he said.

"No," I said, biting off the automatic 'thanks' I would have given to anyone else.

"She'd rather eat with me," Fox said, sidling up next to me and I wondered where in the hell he'd even come from. He slid his hand into mine and I looked down at it incredulously.

Beckett stepped up to Fox, ignoring me once more and proving yet again that this wasn't about me. Beckett was all ice-cold hatred ready to burn Fox from the inside out. Fox was all amused defiance waiting to see what his king would do while he held my hand.

As Beckett snarled, "Do not touch her," at Fox, I yanked my hand out of Fox's.

"Something we can agree on," I muttered, and they both turned to look at me.

I looked them over and felt the push-pull in me. Fire back. Keep quiet. Stick up for myself. Protect myself. Stand out. Stay under the radar. My inner monologue and the person I was conditioned to be around these people warred in me.

This wasn't Jaeger being a somewhat entertaining dick when it was just the two of us and I could sass back at him and make him smirk in amusement at the little pleb thinking she made a difference to the mighty Royal. This was the king and his heir battling it out for something I didn't understand. Something that was clearly bigger than your average high school popularity contest. Something that the outsiders weren't privy to.

Like it was at all on the same bar, I took Sam's hand and headed to the dining hall.

I could feel Fox's and Beckett's eyes on me as I walked away, but I squeezed Sam's hand harder and told myself not to turn around. Thankfully, my best friend did it for me.

"They're both looking," Sam whispered.

I shrugged, but he saw through my nonchalance instantly. "They can be the ones to appreciate my arse for once."

Sam snorted, then turned back around like he didn't want Fox or Beckett to see him smile. He slipped his hand from mine and put his arm around my shoulders.

"Sometimes, I wonder if life would be easier if I liked you," he said, and I knew what he meant.

"We could still get married and save each other a butt load of trouble?" I offered.

"Is that you asking?" he asked with a warm smile.

"How about this? If we're still single at thirty, we pity marry. Try the whole IVF thing and co-parent while we try out a bunch of sordid affairs."

"You just want to take your affairs in my dad's helicopter."

I nodded. "I do want that. I want to *Fifty Shades* those poor innocent bastards," I laughed.

Sam joined me as we dropped at the end of the food line. "Okay. Deal. But is thirty too early?"

"If you want me to have your babies, no." I patted my hip bone.

"These puppies are only good for so long."

He nodded. "Yeah. All right then. What if we get you pregnant, then find our The One?"

"Then we have the makings of a hilarious and bestselling rom-com on our hands."

"I can get behind that."

I nudged him companionably and he grinned at me.

We met Hunter for Recess, where there was no more talk of our new pact, then it was just us again for double Maths, and back to meet Hunter for lunch, then Hunter and I left Sam to his free and went to Biology.

I didn't know why I'd chosen Biology. I had no plans to do it or probably anything science-related at uni, but I enjoyed it, and it was, weirdly, something I was good at. I liked cells and genetics and all that stuff. Which was about all we'd got to at the beginning of Year Eleven.

As we walked back out of the biology lab, Preston Worthington-Smythe and his overly tight, tailored, cropped trousers sighed as he pushed off the wall as though he'd been playing guard duty for his king. I wasn't sure who was less impressed with the duty, though; me or him.

Apparently, the Royals weren't just arseholes, but clichéd arseholes who hadn't got the memo that you could in fact stand around in a corridor without leaning against a wall. Although, where Beckett favoured the 'side-on, shoulder-to-wall and foot crossed at the ankle' lean against a wall, and Jaeger liked the 'back-to-wall with one knee bent and a foot on the wall' lean, Preston went for the 'back-to-wall and foot crossed at ankle while looking like you were trying to keep that rod up your arse with nothing but your sphincter muscle' lean.

Hunter looked him over and I almost thought he was going to do or say something to the snooty Royal.

Preston was well known for his brains, not his brawn. At least, we assumed he had brains in his head considering the most impressive fight he'd ever been in involved him swaying away from flailed fists, kicking his attacker to the floor with his expensive boat shoes, then smacking him on the back with the end of his cane like he was swatting a fly. He'd walked away from that altercation easily and without batting an eye. His attacker hadn't been so lucky.

"I am to walk you to Psychology where Rowan will meet us and ensure Fox sits as far away from you as possible," Preston drawled, like the whole thing was beneath him. Honestly, it probably was.

"Has Beckett got *all* of you wasting your frees on me now?" I asked, aiming for a joke because, to be honest, Preston was the one who made me the least comfortable. I had no history with him, he gave less away than Beckett, and I had no idea what was going through his head.

Preston's nose wrinkled slightly, and he sucked his teeth apathetically. "Yes."

Well. I had nothing to say to that, and Hunter had to go in the opposite direction for his lesson, so I let Preston wordlessly lead me to Psychology.

Rowan was waiting for us with a barely hidden snarl tugging at his lips as he looked me over like I was more trouble than I was worth. I had a tendency to agree with him on that one. But he took up his station outside my classroom and I wasn't the only one who kept an eye on him through the whole lesson; Fox kept a watchful eye on Rowan, and the teacher clearly wondered what in the hell Rowan Finch was doing outside his classroom. The fact he kept looking at me suggested he knew or at least guessed the answer to that question.

So, I escaped at the end of the day as fast as I could and made for my room to get my bathers. After a day like that, I needed the pool. I needed to swim, to try to calm myself down and stop thinking about Beckett Maxwell and the whole shitty situation.

Thinking I was terribly clever, I made for the back stairs of the girls' dorm. It was rarely used. I had to go out of my way to get to it or from it to anywhere else. On my way out, I headed that way again. It was really designed as a fire escape, but I hoped Beckett wouldn't think of it.

Naturally, all hopes were instantly dashed as I turned down the next flight of stairs and ran straight into him. My hands went to his body like I needed it to steady myself. His kept his hands off me like he knew I wanted the exact opposite.

Beckett and I stared into each other's eyes. I knew his were a challenge. A challenge I very much wanted to meet, but I kept my mouth shut in the hopes it got the game over quicker. But the way he searched my face every time he looked at me now, I was sure he could see written in my eyes as plain as day my attraction to him. The way there was this small hint of something like victory in his eyes as he stared into mine. I knew he knew. And it helped me keep my mouth shut even more because, if I didn't voice it aloud – again – maybe he'd eventually think it was a mistake on his part.

I breathed heavily as Beckett looked me over and felt the nerves cause me to bite my lip. Like we all knew I was going to say something stupid given half the chance. I took a step backwards and felt the wall at my back.

Beckett's face inched closer to mine, veering at the last second to touch his lips to my ear. "Go on," he purred. "Say it."

I fought the instinct to sass him, but still said, "Say what?"

"Yes," his voice slid over me tantalisingly, seductively. It was almost pleading. "Give in now, and you won't regret it."

Well, that was both true and false at the same time.

My body wouldn't regret it, my head would. I was all for meaningless sex if it was on offer, but there was no way that sex with Beckett Maxwell would be meaningless. It wouldn't be meaning*ful*, but it would definitely mean *something*. And without knowing exactly what that something was, it was far too dangerous a thing to give into. Whether it meant my life back or not.

But, God, I wanted to. So badly.

His hand ran down my side, hugging my thigh like he wanted my leg to hug his hip. My leg wanted that as well, but it only buckled a little and I was very impressed with my restraint.

"You want to," he said as he rocked his hips into me. "You want me to."

Well, yes. Very much, but… Fuck, it was such a bad idea.

My body did not get the memo.

My head lay back against the wall at my back and my hand lay on his arm in the very opposite of pushing him away or telling him no.

Beckett took that as an invitation and picked me up effortlessly to press me against the wall with nothing but his body holding me up. He was perfectly aligned between my legs, with our faces at a very opportune height for kissing. Jesus, but having sex with him now would have been easy and effortless.

Undo that loose zip of his, slide aside my undies, and…

He dropped his lips to my neck and goosebumps flared to life across my whole body as my nipples tightened. He ran his hands up my sides firmly and my traitorous body wrapped my arms around his shoulders and threaded my fingers in his hair as my clit throbbed.

I took a deep breath, but it did nothing to still the frantic, desperate flutter of my heart.

He thrust his hips lazily and it did nothing to help me want him to put me down.

Beckett looked me in the eyes as his fingers found the buttons of my shirt and deftly started undoing the top one. My chest rose and fell heavily, much heavier than his. If this was affecting him as much as it was affecting me, then he was a damn sight better at hiding it than I was. Which I knew was only giving him the upper hand, but I couldn't help it.

As his fingers trailed to the next button, my hand wrapped around them to stop him.

He looked at me quizzically, humour dancing in his eyes.

"No doesn't mean yes, Beckett," I told him, embarrassingly breathlessly.

"And you don't mean no."

He wasn't wrong. I wanted to say yes, but I wasn't and he was going to have to deal with that.

His nose nuzzled mine as he whispered, "We both want this. You want me. I want you. And I always get what I want, Eden."

A part of me knew it was only a matter of time before he did get what he wanted, if he did actually want me. My restraint only went so far and, if he kept up this sort of thing, there would come a time when I was sick of saying no and just deal with the consequences after.

Another part of me very much wanted to show him that he didn't, in fact, always get what he wanted. It was a petulant part who was instantly despised by the rest of me who thought just fucking him there and now would be a great idea. But the petulant part was stronger.

"Giving me what I want only gets you what you want," he

continued, and I almost fell for it.

"No," I said, sounding more believable than I felt.

He dropped me gently, almost tenderly, to the floor but didn't step out of my space. One heartbeat. Two. I wasn't sure what he was going to do. I only wanted him to do things that were such a damned bad idea.

"I will get what I want, Eden," he said as he finally took a single half a step back.

I clenched my jaw, knowing that anything else I might say now would land me in hotter water.

His gaze seared me almost as much as his hands, as his lips.

All I could do was bite my lip again, hurry out of there as quickly as I could, and be glad I was already heading for the pool.

He didn't follow me, but I felt like someone was watching me through my whole swim. It totally defeated the purpose of the exercise, but I was still feeling a little bit less stressed by the time I got back to my room.

# CHAPTER SEVEN

Another week had passed and Fox and Beckett were still at it.

It was getting tiresome.

Fox was easy to brush off and he hadn't taken it as badly as I'd expected, which made it less annoying than it could have been. The cynic in me firmly believed he was playing the long game.

Beckett was less easy. In every way. There was more testing and teasing, and me putting my foot in it when I didn't know he was listening. I kept trying to tell him no, but my restraint was wavering violently and he knew it.

By Saturday morning, I was looking over my shoulder before I said anything to anyone. I stomped to meet Mum at the pool.

"Here," she laughed when she saw me, and passed me the travel mug of coffee.

I nodded. "Thanks."

"*What* is keeping you up so badly?"

I was not about to tell my mother – as progressive and laid back as she was – that two of the Royals were in a competition to get in my pants (to be honest, she probably already knew and kudos to her for saving me some dignity and not bringing it up first). Nor was I going to tell her that one of them was very close to winning, and it was thoughts of him that were keeping me up, or waking me up, most nights.

The efficacy of a cold shower had diminished drastically after

Isabella and a few of the other harem had cornered me in the girls' bathroom one too many times and tried browbeating into me that Beckett was off-limits.

No amount of continued reminding them I didn't care, because I didn't want him, made any difference. They hadn't actually threatened me with physical violence, it was all verbal, and I wasn't all that concerned about them in the grand scheme, but it was annoying and something I preferred to avoid.

"Just not sleeping."

Mum put the back of her hand to my head. "You coming down with something?"

*Royal-itis? Or maybe just a Beckett Complex.* "I don't think so," I said with a shrug.

"Hm. Okay, but if you're still not sleeping next week, I want you to see the nurse."

I nodded, if only to placate her. "Sure. I will," I told her, knowing there was a fair chance I'd still be not sleeping and I wasn't going to be telling the nurse anything.

She smiled. "All right. Thank you. How's the year going so far?" she asked as swimmers trailed in and out in various states of dress, or undress.

Some kids came to the pool in their bathers. Some of those left the pool in their bathers – in any weather – and changed in their dorms. Others brought something dry to leave the pool in. Some kids came in clothes and changed at the pool. Others did a combination of many of the above. It was a free for all.

"We've only had three weeks," I reminded her. "It's going as good as it's going to get."

She smiled. "Fair. How's Psychology?"

I shrugged noncommittally. "It's okay. I don't think I'm going to like Stats."

"Stats is the best bit!"

I frowned at her. "If you're so good at maths, why did you go into sport?"

"Because I was better at sport."

I rolled my eyes. "Well, if you were going to hog all the talent, you could have at least passed on some of the brains, then."

She gave me a one-armed hug. "You've got plenty of both."

"Tell that to my maths grades."

"You didn't have to do it this year," she reminded me.

"Thank you, Madam Logic. But Sam was always doing maths."

"You *are* allowed to pick subjects that your friends aren't doing."

I fake gasped. "Blasphemy. How dare you suggest I could be my own person!"

Mum smirked. "Look, I don't mind that you're keeping your options open. It's practical. Just promise me that, if you settle on what you need for uni, then you'll just do those subjects."

"Of course, I will. But, until I have any idea what I want to do with my life, there's living vicariously through my friend…and an Arts Degree."

"Just so long as you have it all planned out," she chuckled.

"I do. If Rivermont's good for one thing, their Futures team is very…dedicated and communicative."

Mum laughed into her coffee. "That's very political."

"Maybe I'll go into politics."

"What'll your platform be? Vote one Democracy Sausage?" Mum teased.

"Yes," I told her, deadpan. "The Democracy Sausage is an integral part of Australian Politics."

Mum nodded, fighting a smile. "That it is."

"Coach?" one of the swimmers came up for Mum's attention.

"That's me," she answered as he put her hand to my arm, her non-verbal way of saying, 'Sorry, got to work. Back to you later'.

I returned the gesture for a, 'No worries, have at it', and headed over to the bleachers. My eyes roved over the pool. Over the various swimmers in their groups, warming up or chatting, or just still waking up. I was the only one in the bleachers, but no one paid me any more attention than they did any other week. Which was none.

Except one.

The previous week, it hadn't even occurred to me that Hunter was supposed to have been at practice in week one. I'd totally forgotten that he was apparently now a swimmer. So, when I saw him across the pool, ready for practice, that morning, I was still surprised to see him.

He gave me a huge grin and a wave, and I smiled politely as I shifted in my seat.

"Aw, that's cute," Jaeger said as he appeared beside me on the bleachers. "He thinks you're actually likely to fall in love with him now."

"Isn't your arse cold?" I muttered, my eyes darting to his barely budgie-smuggler-covered butt cheeks on the cool metal of the bleachers.

"It's damn hot, and you know it, Harlequin," he said with a mischievous smirk. "Doesn't he know you're not into swimmers?" Jaeger leant into me and put his arm around my shoulders as he looked at Hunter. "Otherwise, you and I'd have sealed the deal years ago."

"I thought your king wasn't going to tell you twice?" I asked as I rolled my eyes and pushed him off me. "Won't he take issue with you pretending to flirt with me to annoy Hunter?"

Hunter frowned at us from the other side of the pool and Jaeger chuckled.

"Lover boy takes issue with me talking to you, it seems," he said, waving to Hunter obnoxiously as he leant back on his other hand and crossed his ankles in front of him.

"Hunter's my friend – which is more than can be said for you – and he doesn't want to see me get hurt – which is also more than can be said for you."

Jaeger scoffed humourlessly as he sat up straight again. "I promise you. I care more about your health and wellbeing than your *friend* does."

"Hunter doesn't trust you and I don't blame him," I replied, ignoring the insinuations heavy in Jaeger's words.

Hunter's distrust was written plainly on his face. It wasn't just distrust. It was bordering on hostile fury, and it was all directed at Jaeger. I think Jaeger and I both knew it wasn't just about Jaeger, though. Somehow, I seemed to read on Hunter's face the 'keep your king away from her' threat.

But then, that was how Hunter had taken to Fox and Beckett paying me attention. He'd been pissed. Like unusually pissed off about it. He was on the verge of territorial. He acted like he was going to actually put Beckett-freaking-Maxwell in his place. It didn't seem that much of a stretch to imagine that he'd consider putting Jaeger in his place…in Beckett's place.

Jaeger frowned at Hunter, and I saw the warning in it. "Beckett will not suffer another man to encroach on his territory. Tell your friend to keep his insolence in check."

"Yeah, and how's that going with Fox?" I asked Jaeger.

"It's better not to talk of things you don't understand, little Quince."

"I understand arrogant cavemen fighting over something that isn't theirs," I told him. "What I don't understand is why."

"And you don't need to," he said simply.

"Why?" I scoffed. "Because it's not the women's place?"

Jaeger turned a stern eye on me. "We Royals are a lot of things, Quincy. But what we don't tell you, keeps you safe. The way you should be kept. The way your *friend* over there would never consider keeping you. Beckett wants more than just your body, wants more than just not letting Fox have you. It's deeper than that, Quin."

I rolled my eyes. "Do you hear yourself?"

He nodded. "I do and I mean every word. Beckett's not just motivated by jealousy. Not like some people," he finished, cryptically. Then he stood up and voluntarily headed over where Mum was starting practice.

I watched him go and wondered at his words.

From what I knew of the Royals, Jaeger's words were…foreign and *should* be considered weakness. It didn't track. The only thing I could think of was that this was him playing wingman. I wasn't sure or not whether Jaeger was likely to lie in the effort to get me to choose his king, but he would definitely stretch the truth.

Either way, the extent he was going did nothing to make me want to choose Beckett – like there was actually a choice – and everything to convince me more that this was just some bogus status operation that was way above my paygrade or care levels.

As I mused on Jaeger and Beckett and Fox, I watched Hunter pushing himself to keep up with Jaeger in the pool. His splashes made his efforts look frantic. A stark comparison to Jaeger's effortless clean lines.

A part of me was amused that Hunter's instinct was to try to beat Jaeger in the pool. A guy who'd barely stepped foot in the pool in the last three years thinking he could beat a guy who'd grown up in the pool and been in it everyday for at least the last four years.

There was another part of me that wondered why Hunter was getting all aggro like that. There was indignation on my behalf, and then there was this weird almost jealousy that seemed to make his whole body vibrate.

Sam had taken a very different approach to the whole thing. As evidenced by a message I got on my phone while Hunter fell a full half-lap behind Jaeger.

**Samwell Kap-gee**

How you doing? Sleep any better?

**E-denQ**

Goooob morning.

Not really. How about you?

**Samwell Kap-gee**

Gooooob morning to you.
Slept like a damned baby.

**E-denQ**

Oh, look at me, I'm Sam and I sleep

well.

Way to boast.

**Samwell Kap-gee**

If it makes you feel better, I'm very close

to pity fantasies.

**E-denQ**

*snort* I'm not sure that does make me

feel better.

**Samwell Kap-gee**

I actually dreamt about Beckett last night. Are his hands as soft as you'd think they are?

I snorted out loud this time.

**E-denQ**

Yes.

**Samwell Kap-gee**

Damn.

**E-denQ**

Yep.

And that summed up Sam. He was getting as tired of it as I was because he knew it annoyed me. But he just cared how I was coping and was there as a sympathetic ear. He knew if I wanted him to do anything, I'd tell him. Not that he was really a do anything about it kind of guy. He could let rip with the verbal sparring as well as anyone. In debate. When he'd learnt and practised his speech. In an actual argument, he got all tongue tied and couldn't think of anything remotely witty to say.

**Samwell Kap-gee**

Ah well. Lunch later and we can commiserate about Beckett's baby-like hands together?

**E-denQ**

They're soft, but they're huge.

81

**Samwell Kap-gee**

*fanning GIF*

Don't tell me that!

Now all I can think about is how big his

dick is!

**E-denQ**

I think it's pretty decent.

**Samwell Kap-gee**

Is this your personal opinion, or just
your best guess based on the
information you've been given thus far?

**E-denQ**

There will be no more gathering of

evidence. Survey is closed. But it's my

best guess based on my leg's feedback.

**Samwell Kap-gee**

Hot damn, woman.

Forget pity fantasies. I'mma just
fantasise on my own.

**E-denQ**

Have at it. Someone may as well enjoy

it.

**Samwell Kap-gee**

...you... you could be...

**E-denQ**

In theory, I could.

**Samwell Kap-gee**

In theory, communism works.

In practicality, you could just take his highness for a test drive.

**E-denQ**

I don't think us lowly mortals are the ones who do the driving.

**Samwell Kap-gee**

Just how I like it.

**E-denQ**

What if I want to drive?

**Samwell Kap-gee**

Get yourself a potion that makes you miraculously attracted to someone not Beckett Maxwell.

**E-denQ**

I'm attracted to people who are not Beckett Maxwell.

**Samwell Kap-gee**

Name one.

**E-denQ**

…

**Samwell Kap-gee**

Didn't think so.

**E-denQ**

I'm thinking!

**Samwell Kap-gee**

Thinking how to lie to me maybe.

Damn him for knowing me so well.

**E-denQ**

Fine. I can't currently think of any. But

there have been others!

**Samwell Kap-gee**

If Lord Gets What He Wants always gets

what he wants, why can't you have what

you want?

It was eerily close to what Beckett had said to me. Coming from
Sam, it sounded much less easy to disregard. To the point that I was
about to agree with him, but…

**E-denQ**

Whose side are you on?

**Samwell Kap-gee**

Yours.

Always.

**E-denQ**

Mine or my libido's?

**Samwell Kap-gee**

*taco por que no los dos ad GIF*

**E-denQ**

Not helpful.

**Samwell Kap-gee**

*Road to Eldorado both GIF*

**E-denQ**

Fine. I'll fuck him. Then you'll be

singing a different tune.

**Samwell Kap-gee**

I mean, I won't. But we can give it a

shot?

I smirked as I put my phone in my lap and looked back over the pool.

Sam had always been a shit-stirrer when it came to me, but that didn't mean he wasn't talking some sense in theory.

In an ideal world, I'd totally give Beckett a go and satisfy my curiosity. Then I could go back to my life and leave their little power struggles to themselves. But I didn't live in an ideal world. I lived in a world run by the Rivermont Royals and their arbitrary hierarchy.

**Samwell Kap-gee**

You never answered about lunch.

**E-denQ**

Lunch is a definite.

Fucking Beckett is a definite no.

**Samwell Kap-gee**

Well, one out of two ain't bad. I'll see you then.

**E-denQ**

Not coming to my game? ;P

**Samwell Kap-gee**

I guess I'd best. Who else is going to give you the run down on the Royals' attendance.

**E-denQ**

Shut up.

**Samwell Kap-gee**

You love me.

**E-denQ**

I do.

I slipped my phone in my pocket and went back to watching swim practice.

If Hunter and Jaeger were actually having a competition of their own, I didn't think Jaeger knew about it and he was still crushing Hunter at every turn. As Hunter's friend, I knew I should feel worse for him, but I honestly couldn't bring myself to condone the ridiculousness, even in the privacy of my own head.

Just before the end of practice, I downed the last vestiges of my coffee and headed into the changerooms to get into my softball gear before breakfast with Mum. As I was changing, I heard Regina and Phoenix come in and start talking with someone else on the other side of the lockers and I caught my name.

"Why Eden Quin, though?" the third voice asked.

"Because Fox actually thinks my brother *likes* her," Regina said snootily, and with a note of humour in it, like she thought the idea was as laughable as I did.

"Fox is an idiot," Phoenix, Fox's little sister, said exasperatedly. "He thinks just because Beckett flexed on him over a failed insult to the Quin girl that our king must be weakening."

"So why did he bet with Jaeger?" the third voice asked.

I jumped and banged my elbow on my locker.

Excuse me? Who did what now?

There had been a bet with Jaeger?

I wasn't exactly sure how I felt, but indignant, furious and quite miffed were at the top of my list.

Regina huffed, but there was no humour in it. "Because he wasn't banking on Beckett putting his foot down so early."

"What was the bet again?" Phoenix asked innocently.

"You know that movie 'He's all That'?" Regina said and the others agreed. "Well, it was a remake of some nineties film or something, and the theory is famous among the boys. Take a girl and make her cool so she wins prom queen and then fuck her."

"But we don't have prom queens," the third voice said.

"No, but we have a Royal court and Fox bet Jaeger he could make Eden Quin acceptable, then take her to the formal and then take her virginity."

*Well,* I thought, *joke's on him. That ship sailed a while ago.*

"And Jaeger paid that bet?"

*Get in line, Mum. I might kill Jaeger.*

"Yep," Phoenix said. "Who was going to do it? Jaeger or Fox?" she asked, hypothetically.

I didn't know what was more gross. The idea of sleeping with Fox or Jaeger. No. I did know. There was a morbidly curious part of me that had wondered what Jaeger would be like. I wouldn't have touched Fox with a pole the length of an Olympic swimming pool.

"Then my idiot brother stepped in and put a stop to it," Regina added. "He decreed that no Royal would take Eden to the formal. No Royal would touch her. No Royal would even speak to her."

"Jaeger complied," Phoenix said. "But *my* idiot brother decided on treason."

Jaeger was maybe less in my shit box.

"So, why's Beckett interested in Eden?" the third voice asked. "Why doesn't he let Fox just have her?"

"Beckett can't lay down the law and then let his heir disobey him," Regina scoffed loftily, sounding exactly like her brother. "It's all about power now. Why he made the law to begin with though, I don't even know. I don't get what's so interesting about the Coach's daughter."

It was about that time that I stopped caring what they were saying.

Whatever they said next could have nothing on the revelation they just dropped.

I was just the butt of some Royal power struggle? Well, I knew that. I'd guessed that it was some power play. But it was because of a bet? It wasn't even because there was a part of Fox that was actually interested? It was all for a crown that meant nothing to me.

Suddenly, everything was making a disgusting kind of sense. What did it matter why me? The person wasn't important. Me, being the person. All those advances – Fox's flirting and Beckett's hands all over my body – meant nothing. Were as nothing as me to them. What mattered to Fox and Jaeger and Beckett was who came out on top.

Turns out, Sam had been dead wrong. He might get to be safe in the stands while he watched the Royals' worlds implode, but I was going to be forced to be right in the middle of it. Wanting no part of it was going to make no difference to either Beckett or Fox and whatever plans they had. Had I been a more ambitious person, I'd have wondered which of them I could manipulate more and therefore help them win in order to gain. But I wasn't. I was an introverted kind of person who just wanted to live her life in peace, and I didn't give a single shit about which dickhead ruled the school with their arbitrary laws.

"Oh, hey, Eden," I heard and looked up to see Abby walk in.

I forced a smile I certainly wasn't feeling, but felt real enough. "Hey, Abby."

"How are things?"

Pretty shit, actually. "Fine, thanks. You?"

She nodded. "Getting there. Are you playing home or away this week?"

"Uh, home," I said absently.

I heard Regina laughing and they walked past our aisle of the lockers. Regina looked straight at me, and I was very sure that their conversation had been purely for my benefit. She'd known I was there, and she wanted me to know about the bet.

Why? Who in the hell knew. Who in the hell cared.

It was probably just another way of messing with me. Another way to make me feel powerless in my life. A way to make sure I remained firmly in my place and didn't get any lofty ideas that two powerful men at our school actually wanted little old Eden Quin.

Like I'd trusted them about their sincerity anyway.

Whatever my face was saying, it made Regina smirk before she disappeared.

"Uh, are you okay?" Abby asked me.

I looked at her. "Um, kinda. Okay enough, anyway."

She didn't seem to know what to say to that and I didn't rightly blame her.

Regina might have reminded me how little power I had over Beckett and Fox and the situation they'd put me in. But I'd take back what power I could. They could flirt with me all they liked, Beckett could make me forget my own damned mind and let carnal desire rule me as often as he wanted, but I wasn't going to let them win without fighting in the only way I could.

"Listen," I said to her and she smiled. "We have a few classes together, right?"

She nodded. "Yeah?"

"I've noticed you don't have anyone to sit with. Do you mind if I sit with you?"

She blinked like that hadn't been what she was expecting. "Uh, no. No, that'd be fine. Great even. Your boyfriend won't mind, though?"

I scoffed, assuming she meant Fox. "Fox is not my boyfriend, and he never will be."

"Oh," she seemed confused for a moment, then rallied. "Sorry, I just assumed because of how–"

"He likes to act like he has a chance in hell of getting in my pants?" I offered.

"Yeah, that."

I nodded. "Yeah, that. It's going around but, don't worry, it doesn't have anything to do with me. Apparently, I'm the butt of some Royal power struggle."

She cocked her head to the side in question. "Really?"

I nodded and, despite the fact I was meant to be getting ready for softball, I launched into the whole sordid mess with her. She gasped in all the right places, commiserated with me in all the right places, and agreed that guys in general were arseholes and the Royals in particular were pieces of shit.

"What are you doing this afternoon?" I asked her as we left the changeroom.

She shook her head. "Uh, no plans."

"Sam and I are going for lunch. Want to join?"

Abby's face lit up. "I'd love to, thanks."

As I went out to meet Mum, Abby and I swapped contact details for the Rivermont app so I could let her know when I was done and where Sam and I were heading.

"See you later, Coach," Abby said with a wave as she headed for the doors.

"Bye, Abby."

"Later, Eden."

"Later," I replied.

"You seem more chipper," Mum commented as we headed for the café in the teacher's village.

I nodded. "I feel more chipper. Did you put something in the coffee this morning?" I teased.

"No. Are you sure it has nothing to do with making a new friend?"

As a credit to her, I gave it some serious thought. Maybe it was. Maybe making friends wasn't the worst thing in the world. At least, maybe making friends like Abby wasn't the worst thing in the world.

# CHAPTER EIGHT

By Monday, I was still seething, though I was hiding it as best I could. I *had* told Sam this time, at lunch with Abby after my game on Saturday. He'd been suitably riled along with me, and the three of us had spent the afternoon coming up with revenge plots I would in no way have the balls to enact.

But it didn't mean it didn't fire up my annoyance levels and, the longer I stewed on it over Sunday, the angrier I was.

A bet? I was a fucking bet?

Not just a bet but one that had turned into some ridiculous power struggle between Fox and Beckett?

I was beyond livid.

My life wasn't a joke anymore, it was a fucking fiasco.

Beckett didn't want *me*, no matter what Jaeger was going to try to put on in the hopes I picked his king. Said king just wanted to maintain his supremacy over Fox's little attempted coup, and I was the thing he needed to own to do that. Well, fuck you very much.

He was not getting away with it.

And neither was Fox.

Plus, Jaeger deserved a bit of comeuppance at least for the part he'd been willing to play but for his king's decree.

I just had to work out how to deal with each of them in turn.

Fox was first.

And it wasn't pleasant.

Second lesson on Monday was Psychology. It was another class that Abby and I shared with Fox and no Sam. I made sure to find Abby on the way to the classroom and hang out with her the whole way, so we sat down together. On Abby's usual side of the classroom.

"Thanks for this," I told her.

She smiled. "I should be thanking you, surely?"

My smile for her was a little apologetic. "I feel a bit like I'm using you."

"This was one of the more practical plots from Saturday," she reminded me.

"Still…" I said slowly.

She shrugged. "I like to think of it as me helping you. Help seems a good basis for a friendship. Besides, it's not like you weren't totally honest about wanting me to help you avoid Fox. And it's not like it wasn't partly my idea."

Which was true. Between us, we'd cemented the plan of me sitting with Abby, in classes we shared without Sam, so Fox couldn't sit next to me.

Who was just then walking into the room. His eyes swivelled around the room as he looked for me, and he fixed me with a glare when he found me sitting with Abby. Then it was like he remembered that he was supposed to be winning me over with kindness and politeness and he smiled winningly. Shame it didn't reach his eyes.

"Eden," he said smoothly, his eyes falling on Abby. "I thought we were partners."

I nodded and pulled up my big girl pants. "You did think that. But I'm done, Fox. There is no way in a frozen Hell that I would ever go to the formal with you, and I do not care about being 'acceptable' enough for you or your idiot Royals. Plus, my virginity has well and truly left the building. Turns out, I'm not *all that*, after all."

He understood the reference straight away and his reaction was one I hadn't planned for.

So much for Fox being relatively harmless.

I had never seen such dark thunder on his face before and, unlike with Beckett, it actually scared me. He leant on the desk to get his furious face in mine. "You'll regret this, Eden," he said, his voice low.

I held my own as best I could, standing up to try to even out our physical positions. "I promise you I won't, Fox. I indulged your little fantasy that you could ever be endearing, but I'm over it. I'm bored now. Be a good boy and go lick your wounds where I don't have to look at you."

I didn't know where all that had come from. Probably two weeks of stamped down annoyance and keeping my witty quips to my head.

Fox twitched like his instinct had been to hit me, then the applause started in the room, and he just snarled at me and stormed out of the classroom, nearly knocking over Mademoiselle Teller as he went.

She looked around questioningly, but she soon found out what had Fox Maddox sweeping dramatically out of her classroom. The whole school soon found out. Before the lesson was over, I had a message from Sam that was just a victorious GIF. Followed swiftly by an explosion GIF. Followed just as swiftly by one that suggested I'd just dug myself an early grave.

Support followed by hyperbole followed by reality.

That summed Sam up perfectly, really.

As Abby came with me to meet Sam for Recess, the whole damned school was looking at me and whispering behind their hands as I passed. There were no points for the house of your choice for guessing what they were talking about. The majority of them all thought I was nuts, clearly. Their wide eyes and lack of smiles suggested they also thought I'd dug myself an early grave, and I wasn't inclined to disagree with them.

"I'm so dead," I whined.

"I'm sure it's not that bad," Abby offered.

I looked at her in disbelief. "Everyone knows."

She shrugged. "You were standing up for yourself."

"No one stands up to the Royals. That's the whole point."

"Well, maybe you've started a new trend?"

I didn't start a new trend, but Abby did join us for Recess and, like on Saturday, instantly hit it off with Sam. She even had something in common with Hunter given they were both on the swim team.

The three of them stuck by my side for solidarity as much as they were able. I had Sam with me for the English double, not that it stopped Fox and Gunner giving me a hint of what was coming to me. At the end of the lesson, Fox and Gunner made to beeline to me and their faces told me it was only the start of making me regret my words. Then Fox's eyes darted behind me, and he stopped short. I followed his gaze and saw that Rowan Finch was standing outside the room.

My immediate thought was that Beckett had found out about what had happened in Psychology and sent Rowan to keep an eye on me. I couldn't be sure it wasn't wishful thinking, but it was quite possibly the first time that I didn't mind Beckett's stalker tendencies.

Rowan stood like some immovable mountain with his arms crossed over his massive chest. He kept his eyes firmly on Fox and Gunner as Sam and I hurried out of the classroom, but he nodded to me.

"Get safe," he snapped at me with a coldness even Beckett wasn't capable of.

I'd heard rumours about Rowan, just like there were rumours about all of them. It was said that no one was as ruthless and heartless as the King of Rivermont, but it was also said that no one was quite as evil as Rowan. Beckett was cruel in that he was ambivalent, he was indifferent. But I'd heard Rowan was cruel in that he took a singular pleasure in being so. He enjoyed it.

Looking at him watching Fox like he dared the younger boy to take a step closer, I could believe it. There was a deep sense of satisfaction in his eyes just as his body looked utterly relaxed. It was like he was never more at home than when he was intimidating, or there was chance of beating someone up.

I had to wonder what horrors someone like that had faced. What kind of upbringing they'd had. I didn't doubt there were some seriously twisted individuals in the world – and a significant portion of them were Rivermont Royals – but I also didn't doubt that not all of them got that way just by being born. A lot of them – if not all of them – I was sure were made that way. No doubt by people, who had been made that way as well, in the name of tradition and necessity.

"Uh, okay," I stammered, wondering about the protocol. Did someone like me thank someone like him?

He gave a silent, humourless, scoff. "Thank the order of my king," he said, as though he'd read the question in my mind.

Without bothering to question further, I grabbed Sam, and we practically ran down the corridor. Behind us, we heard the tell-tale clash of bodies. Or, at least, the tell-tale sound of onlookers watching people fighting. At the door, I snuck a look back, and saw Rowan and Gunner were going at it.

Like Beckett had his muscle, so did Fox.

Like Fox was just that much less than Beckett, so Gunner was just that much less than Rowan.

It didn't mean that Rowan didn't give Gunner the upper hand for a moment simply because it made throwing him to the ground, when he finally got around to it, far sweeter. Rowan was clearly toying with Gunner. Gunner was clearly quite serious.

Yet another sign that the second generation of Royals still had a way to go before they equalled the first generation.

"No, you don't," Rowan said.

He whirled, keeping one hand on the back of Gunner's shirt as he reached the other to stop Fox taking a second step after me. Rowan's eyes flitted to follow Fox's gaze and found me standing there.

"Beckett said you had trouble following orders," Rowan said, his displeasure heavy in his voice. "Get. Safe." His tone told me he wasn't going to tell me a third time, and that he'd resort to physically making me if he had to.

I scrabbled beside me for Sam's arm as we shoved out of the doors and into the sun. Its rays on my face somehow lulled my head into some kind of security that my heart wasn't quite feeling.

"Ugh," Sam said, as he looked around. "I'm supposed to have Chess now."

I nodded. "No. All good," I said, totally faking how panicked I felt to be left to myself to go find Abby and Hunter for lunch.

"I can't just leave you."

I nodded again. "You can. Rowan's dealing with Fox. And Gunner. I guess. That should buy me some time to get to the library. I'll hide out there. I know it better than Fox. And, if I know Beckett, he'll find me before Fox does."

Here was hoping, for once, that Beckett was actually still not interested in listening to my very half-hearted protests about his attentions.

"You actually looking forward to Beckett finding you?" Sam

teased, knowing what I was thinking. Honestly, one brain.

"Shut up," I said, trying to hide my smile. "Go, and I'll see you later."

He nodded. "Okay. Okay, if you're sure."

"I'm not afraid of giving Fox a swift kick to his jewels," I said, really hoping it wouldn't come to that and just as equally hoping that I'd be less afraid if it did come to it.

"What happened to ignore them and they'll go away?" he joked.

I smirked. "I think that ship has sailed right along with our virginities."

He laughed. "Yeah, fair enough. Be safe."

"I will."

We hugged and went our separate ways.

So, Fox was dealt with – sort of – even if it put me in a worse position than I had been, but still it was done. Which meant I still had to deal with Beckett after Regina's revelation. I didn't have a plan, but I knew I could do it soon because he'd been following me around for the last three weeks; I knew there was no way he wasn't going to continue that now.

True to expectation, I saw Beckett and Jaeger near the library. I still wasn't sure what my plan was for dealing with Beckett, but I fixed him with a very pointed look before ducking into the library. Also true to expectation, he followed. I angled down to the back of the library, one of the spots well known for the place to go if you needed a little mid-study release. Even the Royals, who acted like they didn't know what a library was for, would have known that. Who better to seduce than horny and stressed teenagers?

Beckett followed me into the furthest aisle, but Jaeger was nowhere to be seen.

Good, because I only had the wherewithal to deal with one of them at a time, and the only reason I had the courage to deal with Beckett just then was that I was buzzing on adrenalin after Fox.

Beckett followed me right to the end of the aisle and looked me over with that unreadable look on his face. He elicited so much in me, and I was just a power play to him. He'd spent weeks seducing me, running his hands over my body and acting like we both wanted it, when I was just a means to an end. I wasn't surprised by that information, I'd known that, but having it confirmed annoyed me more than I thought it would.

I was so over these conflicting feelings that Beckett was making me feel. This constant push-pull. I knew I shouldn't want him, but I wanted him so much. Even in the face of what I now knew. I knew wanting him would only end badly for me, but it made no difference.

I just wanted it to be done, one way or another. When his eyebrow quirked in silent question, like I was the one who needed to be explaining themself, my self-preservation tactics utterly deserted me in the face of my frustration reaching boiling point.

I shoved against Beckett as hard as I could and totally blew all semblance of cool. "Why are you stalking me? Why does Jaeger follow me around when you're not? What is it about me that suddenly has this interest of the Royals, huh?" I wanted to see if he'd admit it.

No surprises, he didn't. "I'd have thought you'd prefer light stalking over what Fox has planned for you," he said, venom in his voice.

"Oh, I know exactly what Fox has planned for me," I spat, and I watched his eyes widen slightly.

"After that stunt you pulled on him, you have no idea what he's going to do to you," Beckett snarled, and fear ripped through me. Not fear of Beckett, but fear of what he was sure would be Fox's retribution.

"Maybe not, but I know all about Fox's little bet with Jaeger over the formal. I know you told them both to back off for some inexplicable reason. And I know Fox refused to obey his king's law and now you've made it personal. What doesn't make sense to me is why? Why you care, why you're feeling me up in the library stacks, and why you're following me around the school all the time."

He took a controlled breath. "I told you, Eden. I get what I want."

"Uh huh. And do you want *me*, or you just don't want Fox to have me?"

He stepped up to me. "Why does it have to be one or the other?"

I scoffed sarcastically, "And why would you give me an actual answer?"

His fury was palpable, and it was sexy. "I can want you *and* want to protect you from Fox," he said, his nostrils flaring.

"Excuse me? You think you're…? Protecting me!" I actually laughed in his face.

Beckett frowned pure ice. "If he gets you alone, your body won't be begging for his."

The end of that sentence was implied; '…the way it begs for mine'.

"Just stop!" I hissed at him, pushing him again. Not that it had a physical effect on him at all. "Enough!"

My full-on defiance seemed to please him and I had to stop myself doing it again just to please him more. "We're going to have to work on our safe words, Eden. We wouldn't want any misunderstandings. In the heat of the moment, it is *so* easy to say no when we really mean yes."

Fucking hell.

Talk about no.

I couldn't do this anymore.

Yeah, I wanted Beckett Maxwell to fuck me raw, ruin me, and throw me away when he was done. But doormat wasn't in my list of personality traits, despite how little I voluntarily entered confrontation. I'd already tried putting Fox in his place, why not make it a two-for kind of day?

"Well, you can go figure it out with someone else. Jaeger seems more than happy to do anything his king asks. See if he'll share his safe words."

"You want me," Beckett said snidely, a taunt.

I mean, yes, but… "I loathe you," I told him.

His knowing smirk had a touch of snarl in it. "There's a fine line between love and hate, Eden."

"Careful, *king*, lest you betray yourself and imply you're capable of more than just contempt." Someone had been reading too much Shakespeare for English. Or maybe that was my Austen fixation.

He leant forward, his lips grazing the soft shell of my ear as he spoke, and goosebumps broke across my skin as my nipples responded. "I feel more than just contempt for you," he purred, and I believed every word right down to my clit.

I knew what he was referring to. I could see it in his eyes. I was sure it was mirrored in mine.

"Lust doesn't count," I informed him, feeling very much in that moment like the complete opposite was true.

He pressed me hard into the shelves at my back and locked his gaze with mine. A battle of grey and brown. I felt him breathing deeply, his chest rising and falling against mine. It wasn't just contempt. It wasn't just lust. It was barely constrained fury. And I wanted more.

"Is that what you tell yourself?" he asked, his words a dare. "You tell yourself it's all right to lust after me because it doesn't count?"

"And what do you tell yourself?" I countered, knowing it did no good to lie to him now. "What justifies the King of Rivermont wanting someone like me? A nobody." They were their words – his words – not mine.

"I get whatever I want, Eden."

"Not this time," I said.

When I tried to push him away again, he obliged to sway backwards. I knew it was only because he let it happen.

As I walked away from him, I could have sworn I heard him say, "Definitely this time," in the sort of tone that implied I'd somehow just given him exactly what he wanted.

As I walked back out into the thoroughfare, I saw Jaeger leaning on a bookshelf as though he'd been on guard duty. He threw a cheeky half-smirk at me as I approached him.

"What?" I snapped, in no mood for his games.

He shrugged, then looked behind me and his smirk grew. "Nothing, Q," he said, looking like he was trying to stifle laughter. His eyes swung back to me and he gave a small fist pump, like he was trying to hide it from Beckett. "Score one for the bad girl."

I didn't need Jaeger Richards' approval, but it sure felt good to have it. Even if he had made the bet with Fox.

As I hit the door to the stairs, I turned for a moment and saw Beckett and Jaeger. Beckett's usual stony expression was trained on me. Jaeger's smirk threatened to overwhelm him as he shook his head. He then grasped Beckett by the shoulders and turned him to walk in the opposite direction.

I watched them for a moment, feeling like a part of me was going with him. But as wrong as walking away from Beckett felt, I knew it was right. I also realised exactly why I wanted him as much as I did.

Beckett was right when he said there was a fine line between love and hate. Not that I thought there was any chance of love blossoming between Beckett and me. But he was all passion. Whether he was angry or annoyed or amused with me, he did it all with a simmering passion that was threatening to spill with potential. It was that simmering passion that I wanted to see translated into the bedroom.

For years, I'd seen the cold, detached, calculated and controlled side of Beckett Maxwell. The one he showed the world. Even when I'd seen him in compromising situations, there'd been something cold about it. About him. Then school had gone back this year, the stupid bet had kicked off my own series of unfortunate events, and I'd seen a new side to him. He was still the same cold and controlled guy, but I saw the passion underneath now. I saw the fire that had the potential to catch flame and burn down my whole world.

And I wanted him to burn my whole world.

A man who hated that passionately and commanded such self-control surely fucked just as passionately and with just as much self-control.

So yeah, walking away from Beckett felt like the one thing I should never do. But I knew it was the sensible thing to do.

For a second, I was starkly reminded of Mum's favourite lecture. The one about some mistakes being the best time of your life. I knew without a doubt that Beckett would be the best time of my life and I didn't need to make that mistake to learn from it, but my resilience in the knowledge that it was a bad idea was starting to collapse.

*Why shouldn't I get what I wanted, too?*

For now, the pillars that held my belief up were still standing, shaky though they were, so I had the strength to not run after him and beg him to show me what it would be like to be his even for one afternoon.

But we'd see how long that lasted.

# CHAPTER NINE

My resolve was weakening. I knew it and I suspected Beckett sensed it.

After the day before, I was starting to forget exactly why I was denying my want for Beckett. I had more arguments for giving in than against, and little interest in arguing against anymore. Then, I walked into the library in my free lesson the next morning and found a very unwelcome sight at my desk. Not in my usual seat, but the one opposite which I thought was…oddly considerate and quite possibly meaningful for a guy like him.

"This has to be a joke," I muttered to myself, sliding into my usual seat.

"I don't joke," he said, fixing me with a glare.

I didn't doubt it. "Don't you have better things to do in this lesson than stalking me in the library?" I huffed.

He leant on the desk towards me. "No."

"No," I chuckled humourlessly. "I suppose guys who are going to inherent trillions of dollars don't have to worry about their grades."

A slight smirk tugged at the corner of his unbelievably kissable lips. "It's one of my frees," he said, and I took note of the fact that he didn't make any mention of his future trillions or my comment about them.

Because of course Beckett had a free at the same time as me. I'd assumed as much and now he'd confirmed it. Why wouldn't he? Why would the fates *not* engineer us both having the same free? The idea we would have totally separate frees was laughable.

"Please don't feel the need to suddenly hang out in the library in your free because of a nobody like me," I snapped as though he hadn't been in there plenty more than that, and his eyes lit up.

"My presence in the library during our free lesson is hardly sudden," he said smoothly. I filed away the fact he'd called it 'our' free lesson, as though we shared anything more than flaming sexual chemistry. He sat back and made himself unnecessarily comfortable.

Against my better judgement, my eyes roved over his body as it reclined in the chair. As usual, he was wearing the shirt, tie, blazer combination he so favoured. His white shirt was thick enough that there was no sign of any potential body hair, but it was tailored well enough that it clung to the ridges and contours of his muscles, hinting at the full definition of those abs. I absently chewed my bottom lip as I looked him over and wondered how much better he'd look naked, sprawled against opulent pillows and…

When I heard him chuckle, my eyes flew up and I felt my cheeks heat in embarrassment that I'd risk ogling him so shamelessly when I knew he was looking right at me. Condescending amusement danced in his eyes and there was a superior, knowing pout to his lips as he looked me over.

"Like what you see, Eden?" he asked.

I swallowed hard. "No."

We both knew it was a lie, and my lying seemed to amuse him more.

Everything about him was predatory and like the actions of those beneath him – when he wasn't indifferent to them – humoured him. He found it adorably pathetic that us plebs did things like lie and work hard to get anywhere and try to be polite to people if we wanted something.

"You've already chosen me," he said. "Why not just admit it?"

"How have I chosen you?" I asked him, pulling my books out.

"You publicly denounced Fox. Ergo I win."

"I told Fox to take a hike, and I'm telling you the same. Ergo *I* win."

His smirk wouldn't be shaken. "We can both win."

It was an argument I'd tried on myself. Why not choose one and try and get something out of it? The problem was, Beckett was not the guy I could manipulate into doing anything.

"You want something, Beckett?" I challenged. "How about just coming out with it?"

"You know what I want."

I sighed. "You're not very good at this whole wooing thing, are you?"

"I don't need to woo you, Eden." He leant on the table again, getting as close to me as said table allowed. "You want me as much as I want you. All I need to do now is wear down your defences until you give in to us."

He was right, of course. Annoyingly. I was sure he knew how close he was. I was surprised I hadn't already given in when I so wanted to. I could hardly remember why I hadn't anymore.

But, "There will never be an us," I scoffed.

"What did you pick for your History essay?" he asked, totally changing the subject.

It took me a second to rally. "You don't give a shit about my life."

"On the contrary, Eden. I want to know all of it."

Stupid flutters erupted in my chest. "You really want to know?" I asked him and he nodded as he settled back in his chair again.

"Tell me all about it," he said, his voice a seductive plea.

So I did, and I was pretty sure he regretted asking as soon as I was a couple of sentences in. But he just sat and listened to me nerd out for a full ten minutes, until I ran out of steam and even my nerd-gasm couldn't be sustained in the face of his stonily sexy silence.

"Well, I guess you'd better get writing then, hadn't you?" Even that sentence was delivered in a way that sent a shiver running down my spine and my skin break out in goosebumps.

I shifted in my seat and got to work, but not because he'd told me to. I did it because I told myself that it would let me ignore his presence. It did not.

I felt him blazing in front of me like a beacon that had the power of bringing me to the only shelter that could save me from the oncoming storm. Which was ridiculously dramatic, but everything about Beckett seemed dramatic and over the top so it seemed fitting.

And I couldn't stop thinking about my revelation of the day before.

I knew why I wanted him now and none of my arguments stood up against the truth of it anymore. I couldn't find a single reason why I shouldn't just stand up, take his hand, pull him into the stacks and see what all the fuss was about.

The chances were high that giving into him would end their power struggle, meaning I would get to taste him *and* get my life back. I was starting to believe that was possible. It could have also been my libido talking.

Fox was the only reason I didn't do just that.

Giving into Beckett might secure him his crown and make him lose interest, but I highly doubted Fox was going to let me walk away so easily. He wouldn't let a slight like that slide. Whether I gave into Beckett or not, Fox would still be out for my blood. Maybe, just maybe, if I didn't give into Beckett, his continued obsession could afford me some protection, as he'd so laughably called it.

Protection he must have been taking very seriously because, after my free, he silently walked me to homegroup. As we walked out of the library, our hands brushed and it didn't feel like an accident. Then he dropped behind me to hold the door open for me.

Fox had held doors open for me in the last two weeks. This didn't feel anything like that.

I tried not to look up into his eyes as I passed him, but I did it anyway. He was looking down at me and something zinged between us. I felt the nearness of his body to mine, just not quite touching, as goosebumps spread across my skin. My breath caught and my heart raced. I watched as his tongue swept out slowly and licked his bottom lip.

Good lord, but his lips were kissable.

His whole body was kissable, and I was in danger of tasting it.

*Was* there a reason I wasn't?

I honestly couldn't remember at that point.

All I knew was that, if I lifted up slightly and he angled down just a smidge…

Our lips were suddenly very close together. A lot closer than they'd been a second before. I could tell because my nose bumped his. My eyes flitted to Beckett's, and I saw he was just as frozen as me. Just as surprised as me that we were suddenly this close.

My heart thudded incredibly slowly. Like it had to force itself to remember how to beat. Tension swirled around us, and I was sure this was one of those moments where a decision was going to be made. I just didn't know what the right choice was.

"Eden…" Beckett said, his voice husky and – holy shit – full of need.

I swallowed hard and turned quickly, but he caught my hand. I looked back at him in question. He said nothing, but his desire was burning in the depth of his eyes.

"Beckett..." I whispered, begging him not to do this. Not now.

It was one thing to be on the verge of just fucking him out of my system, but this was not that. This was something bigger and deeper and much more scary. This was something I felt like I had to be imagining.

Beckett didn't do bigger and deeper. Everyone knew that. And even if he did, I didn't want to do it with him. Did I?

No. Of course, I didn't.

Right?

Beckett dropped my hand gently but neither of us moved for a moment.

Finally, he nodded and kicked his head behind me, indicating I lead the way.

He walked next to me the whole way to homegroup. He was this strong, silent, stoic presence next to me and, for a brief moment, I entertained the idea that this was what life could be like. This feeling of being untouchable and admired. Of being the King of Rivermont's. It was weak of me to indulge, but I didn't hate the feeling.

It wasn't the infamy I wanted. It wasn't the look on those passing us that I enjoyed. It was just him by my side as though it was a message to the world that I was his. Nothing overt. Unpretentious in its simplicity.

Then I remembered that this was Beckett Maxwell and there was nothing unpretentious or simple about him. It didn't stop me humouring the fantasy for a little while longer.

When we got to my classroom, he peeled away from me, as silently as he'd been since we left the library, and went to lean against the wall in his typical fashion. I paused for a moment, and I knew the message I sent him was, 'Are you staying? Please be staying'. Just as I was sure his answer was, 'I'm not going anywhere'.

"Eden, can I walk you in?" Fox asked as he came from the other direction.

There was nothing pleasing or kind or cute in his voice now. It was dripping with sarcasm and thinly veiled hatred. I knew it was all for Beckett's benefit, but it didn't stop me taking a step back.

Beckett put himself between me and Fox. "Do not make me tell you again," Beckett snarled.

"Or, what?" Fox goaded.

Beckett sniffed. Then quick as a flash, he took one step behind Fox and kicked Fox's leg to force him into a kneel. Beckett put his hand on Fox's shoulder and leant to the younger guy's ear.

"Stay away from her," he said, his voice low and cold. "Or that will be the least painful way I make you pay homage to your king."

A thrill ran through me, and I knew I shouldn't have let it. But I didn't think I really had that much control over it. Fox glared at me, and I knew Beckett's peacocking was putting me deeper and deeper on Fox's shit list. I could almost see the new and terrifying ways Fox was currently planning to get his revenge on me.

"Eden, go and find Sam," Beckett ordered.

I did, but not because he wanted me to.

Sam and I got through homegroup, then met Abby and Hunter for recess while Beckett and Jaeger hovered close enough to deter Fox.

"What do they want?" Hunter huffed sullenly.

"They're the only thing standing between Eden and whatever Fox thinks he's going to do to her," Sam snapped, and I was surprised he'd lost his cool so quickly. He sounded scared.

I put my hand on his arm and we exchanged a look.

"You good?" I asked him.

"I think I should be asking you that," Sam said.

I nodded. "You ask me that plenty. It's my turn to ask you."

"Why?" Hunter asked. "You're the one who's being assaulted by a bunch of entitled wankers."

I shrugged. "And Sam cares–"

"Are you implying I don't?" Hunter spat.

I recoiled. "I can see we're all a little on edge today–"

"You're a bet to them, Eden," Hunter said as he leant towards me. "Nothing but a bet. *Nothing*. Yet you seem the least affected of everyone."

I blinked back the hotness in my eyes. "I am. I'm nothing to them and yet," I challenged him, "they've somehow never made me quite feel as small as you did just now."

Thankfully the bell ringing for next lesson sounded as I stood up.

"Eden," Hunter said, an apology seeming on his lips. "That's hardly fair." But apparently not going to be given.

"This isn't about what you think is fair, Hunter," I told him. "It's about me surviving until this all goes away. My *friends* seem to understand that."

As I pushed away from the table, tears of anger threatened. I was well aware that I'd just veered in accusing him of the same thing Jaeger had accused him of over the weekend. And maybe Hunter was right, and it wasn't fair. This whole thing with the Royals was obviously affecting us all and we were all dealing with it differently. I just had to remember that all my friends, including Abby now who was currently hurrying to keep up with me, did care and we weren't going to make it through by lashing out at each other.

Beckett caught me before I got to the door to the dining hall. He stepped in front of me, and I had to pull up very short if I didn't want to run into him. The toes of our shoes were almost touching as he leant his face to mine.

"What did he do?" he asked, his voice low like he didn't want anyone else to hear.

"You almost sound like you care," I spat at him, but we both heard the tears thick in my throat.

"If he hurts you, he won't be walking for at least a month," he growled, and that traitorous shiver ran through me.

I turned my head back to look at Hunter and it made my position with Beckett even more intimate. I could feel his nose at my ear as I saw the fury on Hunter's face.

"Did he hurt you?" Beckett demanded.

"No," I told him, turning back to face him and our noses bumped.

I was sure he knew I was lying. But neither of us seemed focussed on that just then.

We were millimetres away from our lips meeting and that zing was bouncing around us again. Something that made my heart flutter in nervous excitement at the same time it warmed pleasantly. Something that made a smile tug inexplicably at my lips. Something that made me forget that the rest of the world existed or that Beckett was actually a massive douche bag. Something I knew he felt, too.

"I'm late for guard duty," Jaeger whined, breaking whatever spell Beckett and I had fallen under. "And my charge is playing moony eyes. Either excuse me, or let me get on with my orders."

Beckett took a step away from me and cleared his throat. "Fine," he said to Jaeger. "Go. Do not leave her until Preston takes over."

Jaeger snorted. "He's lucky he's only got one free when you don't. You imagine asking him to do this for two lessons?"

Beckett turned a stern glare to his left-hand and Jaeger lost all his jovial jestering.

"Long live the king," he said with a mock-bow. It was sarcastic, but felt more like an in-joke condescension rather than outright defiance.

I turned to head to French, but Beckett took my hand.

"Do not go anywhere without one of us," he ordered.

"I don't take orders from you, Beckett," I told him. "I'm not one of your ridiculous court."

He stepped up to me again, the sexiest anger written plain on his face. "You will do as you're told, or Fox won't be the worst thing waiting for you."

"And just when I thought we were turning a corner," I said as I rolled my eyes. "Come on, Abby." I linked arms with her, and we headed off.

"Yes," Jaeger said with a smirk as he jogged to catch up to us. "Come on, Abby."

"You can stop that," I said to him, and I found him watching me with a twinkle in his eye.

"Stop what? I'm just being friendly."

"Sure, Captain Jack," I snorted, and Abby laughed.

"Who's Captain Jack?" Jaeger asked, clearly feeling like he'd been left out of the joke.

"A horrible flirt," Abby said.

Jaeger fixed her with a winning smirk. "So, the opposite of me, then," he said with a wink.

Abby gripped my arm tighter and cleared her throat and I tried not to smile. Jaeger had the power to make me feel unsettled and amused by his flirting, but I'd never fallen for it. Not really. I did wonder, though, if Abby might.

Then, I remembered that he'd made the bet with Fox, and I was angry with him again. I left him, understandably confused at the sudden change in my attitude, outside my French classroom and ignored any attempts he made to catch my eye through the lesson.

After French, I had to stay back to talk to Mademoiselle Teller, so Abby went ahead to Biology without me. By the time I was done, Jaeger was still waiting for me.

"Harle–"

"Do not start with me, Jaeger Richards," I spat, and he actually snapped his mouth shut as his eyes widened in surprise.

"Have I done something to offend you, Quincy?" he asked and, despite the continued lack of using my actual name, he sounded like he legitimately cared.

Annoyingly, it seemed it was very difficult to stay angry with Jaeger. I didn't know what it was about him, but I just didn't overly enjoy being angry with him. I did my darndest, though.

"You know what you did," I told him, making to turn away.

He caught my arm gently. "Is this about the bet?" he asked.

I huffed. "No," I said sarcastically. "It's about the amount of bleach you leave in the pool!"

He smirked. "It's about the bet, isn't it?"

"Of course it's about the bet, Jaeger! You expect me to not care that you made a bet to make me 'acceptable' so you could take me to the formal and then fuck me?"

He opened and closed his mouth as though the mighty Jaeger Richards was actually speechless for once. "I don't know what to say, Quinjet."

"How about an apology, for a start?" I suggested.

His shrug was definitely apologetic. "It was only meant to be a bit of fun, Harlequin."

I frowned at him. "I'm a person, Jaeger. A person with hopes and dreams and feelings. Not just some pawn to use when you Royals have nothing in your lives to stop you getting bored so easily!"

He scrubbed a hand over his face. "Beckett is *not* going to like this…" he muttered, more to himself than me.

I was sure the list of things Beckett didn't like was hugely longer than the list of things he did, if *that* list even existed. "Won't like what?" I asked.

"What I have to do now. Quinlet, I'm sorry…" he said gently. "I am."

Tears pricked my eyes and I didn't know why.

"Hey," he said softly. "Hey. Look, it's not an excuse, but I honestly didn't think anything would come of it. I figured we'd both lose. But, just in case, I had to take the bet or someone else would."

"If this is another bullshit claim about protecting me, I don't want to hear it. Beckett's already tried that shit on. Besides, did it ever occur to you that I might not need the kind of protection the Royals are offering? Let alone protection at all!"

Jaeger sighed. "I know how strong you are, Quincy. But you don't know our world. You haven't grown up in it. Accepting our protection isn't an act of submission, it's just self-preservation."

"At what cost? What price do I have to pay?"

Jaeger looked deep into my eyes. "He just wants you."

"Does he? Or does he just want to keep his crown?"

"Why can't he have both?" he asked, echoing Beckett's own words too close for comfort.

"Why should he get both when I get nothing?" I asked in a small voice. "Sure, I want him. But even if I let him have me, I could never really have him."

It wasn't something I was aware I actually wanted, but it didn't make it any less true.

"Harlequin…" he said, and I could see him trying to disagree.

"Could I? Be honest."

I could see in Jaeger's eyes how torn he was. "Maybe you can show him how?"

I scoffed. "And exactly how likely do you think that is?"

Jaeger levelled me with an intensely serious look. "I think you're the only one who stands a chance."

Jesus, was I actually considering his words?

Of course I wasn't. Thinking about considering having sex with Beckett was very different to whatever it was I'd found myself talking about with Jaeger.

I shook my head and stepped back from him. "No," I said. "No. This is supposed to be about you apologising to me, not playing wingman for your king!"

"Why can't I do both?"

"What is it with you Royals and having everything? You can't just let someone else have a win without getting one of your own? You can't let it be about someone else for a change?"

"No," he said simply. "That's not how our world works. Be lucky that we've even considered what you might want and are doing our best to accommodate."

I shivered at the finality of his words. "Why are you so honest with me? Or is this your version of lulling me into a false sense of security?"

"I'm honest because I like you. And, even if I didn't, I'm loyal to my king. I've killed for him. Compared to that, using my discretion to give you some understanding of our side of the narrative is a fucking swim in the pool."

I chewed my lip as I thought about it. "You do know that you can champion him as much as you like–"

"Why, thank you."

"–but," I continued like he hadn't interrupted, "actions speak volumes more than words. Your words mean nothing in the face of Beckett's actions. And his actions are *not* backing up your words right now."

Jaeger grunted in frustration. "What can I do to make you trust him?"

I huffed humourlessly. "Nothing, Jaeger. While I'm still just an object in this power play, I will never trust him. I don't know that I would even if I wasn't." I knew one other thing about me, though. "Doesn't mean I won't give in and sleep with him at some point," came out of me unbidden.

Jaeger smirked. "Oh, really?"

I frowned. "Do *not* tell him I said that!"

Jaeger shrugged. "Tell him you said what?"

I had no idea if Jaeger would tell Beckett or not. Half of me firmly believed he wouldn't, but then he'd literally just assured me how loyal he was to his king.

# CHAPTER TEN

Beckett had appeared in the library in our mutual free again on Wednesday – a double lesson. I'd forced myself to sit there and get my work done while he literally just watched me do it, silently, for a full hour and a half.

We hadn't exchanged words. I'd just felt my whole person burning up under the bright flaming sun that was everything Beckett was while I stared at my laptop screen. My cheeks kept periodically heating as the nerves or fantasies took hold of me. And Beckett continued saying and doing nothing. Whenever I dared glance up at him, he was just watching me with that fixed, stony expression and I had no idea what was going through his head.

I wasn't risking another single minute of it on Friday morning, so I decided that I'd just do my study at my desk in my dorm room instead. The theory wasn't working any more in practice than if I'd just gone to the library and let Beckett stare at me for the whole lesson. I kept feeling like his eyes were on me anyway, and my cheeks would heat. I then got bogged down thinking about what would happen if he found me in my room. Then the implications of him finding me in my room and that we would then be alone in my room together. And anything could happen then.

So, what did happen?

Naturally.

I heard my door open – because locks weren't a thing in the

Rivermont dorms. We all functioned on an honesty system and, in my three years in the dormitory, it had worked. Very rarely did the Royals bother bullying kids in their own dorms. Or rather, very rarely did Royals bother bullying me in my dorm.

Thus, my door was unlocked – as they all were – and anyone could come walking right in.

Which is just what Beckett did that Friday morning.

Stupidly, I'd assumed it was Sam wagging to give me some more gossip again. So, I finished my note, then finally turned to find very not-Sam leaning cavalierly against the door frame with his arms crossed and a furiously expectant look on his face.

"Do you mind?" I asked him.

He shrugged, pushed himself off the door, then stepped into my room and closed the door behind him. "Not particularly."

I frowned. "What are you doing?"

"A menial task Jaeger should be doing, but he has class."

"I beg your pardon?" I spat.

"You have it," he said as he looked around the room as though it would give anything away about me that he might not know already.

It wasn't much to look at, but that didn't bother me. My bed was a single and pushed against one wall. My sheets were the standard Rivermont issue of black, white and red with the academy crest. I had a pile of crap on my beside table that I'd been periodically clearing and promptly refilling for the last three years. My little bookshelf was overflowing with all the books I kept in my dorm room, since that was where I spent most of my time. The top of my chest of drawers wasn't much better than my bedside table, a couple of drawers were open a little and I noticed one of them had a bra and pair of undies hanging out of it. Beckett's eyes stayed less time on that than I expected from an eighteen-year-old guy.

I'd stuck posters up all over the room of all my favourite fandoms – TV, film and book – and my corkboard was plastered with my timetables with pictures of me and Sam, me and Mum, and a few of my favourite tombs in the academy cemetery from way back when. My desk was the cleanest thing in my room, and that was only because I'd pushed everything onto the floor to give me room to work that morning.

"This is your room?" Beckett said, as though he didn't think much about that.

I huffed. "And I suppose you have marble floors and velvet curtains and six million thread count sheets that are like sleeping on clouds, huh?"

He smirked at me and something in me definitely melted. "If you want to sleep in my bed, you just have to…*beg*," he said, his voice sultry.

I rolled my eyes. "I don't want to sleep in your bed, Beckett."

He came over to me, putting his hands on the desk behind me so he was right up in my face. He looked me over carefully and there was a visceral sizzle between us. "You want to sleep in my bed, Eden." It wasn't a question.

I wasn't going to tell him that any interest I had in being in his bed had absolutely *nothing* to do with actual sleeping.

"I know you're used to every girl in this school wanting in your bed, but I'm not one of them," I told him.

His nose ran tantalisingly over my face with the barest of touches. "No other girl in this school has a chance in hell of being in my bed," he whispered seductively, and a thrill ran through me.

He was staring so far into my eyes that I knew he saw it.

"I get what I want, Eden," he challenged me. "Give into it. You may as well enjoy it."

His implication was an interesting one. Would he *really* just take it if I didn't give it to him? It didn't hurt to test that theory.

"You keep telling me that you get what you want, and yet you haven't taken me, Beckett. I have to wonder if you actually do always get what you want, or is that you just won't take *me* by force?" My voice was heavy on the implication, and I could see he'd most certainly understood what I was accusing him of.

His face was fury and it turned me on. He growled in frustration and hissed, "My restraint only goes so far, Eden. You do not want to test me."

I leant towards him. "Why, Beckett?" I purred myself. "What are the consequences for disobeying you?"

"You don't want to know," he growled.

I smirked at him, feeling confident. "Or I'll never find out."

"Keep defying me and you will."

My smirk grew right along with my confidence. "Will I, though?"

His lips rippled in a snarl as he took my chin in his hands. "I will have you, Eden. Whether you want it or not."

He pushed away from me and stalked out, totally belying his words.

I could imagine that he'd used that line before, been given the shakiest of consent that was obviously the opposite, and probably just taken what he wanted anyway. But he hadn't done that with me. I wasn't sure I wanted to find out exactly why that was. I did know that it answered one question I hadn't even realised I'd had before then; all those times he'd invaded my space, surprised me, physically come onto me, and I hadn't felt uncomfortable about it?

I felt safe with Beckett.

Of all the things I guessed he was capable, weirdly I felt absolutely no danger from him or his attentions.

For the first time that year, I honestly felt like maybe I could get the upper hand on him. I had something over him and, unless he wanted to ruin any chance that he actually had of getting what he wanted, there was nothing he would do about it.

I took that knowledge with me to the pool that night, for once swimming more because I needed some clarity and time to think than I needed soothing or relaxing. I didn't come up with any more answers, but I hadn't been looking for solid answers. I'd been looking for acceptance and understanding. And I found them.

When I got out of the pool, I was feeling much more prepared to deal with whatever was coming next. I felt better prepared to challenge Beckett on a more equal footing.

I wiped my hand on my towel and picked up my phone to see if Sam has messaged. Suddenly, there was a burst of noise from the door and a, "Get the fuck out," roared from the bleachers above me.

As I pulled my towel to me quickly, I didn't rightly know where to look. Up happened first. And my confused, "What?" didn't make him bat an eyelid.

Jaeger was striding down the bleachers, his long jean-clad legs fully capable of just letting him stroll on down. His eyes were focussed on the door, making me follow his gaze.

There were a few confused peopled huddled in the doorway, looking around.

"Seriously?" Jaeger scoffed. "I gotta tell you twice?"

The people practically fell over themselves in their rush to get back out again.

"What are you doing here, Jaeger?" I asked, half-miffed and half-resigned.

"Making sure no one but Beckett sees you like that," he said simply.

His eyes were still trained on the door as he came down the final few bleachers.

"So, you're planning to, what? Burn your eyes out later?"

He dropped, feet together, off the last bleacher to land beside me, still facing the door. Finally, he turned just his head to me. He looked me down and up in my two-piece bathers.

"I would never go for another man's girl. That's piss-weak."

I started towelling my hair. "Firstly, I am not Beckett's girl–"

"It's cute you still think that," Jaeger interjected, bopping my nose with his finger, but I ignored him.

"Secondly, how long have you been here?"

"How long have *you* been here?"

"A bit less than an hour," I said, wondering where this was going.

"Then, a bit less than a bit less than an hour."

"How did you know where to find me?"

"I have my ways."

"Are you following me?"

He shrugged and dropped onto the bottom bleacher. "I do what I need to do. I'm a good little guard dog."

"I thought you cleaned up Beckett's messes?" I scoffed, towelling my hair.

He leant towards me with a winning smirk. "That'd be Rowan. I *make* Beckett's messes."

I looked down at his knuckles, which were covered in bruises and cuts as always, and believed it.

"Of course. Heaven forbid the King get his own hands dirty."

"He'd get them dirty for you."

"I don't know what's so special about me," I huffed.

"You really don't, do you?" he asked, like he knew a secret I didn't.

"No," I sighed resignedly. "But I'm sure you're going to tell me."

"I'm so glad you asked," he said gleefully.

"I didn't–"

"Beckett's never claimed anyone, Eden Quin. Not before you."

I laughed. "You mean no one's ever turned him down before."

He shook his head gravely as he leant back against the bleacher behind him. "No. I mean he's never wanted anyone. He's never… You've got him in knots, honey." Jaeger seemed inordinately pleased by that.

I rolled my eyes. "I haven't got Beckett Maxwell in *knots*, Jaeger." I looked him up and down. "Why are you like this?"

Being Jaeger, he knew exactly what I meant. "You're my king's lady, you get to see a side of me no one else does."

"You mean because you're not going to try to sleep with me? Anymore," I added pointedly.

He gave a half-shrug, half-nod. "Swings and round abouts, QT."

"Was that an *IT Crowd* reference?" I gasped.

Jaeger's face paled for a second. "No…"

I failed to stifle a snort. "It was."

He seemed to see the sense in not arguing. He sniffed as he looked back at the door like he thought someone might come through it and save him. "I don't make a habit of keeping secrets from my king, Quincy…" he said slowly. "But if we could keep that between us, I'd consider it a personal favour."

"One I can call in at my choosing?" I teased, but he nodded solemnly.

"Yes." He was deadly serious. I do this and Jaeger Richards owed me. I knew enough to know that meant a lot.

"Oh," was all I could say.

Then he turned his cheeky smirk on me. "Now, let's get you

dressed."

"I *am* capable of dressing myself."

"I'd hope so. Beckett would kill me if my naked skin touched your naked skin."

I frowned at him as I wrapped my towel around me more securely. "Talking about it less suggestively is probably a good start."

He dropped against the wall outside the doors to the ladies' changerooms. "Maybe," he agreed.

He left me to it, and I wasn't sure if he'd still be there by the time I was done.

But, as I walked out of the changeroom in my shorts and Rivermont tracksuit jacket, Jaeger fell into an easy step with me. "Beckett wants to see you."

I openly laughed. "If Beckett wants to ask me out, I'm sure he can do better than getting his friend to ask. Maybe one of those old-school notes. 'Do you like me? Yes or no.' I'm good at crossing boxes."

"He's not asking, Quinjet," Jaeger said pointedly. His tone was hard, but there was humour in his eyes at my sarcasm.

"I know, Jaeger." I sighed. "Even the idiots in your harem know Beckett's not the dating type, let alone the 'anything less than an order' type."

"He still wants to see you."

"I gathered from the first time you said it."

"He *needs* to see you."

"Is that you using your discretion?" I teased.

"It's me saying what he can't."

I stopped walking and Jaeger stopped as well. "Well, too damn bad!" I told him with a huff. "I'm not one of your harem who you can order around, and I'll gladly drop to my knees to thank you for the honour of your attention. I don't do obedience, Jaeger. Certainly not for the likes of Beckett Maxwell."

"Just go and see him. Please? It's really not a good idea to annoy him more than you already do by just existing, Harlequin."

I wasn't sure what he meant by that. He seemed sincere in his concern, and sincere in whatever effect I had on Beckett. It mattered very little to me, though. If Beckett wanted something, he could learn that he wasn't always going to get what he wanted just by wanting it.

"If Beckett thinks he's protecting something, the least he can do is do it himself," I told Jaeger. I knew it was a stupid challenge, but I was going to issue it anyway. "Tell your king, I don't do summons and I don't do being stalked. If he wants to see me, then he can come to me. My dorm room is literally always open, regardless of my feelings on the matter, as he well knows." I flailed my arms and then headed off for said dorm room.

The annoyance that had started simmering with Jaeger's pronouncement, had reached boiling point by the time I got to my room. It was enough to make me think of heading back to the pool, but I was a little worried that the kids Jaeger had scared off might have gone back once the threat of Jaeger had passed.

How dare Beckett try to order me around! Like, honestly. It was one thing stalking me around the school under the guise of 'Fox will do worse'. Fine, I accepted – annoyingly – that there may have been more truth to that than I would have liked. A case of the lesser evil in this case. I had no doubt that Beckett was the larger evil in the grand scheme of the entire universe and the danger he posed to my world in general. But he was the lesser evil in the face of Fox in relation to my immediate person. I wasn't going to like it, but I could very begrudgingly accept that Beckett may have actually been protecting something.

I stomped up the stairs in the girls' dorm, relishing in my anger and my accompanying petulance. I pretended I was working through my lack of control over pretty much everything in my life just then, when in reality I was just wallowing in it for a bit. It was no less cathartic and possibly necessary, but it was less helpful for what I found waiting for me at my dorm.

*Two times in one day?*

I pulled up short as I opened the door and found Beckett lounging on my bed. He looked ridiculously large in it, and I told myself not to find it sexy. Wearing a black tee and black jeans with pure white sneakers, he had one hand behind his head and his ankles crossed. The fact that I kept traitorously imagining myself climbing on top of him just compounded my already burning anger.

"What are you doing in my bed?" I asked, slamming my bedroom door shut and throwing my swimming bag against the wall to my right.

"You wouldn't come to mine. I thought this a decent compromise." His indifferent calm annoyed me even further.

I had no explanation for what I did next. It was utter lunacy. I did it anyway.

Under my zip-up tracksuit jacket, I was still in just my bikini top. So, I practically ripped off my jacket, throwing it on the floor with my bag. He half sat up in interest and obvious surprise. I climbed up the bed to straddle his lap and pushed him back into the bed. He went satisfyingly willing, as though he was at my mercy for once. His face was set, his jaw hard, but his eyes spoke volumes about the unexpected turn this situation had taken, which told me a lot about his expectations – or, lack of – and I didn't hate that.

"Is this what you want, Beckett?" I asked, all venom in my low tone, not at all concerned about showing him everything I was.

Moody.

Temperamental.

Sassy.

Strong.

So very over all of his shit.

He could have it all and see what he wanted to do about it. See whether he still wanted it afterwards.

I ran my hand up his body and leant over him, my nose brushing his. My hips rocked against him, and I felt his cock harden under me. I ran myself over him again for good measure and I watched the wariness in his eyes. His hands were very carefully not touching me, like he knew this for what it was; teasing.

"You want this? Us? Any bed will do?" I purred.

I rubbed against him again and couldn't bring myself to regret it. It was quite possibly as dangerous for me as it was for him. Pleasure zinged through me, and I was definitely considering seeing this through to it's delicious finish. I held myself together, though. Just.

"Do you want to bury yourself deep inside me?" I continued, my lips too close to his to not feel a desperate need to kiss him. "Feel me come undone for you, make me tremble as I cum on your cock, over and over?"

I could see in his eyes that was exactly what he wanted. I wanted that, too, but I refused to give into him just because he demanded it. It didn't mean I wasn't going to keep teasing the both of us to our very limits, though.

"You want it, Beckett?" I challenged. "Then take it."

Finally, he touched me. His hands ran slowly up my thighs and even more slowly over my arse. When they lighted on the naked skin of my lower back, he sat us up. In his eyes was a dare I was close to meeting.

He ran his hands over my back, my waist, teasingly tugged at the clasp at the back of my bikini. His nose trailed over my face as he whispered, "I'll take it when you actually plan on giving it, Eden." He rocked his hips so we rubbed together again, and an embarrassing gasp tried to escape from me.

I saw the look in his eyes; he noticed. He liked it, and we both knew we could put an end to this here and now. If I just owned my desire for him, then we could both get what we wanted. Which, in the heat of the moment, didn't seem like such a bad thing after all.

And God, how I wanted it. My clit throbbed with a need only he could sate. My nipples tightened just thinking about the fact that, at one word from me, we could get rid of the rest of the clothes between us and he could finally ease this craven want in me.

Like we both knew I was so very close to actually giving it, our hips rolled together in sync. I knew the desire and pleasure was written plain on my face and in my eyes. I also knew Beckett saw every detail of it. Because we were staring at each other like the world might end if we stopped. So, I also knew he felt the same. He liked it.

We rolled together again, still like we were both testing the waters, seeing what the other one would do. And once more. I pressed my body into his as we rubbed together once more.

My hand went to his arm like I needed to steady myself. It wasn't totally unnecessary.

Beckett tipped his lips to my neck and my whole body hummed for him. His hand rested firmly on my lower back, and I couldn't be sure if he arched my body against his or if it was all me and he was just following.

As though we were done testing the water and both just wanted to get it done already, our bodies rocked together without any pretence as he kissed and licked and sucked my neck. My arms wrapped around him, and the pleasure mounted in me as I basically rode him. My clit tingled and warmth flooded me. My breathing grew shallower as my hands gripped his back tighter.

I felt his smirk as his hands tightened on me.

Just as I was balancing on that precipice and totally ready to tumble over it for Beckett of all people, he grabbed my hips and lifted me off him just enough to remove all delicious friction.

I wanted to glare at him for denying me, but I was supposed to be teasing him here so getting any pleasure out of him was hardly the point and definitely wasn't going to give me the upper hand. Then again, him being in the position to deny me was certainly not giving me the upper hand either. And he knew it.

"I'll give it when you do," he moaned in my ear, then nipped my ear lobe.

Then he stood up, dumping me on my bed. I glared at him, but he only looked down at me with cocky humour.

"You've felt how effortless this could be, Eden," he said, rearranging his jeans like what did it matter to him that I'd given him a raging boner. "If it was that easy for me without trying, imaging what I could do to you when that's my only goal. You just have to say yes."

I bit my lip. I couldn't say yes now, but I also wouldn't say no anymore.

"Or are you still pretending it's a no?" he asked.

I couldn't keep lying to him. Not after that display.

"That's what I thought," he said with a languid smirk when I still didn't say anything.

He left me sitting on my bed feeling very much like he had me right where he wanted me. Which I wouldn't have minded so much had the whole point not been for me to get the upper hand for once.

# CHAPTER ELEVEN

After what I did to us in my dorm on Friday night, Beckett changed tactics. Instead of getting me all hot and bothered, the plan was obviously to show me – in sordid detail – what I was missing out on.

As a tactic, it was unexpected. I'd thought he'd be worse, more teasing, not let me sit cold turkey. And I was sure that's why he'd chosen it.

On Monday, Rowan walked me to homegroup with Fox trailing behind us and making my neck prickle uneasily the whole way. When we got to the classroom, Beckett was locked in a very tight embrace with Isabella just outside the door, so I had no choice but to see it.

The strong independent woman in me wanted to say the little green monster of jealousy didn't rouse its head curiously. And it didn't. It full blown stood up and wanted to smack Beckett in his smarmy, sexy, obnoxiously good-looking face.

Rowan put a hand in front of me, like he could feel the insane possessiveness rear in me and knew, better than me, that it was a mistake to act on it. Which interested me because I'd have thought Rowan would be all for giving Beckett exactly what he wanted.

Sam was coming from the opposite direction, and I saw the question on his face. I hoped mine told him I'd give him all the answers I had as soon as I could. Not that I had many.

As Isabella finally pulled away from Beckett, she smirked at me unpleasantly as she wiped the side of her mouth, as though she'd been doing something far more scandalous with it. Based on the look of victory on her face, she thought she'd won. She firmly believed that Beckett was over whatever temporary madness had made him come after me, and she was back in line for her obnoxiously extravagant wedding to Beckett Maxwell the fourth.

I stood there, a little dumbfounded over Beckett's behaviour, even as I told myself it really shouldn't have been a surprise. I had to remind myself that Beckett never wanted me, so this was just yet another level of the game to him.

Fox walked up behind me, pausing before he went into the classroom. "My cock's always waiting, Eden," he said snidely.

Beckett stood at his full height and snarled at Fox, which I thought was a bit rich given he'd just been basically fucking Isabella against the wall.

"The missus and the mistress," Fox whistled to Beckett. "Daddy making you get it all lined up already? I think Isabella's already picked out her dress. Are you going to invite your mistress? Or just keep her locked in a cupboard to use when you feel like it?"

Beckett took a step towards Fox, but Fox just laughed in his face.

It was hard not to respect Fox's gall. Seriously. Beckett looked like he was going to murder him there and then.

"What does it say about this little attempted coup of yours that she'd rather be my *mistress* than choose you?" Beckett's smirk was all humoured insult.

Fox's humour fell. "But she hasn't chosen you, has she?" Then he stepped away and went into the classroom.

And that wasn't the end of it.

Fox sat behind me in homegroup.

Isabella flaunted her assumed return to station with every look she shot me.

Beckett stood outside the classroom like he was going to kill more than just Fox over this whole thing.

Part of me wondered if he was rethinking his new tactic. Fox had definitely been intimating that I wasn't going to stand for it, so maybe Beckett was seeing the sense in that.

That part of me was set to rights while we sat at our tables in the dining hall at Recess.

Staring right at me, Beckett dragged Isabella into his lap and just pretty much dry humped her in the middle of the rest of the school. Sam was still confused, as was Abby, but Hunter seemed to both be inexplicably delighted and even more infuriated by it. Thankfully, he kept whatever his thoughts were to himself as we all pretended we weren't dying to talk about it.

"I've gotta pee," I said as I pushed myself to standing. "I'll see you in class?" I asked Sam.

His eyes darted to Beckett like he knew my true feelings were conflicted about the whole thing, then back to me. Sam nodded and didn't say anything about that. "Yeah. See you there."

Rowan was obviously on duty again after Recess. He stood up from his table as he saw I was on the move, and followed me as I stormed out of the dining hall.

"You would do well to calm the fuck down," Rowan said, his voice gravelly and low like he was used to speaking secrets. His tone was terrifyingly even, like the lack of inflection was proof of the lack of emotion in him.

"*You* would do well to stay the fuck out of my business," I snapped.

"Indifference would serve you a lot better," was his answer as we reached the girls' bathroom.

I whirled on him, a hand on the door. "I *am* indifferent, Rowan. I don't know if it escaped your notice, but I don't want your king."

Rowan's eyes told me he very definitely didn't believe me. "Don't give him what he wants now."

"Why do you even care? Aren't you all loyal to your king and your sole purpose is getting him what he wants?"

The smirk that crossed his face was chilling in the coldness in his eyes. "He will get what he wants, but it doesn't hurt him to suffer for a while longer."

"You want your king to suffer?" I asked, surprised.

His smirk deepened, but there was still no warmth in it. "His suffering ensures your suffering."

I blinked. "Well, I seem to be the only one suffering at the moment." My surprise at the workings of his mind made me totally honest.

Rowan looked me over. "Then make him suffer as well."

Looking him over now, Rowan struck me as the kind of guy who'd set the world on fire just to watch with utter glee as it burnt. He liked chaos for chaos' sake. He might have been loyal to his king – I'd go so far as to suggest that he liked Beckett, as much as I believed a guy like Rowan could like anyone – but he was still a sadist who was never happier than when even his own friends were hurting.

"Who messed you up so bad?" I heard myself whisper, awed and floored by him.

He leant towards me. "It's difficult to develop healthy emotions when you're wading through rivers of blood before you can even walk."

In his eyes was pure madness. Pure-fucking-madness. And yet, right in the middle of his eyes, was this tiny point of cold lucidity. Like he knew how fucked up he was, like he could easily flick the switch and be more human, and he didn't want to.

I shivered. "I'll bet."

"I don't need your sympathy," he snarled. The first sign of something other than apathy.

"Trust me. Sympathy is far less high on my list of priorities than the loo. I do actually have to pee."

Rowan searched my eyes, but I don't know if he found what he was looking for. "You have the power to bring him to his knees, you know." Somehow, he managed to make that sound more like a threat than support. Or maybe it *had* been intended as a threat.

"I highly doubt your King bows to anyone," I told him as I went to go into the bathroom.

As the door closed behind me, I heard his reply. "No. But he would bow to you. Do not disappoint me."

I didn't believe him, but he didn't bring it up again as he walked me to double English.

Then, Preston was up after lunch. The only expression of his displeasure came in the up turn of his nose and heavy sighing as he walked me to softball practice.

"If Beckett thinks Fox is coming at me at softball, then I think he overestimates even Fox's obsession for the crown."

"I was told to bring you to Beckett at the softball pitch. The king's law is apparently more important than the state of my shoes."

I sighed. "Like you don't have the money to just buy new ones."

"That is hardly the point, Eden."

"Then what is the point, Preston?"

He was somehow much less of an unknowable enigma – and so much less scary – when he was bitching about his shoes, of all things.

"That my king is making me demean myself for you," he said loftily. "If you just give him what he wants, then I wouldn't have to do this shit."

"Well, I'm terribly sorry that my morals are messing with your wardrobe."

"Is it morals, or just spiting yourself at this point?"

I frowned at him because I didn't want Preston Worthington-Smythe of all people making sense. Least of all the kind of sense that had me giving into Beckett now.

Maybe I *was* spiting myself, but I would be damned if I gave in now. This was now a test of wills. Was I stronger than Beckett? Probably not. But I wasn't giving in without him giving me a little something, too. Something that suggested he actually wanted me. Something that I could at least pretend meant I wasn't *just* a pawn in his game.

I suspected it was probably because I knew I'd never get that from him, so that made me safe.

Ergo, I would never give into him, and therefore I'd stay safe from Fox as well, all because Beckett would never give me anything in return. Because, much like lust, rocking my damned world and giving me the best sex of my life didn't count.

We finally got to the softball pitch without much more talk from Preston, and nearly ran into Sienna.

"Sienna," Preston said, his voice all haughty and self-important.

She looked him over like he didn't impress her. She'd be quite possibly the only one. "Preston." Her eyes dropped to his loafers. "You have mud on your shoes," she told him like there was nothing worse, then kept on her way.

I failed to fully hide my snort and I felt Preston's ire heating beside me.

"You know," I told him. "I'm starting to think that you Royals are not all that, after all."

He straightened his waistcoat with a huff. "Just because we haven't shown you the full force of what we could do to you, do not assume the rumours about us are false. Beckett curiously might not raise a hand to you, but Fox will do more than that. He won't care if you're black and blue, he'll still take what he thinks will get him the crown."

I swallowed hard and fought the tremor that snuck through my body as I watched Preston go to join the other inner sanctum on the bleachers.

On Wednesday, Beckett fell into step beside me as I headed for the dining hall doors to go to the library before my free, and I couldn't help sneaking a look back to Isabella. Confusion marred her features, but I could tell she was thinking that nothing good was coming my way.

"Watch out, or your missus will get the wrong idea," I said to him.

In one smooth motion, he pushed me against the wall and crowded my space. Everything in me zinged and fluttered, and my hand went to his chest. I just didn't know if it planned to push him away or pull him closer.

He dipped his nose to my jawline as he ran his hand up the side of my leg.

I knew Isabella and the whole damned dining hall was watching us, but I didn't care. His head obstructed my view of the room, and I was quite happy pretending it was just the two of us.

"Then let her get the wrong idea," he purred in my ear as his hand slipped up under my skirt and he pressed himself into me. "You can only deny me for so long, Eden."

If I didn't know this was Beckett, I'd have almost believed he sounded desperate. But desperate wasn't a word associated with Beckett Maxwell. He was far too controlled and superior to ever need to wait long enough for anything he wanted to know what desperation was.

Wasn't he?

The hand on his chest pushed him away and he went, though very reluctantly.

"You really think I'm going to give you anything when you're all-but fucking Isabella in front of me at every opportunity?"

"Would you rather it was you?" he said, thinking he was getting the upper hand here.

I mean, yes, but I scoffed. "It's irrelevant. Whether I do or not, I'm not giving anything to a guy with a *girlfriend*." I used the word mainly to get a rise out of him. I wasn't prepared for the rise I did get.

"She's not my girlfriend."

"No? Could have fooled me."

He grabbed my arm tightly. "She's not my girlfriend, Eden. I don't want her."

I looked up at him and our noses almost brushed. In his eyes was the end of that sentence. In his eyes, he said what he couldn't – wouldn't – voice out loud. He didn't want her. He didn't want anyone else. He wanted me. My heart hitched in my chest, and I told myself not to fall for it.

"Does she know that?" I asked quietly, wanting him to know I wasn't arguing for once. It was a proper question.

He licked his lip before he replied. "She doesn't want to know that."

"Have you tried explaining it?" My tone was a little more terse than I'd intended.

But Beckett's eyebrow just quirked along with a slight rise in one corner of his lips, like he found that interesting. "I've tried."

"How hard?"

The humour lit his eyes as he looked me over. "Jealous?"

I frowned and pulled away from him. "Not doing this, Beckett."

"That would be a yes."

I whirled to face him, my finger in his chest. "I'm not jealous, Beckett. Whatever dance you *think* we're doing, I'm not doing it with three."

He leant towards me, his lips tantalisingly close to mine. "You'll do it with as many as there are, Eden."

What power did he have that made me simultaneously hate him and crave him? Made me want to thump him and then beg him to throw me against the closest wall. And why did he exercise it over me? Why couldn't I be one of those girls who just craved him? Or better yet, why couldn't I go back to just hating him from my invisibility? Anything would be better than this push-pull.

Well, I could fake it until I could make it true.

"No, Beckett. I won't." I turned and headed down the hall.

"You think you can walk away from me?" he called after me. It was almost imperceptible, but his voice rose. By his standards, it was a yell.

I smiled to myself as I continued to walk away. "Watch me," I called back without turning around.

# CHAPTER TWELVE

The next Monday was a public holiday. Adelaide Cup. It was another one of those days the Royals held a party. This time, it was in the boys' dorm in one of the rec rooms because it was raining. Which was why I was heading up to Sam's room with Abby.

The rain. Not the party.

Speaking of the party…

"You're coming to the party, right?" Jaeger said as he was coming down the stairs with a slab of drinks in his arms.

"What party?" Abby asked, looking at me like I'd been withholding.

"The Cup *extravaganza*, of course," was Jaeger's flamboyant answer. "You know…" He paused and looked around like this was going to be a really juicy secret. "*I'm* going to be there."

"Oh, well! If you'd led with that, the answer of course would have been 'yes'," I said sarcastically as Abby and I shared a smile.

"Excuse me, Quincy," he said pointedly. "I'm not flirting with *you*, am I?"

"No," came Beckett's hard voice and we all looked up the stairs to see him frowning at Jaeger, fully unimpressed.

"Do you need a hand with that slab?" Abby asked Jaeger quickly.

"Yes, thank you," he told her.

"Don't leave me here," I begged her.

She shrugged in apology, he grinned cheekily, then they both left me while he prattled about God knew what.

Beckett strode down the stairs. "You're coming to the party?" he asked, and I couldn't get a read on his monotone expression.

I expected, "I wasn't planning to," to be the answer he wasn't looking for.

He surprised me. "Good."

I frowned at him. "Good?"

He nodded. "Good."

"Why? You want free reign to fuck as many other people as possible without me knowing about it?"

He stepped closer to me. "Be careful, Eden, lest you betray your jealousies." His low voice slid over my skin, making goosebumps break out everywhere and tingles chase themselves decidedly down my body.

Damn him for turning my own lines against me.

But, I scoffed, "I'm not jealous, Beckett. I'm amused that you could possibly think I'd hook up with you when you're off hooking up with other people."

"Does it *amuse* you to know that I haven't touched anyone else since you?"

I snorted. "Since me, *when*? Since you last had your hands down Isabella's pants?" Although, I hadn't seen him and Isabella together since I'd accused Isabella of being his girlfriend.

He boxed me against the banister. "Since the first week of term. And Isabella doesn't count."

I nodded. "That's right. We already established that lust doesn't count, didn't we?"

He growled at me, and my whole body liked it. "I couldn't care less about Isabella."

"Do *not* pretend you care about me. You just have fun at your party and make sure you have enough condoms.”

I made to walk away but he stopped me. “The only risk to my condom supply is you.”

As far as Beckett and comebacks went, I thought it was a little lame. I told myself not to read into it, and especially not to read into it that it was sign I was cracking that stony composure of his.

“What, Beckett?” I scoffed. “You think, if I come to that party, that’ll be it? Bye-bye restraint. You just won’t be able to help yourself?”

“Yes,” he growled, glaring at me like he hated me for it.

Then, like he was annoyed at himself for admitting it, he grunted and pushed away from me before jogging down the last few steps.

Well, if that was the way Beckett was going to behave, then I’d go to the party, and he could deal with it.

I burst through Sam’s door, and he looked up at me in surprise.

“Where’s Abby?” he asked.

“We’re going to the Royals’ Cup party.”

He blinked. “Are we?”

I nodded. “Beckett seems to think he won’t be able to help himself if I go. So, I’m going to go, and he can suck it.”

“Literally…?”

I rolled my eyes. “No.” *Maybe.*

“Okay. What am I going wear?”

“Who cares,” I said. “What am *I* going to wear?”

Abby found us a little later, with no word on what she and Jaeger had filled the time doing, and I informed her we were going to the party. She took less convincing than Sam, and we both teased her that it had something to do with a certain bleach-blond shit-stirrer. We spent the rest of the morning working out what to wear and getting ready. It was only when Hunter messaged Sam to ask where he was that we thought to clue him in, and he said he'd meet us at the party.

By the time we walked into the rec room, I was feeling like no one in there would be able to help themselves. I didn't make a habit of dressing up – I was a shorts and tee kinda girl – so my options for outfits were limited. Luckily, I was only a size bigger than Abby, and she was more than willing to help out.

She's put me in a slouchy cropped tee that my boobs were trying their damndest to bust open like I turned green if I got too mad. She paired it with a flared black skirt my arse was going to peek out of if I bent over too far. To finish it off, my hair was left to dry wild, and all I had to do was wear my usual low top Chucks. I felt fabulous and gorgeous and me, and so ready to prove to Beckett that he didn't tell me what to do.

So, what did he do as soon as he saw me?

Well, drown out every other person in the whole room for starters, as well as send Sam and Abby bustling a very indignant Hunter and his protestations away.

But did Beckett come up to me and tell me I looked nice? Thanks for coming? Help yourself to a drink?

Yeah no, he crossed the room like it was the damned parted Red Sea, and tried telling me what to do.

"You talk to no one unless it's me or Jaeger," he said as he looked me over.

I knew when he said 'anyone,' he actually meant 'guys'. He was now dictating who I talked to.

"I talk to whoever I want, whenever I want."

He shook his head. "No. You don't."

"Sam has been my best friend for far longer than you've had this weird possessive streak, and he'll be my best friend long after you lose interest and move onto the next girl who turns you down."

"You're wrong."

I huffed. "I'm talking to Sam and that's the end of it."

"I wasn't referring to that."

Now, I frowned. "What were you referring to?"

"Are you sure he's been your best friend longer than my possessive streak?"

He sounded like he knew something I didn't. At the very least, he was implying something. It couldn't have been that Sam wasn't my friend. That was one of those truths on which you founded your life. It definitely wasn't that. The only other thing I could think of was that he was implying he'd had the possessive streak for a while. Certainly longer than I'd thought. That couldn't have been true either.

Before I could clarify, he spoke again.

"And there will be no losing interest and moving onto the next girl who turns me down." He leant in close and put his hands on the wall on either side of me. "There will be no next girl given a chance to turn me down."

My heart skipped a beat at what he was implying, but I told it to calm down and reminded it that he couldn't possibly mean what that had sounded like. Heat pooled between my legs at his closeness, and I hoped he couldn't see just how much I wanted him.

"The rest of your life is a very long time to have blue balls, Beckett," I warned him.

The tip of his lip quirked up in almost a half-smirk. It was all cocky. It was all sexy.

"I can wait the time it'll take for you to give into this," he told me. "Into us."

A shiver ran over me, and I feared my true feelings showed bright and clear in my eyes that he was searching so deeply.

"You are mine, Eden," he told me, pressing his knee between my legs. I fought the urge to open them for him right there.

"Beckett!" someone yelled.

Beckett didn't react, his eyes bore into mine. "Remember that and we won't have a problem," he said before pushing away from me and stalking off through the crowd.

My lack of arguing with him had nothing to do with him walking away before I had a chance to reply. It had everything to do with the fact that there was something inexplicably thrilling about him calling me his.

I wasn't thrilled by the idea of being owned, but I *was* thrilled by what being his could mean. Physically. I had no interest in being his in any other way. I wasn't property. But I was *so* turned on by him. I was *so* attracted to him. I wanted him to show me all those things I thought I liked the sound of and let me see if I really did like them. Because there was no doubt in my mind that Beckett was as domineering – if not more – in the bedroom as he was in the rest of his life.

I lay my head back against the wall as I tried to breathe my heart back into a semi-normal rhythm and the heat out of my pelvis.

Beckett had me all up in knots and I knew it was only a matter of time before I did give in. I wanted him. Badly. By now, I wanted him so much that it really did feel like me denying him was hurting me far more than him now. It felt like the roles were reversed. That he was the one getting off on my withholding instead of me.

A little contrary part of me wondered why I shouldn't just do it. Just give into him. Maybe if I did, I could get over it. Maybe I could stop wanting him so much and go back to feeling like I had the upper hand in my rejection of him. Maybe I could feel again like I was getting anything out of my so-called strength.

Having had the thought, I couldn't be sure that I was going to actually go through with it. I could, though, be sure that I could stick the proverbial 'it' to Beckett in the meantime.

So, I spent the next hour talking to as many guys as I could as I nervously downed a few beers, and I didn't care that Hunter objected because it didn't matter what *he* thought about any of it.

Half of them were just me playing wingman for Sam because, despite the wit and sass that lived in my head, I wasn't actually all that confident talking let along flirting with just anyone. Hence the Dutch courage. But Beckett didn't need to know that.

And I could feel the king's ire as it followed me around the room.

I laughed obnoxiously loudly at their jokes.

I touched a hand to their chests as I batted my eyes at them, and said whatever remotely flirty nonsense came to me.

I strategically tugged my top down slightly as I pushed my breasts forward to make them strain even further against my clothes.

All things I saw other people do when flirting and it seemed to work. All things Sam and I had seen over and over in our rom-coms. I had to hope that theoretical knowledge was as good as practical experience in this circumstance.

It was certainly not wasted time.

As I was giggling at Tom, a hand slid into mine and then Beckett was pulling me to him. He pulled me hard against his body and I felt it thrumming with anger. "Fun's over," he growled.

I felt emboldened. Beckett was clearly asserting his dominance – and there was something very sexy about that – but I had the power to knock him down a peg.

"Fun's just getting started," I told him pointedly.

"Fun. Is. Over."

"What's the matter, Beckett? Did your horsey lose?"

Oh, he was furious with me. Had he been a different man, I'd have said he was about to hit me into submission. As it was, hitting me was not what I was afraid Beckett was going to do to me.

Beckett leant his lips to my ear and said quietly. "Your defiance is a lot less cute than you think it is."

"Your possessiveness is a lot less cute than you think it is," I countered.

He actually hissed in annoyance. "Do as you're told, Eden. You won't be the one to suffer," he threatened.

"If you have a claim to stake, Beckett, it is perhaps better done with lips than fists." I pulled away to look in his eyes and watch my words sink in.

They did, and the confusion I was expecting lit his eyes as they searched mine. I licked my lips slowly, not caring that there was no doubt a room full of people pretending not to notice this display between the King of Rivermont and a little nobody like Eden Quin. The loud music – not the only thing swirling around us – would only hide so much.

"You think I'm yours, Beckett?" I taunted. "Actions speak louder than words. Don't you think?" I cocked my head to the side and watched him, feeling a sense of superiority.

I might have wanted him to kiss me more than I cared about breathing just then, but it was going to be on my terms. He might have decided I was his, but it was going to be my hand forcing him to prove it.

He snarled, then roughly took my cheek in his hand and crushed his mouth to mine to claim me in front of everyone there. There was absolutely nothing soft or gentle or romantic about it, and that suited me fine.

It was, for want of a better word, perfect.

A veritable thunderstorm pouring down in the desert that had been nearly two months of build-up to this moment.

My stomach bottomed out, heat pooled everywhere, my heart stuttered, my skin broke out in goosebumps, and I forgot anyone else in the world existed outside the two of us.

I reached up, winding my arms around his neck to thread my fingers in his hair, as I gave back as good as I got. His hands went to my hips as he held me as close to his body as he could get me. Beckett's tongue swept into my mouth, searching for supremacy and instead finding a battle of wills I was determined not to lose.

Suddenly, Beckett broke the kiss and looked around. I didn't know what he was doing. Even when he kicked his head behind me and pushed me like he wanted me to lead the way. It was a rough enough push to imply urgency and still be sexy, without it hurting or threatening me.

I took a step backwards and frowned in question.

He nodded, forced me to turn around and guided me quickly out of the room, his front hard up against my back.

"Boss?" Jaeger asked as we passed him.

"Not now," Beckett growled at him.

Jaeger saluted him and tried to hide the smirk as he looked at me, like he knew what Beckett was planning on doing to me as soon as he got me alone. I frowned and Jaeger's eyes twinkled. I wanted to say there wasn't something just a little bit endearing about him, but I was distracted by Beckett pushing me up the stairs.

"Where are you taking me?" I asked him.

As though he was annoyed with the rate of my progress, he grunted and skipped around me. He took my hand and started pulling me.

"Beckett," I protested when he didn't answer.

"Somewhere we won't be disturbed," he said, his voice low and gruff and full of need.

We got to a floor with less doors along the hall than I was used to seeing in the Rivermont dorms. But then I'd never been to the Royals' floor, and everyone knew they'd refurbished the place so each room was the size of at least two and all had their own bathrooms. I heard they even had locks on their doors. It had cost someone a shit load of money, and I doubted the Royals' families had footed the bill.

Beckett got to a door, and I saw a gold door plate with the name 'MAXWELL IV' engraved in it. He pushed it opened, dragged me inside and used my body to close it behind us. As his lips found mine again, I felt him locking the door beside us and all there was, was him.

I was done. Me coming to the party *had* been it, but it was me who couldn't help themselves. Maybe he couldn't either. It didn't much matter right then. All I wanted was him and me and an end to all this unresolved tension.

"I will have you, Eden," he growled against my lips.

"Then less talk, more do," I said, breathlessly.

Beckett clearly liked that answer. His fingers went straight to my clit, rubbing me over my undies, and I melted between him and the door. This. This was what my body had craved for weeks. For weeks now, all I wanted was to have him ease this ache in me and I didn't rightly know how or why I'd resisted for so long.

As his hand slid under my undies and found the wetness of my centre, his lips trailed my down cheek and I lay my head back against the door to give him better access to my neck. He ran over me slowly, building up even more tension in me until I grabbed a handful of his hair and demanded, "Stop teasing me."

He nipped my neck playfully. "You've spent months teasing me, baby. Why shouldn't I return the favour?"

"Giving me what I want gets you what you want," I told him, throwing his words back at him petulantly.

"Now you want to play ball?" he teased as he found my clit again and rolled it between his finger and thumb.

I rocked my hips, desperate for more. "Give me what I want, and I'll give you what you want."

He pulled back to look at me with a sinful smirk lighting his eyes. "I want to be inside you, Eden. Are you really ready to give in?"

In frustration, I dropped my hands to his belt, desperate enough that I was about ready to show him how much I was willing to give to get what I wanted from him. But he gripped my wrists with both hands and raised them above my head to hold them against the door. He rolled his pelvis against me, and a breathy whimper escaped me.

"Tell me," he demanded. "Tell me you're mine."

"No one owns me, Beckett."

He rearranged so he was holding my wrists with one hand and the other went to my throat. "Admit you're mine and I will give you everything you want and more," he purred in my ear before pinning me with his fierce chocolate gaze.

I swallowed hard and felt my throat bob against his hand. But I liked it. I saw in his eyes that he'd seen in mine just how much I liked it. The smirk lit his face, then he was turning me around and roughly forcing my legs to part. He held me against the door with his body weight, and I wasn't sure I'd have been able to move if I'd wanted to.

Beckett's left hand trailed slowly down my stomach, to the bottom of my skirt and up into my undies again. His finger ran over my slit, then plunged into me as his thumb found my clit. I gasped and my hips bucked against him.

"When I'm done with you, there will be no question who you belong to," he said, his voice low.

"Are you going to fuck me into submission, Beckett?" I asked lazily.

"I'm going to fuck you into submission, Eden," he agreed as his finger pumped me. His right hand took my right hand, our fingers intertwined then rested on the door by my head. "You're not walking out of here until you admit you're mine."

"What?" I sassed. "You think you're magic in the bedroom?"

His finger slid out of me to lavish attention on my clit and tingle shot around my body, making me grip his hand tighter where it rested on the door.

"My sole purpose is your pleasure, baby," he growled in my ear, but it was a sexy, needy kind of growl. "I don't need magic to lay you bare before me."

I shivered as the pleasure mounted. "Shit. Beckett…" I panted, pressing my head into the door and my arse back into him.

"Are you going to come for me, Eden?"

I nodded, not sure how I hadn't already. Tingles zinged and shot all over me, everything fizzled pleasantly, but there was no big bang I usually associated with an orgasm. No final conclusion. Instead, it ebbed and flowed. It crested and waned. Like the occasional slightly bigger firework among a whole bunch of smaller ones that had my whole body shaking and moaning.

And Beckett wrang them from me over and over and over until I had to put my hand over his to give me a moment to breathe. He peppered kisses over my shoulder as I breathed heavily, feeling my heart pounding in my chest. I knew it wasn't all physical exertion.

My respite was short-lived.

Beckett flipped me around and lifted me up to claim my lips with his once more. As he did, he rubbed the very hard erection of his cock along my slit, and I sighed against him. My hands went to his hair and his ran up my body. Our kiss deepened and grew more frantic. He cupped my breast and squeezed. I felt my back arch into him, and he squeezed harder.

I moaned softly and I felt the smile as his lips blazed fire down my jaw. With one hand squeezing my breast, he bit me and holy shit. His other hand went to my upper thigh and gripped it firmly as he rubbed against me harder. My nipples tightened and I felt that coil start winding in me again. He pinched my nipple hard as his teeth grazed the skin of my neck again and I practically shattered for him.

His name left my lips in a breathy groan that left nothing to the imagination.

It was all I wanted but I still wanted more.

"God, Eden." His voice was almost reverent and sounded as needy as the throbbing between my legs made me feel.

He got my top off me as he dropped me gently to the ground. My hands went to the bottom of his tee and made quick work of getting it over his head and then I found his lips again and demanded more from him. His hands on me were firm. They were hard. They were a fair bit tighter than I'd have asked for, and I loved it.

I hooked my fingers in the waistband of his jeans and tugged him towards his bed. He didn't need telling twice. As he walked towards it, he picked me up, then threw me. My heart skipped in my chest, and I caught his eye as I landed among his pillows. I saw the inexplicable smile on my face mirrored in his eyes as he stalked towards me and climbed on to the bed.

Beckett only got as far as my waist, where he pushed my skirt out of the way and made short work of getting my undies off me. Then his mouth was over me, he was sucking my clit hard, and I was gripping handfuls of his sheets as my back fully arched off the bed in pleasure.

One of my hands went to his head as my knees clamped around his head. Unsure if I was trying to get him to stop or go harder, I took a second to breathe. Then Beckett was roughly pushing my legs open so he had free reign to do what he wanted; which was give me what I wanted.

Pleasure assaulted me in the best possible way.

I writhed and wriggled on his bed, his hands holding my hips in place so I was at his mercy. His scent surrounded me. I felt the stubble of his beard against the tender flesh of my thighs. His hands were warm, sure, and steady on me. My heart felt like it was going to bottom out, that my body wasn't the only thing in danger of being at his mercy.

I cried out as I came hard, the force of it making me nearly sit up. But Beckett wasn't having that. He crawled up my body, pushing me down into his bed with that predatory look in his eyes that made a thrill run through me. I was usually wary of what could happen when he looked at me like that, but not now. Now I wanted to know every single detail of it.

He settled between my legs and kissed me hard.

I wrapped my whole body around him and gave him back twice as good as I got. We were locked in a battle of supremacy, and I wasn't sure either of us could win. I did know what was about to happen and, while I wanted it so badly, I also wanted to set some boundaries around expectations.

"Wait, Beckett. Wait," I panted, like this was my last hail mary.

He pulled back as though I'd stung him. "What's wrong?" For a second, he sounded like he cared.

"No. It's just… I'm not a virgin."

"So? Neither am I."

Like I didn't know that. "So, you don't gain anything by sleeping with me."

"On the contrary, I gain the pleasure of banging you out of my system."

"So, I'm just a problem you want to be rid of?"

"Did you want more?"

I didn't have to think about that to know the answer. Beckett was nothing I wanted. Nothing except for this pesky attraction I seemed to have with his physical features and the way we both seemed to get off on riling each other up. I had no interest in being a part of his cruel world. He was arrogant, condescending, haughty, rude, and shallow. He was a bully, and nothing I was interested in being with. So, no. I neither wanted more, nor was more even a remote possibility between us.

"We can't be more," I answered.

"No, we can't." He buried his nose in my neck. "Do you still want me to fuck you?"

I also didn't need to think about that.

"I take issue with your word choice, but yes."

"Yes, what?"

"Yes, I want you to fuck me."

"Not what I was looking for, Eden," he said, his voice low and demanding.

I looked him dead in the eyes. "I will never call you 'sir', Beckett."

He pulled me to him in a way that would have been aggressive had I not felt totally safe with him, and had it not been such a turn on. "By the time I'm finished with you, you'll call me whatever I want you to."

"Is that a threat?"

"It's a promise."

Our lips went back to battle as his finger found my clit again, and I fought the feeling of rightness that surged through me at the taste of me on his lips. Like kissing him was what I'd been born for. The independent modern women in me rolled over in her freshly dug grave at that one, because Beckett seemed to have made me kill her off without a second thought.

It was irrational and ridiculous and something I'd most likely regret. But Jesus, all I wanted was to be his. All I wanted was to have him own me. Even for just tonight. I told myself I could give him up tomorrow. I told myself I could go back to needing no man – other than Sam – tomorrow. After I knew intimately everything Beckett Maxwell could give me.

Just as my hands were reaching for his belt, the fire alarm sounded. I pushed him off me as I sat up and looked around.

Beckett's fingers played with my clit lazily as his lips went to the spot under my ear and he murmured, "I'm sure it's nothing."

I frowned at him and put him to arm's length. "I'm not burning for you, Beckett," I told him sternly.

The smirk that lit his eyes didn't quite play out on his face. "You already burn for me, baby."

My lips tried smiling to that, but I wouldn't let them. "I'm serious, Beckett," I said as I got off his bed and looked for my top. "What if one of your idiot court got arson-y drunk?" I finally found my top and pulled it on. "You can't have me if I'm dead."

He huffed and annoyance sparked in his eyes. "Fine." He got off his bed and didn't bother looking for his tee.

"Where are my undies?" I asked.

"Surely the risk of dying in a fire is more important than you going commando?" he drawled sarcastically and I frowned at him.

"Your indifference isn't as attractive as you'd like it to be," I told him as I headed for the door.

He stopped me, took my hand and lay it over the raging boner in his jeans. "It's not indifference, Eden," he said harshly. "It's being denied what is mine."

I shouldn't have liked the way he said that, let alone that he had said it, but I did. Too much.

"Try being less of a dick, and maybe you'll get what you want next time," I told him.

His eyebrow and lip quirked. "Next time?"

I did let my lips rise for him this time. "Next time."

He still looked like he didn't believe I'd be anything other than resistant to the idea of being with him again, so I ran my hand up his naked chest as I pressed my body to his.

"I'm not yours, Beckett, but you haven't fulfilled your side of the bargain."

"We are not a negotiation, Eden," he told me in a voice that had me caring just a little less about the fire alarm still sounding.

I reached up and brushed my lips over his as I said, "*We* are very much up for debate. One I'll be more than happy to argue with you, in your bed, another time."

I felt his lips rise against my lips and saw the humour dancing in his eyes. "Another time, then."

I nodded as I pulled away. "Another time, then."

Before I could leave, he pulled me back to him and seared me with a kiss that I knew was designed to have me jonesing for that other time. And it did its job. It was all I could think about as I looked around for Sam out the front of the boys' dorm.

I finally found him, but couldn't find Abby.

"She's fine," he assured me as we hugged. "Jaeger grabbed her as soon as the alarm went off."

I didn't have time to dwell on Jaeger's sudden protectiveness of my new friend because Sam pushed me to arm's length and smirked.

"Now, let me guess," he said. "You and Beckett made literal flames?"

"Nothing happened!" I protested, feeling my cheeks heat.

His eyes slid behind me and I followed them to see Beckett in just his jeans and shoes, talking to Preston. Damn, he looked good. I hadn't had time to appreciate just how good he looked without his shirt on in his room. But I had full view now and I was going to enjoy it. His jeans sat low on his hips and there was a tantalising, thin line of dark hair trailing from his belly button down into the waistband of the underwear that was just visible as he lifted one arm. As he ran his hand through his hair, his eyes slid to me, and I viscerally remembered the feeling of that last kiss. I told myself my cheeks weren't getting even hotter.

"Nothing happened?" Sam asked, clearly not believing me.

I nodded. "Nothing happened."

"And you're sticking with that story?"

"Why do you think something happened? Just because he's not wearing a shirt? That could mean anything."

"You have a hicky coming on," Sam pointed out and my hand flew to the spot I could almost still feel Beckett lavishing attention on.

Sam smirked and I frowned.

"Shut up."

"Was it at least everything we'd hope for and more?"

Now I smirked as well. "Not quite, but maybe next time."

His eye widened. "You're going to let him have a next time?"

I shrugged. "I've tasted him now, Sammy. I can't walk away without tasting it all at least once."

Sam nodded. "Good for you," he laughed. "Good for you."

# CHAPTER THIRTEEN

The next day, I couldn't give Beckett up. I couldn't go back to needing no man but Sam. I still hadn't fully had Beckett, and it was driving me to distraction. Especially when my first lesson on Tuesday was History and Beckett was hanging outside my classroom, looking at me with dark bedroom eyes like he was just begging me to wag and go back to his room with him to finish what we started.

It was oh so tempting, but I wasn't going to be one of those kids who missed class for sex. And certainly not for my first time with someone. What if all our delicious fizzle totally fizzled right on out and the sex was terrible? Then I'd have a potential detention for nothing.

Without words, Beckett fell into step with me and walked me from History to the library for my Free and I didn't miss the way people looked at us. It was only slightly more distracting than knowing Beckett's body was just not touching mine. His hand hung just next to mine. His arm swung just next to mine. His shoulder…was quite a bit higher than mine actually, but the concept is grasped.

Even if the general student populace hadn't all been witness to the scene at the party the night before, they'd definitely heard about it. I wouldn't be surprised if there was a video – or ten – doing the rounds somewhere. Their faces were the usual mix of 'is she insane?' with a bit of 'I wish it was me' and a whole lot of 'what the hell is happening to the status quo?' It was a good question, and I would have liked the answer to that as well, but Beckett was clearly not going to be answering any questions I might have about the status quo or anything else.

As soon as we walked through the main library thoroughfare on the way to my usual desk, Beckett side tracked us down an aisle and pushed me against the shelves, his arm at my back to shield me from the edges of the shelves in question.

"Beck–" I started but he just kissed me like I was the drug he was jonesing for.

He was pressed right into me, and I felt his cock harden between us as we kissed. I throbbed and tingled and was so ready for him. I wanted to know what it felt like. He wanted inside? I wanted him inside as well. I had no qualms about it being in the school library, but I just wasn't quite so confident as to make the first move about it.

Beckett rocked his hips against me, and his cock rubbed me in all the right places. My arms around his shoulders tightened and our kiss deepened. As though the night before had flipped a switch, he threw away all pretence or teasing as we just rubbed wantonly together. All-but fucking right in the middle of the library where anyone could find us.

I breathed heavily and moaned against his lips as the pleasure in me mounted.

"Cum for me, baby," he demanded.

He dropped his lips to my neck as our pace increased. I dropped my head back and rode it out as the wave crashed through me and I tried to wrap my whole body around him. His lips found mine again as he thrust languidly against me while I came back down.

"Why are you wearing make up on your neck?" he murmured against me.

"Because you gave me a hicky last night."

"I like to mark what's mine."

"Do you also like risking jizzing in your pants?"

He made a noise that might have almost maybe been a laugh. "Not particularly."

I smirked against his lips as I breathed heavily. "I'd have thought you grew out of dry humping years ago," I teased, and I felt his lips tilt. I ran my nose over his and he sighed contentedly. "Is it true they give you Royals your first prostitute at thirteen?"

"Some of us." His voice was hushed, and I didn't know if he was as lost in the moment as I was or if he was about to let me into the secrets of his world. Maybe it was both. "I was fourteen. Rowan was eleven."

My heart constricted. Even for someone as twisted as Rowan. But then, I could see now at least one reason for why he was that way.

I tried for humour. "Were you a late bloomer?" I sassed.

His lazy smile grew, and I was sure he huffed the smallest laugh. "I lost my virginity at thirteen. The prostitute was a gift."

"Some dads just get you a bike," I commented dryly.

He ran his nose over my jaw and my neck as he nodded. "In many ways, she was."

I snorted, though I felt bad about it. "When I was fourteen, I was lucky to get a new phone. I wanted a skateboard. Sex wasn't even really on my radar."

"Sex is power, Eden," he said slowly. "We're taught young to use it to our advantage."

"Is that what this is?" I asked, not even affronted because I kind of hadn't expected any less. "Power?"

"This," he answered before nipping my neck. "This is…" He brought his face up to look at me. "Desire. This, I want. Fortunately, it gives me power as well."

"Over me?"

"Over everyone."

"What's so special about me?" I asked him, echoing my words to Jaeger.

"Everything," he answered before he kissed me again like he refused to say anymore and possibly would have even without me asking him anything more.

Finally, he put me down gently, brushing hair from my face and running his fingers along my cheek. "I expect you'll have some very uncomplimentary things to say to me if I keep you from your study any longer."

My eyebrow quirked. "Here I assumed you liked it when I had uncomplimentary things to say about you."

His eyes shone with something as he looked me over. "Why would you think that?"

I smirked at him. "Because you give me so many opportunities," I sassed as I picked up my bag and started for my desk.

He stepped up behind me and wrapped his arms around my waist. With his lips at my ear, he said, "Realise I respect your reserve, or I would have you right here."

"My reserve, Beckett?"

I felt him nod as his arm around my stomach tightened. "Not wanting to fuck in the library."

I smirked as I leant back against him. "Who said I didn't want to fuck in the library, Beckett?"

I felt his groan against my back. "I thought we were done teasing, Eden."

I reached my arm around to hug his head. "We'll never be done teasing, Beckett. And I *will* fuck you in the library." I took his surprise as the opportunity to slip out of his slackened arms. I turned to face him as I walked backwards to my desk. "Just not today."

He growled and I saw the fire burning for me bright in his eyes. Maybe Beckett was right, and sex *was* power. And maybe that didn't have to be a bad thing. Him looking at me like that certainly made me feel powerful. It wasn't about ownership, but it was about possessiveness. It was about desire.

And I just let him simmer in it for the rest of the lesson until I finally left his side for Sam's at Homegroup, throwing him a look like I knew exactly what I was doing to him. If he wanted what I had, then he was going to have to do it on my terms. And I was going to milk it for all it was worth. He'd either stick it out and prove he wanted me, not just someone to beat into submission. Or he'd move on, and I'd have my answer. Beckett glared at me as Sam and I walked into the classroom, leaving no doubt in my mind that he was going to stick it out and he was going to make sure I know how much he hated every second of it.

"So, news," Sam said as we sat in our chairs at the beginning of homegroup.

"News?"

He nodded. "News. You remember the fire alarm last night?"

I nodded. "Painfully."

Sam smirked, his eyes darting up to Beckett. "No doubt. Well, it was pulled. On purpose."

I looked at him with a surprised frown. "What?" He nodded. "By who?"

"Hunter."

I blinked, my mouth gaping like an open fish. "What? Why?"

Sam rolled his eyes. "Okay, be prepared because it's full-on, like, daytime soap drama." I snorted and he pinned me with a 'no, I'm serious' look that sobered me up. "He was saving you from Beckett."

I blinked again. "Saving me from…" My eyes darted to Beckett again, who frowned like he knew we were talking about him and didn't like that either. I pulled my eyes back to Sam. "…whatever consensual activity was occurring between me and another person?" I clarified and Sam nodded.

"All that. He's very proud of himself, so just… Yeah. There's that. Have fun with it."

I huffed as I sat back in my chair and homegroup started. As the roll was called and notices read, I chewed on my lip and kept sneaking looks at Beckett. I didn't even care that Isabella was shooting me death glares or Fox was buzzing in his seat like he was trying to work out how quickly he could get to me and what damage he could do before Beckett got to him.

I cared slightly more at Recess when, before I'd had a chance to confront Hunter, Isabella actually pushed me onto the floor of the dining hall.

"You think he won't get bored and move on?" she sneered.

"Well, you'd know *all* about that," I muttered sarcastically as I pulled myself off the floor.

She screeched. "You're nothing! You're less than nothing. You don't even belong here, you fucking worthless little pleb."

I nodded. "Couldn't agree with you more. But I'm stuck here. Same as you. I'm sure any of these rich arseholes would marry you and I'll bet that almost all of them will treat you a damned sight better than Beckett could even if he wanted to."

Yeah, Beckett could hear me. I was sure of it. But if he thought I was under any delusions about what we were to each other, then he could be put to rights.

"Then you'll back off and leave him to his own kind," Isabella spat. Quite literally. And it wasn't a question.

"Tell you what," I said to her, nodding in Beckett's direction. He leant forward at his table, watching me carefully and giving nothing away about his thoughts. "You go and tell His Highness who he's allowed to pursue, and we can all go our separate ways."

The corner of Beckett's lip tipped for a split second, and I almost thought he was proud of me. Or impressed with me. Or damn it, maybe even liked me. The feeling was short-lived as Isabella's fist crashed into my cheek and whipped my head sideways.

I stretched my face out, not feeling anything bleeding thankfully, and looked back at her slowly.

"You want to play at finding a husband? Grow up," I said to her before turning and walking away.

"And imagine," Hunter said proudly as I sat down, "how much worse it would be if he actually touched you last night."

The hicky on my neck, that this very morning in my bedroom mirror had been even worse than last night and was now smothered in concealer so no one noticed, belied that statement totally. But I wasn't going to set him to rights when my cheek was smarting something shocking.

I caught Fox's eye from across the room and shivered in fear at the knowing smirk on his face. It told me nothing good was coming my way and I deserved every second of it. It worried me so much that I was actually glad when Jaeger met me and Abby on the way out of the dining hall, and stepped slightly closer to the protection he offered.

"Beckett liked that," he said simply.

"Two girls coming to literal blows over him?" I scoffed, thinking that was about right.

"You."

"Me?" I said as I looked at him and he nodded. "Taking a punch for him like you or Rowan?"

"Taking it graciously, and not having to resort to punching back."

"Yeah," I huffed. "Because only weaklings walk away."

"Because only leaders walk away. You put her down with nothing but words and your own sense of superiority."

"That *is* Beckett's thing," Abby pointed out and I flashed her a 'whose side are you on?' look.

"Well," I huffed to Jaeger. "You can tell your king that, next time he likes it, he can come and check on me himself. I'm not a punching bag, Jaeger. I thought you were supposed to be offering me protection?"

"That you continue to resist," he pointed out. "And women's business is women's business. That shit's between you."

I rolled my eyes. "Fine. Then you tell Beckett that if he gives any other girl cause to come at me over him again, then I'm coming for his—"

The next thing I knew, Jaeger disappeared. I looked around and saw Gunner and Clint holding him against the wall with Locksley standing by, and Fox was stepping up to me. My heart pounded at the look on Fox's face, and fight or flight was heavily engaged. Abby took my hand like sisterly solidarity was going to be enough to stand up to him. Jaeger thrashed against the two holding him and Locksley dealt him a swift blow to the gut.

Jaeger's head dropped for a second, then he rallied like the pro he was.

"Three against one?" Jaeger wheezed, still as peppy as usual. "Come on, boys. Give yourself a fighting chance. Where's Frogmartin? How about Rockefeller? Fuck, even Mariana packs more punch than you morons."

"If you think I can't get to you, Eden," Fox said quietly, ignoring Jaeger. "Then you're even more delusional than I thought. I haven't touched you – *yet* – purely because I'm benevolent. But I won't wait much longer."

He laughed, snapped his fingers and walked away. As soon as he was far enough away, his cronies let go of Jaeger. He lunged at them, and they laughed as they ran after Fox. My heart still pounded, and it didn't settle as Jaeger came to my side.

"Are you okay?" Jaeger asked.

I nodded, my eyes still on the others as they disappeared down the corridor.

"Good. No, I'm good, too. No worries. Thanks for asking," he muttered.

"*Are* you okay?" Abby asked him, and I heard the humour in her voice.

Jaeger smiled but didn't take his eyes off me. "I've had plenty worse, and I'll take worse yet before this is done."

"Don't tell Beckett," I told him, finally looking at him.

Jaeger frowned as he searched my eyes. "Why not?"

Because I didn't want it to change anything? Because I didn't want him more focussed on revenge than me? Because it wouldn't matter if he did? Because maybe it would matter if he did? I didn't know what was true or what would keep Jaeger's mouth shut.

"Consider it a favour," was what I went with.

I saw understanding light those bright green eyes and he nodded. "But, keep the favour, Quincy."

I didn't know whether Jaeger had kept his mouth shut or not. Beckett either wouldn't or couldn't keep his eyes off me whenever we were near. That could have been because he was worried about Fox encroaching on his territory. Or it could have been the still unresolved tension swirling around us that I felt crowding me like a suffocating blanket.

The looks between us were starting to feel an awful lot like the lingering, longing kind by the end of the day on Tuesday. They held a whole lot of unsaid things that made my stomach twinge, my clit heat, and my heart flutter. I found myself biting my lip in case my face tried giving even more away. Beckett followed the movement, and I could see he liked it. Or rather, he liked what he did to me. I told myself that I wasn't having even remotely the same effect on him, but even what *should* have been true couldn't make me lie to myself quite that convincingly.

And as though Fox knew what was happening between me and Beckett, he was even less pleasant than that over the next few days and that was the end of Beckett getting me off in the library. Or anywhere.

Fox wasn't the only one who was verging on insufferable.

Except Hunter had taken a very different tack.

He strutted around the school like he really had personally saved me from Beckett. As though he'd literally swooped in and pulled me from Beckett's talon-like clutches to whisk me to his 'knight in shining armour' safety.

And all he'd done was pull the goddamn fire alarm and cock block me in the most annoying way possible. Not that I would even suggest such a thing in his presence. He was volatile enough about the whole Beckett thing, I didn't need to give him more ammunition.

Beckett had stepped up the 'guard detail' and he spent more time watching over me personally than he had previously. There seemed something slightly more agitated and tense about him. To the point that I was sure someone was keeping an eye on me even when I was in my dorm room. I'd seen Rowan and Jaeger hanging around the front of the girls' dorm, but Beckett was never there, almost like he was worried about what might happen if we were alone in there together and that would somehow – what? – put me in more danger?

On Wednesday, Rowan was threatening to actually be in my English lesson with us, although Sam wasn't complaining. Jaeger had one of the inner sanctums' cronies with him for French and he helped Jaeger give Fox a stern talking to about appropriate behaviour in the corridor. Along with a swift knee to the stomach. Recess and Lunch saw one of the inner sanctums' muscle hovering at our table in the dining hall. Double Psych had Rowan actually sitting with Fox in the classroom, much to the teacher's surprise. And Beckett seemed absolutely immune to the sexual tension burning between us in my last lesson double Free to the point I was wondering if I'd imagined it all until then.

On Thursday, it wasn't much better. By Lunch, Hunter was vibrating with the indignity of having Royals and their muscle around me pretty much twenty-four seven.

"It's ridiculous," he hissed at me.

I shrugged. "It's harmless."

"They're invading your space," he snapped, doing just that over the table.

I sat back from him. "I don't know Fox that well, but I'd rather Beckett and his lot getting in my space than anyone who follows Fox right now."

"You're fine with just me and Sam."

"And Abby," Sam said pointedly. "And she's not."

"I'm useless," Abby offered helpfully. "Fox scares the crap out of me."

Hunter scowled over to the Royals' tables. "He doesn't scare me."

"No?" Sam said. "How about Beckett? Jaeger? Rowan?"

A touch of fear did light Hunter's eyes at the mention of Rowan, and it was probably the most sensible reaction he'd had all day.

"How about Beckett's reaction when Fox steamrolls right over us and does God knows what to Eden?" Sam continued. "Because I don't know about you, but I'm better suited to fucking Royals than fucking them up."

It was colourful language for Sam, outside the privacy of just us two, and even Hunter's indignation saw how serious and important Sam thought this was.

Hunter threw some food into his mouth sullenly. "I still don't like it."

"No one *likes* it," I told him.

"We'd all rather they just go back to bullying Edie for being the swim coach's scholarship daughter," Sam added. "But they're not going to. Nothing's going to be the same again. Even when Beckett wins, nothing's going to be the same."

"What do you mean *when* Beckett wins?" Hunter asked, frowning.

"Which do you take issue with?" Sam asked him. "That Beckett's going to win or that he very nearly already has?"

Hunter looked at me suspiciously. "What do you mean nearly has?"

I sighed, not about to go into the details with Hunter of how close Beckett was to winning. "There is no way I'm picking *Fox*," I huffed, realising too late that I'd put the inflection on the wrong word. I tried backpedalling before Hunter made any more assumptions, even if they were true. "As long as I don't pick Fox, then he loses." I shrugged, hoping that was as simple as it had to be.

Hunter's brain was whirring. I saw it in the calculating way he was looking between me and the Royals' table where Beckett sat. I turned and found Beckett watching me carefully. For a moment, everything else melted away and it was just me and him.

The things I'd say to him in another world. At another time. The things I'd ask.

The first of which would be why.

Because it felt to me like his protection was about more than just beating Fox. He could have beaten Fox easily weeks ago. He could have done it with brute force and the full impact of his personality. But that would have hurt me – physically, mentally, emotionally – and he hadn't chosen that path.

I didn't know if I was getting lust confused with other things, but it felt to me like maybe this something more between us was just that. Something more. Or at least it had the potential to be something more. Something amazing.

"Just so long as you don't do something as stupid as picking King Fuckwit," Hunter muttered sarcastically, and I was slammed back into the present reality.

I cleared my throat and took my eyes off Beckett. To save me answering, Abby loudly asked Hunter if he was ready for the next swim meet and he was suddenly less worried about what I thought about Beckett and more worried about showing me how into swimming he was.

I snuck looks back at Beckett for the rest of Lunch, and he was watching me every time. I wouldn't have minded so much if I wasn't so unsure about where we were now. Did he still want me as much as I wanted him? Had he moved on? Did I go to all the effort to muster up the courage to just ask him, and risk the King's indifference and coldness?

Ugh. I hated everything about that week.

And walking to Biology after Lunch made it so much worse.

"Now we have a fucking flank escort?" Hunter muttered and I was sure he didn't mean to let Beckett hear him.

But it was Beckett, of course he did. "Who else is going to protect Eden?"

"*I* can protect Eden," Hunter said, his tone heavily suggesting he already had.

Beckett's eyebrow quirked in condescending surprise. "Really?"

Of course, Hunter rose to Beckett's disbelief and supposed disinterest. "I already have."

Beckett huffed in fake humour. "Was she in danger from a falling leaf?"

"Her *virtue* was in danger from a piece of shit," Hunter said, and I thought that was a bit rich.

Not that he was calling Beckett a piece of shit. Beckett may have been protecting me from Fox, but I was under no delusions he was a good guy. But my virtue was my business, and I could throw it around wherever I wanted. It wasn't in any more danger from Beckett as it was at risk of swallowing Beckett whole and loving every minute.

Beckett took a step towards Hunter and Abby took my hand. "Eden's *virtue*," he said the word dripping with sarcasm, "is safer with *me*."

We all heard the insinuation. We all understood the insinuation. Well, I understood it as far as what it was. Beckett meant my virtue was safer with him than it was with Hunter. I didn't know why Beckett had made the insinuation in the first place.

Hunter tried his best at a growl and lunged at Beckett. Rowan was there in seconds to hold Hunter back, but Hunter's face was contorted in anger. Beckett took another step towards Hunter and the two of them faced off against each other in a moment I did not understand at all.

Hunter was livid. He was straining against Rowan, who held him easily.

Beckett found Hunter's ire endlessly amusing.

"Go on," Hunter challenged. "Dismiss your muscle and fight me yourself!"

"Hunter!" burst out of me, my hand tightening on Abby's, but Hunter ignored me.

Beckett's smirk rose slightly. "I will kill you," he whispered to Hunter, and I felt like there was another message there that went straight over my head. Like there was a stipulation other than just if they went at it in a fair fight.

I slipped my hand from Abby's and put it on Beckett's arm. "Okay, guys…" I said slowly. "Enough."

"For now," Beckett said, then kissed me hard like that was supposed to prove a point before he stormed off with Rowan following.

I looked at Preston. "I think we'll be fine from here."

Preston huffed a humourless laugh. "Then, you think wrong," he drawled as he dropped against the wall to take up sentry position.

Hunter made to point at Preston, but I smacked his hand down and pushed him into the classroom as Abby followed.

"You raging idiot!" I snapped at Hunter as we sat down.

"Someone has to stand up to them."

"I need you on my side, Hunt," I said, and he finally looked at me.

As he did, his eyes softened. "I *am* on your side, Edie. That's why I had to say something to him."

I shook my head. "No. I need you on my side, which means we just have to deal with the annoyance of the inner sanctum. For now. You aggravating them will only make everything worse."

Hunter nodded slowly. "Yeah… Okay, Edie."

I gave a singular nod as I rearranged in my chair and looked out at Preston and his haughty, knowing smile. "Thanks."

# CHAPTER FOURTEEN

Beckett's agitation and distraction all proved understandable on Friday when Jaeger was nowhere to been seen after French and Fox took that as his opportunity to follow through on the threats that I'd seen in his eyes all week.

He pushed me roughly against the wall and crowded me in much the same way Beckett would, but all I felt was revulsion. My skin crawled and panic clawed at my chest. I tried to push him away, but he was too strong for me, and he had his whole body weight behind him.

"Get off me, Fox," I demanded.

"I might just take what I want right here in the corridor," Fox sneered as his fingers toyed with the bottom of my skirt.

I shied away from him and fought the stagnation in my head.

"Fox!" Abby yelled, sounding as unsure about interfering as I was about her interfering. "Stop it!"

"You think either of you can stop me?" Fox smirked at me, but it wasn't pleasant. "You're the symbol of the coming end of Beckett's reign," he purred, but the only reaction my body had was to shudder in disgust. "When you belong to me, so will his crown. He'll be done and I'll be king. Give in to me now and I'll show you how *deeply* my gratitude runs."

I shivered, but my train of thought restarted and I held my own. "I don't care what play for power you're making, Fox. I'm not for winning or losing. It makes no difference to me which of you arseholes sits on your make-believe throne with your imaginary crown–"

Fox's fist flew back, and I knew what was coming. I cowered, but the blow never landed, and I felt Fox jerk away from me. I opened one eye cautiously and saw Beckett holding Fox's arm behind his back. I'd thought I'd seen fury on his gorgeous face? That was nothing compared to the thunderous shitstorm he was about to rain down of Fox.

"Still making threats you're too weak to follow through?" Beckett sneered at him.

Fox apparently wouldn't be cowed by his king any longer. "I learnt from the best," he jeered, grinning.

"You want to try that again?" Beckett asked, pulling Fox's arm tighter.

Fox grimaced against the pain, but didn't lose his impudence. "When she's mine, *I* won't hesitate when she needs to be put in her place."

We all heard the insinuation. We knew what he was saying about Beckett. I was starting to see – to believe – why I was the symbol of Fox's coup. It was what Regina had said that day in the changerooms and, whether there was truth or not to it, Fox still believed it. He thought Beckett had gone soft over me, was losing his touch and therefore his clout and his reputation. His strength and ruthlessness and, with it, his legitimacy to rule Rivermont. And it only took one to agree with Fox for rumours and dissent to spread.

"This ends now." Beckett pulled Fox's arm tighter. "If anyone is going to own Eden, it will be me," he snarled then pushed Fox away from him.

Fox smirked. "And why her? Why now?" he asked, and the rest

of the corridor was paying attention. "You can have anyone you want, pick of the litter, and you *suddenly* decide you want the one person I do?"

"To remind you where you belong," Beckett replied, stepping right into Fox's space and towering over him with far more than height.

"You sure it's not because you have *feelings* for her?" Fox asked, his tone reminding everyone listening exactly what the Royals thought about *feelings*. He was clearly done insinuating and had moved onto outright accusation.

Beckett's face was as calm and stony as usual. No emotion. No feeling. No hint of what was going on beneath the surface. Even when he slammed Fox into the wall behind him, he did it with a callous nonchalance like it was merely a minor inconvenience in his day.

"You seem to forget who you're talking to," Beckett told him coldly, a tinge of sarcastic humour about him. "You seem to be labouring under the misapprehension that I care what you want. That you can have what you want." He leant up close to Fox's ear. "But you have a long way to go before you can be king." He raised his voice ever so slightly. "Eden Quin is mine," he told all those listening. A decree. Right from the mouth of their King. The unspoken order was to disseminate it through the kingdom.

Fox's smirk wouldn't quite be dashed. "Is she?" he challenged and the whole corridor went deathly still. "She hasn't chosen you...has she?"

I wasn't the only one who held my breath like I had no idea what was going on, despite being literally the person they were talking about. I was still looking between them like they were going to tell me what was happening, who was in charge, and who this Eden was going to pick.

Beckett looked unbothered by Fox's insinuations. "Yes. She has."
He turned and looked at me expectantly. "Eden, come."

Usually, I would have argued with him about ordering me around, but the alternative was to be stuck with Fox and lose the only protection I had against Fox. If I didn't back up Beckett's claims here, then he'd lose his remaining authority over Fox and who knew what Fox would try to do to me then. Beckett at least had boundaries. Beckett at least didn't force himself on me when I said no. I couldn't be sure Fox would afford me the same courtesies.

So, I did the only thing I could do.

I chose.

Not that it had ever really been a choice.

I walked quickly over to Beckett and let him take my hand before dragging me away. As he did, I snuck a look back to Fox, who waggled his fingers at me in a threatening mockery of a coquettish wave.

Those gathered in the corridor already had their phones out – a couple of which were teachers – to pass the news along the Rivermont grapevine. I was Beckett's. His crown and – hopefully – I were safe from Fox, but I knew that wouldn't be the end of it. The lion might have won the battle, if only by a tenuous margin, but the fox was still at war.

Beckett didn't stop until we were in his room with the door locked. He didn't speak to me. He didn't reassure me. He didn't try convincing me he was in the right. He just paced as he raked a hand through his hair, as animated and emotional as I'd ever seen him. Which was something given how expressionless he still was.

He might not have said anything to me directly, but I knew what this was. He was regretting his actions. He didn't think he should have saved me. He should have just let Fox do what he wanted. He was starting to doubt that 'saving me' had had the intended effect. He was starting to believe it was just proving Fox's point.

"You didn't have to stop him," I said, annoyed at the feelings that realisation was eliciting in me.

"And maybe I shouldn't have," he spat, confirming my suspicions. "I should just let Fox have you and save myself the trouble."

"None of this is my fault, Beckett," I told him.

"*All* of this is your fault, Eden!"

"You can only blame me for so long, Beckett!" I snapped.

"I assure you, I can blame you eternally."

"A normal, well-adjusted person would just tell me they loved me," I said, being completely facetious and purely aiming to get a rise out of him by being the second person that day to dare suggest he had feelings like he was some kind of commoner.

I got the rise, just not the one I was expecting.

He gave a devilish smirk, full of knowing taunt. "And where would be the fun in that?" he asked me, the real meaning of his words remaining *heavily* implied.

My heart did something weird, like it was fluttering and stopping and crumbling and starting all at once. I think I hid it well enough. "The fun would be in me not walking away," I told him, making to do just that.

He caught my arm and pulled me back to him. Not that he had to do a lot of the work, my body went to his far too willingly. There was torment in his eyes, and it was mirrored in the gravelly tone of his voice when he spoke.

"I can't stay away from you, Eden. Fuck knows I've tried. I've tried not wanting you. I've tried getting over you. But you are mine and I don't want to try staying away from you anymore."

My whole person zinged at his words, but I cautioned myself against falling for them entirely. I licked my lip slowly as I fought to keep my composure.

Falling for Beckett was likely the stupidest thing I could ever do. We had no future. We wouldn't work. I wanted a relationship built on trust and kindness and friendship. One filled as much with laughter and shared jokes as passionate need and nights spent enjoying the pleasure of each other's bodies.

Beckett was a monster that I doubted was capable of laughing, let alone loving. He looked down on everyone around him. He was entitled, arrogant, infuriating. He was cruel, ruthless, cold. His world held no interest to me.

But I wanted him.

No.

I needed him.

No matter how often he pushed me away, or demanded my supplication, or flexed his authority over not just me but the rest of the world. No matter who he was or what he was, I felt like my world would crumble if I made him stay away from me now.

"Then don't," I whispered, scared as much of what I was asking for as what he might give.

"Eden..." he breathed, questioningly, almost reverently.

I shook my head as I wrapped my arms around his shoulders. "Don't be a dick and ruin it."

To stop him doing just that, I kissed him. Hard.

My hands went to his tie and started pulling it off. His pushed my blazer off my shoulders and it landed at our feet. His followed shortly after. We undid each other's shirt buttons only enough to be able to pull them over our heads.

As our lips inevitably had to part, his mouth opened like he was going to say something.

I dropped his shirt on the floor and stepped back up to him. "I told you not to ruin it."

He brushed some hair from my face then cupped my cheek. "I just wanted to ask if you were sure about this."

"What part of me desperate to get you naked made you think otherwise, Beckett?" I asked.

I saw the humour in his eyes, but it didn't reach his lips. "The fact your body and your voice have been saying very different things for months now."

"They're not saying different things now, Beckett. I want you. I want this. I'm saying yes. Don't second guess me now." I reached up and grazed my lips over his as I finished, "Or don't you want it now that you have it?"

He wrapped me up in his arms. "I want you," he told me, his voice full of what he wouldn't or couldn't say.

We kissed as we awkwardly kicked off our shoes and he deftly got my skirt off me. I stepped out of it, pushing him towards the bed. I felt him smirk against my lips as his hands ran over my now near-naked body. He picked me up, our lips barely parting for a moment, and my legs wrapped around his waist.

"You ready, baby?" he asked, his voice deliciously husky.

"For what?" I asked.

He threw me on the bed, and I felt myself smile.

"Favourite move?" I teased as I leant back on my elbows and looked him over.

"I've never seen anyone enjoy it the way you do," he answered as he took off his trousers and – be still my throbbing clit, of course – boxer-briefs, then crawled over me.

My defiance up to that week seemed so arbitrary and childish now in the face of whatever was between Beckett and me. Jaeger had told me weeks ago that we all knew it was there. He'd told me I was Beckett's girl. Maybe he'd been right about it all in a way.

Beckett certainly had a way of making me feel, of making me accept without question, that this was right. That he was right. That together we were right. Maybe that was what it meant to be his? Just that it was right. Maybe it wasn't something I had to fight. Maybe it didn't need questioning. Maybe it didn't need overthinking either.

So, I let it all go as he kissed me again. I just felt. And it felt amazing.

He dragged his lips down my body aching slowly. He nipped my thigh playfully as he pulled my undies down my legs. As he worked his way back up, his hand slid firmly up my legs, my stomach, to cup my breasts as he sucked my clit, and I pressed my head back into his pillows.

They smelled like him. It surrounded me with softness and might not have been quite like I imagined lying in clouds would be, but it was amazing and far more intimate than I'd had time to realise the last time we were here.

Beckett ran his tongue through my slit and a shiver ran through me as he flicked my clit. So, he did it again. And again. And again, until I was dripping for him. He held me to his face and didn't let up until I was indeed lying bare for him. Pleasure slammed into me hard and fast, and I saw his efforts for what they were; this foreplay was just something to get out of the way before the main event. Usually I'd have disagreed, but we'd done this dance on Monday night and we could do it again later. I wanted the main event now.

Becket sat up, wiping his hand over his mouth as he looked at me hungrily. His hand went to my chin, and he coaxed me to sit up and meet him. He kissed me as he reached over to his bedside table for a condom and his lips didn't leave mine as he sheathed. Then his fingers toyed with my clit as he gently lowered me onto the bed.

He stoked my clit as he positioned at my centre, his eyes locked with mine.

"We do this," he said sternly, "and you're admitting you're mine."

"I don't recall there being a contract."

He planted a hand next to my head. "I've told you, we are not a negotiation, Eden." His voice was growly and told me not to argue, but I was feeling bold.

"And I told you I'd be happy to debate that with you." I reached up to him. "So, *debate* with me, Beckett," I said, seductively and suggestively.

I wasn't going to flat-out disagree with him. If he wanted to take me sleeping with him as me accepting that I was his, then he could go right ahead and do that. Part of me was quite happy with him making that assumption. I wasn't sure what the other part of me thought in contrast, I think I just didn't want to totally approve of him claiming me. Modern independent woman that I was, and all that.

He crushed his lips to mine as he pressed inside me. He went slow, easing into me and allowing me time to acclimate to him. With each thrust, he slid deeper and deeper until I'd taken him to the hilt, and he paused to look down at me with something I'd have said a man without emotions couldn't possibly feel.

He took my hand, lacing his fingers with mine, and held it by my head as he looked me in the eye, and I felt everything flutter dangerously. But I was just feeling, so I didn't ignore it or push it away. I let it in, and I saw something in his eyes soften even further as he watched me.

As he thrust into me slowly, steadily, deeply, he dropped his head and kissed my neck. My fingers gripped his back as I arched into him. The hand that wasn't holding mine, pushed my leg up further and he slid even deeper. We both moaned softly and his hand in mine tightened.

Forget the man without emotions, I was in danger of feeling things here. Things no sane person felt about Beckett Maxwell. Things like warm. Safe. Happy. Things that made me dangerously close to saying his name in ways I really shouldn't. Things that made me hold him close to me just so he wouldn't be able to see on my face those very things.

But when he moaned, "Eden, baby," in my ear, I fell over two precipices: one carnal and one emotional.

His name left my lips and I know he heard it. 'It' being all those things I was hoping to hide from him.

He pushed himself up to look at my face and I hurriedly looked down in the hopes that maybe he wouldn't notice. But he paused and tipped my face to force me to look back at him. I went all in, and my eyes found his. Grey and chocolate brown. So, I saw as they widened almost imperceptibly; he'd seen it and it surprised him.

His only response was to thrust into me deep and strong and capture my lips with his.

Had he not cared? Had he – dare I even think it – been okay with it?

Then his pace increased and all concerns about what he was thinking swiftly vanished in favour of the pleasure building in me again. His fingers dug into my hip for leverage as we rocked together. He kissed me roughly, his stubble grazing my face. Were he anyone else, I'd have said it wasn't just passion but desperation as we thrust faster, our rhythm getting jerkier as we both got closer to release.

My whole body constricted around him as I came moments before

I felt him tense and throb strongly inside me. As we both got our breath back, he looked down at my neck and ran a finger just above my collar bone.

"Do not dare cover that up this time," he said, his voice thick with something.

"Why?" I challenged. "You want everyone to know I'm yours."

"Yes."

"I'm not cattle, Beckett."

He shook his head as his lips brushed over my shoulder and he pulled out of me. "No, you're not."

As he dealt with the condom, I sat up and watched him curiously. He was often cryptic with his words. Very rarely did he say anything that couldn't have like ten meanings. This, though, I didn't think I was brave enough to decide what it meant.

Beckett was back moments later and tackling me back into the bed. He kissed me lazily for a few minutes, then obviously decided that I'd had enough of a breather. He made me see stars twice before he was reaching for another condom.

Our second time out was far less gentle. Although, I wasn't sure exactly where one ended and the next one started.

Beckett plunged straight on in with one thrust and had me what felt like the proverbial six-ways from Sunday. By the end of it, I was totally easy to position because the pleasure he'd ploughed me with had softened me into little more than a ragdoll. If someone told me I wasn't a little puddle of delicious satisfaction snuggled on the floor, then I would have been very surprised.

After he dealt with that condom, he lay on the bed breathing heavily.

"Anyone would think your famous stamina has been greatly exaggerated," I said.

He threw me a look that told me what he thought not only of that but of me for bringing it up. "Anyone else might appreciate that it's very difficult not to blow my load just looking at you after the months leading up to this."

I climbed onto him and watched him look me over in interest. "Do I test your restraint, Beckett?" I teased.

He sat up and wrapped his arms around my waist as his nose bumped mine. "You shatter it, baby."

The bell for the end of lunch sounded and I gave Beckett one last kiss before I stood up to look for my closest piece of clothes. They were somehow spread all over his floor in a very definite line to his bed. Beckett caught my hand, and I looked back at him in question.

As he started pulling me back towards him, I laughed, "I have to get to class, Beckett."

He shook his head, and he dragged me back into his lap. "No. You don't."

I felt his cock hard against my slit and, despite the pleasure he'd just wrung from me, I wanted more. He thrust lazily. He rubbed over my clit, and I was starkly reminded of two weeks earlier when we were in a similar position, and I'd wanted this little clothes between us. I was starkly reminded of just a few days earlier when we were so close but been denied each other.

I leant my head on his shoulder as he continued rubbing me and the pleasure built in me once more. "Beckett," I breathed. "I really need to…" I gasped as I felt his finger slide into me.

"Need to what, baby?" he asked, humour in his voice as his lips brushed over my neck.

My hips rocked with his rhythm as I started fucking his finger. "Need to…"

"Need to cum for me again?"

I was so close. I was so sensitive after nearly an hour of him lavishing me with stimulation, that it was going to take very little effort on his part to get me to finish. I wouldn't miss that much History. It had already happened. It wasn't like it was going anywhere.

So, I wrapped my arms around his shoulders and nodded.

"Make me cum, Beckett," I moaned.

I felt him reach over for something, then he was flipping me over. I didn't have time to ask him what he was doing because he'd re-sheathed and was pressing into me and pleasure crashed over me like he knew he'd timed it perfectly.

Beckett pounded me hard and my next orgasm was building before I was properly over the previous one. I didn't want to tell him to stop now.

He looked down at me with a sinfully cocky expression like he knew what I was thinking. "You didn't say how," he pointed out.

My hands fisted his sheets, and I nodded as the coil in me shivered at breaking point again. "True."

One more thrust was all it took to snap the coil. My body arched full off the bed as I came with his name ripped from my lips once more. Talk about seeing stars, the amazing tingly aftershocks seemed to zing and shoot around my whole body with no signs of stopping any time soon.

Beckett groaned like I was testing that restraint again, so I rolled my hips more strongly. I nipped his ear lobe and moaned in his ear, "You want me to be yours, Beckett?"

"You *are* mine, Eden," he said, and I felt his body tense and his cock throb as he came hard.

"Are you asking to go steady?" I teased.

He thrust lazily once. Twice. Then fixed me with a deep stare.

"Would you say yes if I was?"

My heart fluttered. "Why don't you ask and find out?"

"Why don't you just say yes?" he retorted hotly, and I knew I was frustrating him again.

I leant up to his face and said against his lips. "I'm not saying no."

"That's not a yes, Eden," he said carefully.

"You seem awfully concerned about consent for a man who always gets what he wants," I told him with a cheeky quirk of my eyebrows.

He sighed as he rolled off me, pulling off the condom and throwing it on his floor carelessly before lying on his back in full display with his arm over his eyes. "Will you ever make things easy?"

I shook my head as I rolled over and put my hand under my chin to lean on his chest. He snuck a peek at me under his arm.

"I'm not one of your court, Beckett," I reminded him. "If you don't like that, then show me the door."

His next sigh was far more exasperated. "I will not be lowered to the standards of your plebs, Eden."

"Are you talking about feelings or dating?" I asked, aiming to sass the shit out of him.

"Both," he answered honestly.

"Well, if you want something, Beckett, then you're going to need to lower away and ask for it."

He opened his mouth and I lay my finger over it. He dropped his arm and looked at me incredulously.

"Not demand," I clarified. "Ask."

"I don't ask."

I mean, he did. But I could meet him halfway. "Did you want this thing to be exclusive, Beckett?" I asked him.

He glared. "If another man touches you–"

I patted his chest as I sat myself up. "I don't just mean me," I said as I made to get off the bed.

He stopped me and I turned back to look at him. I knew my expression was expectant. Because I expected him to say something. Anything. I hoped he'd say 'yes', but this was Beckett-fucking-Maxwell, and I wasn't sure words like 'exclusive' and 'monogamy' were in the vocabularies of people like him.

I leant towards him teasingly. "You want me to be yours, Beckett, then you need to give me *something*. It doesn't have to be now. Today. But this thing, whatever it is, has a bloody short shelf-life if you don't give me something."

"Exclusive," he said, and I wasn't sure if it was a question or not.

"Is the concept foreign to you?" I joked.

The corner of his lip threatened to tip, and he stamped it down. "You want me to tell you this is exclusive?"

I shook my head. "No. This thing is only a thing if it *is* exclusive."

He took a deep breath. "Then, it's…a thing."

I tried to hide my smile by biting my lip, but I knew he wasn't deceived. "Then maybe I *am* yours, but I still have to go to class."

He shook his head and dragged me back into the bed. "Oh, you're not going to class now."

"I'm going to class."

"I'm not asking, Eden."

I laughed as he smothered me in kisses.

One skipped lesson in four years wasn't going to jeopardise my entire future.

# CHAPTER FIFTEEN

Beckett claiming me for all the school to see hadn't made my life easier. I can't say I honestly expected it would, but I think a part of me had still been hopeful.

The weekend had been fine.

I hadn't left Beckett's room until the wee hours of Saturday morning; just enough time to change before meeting Mum at Swim practice. And that had only been after Beckett demanded I shower in his bathroom with his company, but he made it very worth my while. Which made his insistence on following me to my room then to the pool slightly less annoying that it could have been.

I then spent the weekend drifting between the protection of Beckett's arms, and the protection of Sam and Abby. I'd been kept relatively sheltered from what the rest of the school thought or felt, or their reactions. I seriously suspected that Beckett had a more-bruised-than-usual Jaeger, Rowan and their hired goons running interference to keep the worst of it away.

Jaeger certainly seemed to be focussed more on me than swim practice, much to Mum's chagrin.

"I don't like this, Edie," she told me.

I nodded. "I know."

"Are the rumours true?"

I scratched my ear lobe absently. "That probably depends on which rumours you've been hearing."

"That Beckett claimed you in the school corridor and now you need round the clock guarding from Fox. And I'm not going to get started on the sordid stories that are going around about you and Beckett missing class after."

I felt my cheeks heat, but thought I hid it pretty well. "Uh, then. Maybe. A little. Yeah."

"Jesus," she breathed. "Are you sure you're safe?"

I shrugged. "I suspect I'm safer here than anywhere else. That I can live my life here."

"I hate these Royals and their…" She sighed. "Suffice to say, the staff know a bit more about it. And no," she added when she saw I was going to interrupt. "I'm not telling you anything except the lot of them could do with a visit from the law, but their pockets are so deep that's not going to happen. Just… I can't believe I'm even thinking this. Do what you need to survive." Then she scoffed and changed her tune. "How bad can it be anyway? They're just kids."

I could tell she didn't really believe that, but she was doing her damndest to make both of us believe she did. I think it said a lot about the side of the Royals I hadn't seen that my own mother was trying to turn the other cheek and pretend it was just the usual drama of teenagers. Then again, maybe it was, and I'd blown the whole thing way out of proportion.

But on Monday, it was back to reality and, even with Jaeger and Rowan shadowing me in the morning, Isabella still made a pass at me in homegroup.

She slapped me full across the face and snapped, "How dare you, slut!"

I blinked, but held up a hand to keep Jaeger where he was. "How dare I?" I clarified.

She nodded. "Beckett's mine."

I didn't know how much to play it up. After Friday night, it kind of felt like Beckett and I were sort of semi-dating. Maybe. And I wasn't above embellishing to my advantage.

"It would seem he's mine," I told her, and I saw Fox watching me.

Isabella might not have been so concerned with Jaeger's retribution, but Fox clearly was and he did nothing more than shoot me a death glare on his way out of the classroom.

"He'll get over this weird insanity and come back to me," Isabella said. "We're meant to be together."

I rolled my eyes. "If a guy fools around on you or doesn't want you, might I suggest that your anger be better directed at him? It's not my fault that Beckett claimed me." That bit was at least entirely true.

She huffed, then turned on her heel and stormed out.

"Well, played," Sam said to me quietly, keeping his own eye on Jaeger as we headed out to Recess.

"But how much of that was true?" I muttered, hoping it wasn't going to come back and bite me.

"He basically asked you out."

"Basically being the operative word."

"For a Royal, that's pretty much a declaration of undying love."

I snorted. "I'd prefer the declaration."

"Then quit boning a Royal."

"One weekend does not 'boning a Royal' make. And those in glass houses shouldn't throw stones," I pointed out and he nodded.

"Fair."

Except, if Beckett had pretty much declared his undying love for me, why was there a sudden return of the Ice King?

He wasn't at my homegroup and, when I did finally see him in the dining hall, he skipped right past me, dodging to make sure that our bodies wouldn't even risk bumping. On the way out, we legitimately did collide while I was busy making sure I didn't even look in his general direction.

He crowded my space as he bared down on me, and I wasn't sure what this Beckett would do. Sam, beside me, slipped his hand into mine. Beckett's eyes dropped to the movement for a second. My heart thudded in my chest. I didn't even bother wondering where the Beckett of Friday night was. I was under no delusions that I would ever see even a similar Beckett in public. But I hadn't been expecting such a frosty reception. Finally, he just lifted his lip in a snarl, then swept away.

"What's his problem?" Sam whispered as we hurried to class, with Rowan trudging along behind us like the Furies themselves were motivating him.

I shrugged. "Probably just can't deal with how much he loves me," I said sarcastically.

Sam shot a look backwards. "Looks like he's not the only one."

I followed his gaze back to Rowan. "He's probably just miffed no one's suffering more."

Sam snorted, but we were still paying attention to Rowan so didn't notice where we were going until I literally ran into Regina Maxwell.

Two Maxwells in as many minutes. That wasn't something I ever wanted to repeat.

She looked stunning in her Rivermont summer dress with crossover tie and cardigan, with her hair spilling in full curls down around her arms, the front pulled back with a satin scarf in the Rivermont black, red and white tartan. Phoenix, to her side, looked no less stunning as she rocked the black summer shorts, a short-sleeved button up shirt and tie.

Neither of them looked impressed that plebs like us had dared even be in the same corridor, let alone actually touch them.

"I hear you chose my brother." It wasn't a question.

I had no idea what to say. Regina was a whole different kind of terrifying than her brother. She was the kind of intimidating only another woman could be to me. She impressed me with how strong and confident and just all around kickarse she was. Even if she was also a gossip-mongering popularity snob, it still made me wish I could carry myself with half her self-esteem. But all of mine deserted me in the face of her.

Regina looked me over like she wondered what in the hell her brother saw in me. It wasn't the first time that I wondered that myself. I also wondered what *I* saw in *him*.

"Consider this a warning, then," Regina said, her tone implying she was bored. "If you think you can wear the Rivermont Queen's crown, you're going to need to buck the fuck up and make Beckett submit to you." She looked me down and up. "Do you actually think *you* can manage that?"

I had no words. I still didn't know what to say to her. She was somehow both threatening and also seemed to be giving me an actually sincere warning. I figured making a deal out of the latter would get me smacked for my troubles, so I didn't mention it.

Not that Regina seemed to need an answer. She gave me a stiff nod, then went on her way.

"Don't forget your place," Phoenix told me harshly. "Plebs who play with Royals get reduced to ash." She gave Sam a stern frown, then her long legs carried her after her princess with ease.

"I get it," Sam said. "Because she's Phoenix."

I nodded. "Witty."

"She goddamn terrifies me," Sam admitted.

"If you don't get your arses to class, I will give you something to fear," Rowan said quietly, and we jumped to find him right behind us.

"Trust me, you're terrifying simply in your existence," I assured him.

There flashed that madness in his eyes. "Good."

I was still holding Sam's hand from the dining hall, so I gripped him closer, and we hurried into the classroom. The door closed behind us, and I heard the tell-tale sound of it locking.

The non-Royal dorm doors didn't have locks, but the classrooms did. Said a lot about the priorities of the school if you asked me.

Fox appeared in front of me, and I looked back to see Gunner behind me.

"Can your king's goons get to you in here?" Gunner sneered as there was a loud thump on the door.

Fox stepped up close to me and I felt Sam's hand ripped from mine. "How much damage do you think I could do to you before Rowan gets that door open?" he asked as he trailed his hand down my cheek. "I'd give him a good couple of minutes. Plenty of time."

Fight or flight kicked in, and fight seemed to get the upper hand for once. My body just acted. My hands went to Fox's shoulders, and I saw his victorious smirk just as I smashed my knee between his legs. Then hands were in my hair and Gunner threw me back against the door. My head cracked against it, and I saw very different stars to the ones Beckett had showed me over the weekend as I slid to the floor.

Fox grimaced, his hands between his legs as he was bent over. "You think the king has a golden cock, Eden?" he snarled.

"I think yours is decidedly more ruddy in colour," I said, holding my head.

I felt something wet and pulled my hand away to find a little bit of blood on it.

"You will be mine," Fox growled, but there was nothing sexy about it. "And we'll see whether the rejected King still wants what's left of you after I'm done."

Sam yanked me sideways just as the door burst open.

Rowan stormed in, pointing at Fox. "She bleeds, you bleed," he said, his voice like Death itself.

"Gentleman!" the teacher said as they walked in. "I don't want to have to send anyone to the office today. So can we go back to our corners until Lunch, please?"

Figures that a Rivermont teacher's response to classroom violence was to pass the buck, preferably to a time and place where they didn't have to bother about the paperwork.

The rest of the day got no better. Kids purposefully bumped me as they passed. They whispered about me. Things like 'who does she think she is?' and 'what's wrong with her?' and 'doesn't she know her place?' and 'maybe she drugged him?', and that's just what I heard. They made me paranoid with their suspicious glances. Like, what? Did they think I had some sort of magic hypnotic vagina or something and I was the one seducing Beckett here?

By the end of the day, I was feeling unbelievably irritable. My lengthy swim did very little to assuage that, and I was going to get no other physical relief because I refused to even speak to Beckett after the way he behaved all day. Not that it was difficult because he was around me as little as possible. I wasn't sure if I was glad he didn't have any frees on Monday or not, but he wasn't even at softball practice. Rowan had met Preston and I there and that was the extent of the Royals at my practice.

The next morning, the exacerbator to my mood was made obvious; my period hit. Between that and more bumps and harsh whispers, my day went from bad to worse to worst very quickly.

Gunner was waiting for me in the library after my free lesson, but it was Preston angrily watching over me. And he kept his distance.

"How are Fox's balls today?" I asked Gunner.

"It's not too late to make the right choice," Gunner told me snidely.

I frowned at him. "Fox isn't the right choice."

"And you think Beckett is? Where exactly is your knight in shining armour? I don't see him coming to save you now."

I pulled every single pair of big girl pants on that I owned. "Beckett's won. Neither he nor I need to waste our time showing Fox just how badly he lost."

Gunner pushed me hard. "If you think this is over, you've got another thing coming."

"Tell Fox, if he thinks I'll be beaten into submission, he's wrong. He had more chance with his transparent nice-guy act. At least he was a semi-decent human being to hang around then."

Gunner pushed me harder, and I stumbled backwards. Right into Preston, who caught my arms none too gently.

"Touch her again and I'll be forced to touch you," Preston said to Gunner over my head with the least amount of cares in his tone.

Gunner scoffed. "If Beckett thinks you scare me, he's more than just lost his touch. He's lost his fucking mind."

"I'd be more than happy to go looking for any spot of skin Rowan accidentally left untouched," Preston told him, and a shiver ran down my spine at the cavalier venom in his voice. "She bleeds, you bleed."

I wasn't going to point out that I *was* bleeding, just through the fault of no one but Mother Nature.

Gunner stepped back and Preston finally let me go. I ducked my whole person as I hurried towards homegroup.

"How much longer are you going to let this go on?" Hunter yelled at me as he fell into step with me.

I saw Beckett heading our way and promptly tried ignoring him. Not that it worked very well because just seeing him had the power to make me want to thump him and simultaneously beg him to throw me on his bed again. And again. Either of which would put me more at ease after his coldness of the last two days. I was jonesing for some of that fiery Beckett passion, and I didn't care if what I got was anger or desire. Preferably both.

I don't think he noticed any of what he made me feel though, because he seemed to be ignoring me as well.

"You know," Hunter continued. "Maybe Isabella's right!"

I blinked and dragged my eyes off Beckett. "Excuse me?"

"Do you just plan to open your legs for anyone now? Or is it just the dickheads who'd rather beat you into submission that make you wet?"

"I don't know what you think you know—"

"I know it will all be ten times worse when you finally give it up to him. You think he's an arsehole now? He's not worth it, Eden. But then, if you're even considering it, maybe it's you who's not worth it."

Everything compounded and tears pricked my eyes. "What is *wrong* with you?" I said softly.

"Oh, now because I'm a nice guy, who cares about you, there's gotta be something wrong with me?"

"No. Now that you're being a total twat, there's something wrong with you. None of this is on me, Hunter."

"No. You'd just rather make puppy dog eyes at the world's

biggest jerk while he couldn't give two shits about you."

"You know nothing about what's going on in my head. And what goes on between me and anyone else is none of your business. *And,* I don't make puppy dog eyes at anyone!"

Embarrassed that this was the thing that had me threatening to cry in the very public school quad, I rushed away from him. My path forced me past Beckett, but I didn't much care at that point.

This time, Beckett didn't stop me to ask if Hunter had hurt me. He didn't do anything more than make sure I saw him actively not looking at me like a petulant child who's punishing you for something and wants to make sure you've noticed.

What was Beckett punishing me for? The little I knew, and the lot I guessed, about Beckett, it was something as stupid as he *was* actually falling for me and didn't know what to do about it. Then I laughed because the idea of that was laughable. Then I nearly cried because what in the hell had I done in a previous life to rain this much shit down on me?

The whole incident with and surrounding Hunter had clearly been the straw that broke this camel's back. He'd stressed and provoked and annoyed me to the point I snapped at both Jaeger and Preston between Recess and Lunch, then let rip on Rowan after lunch.

"Our King might rest between those golden legs, Miss Quin," Rowan said smoothly. "But you will not speak to me like that again."

I blinked and bit back my childish retort. "Fine. Sorry," I gritted out.

He shrugged. "Don't be sorry. Get even."

I wasn't sure if he was referring to Hunter or Beckett. Or both. It didn't really matter.

"And how do you suppose I do that?" I asked him sarcastically. "Hope everyone's cycle syncs up?"

He looked at me like he had no idea what I meant, and I didn't blame him.

"Just," I sighed. "Never mind. I have homework to do."

I stomped off to my room and didn't even bother to leave for dinner. Sam and Abby totally understood and told me to tell them if I needed them to bring me anything. I promised I would, but I had a stash of chocolate in my room that would tide me over when the cramps and bloating wore off enough for me to get hungry.

In the meantime, I was going to distract myself with study and I'd be damned if it didn't work. But while I was studying, the door of my bedroom burst open, and I looked up to see a panicked Jaeger and a stern Beckett.

"Jesus, Mary and motherfucking Joseph," I muttered, trying to breathe my heart back to its regular rhythm. "What are you two doing?"

"You weren't at the pool," Jaeger panted. "Looked everywhere–"

"Out," Beckett told him firmly.

"It's my room," I told Beckett, feeling both excited and irate to see him, let alone seeing him pretend to care. "I decide who stays and goes. Jaeger can stay. You can go."

"The fuck I will." He turned to Jaeger, grabbed the front of his shirt and hustled him out my door. "Get the fuck out." Then he slammed the door in Jaeger's face and locked it.

My door had a lock?

"Did you put that there?" I demanded.

"I arranged it," he answered in a tone that told me I wasn't finding out any more about it now.

"What do you want, Beckett?" I sighed, knowing that even if I was angry with him, for even more reasons now, it would make very little difference to him.

"Where were you?" he asked.

I frowned and crossed my arms. "Last I checked, this was a free country and you're not in charge of my itinerary."

"Where. The. Fuck. Were. You?" he asked carefully, walking towards me with each step.

All right, so it was a little bit – a lot – sexy.

"Here. Where did you think I was?"

"Why weren't you at the pool?"

"Why would I have been at the pool?" I asked him.

He leant on the arms of my desk chair and got his face right in front of mine. "Because you always go to the pool after days like today."

What did it say about me that I kind of liked that he paid attention to me? To my moods, how things affected me, what I did to relax. Even when he was pretending he didn't give a shit about me. On the other hand, there was a slightly stalker feel to it as well. All the better to control me if he knew me, kind of vibes. Push-pull. Again.

"Yeah, well not today," I muttered, standing up and pushing him away from me.

"Why not today?" he growled.

"Have I personally offended you by not sticking to my allotted timetable or something?" I snapped.

He stepped into my space and bared down on me. "You've personally offended me by making me worry about you. You could have been dead for all I knew."

I flicked his nose. Yup. I did that. But it was that kind of day, and I was in that kind of mood. "It's not my problem that you don't know how to deal with your feelings for me, Mr Drama Queen." Because that kind of mood had me fully believing that's what the last two days had been about, and I was absolutely ready to call him out on his shit.

He glared at me, but didn't deny my claim. "I'm happy to make it your problem."

I rolled my eyes, not at all impressed with him despite that being the whole point. "Yes, I'm well aware."

"Why weren't you at the pool?"

I sighed. He wasn't going to stop asking until he had an answer, was he?

"Because I've been riding the crimson wave all day, Beckett. You happy now?"

He frowned. "What?"

"The. Crimson. Wave. Aunt Irma's visiting. I'm on the rag." Still crickets. I rolled my eyes. "I've got my period. I don't like tampons and, even if I did, I've got a thing about potentially leaking in the pool. So, I don't swim, no matter my mood."

His annoyance for me was clear on his face. "Was that so difficult?"

"Telling a guy that I don't particularly like all the nitty gritty details about my menstrual cycle? Little bit."

As he crushed his lips to mine, he picked me up and coaxed my legs around his waist. He tasted like smoky booze and kissed me like his world was ending…or maybe finally beginning. There was only one place this was going with a kiss like that. For a moment, I was lost in it, and all the shit of the last two days melted away. My heart fluttered at the burning passion he communicated in something as simple as a kiss.

But finally, I put my hand on his chest and leant my forehead to his.

"What part of 'on the rag' makes you think I'm open for business?" I asked him.

He ran his nose up my neck and goosebumps broke out everywhere. Instinctively, my whole body tightened against him.

"Would you rather I leave?" he asked, his voice low. It was very dangerous for me when his voice was that low.

"The alternative is a literal bloody mess, Beckett. Port is closed."

His eyebrow quirked and I managed a simultaneous sinking feeling and a rising interest. Sexually. It was like the epitome of the head versus heart debacle, except it was my head versus my clit arguing this time.

Beckett lowered me to the ground gently, took my hand and led me out of the room into the empty hallway.

I frowned. "What are you–?"

"Boss?" Jaeger queried when he saw us.

"Bathroom," was all Beckett said to him.

Jaeger kicked his head up the hall. He fell in step with us until we got to the door then he took up sentry duty.

"You have got to be kidding me," I said as Beckett pulled me inside.

"I don't kid," he answered.

I nodded. "You don't say."

He pulled off his shirt in one smooth motion and that was all I needed to know I wanted this – something – to happen. I was always horny when I got my period. Satisfying that urge was something I'd never done. I wasn't big on period mess. It was already messy enough; I didn't need to make extra mess for myself.

But I knew, intimately, the absolute pleasure Beckett could make me feel. He didn't need to be nice to me to do that. I didn't need to be happy with him for him to do that. And he so clearly wanted to do that. It would almost be rude not to let him.

He went over to one of the showers and turned it on.

"Come," he ordered as he kicked off his shoes.

My feet obeyed willingly, my eyes raking his body as he took off his trousers and boxer-briefs.

There I was, completely clothed, standing in front of a totally naked Beckett Maxwell. His cock was already hard and ready for me.

He cupped my cheek softly as he looked down at me.

"Do I have to undress myself?" I sassed.

The corner of his lip twitched like he was almost about to smile. Without answering verbally, he slid his hands up under my jumper and slowly dragged it off my body. Heat pooled in his eyes as he saw I wasn't wearing anything under it. His thumb grazed my nipple and the tightening sensation mirrored in my clit.

Beckett wound his arm around me and pulled me to him. His kiss was rough, needy, demanding. All the things I liked about him.

When I was about ready to beg him to throw me against the wall, he stepped back into the shower, an arrogantly expectant look in his face.

I whipped off my trackies and super sexy period undies and got in with him.

He pressed me against the wall of the shower, an arm behind my back like he was shielding me from the cold tile as best he could, and kissed me hard.

"A girl might think you *actually* thought she was dead," I breathed as his lips trailed down my cheek.

"The thought crossed my mind," he mumbled against my skin.

I grabbed his hair and forced him to look at me. "Why would I be dead, Beckett?" I asked him.

He didn't shy away from pinning my gaze with his piercing brown eyes. If there was one thing Beckett Maxwell was – and there were actually a lot of things he was – then it was confident. He knew he was the most powerful man in any room he walked into. He wasn't afraid of maintaining eye contact until the other person was forced to look away. I wasn't going to look away.

"Because you're mine, Eden," he said carefully.

Even after he'd basically ignored me the last two days? "Is that a prophecy, a warning or a threat?"

"With enemies like mine, all three."

"I'll play along this once for argument's sake. Did it ever occur to you to live a less fucked up life so as to not put your future woman in danger?"

His eyes were intense. His breathing was deep and even. "No."

"So, my death gets to be inevitable?"

He lay his hand over my throat. "I made one error in the calculation of my life, Eden," he said slowly. "I never counted on you. I didn't expect you. I didn't want you."

"Wow, thanks," I huffed.

He frowned, but more like he was annoyed at himself. "But then you happened. You came into my life. Had you ended up with Sam–"

"I am one penis shy of *ever* being with Sam," I told him firmly.

"–or Hunter," he continued like I hadn't spoken. I shivered at his words, though I didn't really know why. He seemed to make a note of that but kept going. "Then I could have continued to keep you at arm's length. I could have gone on ignoring the way you made me feel–"

"The way you've ignored me the last two days?"

Now he frowned at me and continued like I hadn't interrupted. "I could have let you live a normal life without the dangers of mine. But you are mine, Eden, and I couldn't stand back and risk whatever twisted game Fox would play with you. I will keep you safe.

Whatever it takes, I will always keep you safe."

His eyes were soft, even though his jaw was hard.

I believed him. As dangerous and twisted and arrogant and just generally shitty in the personality department Beckett was, I believed I was safe with him. My person was safe with him. Given all that, maybe my heart wasn't as safe with him as I kept telling myself.

"Kiss me, Beckett," I told him.

He didn't need telling twice. His hand gripped my hip tightly as he crushed his lips to mine once more. My hands were in his hair. Like some switch had flipped between us, suddenly we just couldn't get enough of each other, we couldn't get close enough. It was all fire and passion and just a plain old craven need to express our feelings about the other without the annoyance, permanence, or potential misunderstanding of words.

Hands roamed each other's bodies frantically as our kiss deepened. His fingers teased my clit, and I nipped his lip in protest. I felt him smirk as he growled playfully and lifted me. My legs went around his waist automatically. We rubbed together and my head lay back against the tiles as his tip stroked my clit. His lips peppered kisses down my neck and my hands held his head to my body as though there were any real danger of him pulling away from me. We moved together as we kissed, and it wasn't anywhere near enough. I wanted – no, needed – more of him.

He dropped me slightly so his lips could find mine again more easily and our bodies rocked together closer. I felt him slide into me and the pleasure rolled through me instantly. He thrust hard and I sucked in a heavy breath as my whole body contracted around him. I'd heard that period sex was supposed to be amazing, but I'd clearly never found out for myself before.

"Good?" Beckett mumbled against my lips, and I felt the smile on his.

I nodded and I gripped his head tighter. "Don't stop," I begged.

"Never," he promised as he followed through with gusto.

He bit my neck and my first orgasm threatened to swallow me whole. I knew I wasn't quiet. I didn't care. And Beckett seemed to like it. There was just something so…thing-like about the whole…thing. Feelings were swirling and I'd be damned if Beckett wasn't feeling them, too.

Like he was determined to prove he wasn't, he pulled out of me and spun my front to the wall before plunging into me again. He laced his hand with mine as they braced against the tiles. The fingers of his other hand dug into my hip as he nipped and sucked my neck.

"Are you branding me again, Beckett?" I breathed.

His teeth grazed over my skin. "It has the benefit of marking you as mine and bringing you pleasure."

I couldn't disagree with that, so I just smiled and leant further back into him.

I felt closer to Beckett in that moment than I had to anyone else in my life. It wasn't something you could put into words. I didn't have the words for it. It was like, without knowing anything really about him, I knew who he was. All the bad – and there was a lot of bad – but also the good he was, could be, with me. For me, even.

I came again and he moaned my name before sliding quickly out of me. He wrapped one arm around me and held me tightly against him as he took himself in his other hand and pumped hard. I twisted my face back to his. He breathed out heavily as he kissed me hard, then he tensed, and I felt his cum hot and thick against my leg.

"Oh, my God. We didn't have a condom," I breathed as it just hit me.

I felt him smirk knowingly as he kissed my neck. "Why do you think I pulled out?"

Something else hit me. "Mind you, the chances aren't high that you'll get me pregnant while I'm on my period."

"Is that the only reason to use a condom?"

"Well, no. I'm on the pill," I said as though that was obvious and why did we ever bother with a condom otherwise?

He huffed a rough laugh against my neck. "And what about disease?"

Oh, yeah. That. "Excuse you." I turned in his arms. "I'm clean."

"And how do you know I am?" he asked.

"Ah." I had to concede that was a good point.

"I am. For the record," he said as his lips dropped to my neck once more and his fingers toyed with my clit.

I nodded as the pleasure coiled in me again. "I'll keep that in mind. For future reference."

# CHAPTER SIXTEEN

One may have been forgiven for thinking that that changed things between us. That it had signified some gradual shift in our relationship. If a *thing* could ever really be classified as a relationship.

One should have known better.

Jaeger was at my door as I was getting ready the next morning.

"Jaeger?"

"Eden?"

"Are you following me?" I teased and only too late realised that I was feeling unusually…peppy.

He fell to leaning against the wall with an ease and grace that looked effortless, but I knew took command of a lot of muscles. Once relaxed, he shot me a cocky half-smirk.

"Why on Earth would you think that?" he asked as he shoved his hands in his pockets.

"Jaeger?"

"Eden?"

"*Why* are you following me again?"

"Because my king decreed that I keep you safe."

"And just how much longer do you think we need to do this dance?" I asked him as I pulled my hair into a ponytail.

Jaeger scoffed, but his eyes twinkled. "Oh, to be naïve and innocent."

I frowned at him. "I'm not *that* naïve and innocent."

He leant forward and winked at me. "I know. I've heard you."

A furious blush completely took me over, but I was saved having to think of a comeback or worry about my embarrassment when he kept talking.

"But I meant about our world, Quincy. And, trust me, that's a good thing."

I looked him over as I pulled on my cardigan. "Would you rather be like me?" I only half-teased. "Ignorant about the reality of the darker corners of the world until they decide to have a pissing contest over you?"

Now his scoff was full of mirth. "No. Fuck, no." He shook his head as he pushed himself off the wall, ready to fall into step with me. "Whether by nature or nurture, those of us born into this world are made to survive it. Or we don't. If we do, we're not really suited to your world any more. Even if we wanted to be."

"And Beckett?" My voice was horrifically small as I hurried by him into the hallway, like I was trying to pretend I hadn't asked.

Jaeger shrugged and easily kept up with me. "Beckett has a keen mind. He's inventive. He gets what he wants by any means necessary, even if he has to get murderously creative. But at the same time, he's incredibly unimaginative. Boy couldn't imagine a different world if it was literally parading around in front of him naked."

I could see there was a point he was trying to make. "I don't parade around in front of him naked," I huffed quietly, hoping no one else in the dorms was really paying attention.

"My point stands."

"What about when *you* fall in love?" I asked, keen to move the conversation onto him.

"What about it?"

"Will she be like you? Covered in tattoos, unnaturally skilled with a blade, and have her first murder under her belt by the time she's fifteen?"

My intention was flippant, but he still corrected me. "Twelve."

I blinked but decided I didn't want to know any more about that. "Or will she be a pleb? A normie? And you'll just subject her to a world you know is horrific anyway."

Jaeger's eyes shone with a mischievous knowing as he held the door open for me. "Anyone we fall in love with is only ours because they're strong enough to survive our world," he said. "The trick is trusting them."

I rolled my eyes. "Funnily enough, I think the concept of monogamy is a little firmer for us plebs."

He chuckled. "No, Quincy. We have to love them enough to trust they can survive, and not let our fear of losing them get in the way. Whether they leave because it's too hard or because someone else takes them from us." I suspected he didn't mean by romantic means but deadly ones.

I looked him over again as we headed across the quad for the dining hall. "Another set of very pretty words that could easily explain your king's behaviour, Jaeger. But that's all they are. Exposition in the narrative *you're* writing, not the one that's actually playing out. And," I said forcefully when it was obvious he was going to interject. "Even if I believed that was how Beckett felt, it's irrelevant unless he *does* overcome it." I shrugged. "I can only give him the benefit of the doubt, live with this push-pull, for so long until it *is* going to be too hard."

"He won't let you go that easily."

I recognised the way I liked that fact as a sign that I could fall deeper for Beckett if I let myself forget that this was just a physical thing. It was just a temporary thing. He'd admitted he couldn't – intimated he wouldn't – give more and I'd told him I didn't want it anyway. And maybe that was a way of protecting me from whatever he and Jaeger were so worried about. Maybe it was an acknowledgement that I wasn't strong enough to survive their world.

"Whatever Beckett and I are, has a shelf-life," I said, mainly to stomp out that thrill that ran through me at the idea alone that Beckett wouldn't let me go. "We're not long-term material."

"You are *literally* the only person who's even pretending to still believe that."

There seemed little more to say to that, so we went the rest of the way to breakfast in silence. Jaeger held the door open for me again and my eyes instantly found Beckett at his table. My heart fluttered and I had no idea what my face said, but I felt more than heard the low rumble of smug amusement in Jaeger's chest.

"Shut up," I told him.

"What? I didn't say anything."

"And you'd best keep not saying anything."

But the little bubble of optimism and just general happiness I'd been feeling since the night before was shrinking rapidly as Beckett didn't even look at me. His eyes skipped over me like he hadn't even seen me, the same way they had for the last four years.

Oh, well. It wasn't like I was expecting him to run over to me and swing me around in the middle of the dining hall first thing in the morning. That would have been stupid and overly dramatic for any couple, let alone us who were very definitely not even a couple.

"I'll see you for French," I told Jaeger.

He seemed to realise I wasn't in a joking mood. "Yeah, all right. Couldn't let the Quintet be down a member."

I frowned in confusion even if I still didn't look at him. "What?"

He kicked his head towards the table my friends and I occupied. "You lot. We're the Royals. You're the Quintet. Get it, because you're Quin."

"A quintet has five, Jaeger."

"Consider it a quintet in four parts, then."

There was a part of me that wondered if that was a vague Douglas Addams reference, but I wasn't in the mood to acknowledge it. He gave up.

"Don't leave without Rowan," he said.

I nodded absently, tried to pull my eyes off Beckett, and headed for my usual table.

"Eden," Hunter started as I sat down. "About yesterday–"

I cut him off. "No. It's fine. All good. You're just looking out for me. I get it."

He smiled widely. "Good. Great. Okay. Hey, are you…?"

I stopped paying much attention as Isabella sat down next to Beckett and rubbed herself as all over him as she could manage. The argument could have been made that he wasn't technically doing anything wrong considering he'd assured me this *thing* was exclusive, but he sure as hell wasn't putting a stop to it either.

I felt the annoyance rise in me. Mainly at myself for being so stupid as to believe anything he'd say to me. But I didn't have all that much time to think about him because the reason Jaeger was following me soon became irrelevant, and I was just glad he – and the other inner sanctum – was.

Fox had decided to step up his personal brand of torture. It seemed that whole morning of respite he gave me was just him licking his wounds and re-evaluating his game plan. Gone was the flirt or the idea that he was going to seduce me away from Beckett. It seemed now he was just going to break me. Physically if he had to.

In the quad, on the way from Psychology to Lunch, I heard Abby yell, then Fox appeared behind me and grabbed my hair. He yanked me painfully to him, grabbing my face roughly in his hand and squeezing hard, as his face bared far too close to mine.

I tried to look around, but couldn't see Rowan anywhere. Which was weird because he'd been no more than a few steps behind us since we left the classroom.

"Let her go!" Abby cried and, out of the corner of my eye, I saw Locksley holding her tight so she couldn't move.

"Is Beckett coming to save you now, Eden?" Fox whispered in my ear.

He turned us around and I saw Beckett and Jaeger coming out of one of the other buildings. They hadn't seen us yet. Fox didn't mind.

I felt him nod against my head and then Gunner was punching me in the side. I yelled and, just before I dropped to the ground, saw both Beckett's and Jaeger's eyes turn to find me. I tried breathing heavily to get my breath back, but my ribs just hurt too much.

Fox's foot thumped into my stomach and flipped me over. My head smacked onto the pavement, and I felt the tell-tale sign of blood blossom hot at my eyebrow.

"Eden!" Jaeger started forward like it was autopilot to come to my aid, but Beckett barked something at him. Jaeger's face was full of confusion, as was mine. I couldn't help but stare at Beckett like he'd personally betrayed me.

Wasn't it just the night before that he'd told he that he'd always keep me safe?

Well, what in the fuck was this bullshit then?

Fox picked me up and wrenched my arm behind my back. I cried out against the pain and just hoped that nothing was broken.

Then there was a thunderous roar from the side of us and both

Fox and I were thrown to the ground by a fully Hulked out Rowan. The furious madness in his eyes as he pulled me and Fox apart was terrifying, even when he was – at least, I hoped – on my side. I landed awkwardly on my hand as I tried to catch myself and cursed the day that I ever saw Beckett-fucking-Maxwell.

The next minute, Jaeger was beside me and pulling me slightly more gently away. I looked up and saw Abby safe behind him.

"Eden?" she said, and we huddled together as Jaeger and Rowan ripped through Fox and his cronies.

I pressed my face to Abby's shoulder as she held me tight.

A few minutes later, Beckett's voice was carrying over the noise, "Enough," and I couldn't help looking up at him.

Even Fox and his lackies stopped. Although Gunner was the only one still in sight. I wasn't sure if it just went to show that they actually still deferred to Beckett as their king, or whether it just gave them an excuse to not get punched by Rowan or Jaeger anymore.

All four of them were covered in scrapes and cuts and marks that had the potential to blossom into beautiful bruises.

A couple of teachers were behind Beckett, like they were also deferring to him as Rivermont's King.

"All right," one of them said. "Let's get this lot to the nurse. I assume you'll work out a way to keep them apart in the infirmary?" That was directed at Beckett.

"It is done," he said, his tone cold and his eyes still nowhere near me.

Jaeger limped over and helped Abby and me up off the floor.

"Are you okay?" he asked Abby and she nodded.

"I'm fine. I think Eden might have broken her wrist, though."

Jaeger grumbled something to himself about carrying me in his state, but this was what he did for the people he loved. But Beckett beat him to me. He took a step into my space, and I tried batting him away.

"Do not make me put you over my shoulder," he growled at me, low and vicious.

I could argue with him about his shitty personality later. Preferably while blood wasn't dripping in my eye, and I didn't have any number of aches and pains.

"No, we'll leave that to the bedroom," I huffed at him, unable to not say *something*.

He drew me into him unbelievably gently and it was very difficult not to melt a little at his tenderness. "It would be my pleasure. You just have to ask," he purred in my ear, and this time I cursed his ability to effortless seduce me to the point I was very ready to forget all his shit.

I tried very hard not to snuggle into him as he carried me to the nurse.

The infirmary was a small wing of the main building. There were a few solitary rooms, but also a couple of wards. I'd heard that it had been a big refurb after some big plague a hundred years earlier or something. It had been pretty useless up until a few years ago, but was thankfully pretty useless again.

The nurse had the main ward, which was where we'd find her. A room with five beds down each side and her desk and station with all her basic supplies at the back end.

When she saw Beckett carrying me in with Abby and a bruised Jaeger, Rowan, Fox and Gunner behind us, she clearly guessed what had happened. Seemed the Rivermont grapevine really did make it the whole way around the school. She stood up and started directing us around her ward.

"Right, you young'uns over there and wait your turn. Weapon and

Cleaner, I want you over there. I don't need to remind you that there will be no fighting on my ward?"

"No, nurse," Fox mumbled as he and Gunner went to a corner by the doors and took a seat on the beds.

The nurse fixed her glare on Jaeger and Rowan.

Jaeger finally nodded. "No. Of course not." He tugged on Rowan's arm, and they headed to the other side of the room to Fox and Gunner.

She nodded, then looked at Beckett. "Bring her over here. Gently, Mr Maxwell."

Beckett lowered me onto the examination bed and then stepped away to Jaeger and Rowan. I gave him another glare of betrayal because he knew what he'd done, but Abby was by my side so I felt slightly less alone than I could have.

"Please don't call my mum," was the first thing out of my mouth.

The nurse pursed her lips as she gave me a look that told me she'd have some choice words about who I chose to hang out with were I her daughter. "Let me look you over before I make any promises."

She did her work quickly and efficiently. My wrist needed bandaging and I'd have to restrict my use of it for a few days, but otherwise should recover fairly quickly. The damage to my pride was going to take longer to heal.

"Sprained wrist," the nurse said, typing the notes into the computer. "Bruised ribs but nothing fractured. And a plaster on your eyebrow. I've definitely seen worse after a Royal's done playing, so congrats."

Let it not be said that her bedside manner had ever been the best. She did good medical work and probably saw a lot more shit than we gave her credit for, and had been doing so since our parents' day. I didn't blame her for being a little blunt and cynical by now.

She looked up at me. "Probably best to skip practice tonight. See how you feel for the game on Saturday. I'm going to have to let your mum know, but I'll tell her it was nowhere near as bad as that ball you took to the jaw at practice two years ago."

Upon her prognosis, without a word or a look at me, Beckett swept out of the room, forcing a very surprised Sam out of his way. I couldn't be sure if the coat rack he tipped over on the way out had more to do with his annoyance that Fox got to me, or annoyance that he cared that Fox got to me, or maybe – and seeming more likely as the minutes passed – annoyance that he felt obligated to care after he told me he would.

"Edie! Abby texted. I got here as quick as I could," Sam cried as he hurried over to me, his eyes darting nervously to Gunner.

I knew that look. I felt that look viscerally. It was the look of the enamoured in spite of the shittiness of their personalities. I had no doubt that I'd been looking at Beckett in the exact same way only moments earlier. And it sucked.

Abby, Sam and I had a group hug, and I breathed the tears away. Or tried.

"Hey," Sam said as he pulled away. "Does it hurt that much?"

I shook my head. "Not physically. I can't believe I trusted him!" I fumed.

Abby and Sam exchanged a sympathetic smile.

"I don't know what's going on in his head," Abby said. "But…" She sighed. "I don't want to be the one to say give him the benefit of the doubt."

Sam nodded. "Okay. I'll do it. Expect he's going to fuck up, because he's a goddamned Royal. But if he actually likes you, Edie, then give him a chance to work out how to show you, yeah?"

I took a breath. "That's the question, isn't it."

"You can take her back to her room," the nurse told Sam and Abby.

Sam put his arm around me as they guided me out. Jaeger nodded to me, and I paused.

"Is Preston waiting outside to walk me back?" I sassed.

He gave me a smirk that didn't reach his eyes. "You'll be fine for a few hours with these two." He indicated Sam and Abby.

I gave him a nod and let my friends take me to my room. They stayed with me until the end of Lunch when Mum, who had popped in to check on me, forced them to go to class as she left. It was my double free, so I just curled up in bed and slept thanks to the painkillers the nurse had given me.

I woke well after the end of the school day and realised I hadn't been to the bathroom since after breakfast, and Mother Nature was calling.

I tried my door. It was locked. From the goddamned outside and I couldn't open it.

"Oh, this is not going to be a thing!" I muttered.

I looked around my room, like going out the window would actually be an option. With no other options available to me, I resorted to banging on the door because I knew one of them was out there by now.

"Some of us can't pee in a bottle, boys!" I yelled.

After a moment, I heard the door unlock and Jaeger was pulling it open.

"This shit will not fly," I told him.

He looked me over. "Boss isn't taking chances."

"Your 'boss'," I even used air quotes, "fucking stood back and watched it happen!"

"Quincy–"

I shook my head as I pushed past him, all thoughts of the loo forgotten. "No. Nuh uh. Where is His High and Mighty Arsehole?"

Jaeger caught my arm gently and I stopped.

"What?!" I huffed.

"Please don't antagonise him any more than you have to."

"Oh, trust me. I have to."

"He wants to keep you safe."

"If that were true he'd have stepped in today. He wouldn't have *stopped* you from stepping in!"

Jaeger actually looked chastened. "Quincy…"

"Don't 'Quincy' me, Jaeger, and think I'll just agree with whatever you're saying. Beckett doesn't own me. I'm not property or a trophy to be gaoled and sat on a shelf behind bullet proof glass. I'm a goddamn human being who wants to live her life!"

Jaeger's green eyes searched my own carefully. "He's doing his best."

"His best fucking sucks."

He huffed a humourless chuckle. "Yet his old man would literally feed you to Fox on a gilded platter just to prove he owns you. Beckett's doing the best he can with what he's been given."

I swallowed hard as I thought about that, and about the implications of that. "Seriously?"

Jaeger nodded. "Yeah. Do you get it now?"

I certainly didn't want to. "I don't 'get' anything, Jaeger. This door will not be locked on me again, do *you* get it? I'm not a prisoner and I will not be gaoled just because Beckett would rather kick down my sandcastle than admit he's falling for me." I held my hand out. "Give me the key."

He shrugged. "I'm not allowed."

"I don't care how many people you've killed or will kill in your life, Jaeger Richards," I said, my voice deadly cold and still not sure I believed a word of what I was saying. "I don't care how many of those people Beckett will be responsible for killing. I will kill you both if you keep thinking you can do what you like with me."

Jaeger nodded slowly. "Okay, Quincy." He pulled the key out of his pocket just as slowly. "You got it."

I snatched it from his hand and slammed the door in his face.

I leant against the door and took a deep breath, trying not to think about what Jaeger had said about Beckett's dad.

I didn't need any reasons to think that Beckett and I were honestly more than some *thing*. But Jaeger seemed insistent on giving Beckett layers and depth and motivation that I kept reading into his behaviour. It was all stuff I could easily believe was there, but how much of that was just Jaeger making me imagine things, and how much was Beckett actually giving me?

I slid to the floor and put my head in my hands.

As long as I remembered that Beckett and I would never be more than we were, I was going to save everyone an awful lot of heartache. As long as I remembered that actions spoke louder than words – especially someone else's words. And as long as I remembered that five good things did not erase five bad things… Maybe I could be saved that heartache.

But, as I lay my head back and forced myself to breath deeply and evenly, I felt it. A tiny point in my heart that wondered, that believed, that wished. Maybe Beckett really was doing his best with what he had. Maybe he was falling for me. Maybe one day his best was going to get it right. And I couldn't make it stop no matter what I told myself.

Beckett was there in the morning. He walked silently beside me to breakfast then to History, then to homegroup, and Recess. He said nothing, just made me exceptionally nervous with his stoic and intimidating stature.

Then I didn't see him for the rest of the day.

I'd taken to locking my door since Jaeger gave me the key. It felt weird to be doing it after so many years of not, but my injuries were still vivid enough that I could do with the security. So I was in my room, with the door locked, with Jaeger outside as far as I knew, before dinner that night.

I heard my door open and turned with a furious frown on my face. "Jaeger, I told you—"

Only it wasn't Jaeger. It was Beckett. Clearly, he'd given up on locking me in but wasn't above letting himself in. But I wasn't going to do this. I was angry at him. I wasn't ready for apologies or whatever nonsense he'd spout to justify himself. I didn't want to risk him saying anything that would take away the fantasy Jaeger had planted in my head. I didn't want to know that the Beckett who didn't protect me was the real Beckett.

So, I shook my head. I got up from my desk and wordlessly pushed past him as he was coming in. I didn't ask him to leave. I didn't remind him where the door was. I walked right on out that door, shut it behind me and locked him in.

"See how you like it," I muttered to myself as I pocketed the key and wandered off down the hallway with a cavalier nod to a very surprised Rowan.

I heard a loud thump on my door but knew it was beneath him to yell after me. A moment later, I heard his very calm, "Eden," in that tone all were expected to obey.

My body thought about stopping like it was addicted to him, but I wrapped my arms around myself and forced myself to keep walking until I got to Abby's room. She took one look at my face, bustled me in and put on a movie marathon until we wandered to dinner.

I'd expected Beckett to follow me. The more cynical side of me presumed he didn't want any more people to witness me flagrantly disobeying him than necessary. That stupid little point of hope in my heart wondered if it was him, for once, regarding my wishes.

If it was the latter, that only lasted one more day.

On Friday, I avoided Beckett as much as possible.

Jaeger kept telling me Beckett wanted to see me. I kept telling him Beckett could take a hike.

Beckett found his way into my messages. Unsurprisingly, he didn't lower himself to the common pleb and actually apologise.

I made sure to open every single one as soon as I got it and then left him on read.

That night after dinner, Beckett had the gall to come to my room again like that was a thing we did. Before I could leave again, he pulled me to him without words and kissed me deeply. It took me a second to pull my shit together and push him away.

"What's this?" I asked sarcastically. "I assumed you had your booty calls dragged to you."

"When my woman won't come to me, I have no choice but to go to her."

"Seriously?" I looked him over, as unimpressedly as I could muster. "You think you're going to get lucky tonight?"

"I get what I want, Eden."

I shoved him. "No," I told him firmly. "Not this time."

"No one says no to me, Eden."

I scoffed. "I do. And after this last week, I am so fucking done with your games. You," I shoved him again. "You don't talk to me. You don't look at me. I want nothing to do with you."

Fury emanated from his whole person. "You are mine."

Damn that little thrill that still ran through me at those words. "So, my body should just be here, waiting for whenever you deign to want it?"

"You want me as much as I want you."

I mean, yes, but I shook my head and stepped backwards so my body didn't try to step towards him. "Not after your bullshit. I still have the bruises Fox gave me, Beckett. The ones you stood back and just let him give me. I joked that you just don't know how to deal with your feelings for me, but you've convinced me that's exactly what this is."

"I think you have me confused with one of your little pleb boyfriends, Eden."

I rolled my eyes at him. "Oh, I know who you are, Beckett. I don't expect you to be a good guy. I don't care if you still beat up other kids because it gives you a power trip. You can do whatever little shady shit your world demands of you. But I will not be treated like shit then have you claim ownership of me. That's not how it works. If you want me, Beckett, don't treat me like shit just because you can't deal."

He looked me over at the end of my tirade, his face unreadable. He looked a bit like he was considering my words. Then he spoke and, much like he was wont to do, ruined it. "You think the heir to the Maxwell empire, the King of Rivermont, Beckett Maxwell the fourth suffers such trivialities as *feelings*? And for you, no less?"

Whelp, I'd given him the chance. Everything in me screamed at me to ignore his shittiness. Ignore the parts where he treated me like shit because the good bits were more than worth it. But the good bits were just sex. That's all there really was between us. And I wasn't so far gone out of my mind for him that I'd let myself be subjected to his whims just because I liked the sex.

With a deep breath, I went to my bedroom door and opened it. "Get out," I said simply. I didn't raise my voice. I didn't get overly emotional about it. I levelled my best authoritative look on him and delivered it calmly. Just like he would.

"Eden–" he started, but I shook my head.

"Get out, Beckett. I'm done with this…thing."

He took a step like he was going to move towards me, but I took one away from him and looked at the floor.

"You're making a mistake," he said to me as he walked out.

I closed the door behind him and agreed with him. At least, I couldn't stop myself from agreeing with him even if I didn't want to. Maybe it was a mistake to kick him out. No, it felt very much like a mistake. But I had to take my wins when I was strong enough to make them and tell myself that all I was giving up was great sex.

Tears still pricked, but I reminded them that, if I was falling for anything, I was falling for Beckett's potential. That annoying point in my heart still hoped his potential was worth all of this. It was apparently not willing to just completely give up on him, but it seemed more than likely that there was going to come a time when he fucked it up one too many times and I was going to have to crush its hope.

The next morning, I was still sore enough that Mum and the nurse had organised for me to miss softball. I was a decent player, but not one who was imperative to winning or anything.

"I just thought of something weird," Abby said as I sat with her while she got changed for practice.

"What?" I asked her.

She shook her head. "Nah. It's probably nothing."

I smiled. "Try me anyway. Is it about Jaeger…?" I teased.

She threw me a look. "Sort of, yes."

"Oooh!"

She laughed. "Just not like that. Did it feel like Beckett was keeping Hunter away from you this week?"

I frowned. "What do you mean?"

Abby frowned too. "I don't know. I just kind of feel like…" She paused. "It's probably stupid, but it felt like they all kind of backed off a bit this week when it was just me and Sam with you, but they were literally right next to you every time you were with Hunter."

"Were they?" I asked, thinking back.

Abby shrugged again. "Maybe I'm just making things up."

She went back to yammering about a movie we were planning to watch with Sam that night, and I only half-listened. I was thinking about her words.

Had that been right? Maybe it had.

I remembered Preston and Jaeger being all up in my business while they were on duty, but Beckett and Rowan had been slightly less present. I'd assumed that was on account of who they were; Beckett was playing at just as aloof as Rowan, Jaeger was always happy to be up in my business, and I suspected that Preston was being annoyingly specific about his directions just so he could complain about them more.

Jaeger and Preston were the ones who were around when Hunter was, so maybe Abby was right. At least, there was a correlation. I doubted it meant there was cause and effect, but there was definitely correlation.

"Good morning, lovely ladies," Jaeger said as we came out of the changeroom.

I frowned at him, still pissed off about the events of the week. Abby was stoically on my side, and also gave him the cold shoulder.

"Oh, come on," Jaeger pled, in a very tantalising voice that made it incredibly difficult to stay mad at him. "Let's all move on."

"You can try telling Beckett, but I doubt he'd let us," I snapped.

"Quincy, he's claimed you. There is no moving on now."

I whirled and poked him in his naked chest. "In the real world with the rest of the non-elitist arseholes, we don't claim people. We…court them. We take no for an answer. We don't just expect them to fall in line."

Jaeger almost seemed to think the idea was adorable in how ridiculous it was. "Is that what you want? To be courted?"

"Would it matter if I did?"

He shrugged. "With Beckett, no."

I nodded. "I didn't think so."

"You may not know this about him, but he's very keen on good time management."

"Brilliant. I'm sure he's great with group assignments."

"He doesn't waste his time, Eden." It was the first time I remembered Jaeger using my first name where it wasn't sarcastic or mocking.

"There's a first time for everything."

Jaeger shook his head. "He doesn't waste time chasing tail for no reward."

"How sure about that are you?"

"Sure enough to know that, if he's chasing, there's something there. Sure enough that, if he's claimed you, then you're his." He said it like there wasn't a question, and even I started to believe it.

But I scoffed, "You're all delusional."

"Pot meet kettle."

"What's that supposed to mean."

"It means that, whether you want to admit it or not, there's something between you and he knows it's there. And he'll only wait so long for you to catch up before he takes what's his."

I didn't call him out on it. No matter how much I wanted to, I couldn't because I realised that he was right. I couldn't deny it to myself anymore. There *was* something between me and Beckett. Something I didn't want but may not have been able to stop. The strength and the force of it scared me. The strength and force of him scared me. But I wasn't sure that, when the time came for Beckett to truly take what was his, I'd want to put up much of a fight.

# CHAPTER SEVENTEEN

I heard very little from Beckett for the next week. I wasn't so naïve that I thought he'd taken my words to heart, but he went back to ignoring me the way he had before this whole Fox thing blew up in my face.

The main difference from the week before was that Fox wasn't allowed anywhere near me. Beckett might not have looked at me but, the times he wasn't stuck in avid conversation with Jaeger – their heads bowed together like they were single-handedly creating the world's problems (because those two sure as shit weren't solving them) – then he was throwing his might around to make sure Fox and his buddies didn't go near me. When he wasn't there, Jaeger and Rowan were. Preston needed only swirl his cane near Alexander, and Fox's cronies backed off.

Life was almost back to my version of normal.

Almost.

Jaeger was still my own little shadow out of school hours, following me to the pool or the library or to and from the dining hall. So it wasn't that much of a surprise when there came a knock on my door on Friday afternoon and I opened it to find him standing there. What was a surprise was the massive box in his arms.

"Where are you taking that?" I asked him.

"To you," he said, angling himself in the door and putting the box down on my bed.

"Why are you taking it to me? Is it a present?"

"It *is* a present," Jaeger said as he stood back.

I frowned in confusion. "Why did you get me a present?"

Jaeger rolled his eyes with a smile of fond exasperation at his lips. "It's not from me."

Finally, it all made sense. "I don't want it. You can take it back to him."

"Please open it, Quincy. He's trying to apologise."

I huffed but still started opening it as I complained, "You Royals and being so above normal human interaction. Like seriously. Most people?" I threw a look to him and saw him watching me with amusement. "Most people just come themselves and give a simple 'I'm sorry'. A goddamn text would have sufficed. 'I need to see you'?" I said, dropping my voice low like I was trying to imitate Beckett's. "How about 'Sorry, I'm shit'? It's not that hard, Jaeger."

"Is that all it would take?" Jaeger asked, the amusement dancing in his voice.

"It'd be a bloody better start," I started as I ripped open the last bit of tissue paper, "than…"

I blinked at what I saw in the box. I looked up at Jaeger as though he could offer any insights. He just kicked his head at the box, and I picked up the little envelope nestled at the top. Even the paper felt unnecessarily expensive.

## You are cordially invited to the

## Maxwell Easter Ball.

I opened the invitation and nearly dropped a little piece of paper Beckett had slipped in there.

The date on the invite said the party was happening that night.

My heart did an awful lot of crazy acrobatics as I tried to work out what the hell this meant. Beckett wanted me at his father's party? A party at his home. Where his parents and relations and their sycophantic – and no doubt slightly psychotic – society would be watching me be with him. As in…with him…? Like an actual date?

The first thing out of my mouth was, "He thinks taking me to a family function counts as an *apology*?"

Jaeger's smirk was rueful. "He thinks taking you to a family function will show you what you mean to him "

"This is your discretion again, isn't it?"

Jaeger inclined his head. "He didn't put it in so many words."

"I'm willing to bet his trust fund that he didn't say that in *any* words."

Jaeger just shrugged. "Get dressed. He wants to leave in an hour."

I looked around. "What about me suggests I have anything remotely appropriate for this sort of thing?"

Jaeger kicked his head at the box again. "That's what the present is for."

"This shit," I indicated my whole person, whom I loved, "will need more than just a dress for a freaking Maxwell ball, Jaeger!"

"There are shoes."

I glared at him. "And longer than an hour. Jesus…" I pulled my phone out and texted Sam and Abby with an SOS.

"I thought you were mad at him?" Jaeger teased.

"I *am* mad at him," I replied.

"But you're still going to go."

As far as apologies went…I was going to follow this one through to its conclusion and reserve judgement until then.

I huffed. "I find it very hard to say no to you," I begrudgingly admitted, as though that was the whole truth.

Jaeger gave me a full-on grin. "That's why I told him I'd bring you the dress." He dropped into my desk chair. "He wanted to come and wrestle it onto you himself, but I told him you'd just kick him out again."

"Kick him in his jewels, maybe." I looked him over as he was inspecting his nails. "Is this what you've been whispering about all week?" I scoffed with a little humour.

"No. It's what comes next that we were whispering about all week." He was clearly very pleased with himself.

I allowed him a small smile. "And here I thought you were plotting world domination."

He nodded. "Oh, that, too."

I frowned. "What?"

"Oh, Quincy!" he crowed happily. "If you think he won't have dominated your world by the end of tonight, then I know nothing about love!"

"What's the emergency, why does Abby have her curling iron, and why is he sitting in your chair?" Sam asked as they bust in my door.

"Belle's going to the ball, fairy godmothers," Jaeger announced.

"What does that make you?" Sam asked him as he crossed his arms.

Jaeger grinned like he was very pleased that Sam had asked. "The pumpkin."

I rolled my eyes, ushered them in, gave them a quick explanation that didn't involve Disney, and they set to work. Sam mostly hovered and gave lots of opinions without lending any physical assistance. But Abby was a champ. Forty minutes later, I was awkwardly walking down the stairs in the girls' dorm and hoping no one really noticed me.

And it turns out, maybe I was *all that* after all.

Beckett was waiting as I did my grand descent down the stairs, and I don't know who was more blown away; me or him.

He looked insanely lickable in a black suit that seemed like it had been melted onto his body in honour of the holiday. He wore a ridiculously crisp white shirt with the top button undone. His hair seemed darker than usual, and his stubble was no less visible considering he was about to take me home to meet his dad.

*Shit.*

*His dad.*

I paused mid-step.

No amount of layers and layers of gorgeous pale blue, wafty material was going to hide who I was in the eyes of these people. It didn't matter that the dress fit me like a glove, wrapping over my bust and around my curves with no bunching or excess fabric getting in the way. The sleeves could kiss my shoulders elegantly, and the skirt could fall just below my knees and make my ankles look poised and alluring all they liked. It could even match the silver studded heels in a way that made the whole outfit feel more like me and less like a toy doll.

But they'd see right through me. Their kids saw right through me every day at school, the adults had far more practice rooting out anything that didn't belong. They revelled in it. And nothing the goddamn gorgeous god in front of me could say or do would make me believe otherwise.

"This was a mistake…" I breathed, feeling my lungs threaten to hyperventilate.

My feet took a few steps back and Beckett took a few steps forward.

"Eden…" he said gently as he held his hand out for mine.

I saw the apology in his eyes. Or, at least, I saw what looked like regret and the desire to work it out. Or maybe all the hairspray was making me delusional.

I saw Beckett's eyes flick to Jaeger and that was enough to have me pausing.

It wasn't the sort of look to convey 'get ready to catch her if she runs'. It wasn't a 'make sure she does what she's told'. It was very much a question. Beckett didn't want to fuck this up, but he didn't know what to do and he was asking Jaeger for help.

I took a breath, trying not to chew on my lip and get lipstick all over my teeth. "How are we getting there?" I asked him.

"There's a car waiting," Beckett said, almost stilted like he really wasn't sure what to do or what to say now. "The drive's a bit over an hour."

I nodded and smoothed my dress awkwardly. "Okay. I guess we should get going, then."

Beckett shot a look of pure surprise to Jaeger, who put his hand on my back and gently nudged me forward. I felt like Beckett and I were two incredibly socially inept idiots who needed their friend to help them date. In many ways, I guess that was very much what this was.

I gave Beckett my hand and he led me out to the waiting car. Except it wasn't a car, it was a freaking limo with the…

"Is that your family's crest on the door?" I asked him.

He inclined his head as he pulled said door open for me. "It is."

"It's fancy," was the only thing I could think to say.

He shrugged as he helped me in with as much dignity as a girl who'd had very little cause for dresses and heels could manage.

I liked heels and dresses, but the opportunities for them were few and far between when you were a bit of a tomboy who lived at school. Even for school parties, if I ever went, I never wore heels. Most of them were outside and there was no way I was combining me, alcohol, heels and an uneven ground.

"Did you have plans for the holidays?" Beckett asked awkwardly after a while.

We'd been sitting in silence for a good ten or fifteen minutes while he stared out the window in front of him. I was sitting on the very back seat, and he was on one of the sides like being any closer to me would have had a very different outcome.

I fought the smile his attempt at small talk gave me. "Not really. Mum and I will eat too much chocolate and I'll probably swim and get ahead on my homework."

He cleared his throat. "Sam and Abby are going home?"

"Abby is. Sam opted to stay."

He nodded, but obviously had nothing more to say about that.

"What about you?" I asked quickly.

"Me?"

"Mm. Are you…?" Now, I cleared my throat but only because I just realised what my question might have sounded like. Be rude not to ask in return, though. "Are you at school for the holidays?"

He finally looked at me. "Are you asking me to stay?"

My heart hitched at the look in his eyes. "Do you want to stay?"

He leant towards me. "I want you to want me to stay."

Lipstick be damned. I chewed my lip anyway. "I won't be an obligation, Beckett."

He dropped to his knees in front of me. "You're not an obligation, baby." He trailed his fingers gently over my temple. "That will be the last time Fox touches you."

My heart beat erratically. Was this him finally getting it right, or was this just another chance to let me down? "You said something very similar two weeks ago, Beckett. The next day you let him touch me. This foundation is still hiding the bruise."

"I was raised to be ready for anything," he said softly, almost like he wasn't talking to me. "Everything. Everything except you. I won't be blindsided again, Eden. I want you more than…"

My heart tripped over itself at what it thought he was about to admit. Could I really be worth more than Beckett's crown?

"…the emotionless shell my father taught me to be," he finished.

It might not have been what I'd hoped he'd say, but I wasn't disappointed.

Beckett sat next to me and wrapped his arm around me as his other hand brushed against my face. "Everything I was taught to be tells me to push you away."

I ran my nose over his. "I thought you didn't want to stay away from me?"

He nuzzled me right back. "You're a goddamn mind-fuck, baby." He pulled me into his lap and mumbled against my lips, "But fuck, I want you."

He kissed me and I almost lost myself to it. To him. To the idea of us. Then his hand slid up my body on its way to my head and I pulled away, already slightly breathless.

"Do *not* touch my hair," I warned him.

Mirth sparkled in his chocolate eyes. "Are you going to turn into one of those girls on me?"

I leant into him, my finger on his chest. "I don't care about my hair because I'm yours. I care about it because Abby spent forty-five minutes and half a can of hairspray on it, and I don't want you to ruin it before I can make my very bad first impression at your father's party."

I felt his smirk against my lips. "I don't care what he thinks of you."

"No. I'm sure you don't," I said as I slid off him and pretended that I had any idea about making sure my hair wasn't all sex-ruffled.

"Eden." It was that commanding tone of voice again.

"I'm here, Beckett," I told him by way of answer. "But let's not pretend this isn't going to backfire just as much as it *might* make some amends."

He kissed my neck. "Do you forgive me, then?"

"I might if you *actually* apologised."

"I'm sorry Fox hurt you, Eden," he said and sounded very sincere. "I'm sorry I let him." He laced his hand with mine as he nipped my shoulder. "I will not fail to protect you again." He nudged my jaw with his nose. "Are we good?"

"I don't honestly know what we are to know if we're good anymore, Beckett."

His hand slid tantalisingly over my stomach as his nose trailed down my jaw. "Do you really not?" he asked quietly.

I turned to look at him. "Do you?"

The question surprised him. I could see it in his eyes. I didn't think it was in a bad way, though. More like, he realised he might have to re-evaluate what he'd thought and could just possibly come out with an even better answer.

"I'm working on it," he said.

That would have to be enough for me. For now.

"Tell me," he said, as he pulled me to lean against him, "how you and Sam became friends."

"Why?" I asked with a laugh.

I felt him shrug. "I'm interested. I learnt a lot about you by watching you these last few years, but I didn't notice Sam. Last day of Year Eight he wasn't even there, then first week of Year Nine you two already seemed like you'd known each other for years. I want to know what I missed."

"Your Year Eight and Nine," I pointed out.

"My Year Eight and Nine," he agreed. "Go on."

"You really want to know?"

He kissed my temple. "I really want to know."

"Because you're jealous?" I teased.

"Because he's important to you."

I was going to let that be all we said about it. "Okay, but then I want to know how Jaeger got stuck with you."

I felt more than heard his smile. "Deal."

# CHAPTER EIGHTEEN

So, we shared stories until we arrived at his father's station. Although, 'station' felt like a very mundane and ocker way of describing the sweeping driveway and vast swathes of lawn in the east of South Australia. Horses ran through a paddock to our left like they'd been set loose specifically to coincide with our arrival. Twinkling lights hung through the trees, a combination of the good old Aussie gum and things that felt far more European to my un-green thumb.

The limo pulled up to the front steps and a guy jogged down them to open the door. Beckett indicated he'd go first, then held his hand out to me to help me out.

A lovely cool breeze cut through the latent heat left from the day. Faint music reached my ears along with the sort of polite chatter you hear in the background of parties in rom-coms.

"Beckett," I heard a voice say with loud affection.

I looked up to the door and saw an older woman whose resemblance to Regina was striking. Thick dark brown hair, framing a face that was clearly not subject to the whims of aging. She wore the rueful, commanding Maxwell smirk and carried herself with the dignity – and the chip – I saw in Beckett every day. She wore a long, sparkling gown with floaty sleeves, and dripped diamonds and pearls.

I nearly fell out of the car just staring at her. Only once I was safely completely out of the limo with both feet on the ground did

Beckett take his eyes off me and look to her. His hand tightened on mine, but he didn't hesitate in leading us towards her.

"Aunt Rosalie," he said, inclining his head.

"You brought a date this year," she cooed, and I suspected that wasn't her first glass of bubbles.

Beckett shifted almost uncomfortably, but I heard the humour in his voice as he answered, "I did. Eden, this is Roz Maxwell-Ellis. My father's big sister. Aunty Roz, this is Eden–"

"Your girlfriend?" Roz smirked.

Beckett's small smirk looked like the beloved nephew who knew better than to argue with his doting aunt when she was teasing him. "Something like that."

Roz clucked her tongue and looked at me. "Pleasure to meet you, love. You're the first girl he's ever brought home, so you make you sure he doesn't go around being all ambiguous like that for too much longer." She gave me a wink and ushered us inside.

The place was so opulent. It was like one of those outback houses you saw in movies and on TV with a tonne of money thrown into its renovation and upkeep. The whole house looked like it had been basically rebuilt from the cellar up in materials I didn't even have words for. It looked like light oak and marble and glistening mirrors and everything running off your app kind of stuff. The furniture was all huge, but the rooms were even bigger. People flitted around like the whole house was on display for the party. It looked it. I couldn't rightly believe anyone inhabited it.

Nothing gave any hints about the people who lived there, except they had money. None of the paintings or ornaments. It was all sweeping Australian bush vistas or things I thought I recognised from museums, or expensive versions of the household tat you got down the corner cheap shop. Like a generic figurine of a woman holding a child. Or an artistic interpretation of a cat.

The only thing that was remotely personal was a giant portrait of Beckett and Regina with their parents hanging over the fireplace in the back living room as Roz led us through the house.

"Daddy Beckett's out the back mingling," she told us.

"Regina?" Beckett said.

"She made an appearance as Dictator dictates, then retreated to her room just before you got here."

Beckett touched her arm and leant to whisper. "Mum?"

"Upstairs." Roz patted his arm. "She's taken her pill, so best see her another time."

Beckett nodded once, then turned a look on me that I assumed was supposed to be reassuring, as though everything was fine. And I guessed it was fine. No one we passed seemed to immediately think I was out of place. They all said their hellos to Beckett, and he ignored the majority of them. I wondered what was so special about the ones he did return.

I watched the set of his shoulders as we walked through the party. They were high and square and proud. Here was everything that encapsulated the King of Rivermont Academy. He was truly majestic and regal and commanding. I believed he'd been born to rule the whole damned world.

Which is what I was busy thinking when things were suddenly ever so less fine because Roz was telling her brother that his son had finally arrived.

"You're late," was the first thing Beckett Maxwell Senior said to his son when he saw him.

"I'm here," was Beckett's clipped retort.

"Griffith expected you."

"Griffith isn't worth my time. Or yours."

Mr Maxwell looked at Beckett keenly and I didn't know if he was wary of the power of his heir, proud of him, or riled that Beckett had the gall to tell him who was worthy of his time.

"Bekkie brought a date," Roz said warmly, acting like she had no idea about the mini showdown that was occurring between her brother and his son in the middle of their swanky party.

Beckett's hand tightened on mine ever so slightly. I wasn't sure if he objected to the nickname or Roz telling his father I was his date.

Mr Maxwell looked me over and I had never felt so small or insignificant or utterly lacking in my life. "*This* is your date?" he asked his son, not hiding his initial impressions of me.

"This is Eden Quin," was Beckett's very careful answer.

"Quin? Why do I know that–? Not the *swimming coach's* daughter?"

I could see exactly what he thought about me and Mum then. He may as well have outright called us the hired help.

"Well," Mr Maxwell sighed. "I suppose they all spread their legs the same. We all go through the phase." He looked me over again. "Few of us are *bold* enough to dress them up and play at polite society." The way he said 'bold' sounded exactly the same as 'stupid'.

It was obvious what Beckett Maxwell Senior thought about women. Just the way his eyes glossed over his sister and me. The fact it was clear he thought all we were good for was spreading our legs, as he so pointedly called it. Men like him didn't say anything by accident, even if they wanted you to think it was off the cuff.

"Let the boy have his girlfriends, Beckett," Roz said and I saw the look of– shit, was that panic on Beckett's face?

"You let her call herself your *girlfriend*?" Mr Maxwell asked his son, like the mere idea of a 'girlfriend' was horrifying.

Beckett held his own. "She only does what she's told."

I very nearly piped up at that comment – I was here as an apology after all. But I saw the look of warning in Roz's very slight head shake. I also saw the momentary pride in Mr Maxwell's eyes and decided to give Beckett this one win. He could make it up to me later.

"Good," Mr Maxwell said. The way his eyes roved behind us and his voice trailed off, I suspected an excuse to depart was imminent. "Excuse me, will you."

"Well," Roz said after he'd left, taking a sip of her drink. "That could have been worse."

Beckett seemed stiff, even for him. "Worse could yet come."

Roz waved away his negativity and smiled at me. "Congratulations, love. You survived your first meeting with Daddy Maxwell. Let's get you both a stiff drink and see if we can't loosen you up."

Beckett shook off her encouraging hand. "I'll give Eden the tour."

Roz seemed to think that was code for something. "All right, Bekkie. Have fun, Eden. Lovely to meet you."

I nodded. "You too, Roz."

Beckett's hand in mine tightened noticeably, and he pulled me back inside and away from the majority of the party-goers.

"So, this is my parents' country house," he said, sounding bored by it already.

"Country house? Because you have more than one house?" I asked as I looked around.

He inclined his head. "We have property in every major city. Some minor. Homes in the country, and on the sea and river in multiple states. Not including the number of apartments my father keeps for his toys."

I didn't think, by 'toys', Beckett was referring to cars or

complicated kilometres worth of model train sets. 'Toys' was exactly the sort of word Beckett Senior would have preferred to 'girlfriends'.

"Right," I said slowly as Beckett led me down a hallway.

"This is the kitchen," he said, ignoring the staff who were busy catering for who knew how many people were there.

He pulled me all over the lower floor, showing me with a bored kind of apathy around his parents' house. By the time he pushed open a heavy door, the whole party was outside listening to some speech his father was making before dinner was served.

"And, this is my father's study," he said.

"Let me guess, you bring all the girls here to give a very literal screw you to your dad?" I sassed.

He smirked and pulled me to him. He closed the door behind my back, and I heard the lock click. "Is that what you'd like me to do?"

"Are you man enough?" I teased him.

A vicious mirth lit his eyes. "I don't have to prove my manliness to you. Do I?"

I shrugged cheekily. "A girl could think you're all bark and no bite."

"You might not like how hard I bite."

I had so far. "I can't believe you'd hurt me. Not really."

"Really? And what about me says that exactly?"

"You're too lazy to lift a hand against an enemy. I doubt you'd be bothered with a woman." One eyebrow rose in teasing. "At least in anger."

A slight brightening of humour flashed in his eyes as his tongue darted out to lick his bottom lip. "Is that what you think of me?"

"What else should I think, Beckett? I'd be surprised if Jaeger knew the real you."

His eyes narrowed. "What do you want from me, Eden?"

It seemed teasing was over. "I just want the truth."

He seemed to weigh up not only my words but his response. "And if I told you that what you see is what you get?"

I searched his eyes. "Then maybe I walk."

"What do you think I can give you?"

It was more a test than a question. I knew that. He wanted my answer to be something like 'the world' or a ring, or at the very least his heart. I wasn't going to give him what he wanted. If he wanted this to work, then he was going to have do some of the heavy lifting as well.

"I want what everyone wants. I want to be wanted."

"You think I don't want you?"

"Growling at me and going around telling everyone I'm yours is *not* the same thing."

"Isn't it?"

I shook my head. "Funnily enough, no." I laid a hand on his cheek, and I saw the surprise in his eyes at the simple gesture. "Maybe I'm a hopeless romantic, but I'm the kind of girl who wants to make him lose that stony restraint. I want to feel like I'm wanted, not just owned."

"I was brought up to not show anything that might be mistaken for weakness."

He'd said as much in the limo on the way there. It felt meaningful that he was putting it into clearer words. Like, maybe Jaeger's narrative might not have been a completely different story after all.

"Passion isn't weakness, Beckett. All I want is to feel like I'm not making a mistake. You want me? Show me. Make me feel it. Show me I'm worth losing that composure for…"

"You want me to lose my composure for you?"

"I'm not asking for a ring," I scoffed at his hard tone. "Just a single crack in your famous restraint."

"A ring would be nothing."

I frowned at him and pulled my hand away. "Okay. Well, there's my answer. I guess I'm not the girl to break your composure after all."

I turned to leave. I barely had time to wonder how I was getting back to school after this when Beckett had spun me and thrown me against the wall behind me.

"You're the only one to come close," he said, almost breathlessly.

His eyes searched mine for a moment, then his lips crashed into me, and the breath was entirely knocked out of me. Had he not been responsible for keeping me upright, my legs would have given out.

It wasn't the first time I'd kissed Beckett.

Obviously.

Every kiss had been hot and heavy and left me wanting a lot more.

This kiss was all that and more.

Hot.

Heavy.

Desperate.

I'd never even vaguely thought the word desperate anywhere near a description of Beckett and considered it might be true, but here we were.

I wanted him to want me?

The sizzling fizzing that was shooting around my body told me without a single doubt that he wanted me. And not just in the 'satisfying an itch' kind of way.

Beckett wanted me the way I wanted him.

Like I was water in a desert.

Like I was perfect, precious, irreplaceable.

Like I was the only cure for what was ailing him.

His lips trailed down my neck and I could only lay my head against the wall and feel everything that was him.

"You really want to feel my bite, baby?" he asked, his voice low and thick with need.

I felt myself smile. "You know I do."

He dragged his teeth over the sensitive skin of my neck and my nipples pulled tight. He coaxed my leg around his hip, gripping my upper thigh firmly, and pressed against me. There were too many layers of material between us, but I still felt enough pressure to nearly beg him for more. As it was, a gasp escaped me and even I was surprised by how contented and needy it sounded.

"This. Fucking. Dress," he growled, as he fought the layers of material.

He dropped me gently to the floor and looked me over. His eyes were dark. His face was determined.

"I thought you wanted me," I said to him, affecting a mock pout.

"You have no idea how much I want you right now," he answered, and the truth of it made me breathless.

"And you're going to let something as trivial as a dress stand in your way?"

He looked at me. There was a hint of humoured expectation in the way his eyebrow rose.

"I thought you were Beckett-fucking-Maxwell?" I said, my tone a challenge. "I thought you got whatever you want?"

He wrapped his arm around my waist and pulled me to him roughly, but there was a glint of humour in his eyes. "Unfortunately, even Beckett-fucking-Maxwell has to obey the laws of…what is this? Not physics. Haberdashery?"

I snorted in an effort not to burst into laughter.

"What would your solution be, Eden?" he asked, his voice like velvet as it slid along my body. "That I bend you over my father's desk," his hand lightly grasped my throat, "and remind you who rules your world?"

A little thrill went through me at just the thought of that. At the idea of Beckett throwing me down and really losing control over me. We'd just established that he'd never lost control over me. He'd clearly wanted me, that much had been obvious. But wanting me so badly as to actually, truly lose control? I hadn't thought the notion of losing control existed to Beckett Maxwell, and here we were not just talking about it, but it might be really going to happen.

"Better to ask for forgiveness..." he mumbled.

I was just wondering what he'd need forgiveness for when he pulled me to him roughly and ripped my brand-new beautiful dress right off my body. He threw the remnants on the floor and gathered me into his arms.

I was caught between impressed and annoyed, and a vague question of how I was leaving the room now that my only apparel had been ripped to unwearability. But it was sass I decided to go for.

"You *just* bought me that," I pointed out.

He nodded, the heat in his eyes threatening to combust me right there. "And I'll buy you a hundred to replace it if you so choose."

"Is that losing control or just being domineering?" I asked him.

I saw the corner of his lip tug like he was holding back a smile. "How exactly would you define the two?"

My lips brushed over his as I told him, "Losing control might involve relinquishing it in the first place..." I ran my hand down his face, down to his chest where I grabbed his shirt and tugged him after me.

He followed willingly and I felt ridiculously powerful in nothing but my underwear and heels as I dragged the King of Rivermont

Academy by his shirt behind me. When I reached the couch, I pushed him down onto it and climbed into his lap.

"Is this you trying to be domineering?" he asked with a hint of humour in his voice.

"Why?" I challenged. "You don't like it?"

He wrapped his arms around me. "Baby, I love it."

His hand slid up my back as he pulled me closer and kissed me deeply. I felt his cock harden between us and rubbed along it wantonly.

Beckett growled as he stood us up, holding me effortlessly with just one arm. With the other, he retrieved a condom from his pocket, and shoved his trousers and briefs to his ankles before sitting back down.

"Care to do the honours, baby?" he purred, holding the condom to me.

I bit my lip as I took it from him, and slipped off his lap. His eyebrow rose in question, but he left me in charge.

His cock was thick and hard and, if I hadn't already had it inside me, I might have panicked at being face to face with it. As it was, I knew how good he felt and I was looking forward to having him inside me again.

Slowly, I ran my tongue up his shaft before sliding my mouth over him, as I undid the packet and took the condom out. I slipped the condom between my lips at his tip, then rolled it down, my mouth following my hands. Beckett sucked in a breath, then breathed out a slow, "Fuck."

I smiled as I slowly dragged my lips back up his shaft before standing up. He reached for me eagerly as I climbed on to the couch to straddle him, hovered over his cock.

Beckett held my hips so I couldn't lower myself onto him and looked me in the eyes. "Why does it feel like you've done that before?" he asked.

"Maybe I have," I told him. "Why? Jealous?"

He shook his head. "Your past doesn't bother me, Eden. Only your future."

The depth of emotion in his voice tugged warmly on my heart. It made my stomach fizzle in nervous excitement. It made me wonder if this *was* him finally getting it right after all.

I looked at him and he kept staring right back at me. "What about my future bothers you?"

Beckett bucked up and into me in one easy thrust. My arms tightened around his neck as I leant my head over his shoulder.

"The idea of you with another," he murmured, thrusting again. "Of you raising someone else's children. Of you living your life…without me."

All unattractive prospects just then, I'd admit.

"I don't know how to show you what I feel for you," he said quietly, his lips brushing the shell of my ear.

I gently coaxed his hands to loosen their grip on my hips and ground against him slowly. "That's a start," I told him before kissing him deeply.

He wrapped one arm around my back as the other brushed my hair back, and still his lips didn't leave mine. His fingers on me were gentle and soft as he hugged me close and I rode him steadily and slowly.

Despite being in his father's study with a whole damn party on the other side of the door, we weren't in any rush. When we weren't kissing, we were just staring deeply into each other's eyes, and my heart warmed and buzzed in a way it never had before.

Something sparked between us. Something warm and glowing

and bright. It wasn't flash, white-hot passion. It was something that burned longer and slower. It was the kind of something that forever could be made of.

It built and grew right along with the pleasure in me, until I knew without a doubt that Jaeger had been right. There was no pretending I thought otherwise now. Whatever was between Beckett and I had the very real power to be long-term material. As long as the real world didn't get in the way. But right then, it was just us and it was perfect.

"Beckett…" I whimpered, as needy as I'd ever heard myself.

He nodded against me. "Cum for me, baby."

As my body tensed, he took control of our pace, not deviating from the one I'd set. The pleasure washed over me hard and warm and deep in me. Like it was the roots of everything else between us, taking hold and making their way into my very heart.

Beckett wasn't far behind me. His lips capturing mine again. I took his bottom lip in my teeth, and felt his whole body tense as his cock throbbed. I rolled my hips over him and he breathed hard as he rode his orgasm out.

"I don't want you to move, but I'd best deal with this," he whispered as he brushed a kiss over my lips.

I nodded and slipped off him onto the couch, trying to surreptitiously rearrange my pants. He got up to deal with the condom and his trousers, wrapping it in a tissue and slipping it in his pocket.

"Did you consider how I was going to walk out of here while you were busy losing control?" I asked.

A small smile tugged at his lips. "Strangely, no."

He looked at me, his eyes dragging down and up agonisingly slowly.

"What?" I asked.

He dropped in front of me. "You are almost unbearably beautiful," he said gently.

"I have other good qualities aside from my physical features," I reminded him.

I saw the smile in his eyes. "Oh, your physical features are stunning." He shook his head. "But that's not what makes you beautiful."

Before I could say anything, he shucked his jacket and was slipping it around my shoulders.

"This should get us upstairs," he explained, taking my hand and leading me to the door.

Beckett's jacket was enough to cover me, but not quite enough to hide the fact I was basically naked under it. He ushered me up to Regina's room despite my heavy protests.

He knocked on the door before opening it.

As he stepped in, Regina sat up on her bed.

I was more than prepared for her to be in a compromising situation, but she was just reading.

"What do you want?" she asked her brother, then her eyes roved to me. "Why is your date naked under your jacket?"

"There was an incident," Beckett said, going to a door behind which I suspected was a luxurious walk-in wardrobe the size of my bedroom in Mum's townhouse at Rivermont.

"An incident?" Regina said, looking between us.

"I ripped her dress off."

Regina looked at me, a smirk on her face. "Again?"

I felt myself frown and I took a step towards Beckett like I'd have hit him if he was in reach. "Again?" I spat.

He came back out of the door with a dress. "Don't stir shit, Rexxie. Not tonight."

Regina's smile widened as she looked me over. "I just wanted to see the little kitten's reaction. Most of them wouldn't dare feel entitled enough to be annoyed. Her claws do you proud."

Beckett looked at her like that meant something. "Eden is mine," he told her like that was an answer.

"And you?" Regina asked him.

"What about me?"

"Are you hers?"

Beckett's eyes ran over me like he was looking for something. "Yes." Then he looked back to his sister like he hadn't just dropped an epic bombshell on the both of us and held up a dress. "We're borrowing this."

Regina shrugged. "It was always too short for me anyway. The scraps would make a nice summer top."

Beckett gave her a sarcastic smile. "Ha ha."

I tried to hold in a laugh, but a splutter escaped me and the Maxwell siblings turned to look at me in question.

"Sorry." I waved my hand in front of my face, the other still holding Beckett's jacket closed over me, as I tried even harder not to laugh. "But, for a moment, the two of you actually seemed human."

Beckett didn't seem to like that assessment, but of course he wouldn't. Regina gave me a knowing smirk.

"I see it now, Bekkie," she said gently. "Just be careful."

I wasn't sure if her final words were to me or Beckett, but he nodded.

"That's the plan," he answered, then took my hand, nodded to his sister, and led me out again.

"Now where are we going?" I asked.

"Somewhere no woman has been in about five years."

"Your heart?" I gasped in jest.

As he pushed open another door, he looked back to me with humour in his eyes. "My bedroom."

I shrugged. "Same, same but different."

He used my body to close the door behind us and there went the tell-tale sound of the lock clicking.

"You do so like locking me behind doors," I told him.

"I like having you to myself."

"You sure you just don't want to risk me running?"

"Same, same…" he whispered against my lips, "but different," before searing me with a heated kiss.

I gently put my hand on his chest and he swayed a millimetre away.

"What?" he asked.

"I'm all for the sex tour of your dad's country house." He ducked in for another kiss and I gave into it for a moment. "But I'm less keen on his reaction if he realises you're not at his fancy party."

Beckett ran his nose over mine. "I saw *your* reaction, Eden. It was too much, asking you to be here now. I thought it would…"

He sighed heavily as he pushed off the door behind me and turned away.

"I thought bringing you as my date would show you I wanted to do this properly. That I want the world to see you at my side. An equal. Actions more than words, right?"

I felt the smile tugging at my lips at the knowledge he and Jaeger had been talking, and that Beckett had been taking notes. But I didn't want to ruin his roll, so I just nodded.

He nodded as well. "Right. So, I asked… No. I demanded. And you were good enough to come. But I felt your discomfort. I saw the awe at Aunt Roz. The light dim in your eyes in the face of my father. I don't want you to feel that. Not with me. Not when we could be alone and you can sass the shit out of me or I could feel you tighten on my cock as you breathe my name like it's your only lifeline." He rushed over to me and took my hands in his as he searched my eyes. "I want you, Eden. This thing. Exclusive."

"Well, unless you also have an expiry date, I'm going to have to get used to these parties, Beckett."

He nodded again. "But not tonight. Out there, I'll fuck it up again."

I patted his chest, as my eyes settled on it. "Yeah… We're going to need to have some words about what you said to your dad."

He tipped my face to his. "Do we now?"

"Yes."

"What kind of words?"

"The kind that encourage you to say less like that in future."

He smirked. "Baby, I'm the King. I say what I want."

"You also think you get what you want, *baby*."

"Surely only a queen has such power over a king?"

"Are you asking me to be your queen, Beckett?"

"What would you say if I was?"

"Ask and find out."

"Why don't you just say yes?"

"Why don't you just ask?"

"You're never going to make things easy on me, are you?"

I shook my head. "I've told you I'm not one of your court, Beckett. And, honestly, I don't know how queenly I am either."

"You're not a trophy queen, no. You're a warrior."

"You suggesting that you'll sit on the throne looking pretty and placating the masses while I go off and play war?"

He wrapped me in his arms. "I'm suggesting we go to war together."

My heart fluttered and I felt that forever kind of feeling again. I tried to caution myself, but I was less interested in listening and more interested in getting Beckett naked and pushing him onto his bed.

# CHAPTER NINETEEN

For the Easter holidays, Sam had decided to stay at school with me. Solidarity and all that. Once Hunter heard Sam and I would be hanging all holidays, he decided to stay as well.

Neither of them really needed to bother because I'd sort of semi-hoped that I could just spend two weeks either thinking about Beckett like some sad sack lovelorn idiot. Or being with him, since he'd made me decide that he'd be staying at school over the holidays as well.

Things had changed since his dad's party. He wasn't suddenly a nice, thoughtful guy, but he wasn't cold. Not with me. And it was definitely not just all sex between us. We'd hit that point Jaeger had warned me about. Although Beckett hadn't so much as taken what was his as I'd got with the program. Like we'd met each other halfway, it seemed as though I'd given up denying us but also that Beckett had given me something much more than exclusivity in return.

Not that I could put my finger on what exactly, but it left me with a goofy smile on my face. One that I could almost see mirrored in his eyes whenever he caught mine from across a room.

Like that room. The dining hall. That was almost empty on Easter Monday afternoon.

Along with the majority of the Rivermont student populace, Fox was blissfully gone for the holidays. So was Rowan and Preston and the majority of Fox's cronies. The only one I really needed to bother with was Jaeger, and he was about as concerning as a pop quiz in biology.

Sam sat next to me, as always, and Hunter was on the other side of the table.

I felt my phone buzz and checked it under the table.

**Beckett**

Mine. Tonight.

I looked up at where he was sitting at his own table, his eyes firmly on me. I felt myself smile as I replied.

**Eden**

I told Sam I'd watch a movie with him.

**Beckett**

Are you planning to be there all night?

My smile widened and I ignored Sam's failed hidden laugh. Sam knew who was texting me. He knew who was making me smile. And he was being as goofy about it as me.

**Eden**

Maybe I was going to sleepover?

**Beckett**

You are. At mine.

I don't care how late you are.

I took a screenshot and sent it to Sam.

**Eden-Q**

Naw. Don't you love it when they care?

Sam snorted and we shared a look before I raised my humoured eyes to Beckett. I saw a humour shining in his and the slight tip of his lips as he didn't take his eyes off me. I bit my lip as I dropped my eyes down to my plate.

I felt Hunter looking between us and I knew he was trying to play catch up. There was something going on and he knew he was out of the loop. But what was I supposed to tell him?

'Oh, yeah. Beckett won me over and now I'm pretty sure we're official? I know you hate him but maybe not rain on my parade about the whole thing? Thanks.'

I could definitely see that going well. Not.

Sam and I hadn't talked about not telling Hunter, but Sam and I shared one brain most of the time and I knew he wasn't going to say anything before I finally got around to it. I mean, if Beckett and I were official, then there was only so much longer I could keep that from the general populace. Although, the way we'd gone the last few days, it could be longer than I was expecting.

After dinner, I popped back to Mum's townhouse to let her know I'd be staying over with Sam. She'd long given up on me and Sam doing movie dates in my room in the townhouse over the holidays, and she'd begrudgingly admitted that doing dinner in the dining hall with my friends and movie nights in the dorms even in holiday times was 'boarding school life'.

"Have a good night," Mum said as she gave me a hug. "See you tomorrow night?"

"Definitely," I said with a smile.

Even if Beckett and I were exclusive, it didn't mean I was going to drop my whole life for him. He could demand all he wanted, but I still needed to take time out for my mum. Especially when I wasn't quite ready to go into all the details about any potential relationship I might be in. It was a wonder I'd hidden going to the Maxwell Easter party from her.

Because we apparently couldn't go a few days without seeing

Abby, Sam and I called her for a video chat to catch her up when the movie finished.

"So, you're dating Beckett?" Abby said and Sam smirked.

I shrugged. "I think so, yes?"

"And what does that mean?" Sam asked with a laugh, clearly not impressed with my indecisiveness.

I took a breath, then huffed a shaky laugh. "I honestly don't know. I don't know how long anything with him could realistically last. I don't know how much of it's really just physical. I guess I'm just going along for the ride and enjoying it?"

"Do you like him?" Abby asked.

I made a very non-committal half-shake, half-nod. "What he gives me, I think so. But I'm not sure he's capable of giving me anything more…substantial, might be the word I'm looking for?"

"So, you're just waiting for it to end?" Abby asked, like that sounded sad.

I fiddled with my shoelace. "No. I don't think so. I guess I just figure it's going to have to at some point. I have no idea how or anything." I shrugged. "I guess I'm just a hopelessly pessimistic romantic."

After we got off the chat to Abby, Sam sat me down and I knew some real talk was coming. He had the face on and everything.

"What?" I asked him.

He took a deep breath, and the exhalation was just word vomit. "Are you sure this is what you want? You want him? To be dating a Royal? The good makes up for the bad? He treats you right? Lots of orgasms? There actually is good? All that?"

I looked him over. I could see concern in his eyes, but also love.

"Why haven't you lost the plot about this like Hunter?" I asked carefully, not sure I wanted the answer.

He shrugged. "I too entertain the idea of being swept off my feet by a Royal so, selfishly, I can't tell you to walk away. Living vicariously and all that. But, if you feel you need to, then you should."

I sighed. "I know I probably should…"

He smiled. "But?"

"Either I can't, or I don't want to."

Sam nodded. "Yeah. I get that."

"You do?"

"Edie, I've seen the way he looks at you when he thinks no one's looking. I can only *imagine* the way he looks at you when you're alone. What he says. How he touches you. I also know you. You don't just fall for any idiot. Whether I think it's a good idea or not, there's got to be more to it than everyone else sees."

"So, you don't think I'm an idiot or naïve?"

"I think you're being cautious, but also not letting something potentially good pass you by. Isn't that literally all we can do in life?"

I smiled and we hugged. "Thank you," I told him.

"What else are best friends for?"

"For not leaving you in the lurch just because their 'boyfriend' demands your time?" I suggested.

He scoffed. "Look, if Gunner ever noticed I existed, you know I would leave your arse in the cold in a heartbeat, right?"

I snorted. "Yes. And you'd better!"

He nodded. One brain. "Exactly. Beckett's your Gunner, Edie. Go to him. Make passionate love to him in his hot tub on his private jet or whatever."

I picked up a pillow and threw it at him. "Laugh it up."

He nodded. "Oh, I will."

I left him chortling to himself as I hurried up the stairs to the Royals' floor.

Jaeger was lounging casually about at the top of their flight. So casually that he was rearranging, painfully obvious that he was waiting for me and wanted me to think it was casual.

"Another *IT Crowd* reference?" I teased and he stopped.

"You are going to be the death of my reputation, Qunicy," he said.

I shrugged as I headed for Beckett's room. "Maybe you shouldn't be such a nerd."

"Takes one to know one," he answered back.

I turned to face him, walking backwards those last few paces. "Yes, it does."

"What does?" Beckett asked as he pulled his door open.

"Take one to know one," I told him, grinning at Jaeger.

"Know one what?" Beckett asked, looking at Jaeger.

Jaeger's eyes bugged in silent plea for me not to say anything. I actually couldn't believe that Beckett didn't know that about his loyal left hand's nerd proclivities, but I wasn't going to be the one to rain on that parade.

"Someone trying to make you happy," was the piss weak answer I came up with.

Beckett looked at me weirdly, turned the expression on Jaeger, then shrugged.

"Inside," he said curtly.

"Have you got *grand* plans for me or something?" I teased as he pulled me into his room and closed the door.

His answer was to pick me up and throw me onto his bed just the way he knew I liked.

I lay there among his pillows and watched as he pulled his shirt off impatiently. "Or something," he said before climbing over me and I felt the smile on his face as he kissed me.

****

The next day, I was meeting Sam and Hunter to walk to the pool together. I'd got out of Beckett's room that morning unnoticed by anyone but Jaeger, which didn't really count, and had seen Mum for breakfast and everything. I was feeling quite accomplished.

Hunter was downstairs in the lobby when I arrived, and I smiled at him.

He jutted his chin at me. "I saw you this morning."

Panic set in. "Saw me where?"

"Coming downstairs."

I nodded. "Um. Okay."

"From the Royals' floor."

*Shit.* I tried to laugh it off. "So?"

Hunter's hand grabbed my arm tightly. "Eden," he said forcefully.

I blinked at him. "Hunter, you're hurting me."

He didn't let go. He just stepped up closer to me. "*He* just wants to hurt you."

"What?" I asked, trying to pull my arm out of Hunter's vice-like grip. "Hunter, you're being ridiculous."

"Edie? Hunter?" Sam said as he came down the stairs.

Hunter let go of me hurriedly and stepped away. I smoothed myself over and forced a smile for Sam. He looked between us like he was trying to work out what in the blazes had happened and why.

"Uh, right," Sam said with a nod. "Pool?"

"I can't promise Jaeger won't crash," I said as I took Sam's arm. "I was slipping out of Beckett's room this morning when I was talking to you and Jaeger overheard." No point hiding it now if

Hunter had seen me.

Sam shrugged. "I could be okay with that."

"With hanging out with Jaeger?" I laughed, trying very hard to pretend I didn't feel the awkward blazing beacon that was Hunter fuming on the other side of Sam.

"Yeah. I mean, he's a pretentious twat, but he is clearly besotted with you."

I snorted. "He is not."

"Platonically, obviously," Sam pointed out. "I'm starting to worry I'm being replaced."

"They'll never actually accept her," Hunter grumbled, and Sam exchanged a look with me.

Sam opened his mouth, then shut it. Then tried again. "Edie's got lots of lovely qualities. She'd raise the decency of the Royals tenfold."

Hunter scoffed derisively but didn't say anything more, and neither did Sam or I.

Turns out, Jaeger wasn't just planning to crash our pool excursion, he was already there when we walked in. And so was Beckett. Both of them were in nothing but boardshorts. Jaeger's were short and tight in technicolour rainbow, and Beckett's were knee-length in black.

"What are you doing here?" I asked Beckett as he came over to kiss me.

"Spending the afternoon with you and your friends," was his terse answer. Clearly, he was thrilled by the idea.

"Shall I get you a bucket?"

"What? Why?"

I tried not to smile at him. "Because you sound like you're going to be sick."

"I have seen men killed in front of me. Dismembered and bleeding to death. I think I can manage an afternoon of swimming with your friends."

I patted his very fine, very naked chest. "You let me know how long you believe that."

Sam got the music going, and he and Jaeger spent the afternoon amicably fighting over what songs to play. Hunter was quiet and subdued, especially so when Regina and Phoenix arrived.

"If it isn't the little princess," Jaeger said with his arms outspread.

Regina threw him a look that pointedly said, 'fuck off'. "What else were we supposed to do all holidays?"

"I'm sure there's shopping to do. Your nails might be chipped. Split ends?" Jaeger joked, and Phoenix pushed him in the pool.

Phoenix was about as surly as Hunter, but Regina spared me a small smile that looked foreign on her face. Unpractised. I had to wonder if this was another sign of effort on Beckett's part. Have his sister hang out with us as well like we were all getting to know each other?

It was nice.

At least, Sam and I enjoyed ourselves. But then, we always enjoyed ourselves when we were together. And Jaeger wouldn't be left out. He, out of everyone, seemed to making a real effort to make this whole 'clique merging' work. Beckett's idea of making it work was just not making out with me the *whole* time, apparently.

"You had to wear that, didn't you?" he murmured in my ear as he stepped up behind me and wound his arms round my naked stomach.

I smiled and leant into him. "I have no idea what you're talking about."

I felt him nod. "Of course not. Be lucky I still have *some* restraint when it comes to you, Eden."

He kissed the side of my head absently before moving away. I turned to look at him and saw his eyes were trained on Hunter, who was watching us with a deep, distrusting scowl on his face.

Not that I, or Sam and Jaeger, were going to let Hunter get me down.

****

On Wednesday at dinner, Jaeger took a seat beside Hunter, opposite me. I cocked my head at him in question, but the question was answered as Beckett slid into the spot on the side of me not occupied by Sam.

Hunter glared bloody murder at Beckett, but Beckett ignored him as he put his arm around my shoulder.

"Um. Hello?" Sam asked the table at large.

Jaeger gave him a cocky grin. "Hey."

"Do, uh… Do you sit here now?" Sam asked hesitantly, but there was a teasing warmth in his eyes.

Jaeger kicked his head towards Beckett. "Where he goes, I go. And where she goes, he goes."

"So, it is like official then or something?" Hunter asked testily as he looked between the significant lack of space between Beckett and me.

"It's like official then. Or something," Beckett answered him with zero warmth in his voice.

Hunter levelled an unimpressed look on me like he was severely judging my life choices. "You're dating *him*."

I actually snuggled into Beckett for support, and I got it. "I guess so."

"You guess so?" Hunter huffed. "What kind of piss weak answer is that? It's a yes or a no, Eden. Or are you so stupid that you'd actually throw yourself at a Royal without any commitment from him?"

Beckett leant across the table menacingly. "Don't try to understand things your tiny little child brain couldn't possibly fathom, Gibson. What Eden and I are is of no concern to you. Trust that your *friend* is plenty strong enough to tell me if she's unhappy with what we are and will not hesitate to make me change it."

I could hear the full begrudgment in his voice. It was a thing he hated, but a thing he also couldn't deny.

Hunter scoffed. "Because Eden actually tells *you* what to do?" I could tell he thought that as likely as snow for Christmas.

Beckett's eyebrow rose and I would have been shitting myself if he ever looked at me like that. "If you fail to see the strength and beauty of her character, then it's no wonder you're on *that* side of the table."

There was a hidden meaning in there that I did not understand at all. After a very tense standoff, Hunter got up and swept out of the room.

"Well," Sam said loudly, trying to dispense some of the tension. "Now we're all here, I would like to put in a formal request for a date with Eden on Friday."

Beckett frowned over me at him.

"You do know I'm gay, right?" Sam asked him pointedly.

"We are all aware," Jaeger assured him. "In delicious detail. Is it true you–?"

"Friday?" Beckett interrupted.

"Friday." Sam nodded, dragging his curiosity off Jaeger. I wanted to know what Jaeger was going to ask, too. "There's a new movie we want to see."

Beckett turned his eyes to me. "What kind of movie do you go to without your boyfriend?"

Sam made an unnecessarily obvious 'squee' noise at the previously unmentioned word, to which Beckett actually growled and Jaeger gushed, "I know, right?"

"This is ridiculous," Beckett muttered, then said to Sam, "Fine. Yes. Friday. She's yours."

"Does *she* not get a say in it?" I asked pointedly.

"No," both Beckett and Sam said.

I looked to Jaeger as though for help and he just grinned widely.

So, I was hanging around the dingy alley entrance to the movie theatre complex on Friday night, unusually early after some shopping with Mum, when I got the text from Sam.

**Samwise Kap-gee**

Sorry. Can't make it. You know who

called. Please don't hate me.

Hate him for going after his shot? Never. Be annoyed that it had to happen the first time in my life that I'd ever been early for something. Always.

**E-denQ**

Never. But I will need sordid details.

**Samwise Kap-gee**

Always. Love you.

**E-denQ**

Love you, too.

I blew out heavily as I wondered what I was going to do now. Mum would be back at school and Sam was supposed to be my ride.

I was just unlocking my phone to text Beckett when I heard my name and inexplicable shivers ran down my spine.

"Eden," Hunter called again, and I forced a smile for him before I turned.

"Hey. What are you doing here?"

He shrugged casually. "Heard you and Sam were catching up, then he bailed."

I frowned. Sam had only just told me that.

"I was talking to him when he got the text," was Hunter's explanation. "I was already downtown."

I nodded slowly, feeling my heart racing for absolutely no reason at all. I just had this feeling that I had to get out of there. I didn't care it was irrational, because this was Hunter after all and he was my friend, but I was also going to listen to it because it wasn't really giving me a choice not to.

"Makes sense. Look, I have actually made other plans now, so—"

Hunter's eyes flashed something. "With Beckett?"

I paused. "Uh…"

"It is, isn't it?"

I wasn't really sure what to say. "We are…dating, Hunt. I mean, we're going to…go out and stuff." I don't know why it sounded like a question.

Hunter stepped towards me and shoved me back into the wall behind me.

"What are you—?"

My words died on my lips as he pressed his body into mine.

All I could think was 'EW'.

"Is this what you like about him?" Hunter snarled as his fingers scrabbled clumsily at the bottom of my skirt.

I tried to push his hand away, but he held me firmly as he grabbed my arse and kissed my neck.

Tears were hot at my eyes, and I just froze for a moment, trying to work out what to do. Wondering why he was doing this. Trying to make sense of any of it while desperately wanting to be as far away from him as possible.

A loud burst of laughter distracted Hunter for long enough that I managed to push him away, and I ran. I ran so damned hard and fast that I was sure my heart and lungs were going to explode.

It felt weird to be running away from someone I'd considered a friend for so long. The thought was swiftly followed by the realisation that someone who'd do that couldn't be much of a friend.

I was so engrossed in these thoughts that I wasn't watching where I was going and ran smack dab into a warm, hard body I recognised by touch and smell alone.

His hands went around me and, as annoyed as I was, I also felt safe again.

"What are you doing here?" I asked, my fear and anger directing itself at him.

Looking up at him, I saw his eyes were trained behind me like he was looking for whatever I was running from. Which meant he knew I was running from something, and that something was probably a someone. Even after what had just happened, I didn't want to be Hunter when Beckett found out what he'd just tried.

"Keeping an eye on what's mine," he replied.

"Most people would call that stalking."

"Given the way the night's turned out, you should be thanking me."

"What do you know about the way the night turned out?"

"More than you want."

I pushed away from him. "And exactly what does the King of

270

Rivermont plan to do about it?" I snarked.

He pulled me close to him. "I understand you're scared. I understand your emotions are heightened right now. But don't think I'll let you speak to me that way again."

"I'll speak to you however I goddamn wish," I snarled back.

Something hot flashed in his eyes as his jaw tightened. "Now is not the time." But he said it more to himself than to me. "Come on," was definitely directed at me.

He slipped his hand into mine and I held it tightly as he showed me to his car. He got me in, buckled up, then jumped into the driver's seat. He looked unbelievably pissed off. I felt unbelievably safe and my terror had subsided.

Beckett drove like he belonged in one of the Fast and the Furious movies. His foot slammed the clutch every time he changed gears as he weaved through traffic effortlessly. His face, usually so stone-like and unreadable, was barely contained fury; his jaw clenched, his mouth a thin line, his nose flaring now and then.

"Did you get a manual car just so you could drive like this?" I asked him.

He shot me a look of contempt.

"Don't get me wrong," I continued. "There's something a bit sexy about it."

He gave a rough laugh, but there was no humour in it.

"Something funny?" I asked anyway.

He shook his head ruefully as we roared onto a quieter road that would slowly wind into the mountains. The higher we got, the colder it got, and I wasn't really dressed for it. Beckett put the heater on higher and neither of us spoke for the hours he drove.

Eventually, he turned off the main road, onto a smaller track that rambled through the lush forest. As he slowed, I saw why. A cabin –

no doubt very expensive – loomed up out of the trees, the huge windows – hopefully triple glazed – all shining in the moonlight.

Beckett pulled to a stop, helped me out of the car, and took me to the front door. His arm was wrapped around me as he opened the door, and he only took it off once the door was locked behind us again.

I could see the outlines of furniture and a kitchen in the wan moonlight filtering in.

"Where are we?" I asked.

"My place," was all the answer I was getting apparently.

I watched him fiddle with a control pad on the wall and things were set in motion. Fire flickered to life in the grate in the living room and shutters rolled down the windows.

"Your place?" I asked, still in awe. "What's–?"

Beckett stepped up behind me and wrapped his arms around me. "Questions will wait until tomorrow, darling," he said quietly.

Then he took my hand again and lead me through to the bedroom, lit only by another fire. He climbed onto the bed, totally clothed, and held his arms out for me. Without wondering what he was doing and just trusting him, I climbed on next to him. He drew me down onto the pillows, wrapping his arms around me so I could play the little spoon. I felt protected and comforted all at once and I marvelled at the fact that Beckett Maxwell was making me feel that way.

As we lay there in the dark, I dared to whisper, "How did you know to come for me?"

I felt him take a deep breath. His chest pressed against my back before he dipped his lips to my shoulder. "Obsession recognises obsession, Eden."

Two opposing thrills ran through me. One warm at the thought that Beckett was obsessed with me. One ice cold at the idea that

Hunter was. I think it said something very definite about my feelings for the two of them that Hunter's obsession was unwelcome, and Beckett's wasn't.

"Hunter's obsessed with me?" was what I asked.

"Don't think about him now," Beckett said, his voice hard.

"Why?" I teased, or I might cry. "You won't have me thinking of another man while I'm in your arms?"

"I won't have you thinking of something terrible while you fall asleep," he said quietly and gently.

I didn't have anything to say to that, so I just snuggled up against him and eventually I fell asleep.

# CHAPTER TWENTY

I woke the next morning and felt the familiar weight of Beckett's arm over me.

Then I realised that I was fully clothed, and my eyes flew open. I didn't recognise where I was for a moment. Then the previous night flooded in, and I sat up quickly.

Beckett sat to cradle my body with his. "Shh. It's okay. You're safe."

I took a breath, knowing he was right, feeling it in my gut. I was safe with Beckett. I pushed away all thoughts of Hunter and leant into Beckett.

"So, are you going to tell me anything?" I asked.

He trailed kisses over my shoulder. "Like what?"

"Like where we are or how this is 'your place' or how long we're going to be here?"

He surprised me by giving me actual, simple answers.

"We're almost at the top of Mount Flinders," he said. "This is my place because I bought it. And, yes, I bought it with what *you* would call ill-gotten gains, and we just call income. I hadn't thought about how long we'll be here, but I'd like to take the weekend – maybe Monday – if you'll stay that long. Any other questions?"

"You'll actually answer them?"

"I'll answer what I can."

But, of course, at that moment, I couldn't think of anything I wanted to know.

I felt his smile, like he could tell. "The offer will not expire." He gave my shoulder another kiss. "Breakfast?"

He hauled himself out of bed and I turned to watch as he pulled his long-sleeved tee off. He raked his hand through his hair the way he always did when he got up; like he wasn't that bothered by me seeing the state of it but knew it would be mussed after sleep and had the urge to somewhat tame it.

"I have clothes here," he said, "but there isn't really anything for you."

I shrugged. "Have you got a washing machine, or is that just for poor people?"

He fought the smirk, but humour lit his eyes. "I have a washing machine."

"Okay. No problems, then. But I will need to borrow a shirt in the meantime."

His eyes flashed. "Is this a ploy to wear my shirt?"

I shrugged more coyly now, batting my eyes. "You don't want me in your shirt, Beckett?"

He came over to the bed and leant on it, nuzzling my nose with his. "I'd prefer you naked, but in my shirt is a close second, baby."

He pressed a quick kiss to my lips, then went to the wardrobe and tossed me a shirt.

"Buttons and everything," I laughed.

He nodded. "That's standard, isn't it?"

I stood up to get changed. "Like anything about us is standard."

He didn't say anything so, when I was out of my clothes and in his shirt, I looked at him. He dragged his tongue over his bottom lip as though he really liked what he saw.

"There's definitely nothing standard about us," he agreed.

He took my hand and led me out to the kitchen. Wordlessly, he got me a coffee – just the way I liked it – and started on cooking something.

"I'm not sure where to start," I told him.

"Just pick one," he said with a wry tilt to his lips, obviously knowing I meant I had questions.

"You know how I like my coffee?"

He nodded as he chopped onion. "I'm the heir to a criminal empire, Eden. I know how you like your coffee."

I smiled. "What else do you know?"

His eyes darted up to me. "I don't think you want to know."

I was less amused. "What do you *know*, Beckett?"

"Everything I could get my hands on, Eden." His tone was resigned, like he knew he had to be honest but would rather not.

I was going to leave that where it was, so I just nodded and moved on. "And just coincidentally having food up here?"

"There's no knowing when I might need it. I have people to keep it stocked."

"Of course, you do."

"And?" he pressed, like he knew that wasn't it.

"You can cook?"

The corner of his lip tipped up. "I can cook."

"You don't have people for that?" I teased.

"I have a lot of people for that. I used to have a lot of people to service my every sexual whim, but I can still jerk myself off."

"Used to?" I hedged as I put my cup on the bench beside me, not sure it was a wise question or not.

"Now, there's only one," he said simply.

I looked at him and felt… God, just everything. But, as nice as this was, it was only really working because it was just us again. He'd made an effort at school that last week, but there was clearly still some tension floating around. And not the good kind. For some reason, that didn't sit right with me.

"Why did you bring me here?" I asked.

He looked at me. "What do you mean?"

"Here. You could have taken me anywhere. Back to school would have made the most sense…" I left the sentence hanging.

He shrugged. "You were in danger, Eden. I was on autopilot. There's no conspiracy. I just knew I had to get you safe."

"And safe equals secluded, where no one knows where we are?"

"Yes."

I wasn't expecting such a clear answer. "Seriously?"

"In my world, yes. 'Safe house' isn't just a random term."

"So, it wasn't just about getting me alone again?"

"Not this time, but would it be so bad if it was?"

Which was exactly what had started the niggling feeling in my stomach in the first place. "I told you that hanging out with my friends would be worse than your dismembered bodies," I sighed.

"I…like being with you," he managed to grind out, like it cost him some effort. "Other people…complicate that."

It was as good an explanation as I could have come up with. I still didn't like the way that conclusion felt so inevitable.

"So, we're just never going to be around other people?" I huffed, feeling my emotions starting to fray and fret. I just wasn't exactly sure why.

He sighed and dropped the knife before leaning his hands on the bench. "It's unlike you to not just say what you're thinking, Eden," he said meaningfully.

I breathed in deeply. "What do we really think we're playing at here, Beckett?" rushed out of me and I realised what my problem really was.

"What do you mean?"

Thank God he'd asked. Because then I could answer that for the both of us. "I mean, this. Us. It's all well and good taking me to your father's party, and locking us in your room, and now this running away to a cabin in the mountains. But what actually happens after this? In the real world? Are we honestly a long-term thing?"

He stepped over to me, crowding my space as he looked down at me with an almost feral darkness in his chocolate eyes. "You're mine. Not just for this weekend, but for as long as I say." His tone was icy.

As turned on as I was, I also bristled. "You demanding my supplication like a petulant child will not make it so, Beckett."

He picked me up and sat me on the kitchen bench. He stepped between my legs and placed a hand on either side of me. Heat swirled around us, and my heart skipped as my clit throbbed and my stomach bottomed out.

"You are mine," he said forcefully. "Whether you wish it or not. We are forever inextricably linked now, you and I. No amount of wilful disobedience on your part will change that."

Ugh. He hadn't made me this mad in a while. "And what about choice, Beckett? Don't I get to choose if I want to be with you or not? Be *yours* or not?"

He looked deep into my eyes. "Why should you get a choice when I do not?"

My stomach flipped and my heart felt like it had skipped a step going down the stairs. I knew that was the closest he would – or could – come to putting into words that he was as helpless as me in the face of this attraction, this pull between us. But then, he *had* told his sister that he was mine. So maybe I could argue a little less.

"You want forever, Beckett? Then you don't throw around lines like 'as long as I say'. You want me to be yours? You don't get to just get to call it quits or move on when you get bored."

"You will always be mine," he growled.

"That doesn't mean you won't get bored," I said in a quiet voice.

I knew all about the man who was deeply in love and still strayed. A horrible mistake, the worst of his life, my dad had called it. And there was no guarantee that Beckett was even a man deeply in love. I had no doubts that Beckett had been raised to be the kind of man who would demand my obedience and faithfulness, then not bat an eyelid about being unfaithful himself regardless of promises of exclusivity. He probably wouldn't even consider it cheating because a man like him got to take what he wanted whenever he wanted it.

Something was playing out in Beckett's eyes at my words, and I watched it avidly even if I didn't know what it was. There seemed something almost conflicted in him. I felt like he was trying to decide if he should reveal anything to me. Had he been anyone other than who he was, I'd have said he was tossing up the sense – the necessity – of opening himself up to me. As though Beckett Maxwell would ever open himself up to anyone. The idea alone was laughable.

"I will not get bored, Eden," he said carefully. He ran his hands up my body achingly slowly as he nuzzled my face then leant his forehead to mine. He breathed out heavily as my body fizzled pleasantly. "I will never get bored. I have my pick of women to fuck or toy with, and yet the only one I've wanted, the only one I've craved, I've needed, for the last four years is you."

I blinked and found his eyes. "What?" I breathed.

His hands continued trailing over my body like he felt he had to take the chance while he had it, like he could hardly believe that he was actually able to. His nose ran over my cheek, my jaw, my neck with the barest promise of a kiss as he told me, "I've wanted you since the first time I saw you, Eden. My first year at Rivermont. I was only at the pool because Jaeger threatened to beat me if I didn't show up and support his attempt to get on the swim team. He said he needed it because the new coach was a hardarse. Brilliant, but hard."

Those were two interesting revelations on Beckett's part, but he seemed to find saying the words hard enough without me interrupting and ruining his flow.

He spoke like the words felt weird in his mouth. They certainly sounded weird coming from his mouth. But he was in no way hesitant or unsure about the words he did say. I believed they were true even if it was painfully obvious that he'd never been even remotely that open or emotional in his entire life.

"And there you were," he continued. "Sitting on the bleachers with your hair in two plaits, a pair of denim shorts, a tank top, and Converse. You floored me. I'd never felt the way just *seeing* you made me feel. I'd walked into Rivermont prepared to be not only Rivermont's king but the king of every room I ever walked into for the rest of my life. Then I saw you and, for the first time in my life, I didn't want to lead…" He paused like he wasn't sure how to say the next bit. "I wanted to follow."

My heart seemed to thud with two syllables.

*For. Ever.*

I remembered the conversation at the Royals' party. When he'd sounded like he was asking me if I was sure that Sam had been my friend longer than Beckett's possessive streak. It turned out, maybe Beckett's possessive streak had been around longer.

Beckett finally looked into my eyes, and I saw the apology in them. I didn't know what he was apologising for. It felt like he was apologising for wanting me. Or maybe he was apologising that I made him feel something he'd clearly been raised to never show, let alone feel. It felt to me like he thought he was weak because of it.

"I would have followed you wherever you led, baby," he finished, the look in his eye turning into fear at what my reaction might be. But he'd still said it, even if he obviously didn't think he should have, even if it went against everything that had been beaten into him.

*For. Ever.*

I didn't know what to say to that. I didn't know how to show him how it made me feel, how to tell him it meant something to me, how I didn't think he was weak for wanting me. How did I reassure someone, who was conditioned to not feel anything, that the feelings he did have were good, endearing, welcome?

My head started shaking as I tried to work it out, but it obviously came across the wrong way because he started pulling away. He cleared his throat roughly and my mind scrambled for something to make it all better.

My leg wrapped around his hip and held him to me tightly as I lay my hand on his cheek. "Beckett…" I stalled, hoping some better words were coming to me.

I still wasn't sure how this thing between us could be anything more than it was – a few stolen moments when we were safe from the judgement and reality of the world – but I knew it *was* something. It had already been obvious that we were both powerless to the pull between us, and Beckett had admitted as much only moments ago. But I'd still been willing to believe – to tell myself – it was all physical. At least that's all it could really ever practically be. And maybe that was self-preservation. But now he was telling me, in the only way he could, that he knew it was more, and it made me acknowledge that fact as irrefutable as well.

The man, who had been taught not to feel, felt for me. I could almost believe that he loved me in his own way. And, in that moment, with us in the safety of our bubble, that was all I needed to want to give him all of me. There was a part of me that suspected whatever came of this would have to be rethought – or would disappear entirely – when we went back to school, but I was going to live in the moment. I wanted to know what it felt like to be loved by the King of Rivermont Academy, and I wanted him to know what it felt like to be loved by me.

He was watching me with unsurprising confusion and expectation on his face as I held onto him but didn't say anything.

"I'm yours," I told him. He surged forward and I desperately wanted to kiss him, but I lay my thumb over his lip to clarify, "If you're mine."

I watched him swallow hard. His hands gripped my hips hard as though he was afraid that I'd disappear into thin air. "Then, you *are* mine," he growled, like that was the end of it.

It might not have been the most romantic or swoon-inducing response to my assertion, but it did the job as well as Beckett could. After all, I wasn't into him for his elocution and emotional speeches.

"Then, kiss me," I told him.

I'd expected angry passion and hot and hard, but he was anything but.

Beckett pressed his lips to mine almost reverently. One of his arms wrapped around me tenderly as the other slid up my side softly. His kiss was deep, and fanned the embers in me in a totally different way than usual. Instead of just wanting to rip open his clothes and feel him in me, I felt the whole delicious build up.

A kiss like that definitely had the potential to be real love. The kind that forevers really were made of. My whole body hummed, and this slow zing ambled through me, warming me up from my heart out to my fingers. A recessed part of my head was flashing warning signs, and I happily ignored it.

Beckett dragged my undies off me as he kissed the absolute daylights out of me. I felt him unzip his jeans and take himself out. He was hard already. Then he fumbled in his pocket, and swore.

"What?" I asked.

"I don't have a condom on me. Give me a–"

I gripped him tight with my knees as I ran my nose over his. "You said you were clean."

He looked into my eyes like he couldn't believe I was right there. "I won't lie to you, Eden."

Whether it was a poor choice or not, I believed that of him. I nodded. "Then you don't need a condom, Beckett."

"Do you mean that?" he asked as he dragged himself up my opening.

I held onto him tightly. "Yes."

"You…trust me?" he asked.

I thought it was a weird way to put it, but I nodded. "I trust you, Beckett."

"Fuck, Eden," he breathed, then his lips were on mine again and he was sliding into me slowly.

I buried my face in his shoulder, instinctively biting down playfully, forgetting I wouldn't be biting his shirt. My teeth grazed his skin. I felt his hand grip my hip harder and he groaned.

"Am I not the only one who likes a hicky?" I breathed in his ear.

"Baby, you tell yourself whatever you have to if it makes you bite me again."

I slid my hand up the side of his neck as I brought my lips to the other side. Starting out gently, I kissed him. He responded by thrusting hard and deep into me and both hands were tight on my arse. My teeth grazed his skin gently and his hands tightened on me even more.

With no idea whether I was successfully giving a hicky or not, I just got wrapped up in the moment. I sucked his neck and bit him, dragging my teeth over his sensitive skin and relishing in his groans of pleasure.

Finally, though, his lips found mine again and the pleasure I'd been too distracted to properly feel until then flooded me. My fingers dug into his back as the pounded me. Our breaths mingled as we held each other close.

All the things I wasn't sure we could ever say seemed to pass between us and my heart beat strong and steady, in that moment, just for him.

The coil in me pulled tight as my breathing got more ragged.

"Beckett…" I breathed.

"Eden," he seemed to agree.

The coil burst and I came hard, Beckett not far behind. He thrust once, twice, languidly before leaning his hands on the bench on either side of me, dropping his forehead to mine, and just pausing to get his breath back.

I chuckled and felt him twitch in me.

"Give me a second," he sighed, rolling his forehead on mine affectionately.

"Is it true then?" I asked.

"Is what true?" he replied.

"That sex without a condom is so much better?"

He looked up into my eyes and I saw the humour in his. "Yes, Eden," he said evenly. "It is. Happy?"

I nodded. "Little bit."

He huffed a laugh. "Good."

He pulled out of me slowly, pressing a deep kiss to my lips. As he pulled away, I saw his neck was bright red and splotchy where I'd been lavishing attention on it.

"You'd better not go covering that up," I sassed him, tapping my neck to show him what I meant.

He actually laughed as he shook his head ruefully and pulled me to him. "Never, baby."

My bubble burst ever so slightly as I realised something. Beckett must have seen it on my face.

"What?"

"I need to tell Mum where I am," I said. "She's going to be so mad with worry. God, and Sam."

Beckett just nodded and answered, "They know."

I looked up at him quickly. "What do you mean, they know?"

He sighed. "While you slept last night, I contacted Jaeger. He passed the message on to your mum, and I made sure he told Sam as well, that you were safe."

I slipped off the bench. "I need my phone."

"It died overnight, and I don't have the right charger." His tone was apologetic. "I didn't realise people still used those."

I huffed. "Serve me right for having an older phone, I guess."

He put his arms around me. "No. Serve me right for making assumptions, but I will buy you a new phone if you want?"

"You've already offered me a hundred dresses, Beckett," I said with a wry smirk.

He nodded. "You deserve everything you want and more, Eden. You only have to ask."

"Oh, woe is me. I'm Beckett-fucking-Maxwell and I have more money than I know what to do with," I sassed.

He huffed a laugh. "I'm serious. Although, you're not wrong."

"How about a car, then?" I teased, sliding my arms around his neck.

"I'm thinking AMG G63 in bright green or maybe purple," he answered with a nod, no hesitation.

I blinked. "What are they?"

"They're new but with a classic aesthetic."

I snorted. "And I bet they're a million dollars."

He shrugged. "Hundred and fifty, or so."

I was sure my eyes actually bugged. "Million?"

He laughed. "Thousand."

I smacked him gently. "Beckett, you can't joke about spending a hundred and fifty thousand dollars on me!"

"I don't joke, Eden."

I looked him over. "You don't say," I murmured.

His lips brushed mine as he said, "You only have to ask."

I smirked. "You could just say yes," I teased and felt his smile against my lips.

"You could make things easier for me."

"I could, but I won't."

He wrapped his arms around my waist. "Then don't blame me when you find a new car parked outside your mum's townhouse."

"Beckett–"

But he silenced me with a kiss, and I melted against him. Then he pulled away and manoeuvred me over to his chopping board.

"What are you doing?" I laughed.

"Cooking. With you."

We spent the rest of the morning being ridiculously domestic and I just completely gave myself over to it. Not letting myself worry about what the rest of the world was doing, I enjoyed the here and now. If Beckett was going to be my biggest mistake, I was going to take full advantage of it and properly enjoy it.

Sometime in the early afternoon, I was rugged up in one of Beckett's jumpers and a pair of his socks, with a cup of coffee wrapped in my hands, as I walked past the window and looked out.

"Beckett!" I yelled, my voice ridiculously more high-pitched than necessary.

He came skidding out of the bedroom, his hand going to his waistband like he was used to finding something there in those sorts of situations. I wasn't going to dwell on what that something might have been or why.

"What?" he asked, looking around.

I blinked and pointed out the window. "Just snow, you idiot. I thought it was exciting."

He took a deep breath and visibly relaxed. "You can't just yell my name like that, Eden," he chastised gently as he walked over to me.

"Why? I might be dead again?"

He wrapped his arms around me again. "Yes."

I leant back into him as we both looked out the window at the gently falling snow. "So, my death's still inevitable?" I asked.

He dipped his nose to my shoulder. "I've tried to tell you that my world is dangerous. Why do you think I resisted you for so long? But I will die before any harm comes to you."

I felt the bubble that surrounded us threatening to pop and pushed it away. "So you let the Royals push me around for the last four years to protect me?" I sassed.

I felt the rumble of laughter in his chest. "That was the idea."

"And how did that go for you?"

"It was torture, baby. Watching Jaeger effortlessly interact with you. Seeing them all look at you, see you, when I couldn't." He trailed his hands over my stomach. "All I wanted was to touch you.

To have you challenge me directly. To let you see that I *saw* you."

I span in his arms. "You *saw* me?" I teased.

He nodded. "I've always seen you, Eden." He touched his knuckle to my chin and tipped my face up to his. "I've always wanted you."

"But you could never lose control?"

He shook his head. "Even now, it's a risk I'm hesitant to take."

"Why? You think you'll break me?"

"That I'll break us. If you see…" He sighed and leant his forehead to mine. "If you see the real me. If you get too close…"

"I'm not walking away, Beckett. Not unless you give me a reason."

He shook his head. "God, I should. I easily could. I shouldn't drag you into my shit. But I can't give you up, Eden. Not now. I'm not strong enough."

I put my cup down on the table beside us and took his face in my hands. "Then don't give me up, Beckett," I told him, more begged him really.

I didn't know if this was me deciding I really was strong enough to survive his world. That, if he was actually in love with me, I could live up to it. But I did know it was me wanting to be.

# CHAPTER TWENTY-ONE

The rest of Saturday was spent talking, christening every available surface in the cabin, and learning more about Beckett than I'd expected to in a whole lifetime. Which still wasn't all that much, but it was a pretty good start.

The sound of water running woke me on Sunday morning. Or, at least, that was the first sound I registered. My hand searched the bed for Becket and my half-asleep brain decided he must be in the shower. Not one to waste an opportunity, I slid out of bed and into the bathroom.

God, but he looked stunning. Standing there, stark naked with the water streaming down his unnecessarily tight body. I wondered just what it took to have a body like that. Then I figured, as long as it didn't negatively impact the time he spent with me, I didn't much care.

I stepped up behind him and wound my arms around his body, trailing my hands up his chest. I felt rather than heard the vibration of his laugh.

"Good morning," he said as my hands trailed south.

"Good morning…wood," I said as my hand wrapped around his shaft.

I ran my hand up and down, working him slowly. He put his hands on the tiled wall as though for support as he leant his head forward.

"Fuck. That is hardly fair," he breathed heavily.

"What's not fair?" I asked as I kissed over his back.

"Give a man a taste…" He huffed. "You know what you do to me, and still you tease me."

"That seems like a you problem. Are you suggesting I can't go around rubbing my hand over your cock without you getting something in return?"

His huff was slightly more humoured. "I shouldn't be, I know." He sucked in a breath. "But, Jesus, baby girl…"

I took my hands off him and coaxed him to turn around. Water streamed over his face as he looked down at me and I had never felt more wanted. His eyes were dark and full of desire. His breathing was too deep, too slow and measured, too even, and his cock twitched.

Teasingly, I rubbed my thumb over the corner of my mouth, and I saw the flash of anticipation in his eyes. Slowly, I lowered myself to the floor and took him in my mouth.

"Jesus," he muttered as he basically fell back the final couple of centimetres to the lean on the wall.

Look, my blow job game was probably not the best. I'd had very little practise and it had been a while, to say the least. Plus, I was used to guys who hadn't spent the better part of five years building up their stamina. Beckett was probably brought up on blow jobs under the breakfast table as part of a balanced diet, for all I knew.

Which was why it surprised me when it didn't take long for him to start pushing me away. Surprised and concerned me.

"Shit, was I *that* bad?" I asked as he pulled me to standing.

A full smile lit his whole face. "Trust you to think I stopped you because it was bad."

"So, it wasn't bad?"

He shook his head as he brushed the now damp hair from my face and stared into my eyes. "A whole night lying next to your naked body…? Even if it was bad, which it definitely wasn't, I wouldn't have lasted much longer."

I bit my lip. "Oh."

He nodded. "Yeah."

Then he spun us and pressed my back into the tiles, his fingers skimming down my stomach tantalisingly.

"And it's bad form to cum before she does."

"Somehow, I doubt you say that to all your blow jobs."

He huffed a rough laugh. "No. I've never said that to a blow job. But then, you're not just a blow job, are you, Eden?"

The moment had taken a very sudden serious turn, but the kind I liked. A good kind.

His lips trailed down my jaw. "I still can't believe you're mine," he breathed.

"I thought it wasn't a negotiation?"

I felt his smile against my neck. "It's not, but there was no guarantee I'd ever get to touch you, feel you, make you come undone for me—"

"Come undone for me?" I teased.

"Every day," he said like a promise to a question I hadn't even asked as he looked into my eyes.

"Beckett…"

My words died on my lips. I wasn't sure how to say them. I wasn't sure exactly what I wanted to say. All I knew was that I'd been in free fall over Beckett for months and there wasn't a whole lot of air left under me before it was too late and there was no coming back from it.

I saw the understanding light his eyes. He knew exactly what I'd left unsaid.

He nodded as he took my face in his hands. "I know, Eden. Me, too."

He crushed his lips to mine as his fingers skimmed down my body straight to my clit. My back arched into him, and he wrapped his other arm around me. His lips brushed down to my chest as his fingers sent tendrils of pleasure curling through me.

My hand slid into his hair, the other around his shoulders, holding him close. I was up on tip toes and still didn't think I could get close enough to him. Something told me he felt the same. The kind of something that had him lifting me up gently and pressing into me slowly.

His thrusts were long and steady, languid and lazy. It was everything gentle and soft and tender, and I felt my heart swelling. Our eyes were locked as we rocked together and I felt how deep and intense this thing between us was. This thing I hadn't wanted but, now I had it, couldn't image living without.

As my orgasm built, my body tensed. Like he knew exactly what I needed, Beckett picked up speed. Our eyes were still locked as I came hard and I had never felt something so intimate in my entire life. He thrust faster as he pressed his forehead to mine, and I came a second time. This time, he wasn't far behind me.

It wasn't until we both stopped to catch our breath that either of us dared to speak.

"Eden," he said and I felt all the things he hadn't said.

I nodded, a small smile on my lips. It was a feeling that I was agreeing to, and I tried to tell myself it didn't feel as momentus as accepting something so significant as a marriage proposal.

He kissed me hard as he slid out of me and lowered me gently to the ground, making sure I was steady on the wet tiles before he took his hands off me.

As I cleaned up, I looked down and saw my hips and thighs were covered in faint bruising from where Beckett had held me the day before, bringing a light smile to my lips. I ran my hands over his body and saw he wasn't just a little bruised, but he also had marks where my nails had dug into him, and there was a hicky on his neck as well as one just under his collar bone. Although, what were hickies but just a more specific way to refer to a certain kind of bruise?

"What?" he asked softly, as he brought my body back into his and leant his forehead down to mine.

"Now we both have bruises."

He smiled widely and huffed a laugh.

Now it was my turn to ask, "What?"

He shook his head as he hugged me closer. "Nothing. Just remembering a conversation I had with Jaeger."

"About bruises?"

"Yes."

"Why were you two talking about bruises?" I asked, my eyebrow quirking.

He ran his tongue over his teeth. For the first time I'd ever seen, Beckett Maxwell looked…almost embarrassed.

"Oh, my God," I laughed, batting him playfully. "What were you talking about? Was it me?" Now, I flushed hot with potential embarrassment. "*Was* it about me?"

Beckett tried to hide his smile, failed, and just dropped his head over my shoulder instead. "The topic of kinks came up…" he said carefully, like he was choosing his words wisely. "J suggested you liked… Maybe not rough, but a few bruises. He…"

"What?" I asked, fearing the worst while filing away the knowledge Beckett had a nickname for Jaeger.

"I suspect he was wondering how long it would take you to work out that I…did, too."

I made him look at me, feeling the amusement threatening to burst out of me. "Excuse me?"

He shrugged. "The things I've done behind closed doors – had done to me – I've developed a bit of a taste for mixing pleasure and pain."

"Taking or receiving?" I asked.

"Either."

I was definitely open to exploring. Hadn't I told Sam that I wanted a guy who could show me all the things I liked the sound of to see if I actually liked them? Of course, Beckett was that guy. I'd hoped Beckett would be that guy. All I needed now was the nerve to ask him to show me.

"How *much* pain?" I asked.

"How much do you want?" he asked, his voice and eyes so damned cheeky that I almost didn't recognise that this was Beckett in front of me for a moment.

"Start me off gentle?" I squeaked, not quite sure what I was asking him, but trusting that he'd know what to do.

He turned off the taps, picked me up, and took me through to the bedroom again.

"What are you planning to start with?" I teased.

"I don't have a plan," he said, then threw me on the bed. "Except fuck you absolutely raw."

"I don't know what it says about me that I *really* like the sound of that…"

Beckett crawled on top of me and nestled between my legs. "It says you're perfect for me." He looked down at me, all heat and predatory intensity in his eyes. "You tell me if I go too far."

I nodded.

He flipped me over and pressed me into the bed with his whole body weight and I felt utterly at his mercy. He got his hand between me and the bed and that's when I realised exactly how at his mercy I was. His fingers deftly played over my clit, wringing pure ecstasy from me until I could hardly bear it anymore. But, I wasn't sure that I'd be able to get him off me, even if I'd wanted to.

Knowing I was safe with him, it was thrilling.

A second before I was going to tell him I needed a break, he grabbed my arms. He dragged me onto my knees, holding my wrists firmly behind my back with only one hand as he ploughed into me. With his other hand, he slapped my arse hard. I felt the sting and it made me jump. It was something I was probably only going to want occasionally, but I liked it.

Beckett grabbed a fistful of my hair. Using it and my already bound arms as leverage, he pulled my back to his front and dropped kisses along my neck. I felt heat spread through me as my body got used to the new sensations.

"How you doing, baby?" he growled as the hand left my hair and slid around my throat.

I felt my nipples tighten. "Good."

His fingers gripped my throat tighter as he thrust hard. "Fuck, Eden…" he breathed.

"Still trying to fuck me into submission?" I sassed and I felt him smile against my cheek.

"Oh, you'll submit."

He pushed me back over, his hand on my head as he held it against the bed. My arse was still up and he was driving into me strong and steady. Pleasure was mounting, fizzing, tingling through my whole body.

"God, Beckett!" I cried as my orgasm hit me and my whole body convulsed with the power of it.

He relaxed his hold on me and leant over me, holding me tight but tenderly, so I felt the vibration of humour in his chest. "You're something else," he whispered to me before he gently flipped me over and kissed me as he slid back into me.

I was still sensitive, but I loved the feel of him. Especially as his hand dragged up my leg, over my hip, and gripped my waist firmly. My arms went around his shoulders as I met every thrust.

His lips made their way down my cheek and he nipped my shoulder sharply. I felt like I was getting into the swing of this. It wasn't going to be all lie back and let him have free reign. I scored my nails down his back, more purposefully than before, then shoved against him and he rolled us so I was on top.

"I thought you were going to show me pain, Beckett?" I teased.

He sat up and wrapped his arms around me. "So did I," he admitted.

"Then, what's the problem?" I'd meant to continue being teasing, but I was actually starting to think there was a problem.

He shook his head, his nose brushing against mine. "Nothing. I just… I brought you to bed. A bit of biting, your nails, slamming into you…" He breathed out. "I want to find a way to say that's enough without it sounding like a bad thing."

"*Is* it a bad thing?"

He looked into my eyes and brushed the hair back from my face. "I don't think so. You're plenty dirty for me, baby. I want to spend more time having sex with you than fucking you." He dropped his forehead to mine. "If that makes any sense."

I smiled. "It makes sense. Although, I was kind of looking forward to feeling raw at least once in my life."

He chuckled softly. "Oh, you'll still be raw when I'm done with you."

And I was. Beckett's rebound time was damned quick, and he spent that short time pleasing me in other ways. Until I did viscerally know the meaning of raw – in the best possible way – and we just lay in bed together with my head on his shoulder.

"My mum…" Beckett started as his fingers played with mine.

"What about her?" I asked.

He breathed out. "You heard me talking to Aunt Roz at my father's party?"

I nodded, feeling like I'd been caught out or something. "Uh. I did, yeah."

He gave a single nod. "Our world broke her. My father… My father broke her."

I felt like I knew where this was heading. "Roz seems okay."

"Being five years older than my father gave her a power over him for most of their lives that, while good for Roz, I think he took out on every other woman in his life. Regina's mum. My mum."

"You don't have the same mum?" I asked.

He shook his head. "No. No, Regina was a bastard before my father forced my mother to adopt her. He killed Regina's mum for daring to fall pregnant." He scoffed. "When he was just too fucking lazy to avoid the consequences. But Rexxie's strong. They couldn't save her mum, but they saved her."

There was a lot to unpack in that sentence. "He killed her? While she was pregnant?" I heard myself breathe.

Beckett looked at me. "Does that make you look at me differently?"

I looked into his eyes, and I knew the truth. "No," I told him. "I assumed your world was pretty shady. Although, I wasn't sure how much of that was rumour and imagination, or reality."

"From what I've heard, the rumours are actually pretty tame."

"That's somewhat disconcerting." When he said nothing, I asked, "Does Regina know?"

He gave a humourless laugh. "Of course. Father does so love to lord it over her. He thinks it will break her. He's so buried in misogyny that he doesn't realise she's far stronger than me." He finished so quietly, I wasn't sure I was supposed to have heard. Finally, he rolled to face me. "I will always protect you, Eden."

I saw it, deep in his eyes. Had I not known Beckett better, I'd have said it was terror. As it was, he was worried his world would break me. I was pulled back into that memory with Jaeger. When he'd said that the women they fell in love were strong enough to survive their world. I still wasn't sure I *was* strong enough. I wasn't sure what kind of person I'd have to become to be strong enough. But I was still sure I wanted to be.

This thing between Beckett and me felt... It felt like 'it'. Like the end. Like it *was* the end. Like there would never be anyone after him. There was a finality to it all that made me know – even when the rational parts of my brain were telling me the opposite – that I was Beckett's. Forever.

There were a thousand and one reasons why I shouldn't be with him. And more reasons why it wasn't going to work. But I didn't want to listen to any of them. Because despite all of them, I couldn't shake the feeling of completeness I had when it was me and him.

It was undoubtedly going to bite me in the arse and get my heart smashed to smithereens, but I was going to follow this thing through whether the ending was a happy ever after or a bloody mess.

I leant my nose to his and looked into his eyes. "I trust you," I told him, hoping the meaning in my voice told him more than just my words could.

We spent the rest of the day in bed, only taking breaks to forage for food – or, in Beckett's case, cook me an epic chicken casserole for dinner – or the bathroom. By the time I fell asleep on his chest, I felt like I was really getting to know him. Not just those mundane things like what his favourite colour was or his go-to karaoke song. But who he was and that, to me, was far more important.

# CHAPTER TWENTY-TWO

The next morning, what woke me was hands on my body and lips on my shoulder. It was hard not to just bask in the feeling of rightness that warmed me at waking up with him in this carefree kind of way where we didn't have to rush off to lessons or get me out of the boys' dorm without the wrong people seeing me.

"I could get used to this," I sighed, then laughed self-consciously.

"You've woken up with me before," he pointed out.

I nodded as I snuggled into him. "I know. But this is…"

"Same, same but different?" he suggested, and I smiled.

"Same, same but different," I agreed.

"We could have this…" he said slowly.

I turned to face him. "What do you mean?"

He shrugged as he brushed his fingers over my cheek. "I mean, this doesn't have to stop."

"Are you about to ask me to move in with you?"

"What would you say if I was?"

I bit my lip against a smile. "Why don't you ask and find out?"

"Why don't you just say yes?"

"I'm seventeen, Beckett. I can't move in with you. Like, probably, legally."

He smirked. "If you'll remember, my family doesn't really hold much stock in laws."

"Maybe, but mine does and there are some I won't risk. My mum might kill me if I told her I was moving in with you. Plus, hypothetically, where would we live? *If* you were asking me to move in with you."

"Wherever you want. The dorms. A townhouse in the teacher's village."

"They wouldn't let you have a townhouse in the teacher's village," I scoffed.

"I'm the King, baby, they'll let me have whatever I want. Besides," he said languidly as he got up, "I already own multiple."

I sat up. "What do mean, you own multiple?"

"I mean, the school pays me…rent, shall we call it? To let the teachers live there."

I blinked. "That's… Is that what they call a shakedown?"

He looked at me, seemingly pleased I'd come to that conclusion. "Yes, it is."

I huffed a laugh. "This one of those times you ignore laws and stuff?"

He shrugged. "One of them, yes."

I hugged my knees to my chest. "Just how many laws do you break, Beckett?"

He answered, almost absently, as he pulled two shirts out of the wardrobe and compared them. "A day? Week? Month? Year?"

I took a breath. "A day…?" I said uncertainly.

He picked a shirt and put the other one back. "More than you want to know."

"If I'm…" I started, then stopped.

He pulled on the shirt and looked at me in question.

I tried again. "If this thing continues to be…a thing, how much are you going to hide from me?"

"As much or as little as you want."

"Really?"

He nodded. "There's not point hiding who I am from you."

"I thought you were worried about me seeing the real you?"

He took a deep breath. "I will always fear…losing you, Eden. Of pushing you away, whether because of who I am or by accident. But, if I've learned anything this weekend, it's that I can't hide from you. If you marry me and have my children and we grow old together, it will be impossible for you to avoid knowing me and my business. And, if we have a chance of any of that, then I know I need to let you in now. I'm not good at it, but I'm doing my best."

"The best with what you've been given," I murmured., remembering a conversation with Jaeger of my own.

He inclined his head. "I'm…unused to this, Eden. It doesn't mean I don't want to give it to you. Give you all of me. It only means I don't know how."

I leant my cheek on my knees and looked him over carefully. "You mean that, don't you?"

"With everything I am," he said earnestly.

"Why does this feel like goodbye?" I asked him.

A small, somewhat sad, smile crossed his lips. "It's not goodbye, but we have to face the real world at some point."

"I thought you wanted to keep me all to yourself?"

He huffed and seemed to fight a smile now. "I do. God knows, I do. But you want us to live in the real world. We *need* to live in the real world. As much as I want to just live in a bubble, just you and me, for the rest of my god-forsaken life, it's impractical."

"Not in the least because of your co-dependant bromance with Jaeger," I pointed out, trying to lighten the mood a little so my heart didn't thud into over-emotional.

Beckett chuckled. "Not in the least because of that. Jaeger would hunt me to the ends of the Earth. He'd hunt *you* to the ends of the universe."

"You make it sound like he's more loyal to me than you."

"Sometimes, I think he is." He cleared his throat. "Come on, we've only got a few more hours left here together. What do you want to do?"

I knelt up on the bed and peered out the heavy curtains. "I wanna build a snowman," I told him.

I looked back at him to see his eyebrow quirked. "You want to…?" he started and I nodded. "Okay, Ana…" he muttered, and I gasped.

"Are you *all* nerds?"

Beckett suddenly looked very self-conscious. "I was *eleven* when that came out," he hastily explained. Then he frowned. "What do you mean 'all'?"

I pressed my lips together before saying, "I promised I wouldn't tell."

He frowned as he stalked towards me. "I have ways to make you talk, Eden."

I scurried backwards to the pillows. "He gave me a favour and everything."

Beckett's eyes were deliciously dark and humoured. "I'll give you a favour."

"Try your best, Beckett," I challenged him.

And, I had to hand it to him, he did his best and then some. Like he knew I was excited to get out in the snow for the first time in my life, he didn't drag me down into the bed to be swallowed up by hours of pleasure. But, damn, it was good. So good, even Beckett-fucking-

Maxwell forgot it had all started because he was trying to get information out of me.

The clothes I'd arrived in weren't exactly made for a frolic in the snow, but I'd be damned if I didn't take advantage of it. Luckily, my tights were thick enough to take the worst of the chill off and Beckett made me wear one of his spare jackets over the jumper I'd borrowed.

"The next time, we will be better prepared and there will be appropriate attire," he promised as he wrapped me in his jacket.

"Next time?" I asked cheekily.

He inclined his head. "I thought… Next holidays…?" He cleared his throat.

"You want to take me away next holidays?"

"If you want?" he said, finally looking at me. "I was originally thinking Christmas, but the snow will be gone by then and I wanted you to see it again."

My heart thudded. It was somehow both painful and pleasurable. Christmas was eight months away "You want to make plans for Christmas?"

He ran his fingers of my cheek, my jaw, to cup my neck. "I want to make them for a lot further than that."

I bit my lip against the response my heart wanted to give him. "Okay," I said slowly, making sure the right words came out. "Let's start with next holidays."

I took his hand and pulled him outside.

"Oh, my God," I breathed, letting go of him to spin around. "It's so beautiful."

"Yes, it is," he said wistfully, and I looked back at him to find him staring at me intently.

"Cheesy much?" I laughed.

He nodded as he looked away from me. "It's disgusting, isn't it?"

While he seemed intent on very studiously looking at something, I scooped up a handful of snow. My timing was impeccable. I loosed the snowball a moment before Beckett turned back to me, and it crashed into his cheek.

I pressed my lips together as he stared at me, both disbelieving and clearly impressed with my gall.

"Did you just…?" he asked.

I nodded. "I did just."

His head twitched like he was resigning himself. "All right, Quin. It's on."

"Shit!" I laughed as I looked for somewhere to provide some sort of protection.

Beckett ran at me, and I was too slow to dodge out of the way. He scooped me up, twisted us around and threw us backwards into a pile of powdered snow.

"Oh, my God," I cried. "Shit, that's cold."

"You started it."

I looked at him fondly. "I did." His hold loosened on me, and I scrambled up. "And I'll finish it!" I warned him before grabbing another handful and chucking it at him.

He spluttered a laugh. "Of course, your aim is perfect. You play softball."

I gave him a shit-taking curtsey. "I play softball."

He tipped his head back, a wide smile on his face. "Never making things easy," he murmured before he hauled himself up and came for me again.

I refused to go inside until my lips were blue and I was shivering, and even then Beckett practically had to drag me in. He got me in a hot shower while our clothes did a stint in the dyer, and the sex was slow and passionate. It was perfect, but it was a stark reminder that this bubble was very soon to be popped.

I'd ignored the fact for the last three days but, now it was staring me in the face, there was no more pretending it wasn't going to happen. I'd been gone for three days. Out of contact. And all Mum and Sam had to go on was a, no-doubt vague, message from Jaeger. I wasn't just going to lose the protection and comfort of our bubble, but I'd have to face the anger and fear of my mum and best friend.

It made the drive back to school quiet and somewhat awkward. Not because I didn't know what to say, but because there was just far too much to say.

When we got to school and parked, Beckett helped me out of the car and kissed me hard. It was the kind of kiss that felt like goodbye.

"What's wrong?" I asked, my voice tiny.

"I don't want to leave you, but there's something I have to do."

I looked into his eyes, and he looked back into mine. I couldn't read on his face what was going through his head, but it had nothing to do with the fact he was hiding it from me as he was so wont to do. He was laid bare for once, wanting me to know without him having to say it.

That alone told me it was serious. I just didn't know.

"What are you going to do, Beckett?"

He wrapped me in his arms. "Protect what's mine." He kissed the side of my head, then let me go to take my hand. "I'll take you to your mum's place, then I need you to promise me that you'll stay there all night."

It was still an order, but it was at least a slightly more polite order than usual.

I nodded and something cold ran through me. "Okay, Beckett."

He took me wordlessly to the teacher's village and straight to Mum's townhouse. He even knocked on the door. Mum answered, being very surprised to see me let alone me holding Beckett's hand.

"Edie, I've been worried," she snapped.

"I know–" I started.

"It's my fault, Coach Quin," Beckett said.

Mum looked Beckett over and I wasn't sure what was going through her head either. "Did you want to come inside, Beckett?"

He shook his head. "No. Thanks. I have something I need to do."

Mum crossed her arms. "If it's going to another girl after you've been with my daughter, God knows where, for the last three days, you can rethink the kind of reception that awaits you next time you see either of us."

I was starkly reminded of the time she'd told me that it was all appearances with these Royals; act like you were superior and they'd think you were. And I'd seen her work it on every single one of them. But Beckett wasn't so easily fooled.

The corner of his lip tipped up. "While I appreciate the strength of the Quin women, do not make the mistake that I would allow you to tell me what to do. The fact I have no interest in any other woman has nothing to do with what I *should* do and everything to do with the fact the only one I want is your daughter. You can be sure I'm not going to another *girl*, Coach Quin. Besides, your daughter would never even look at me again if I did."

He kissed the back of my hand, nodded to Mum, then sauntered away as though he had nary a care in the world.

"You want to tell me what that was all about?" Mum asked as we went inside.

"No?" I suggested.

"Think again."

So, I told her all of it.

Fox.

Beckett.

Hunter.

Everything that had happened since school went back.

Minus the whole sex fest part of the last three days.

She'd heard the rumours, of course she had. But we'd always had a policy to separate the rumours from our lives. Mum pretended she didn't know anything she heard through the grapevine – just as if she'd been any other parent not at the school – unless I told her about it. What happened to me at school stayed at school, kind of thing.

But it was time to put both of us at ease.

It was a lot cathartic. Not just about Fox and Beckett, but working through my insistent disbelief that Hunter had actually happened. Telling her let me process it and accept that it really had happened. Hunter had tried to assault me. He was clearly not the guy I'd thought he was. It was a hard admission I didn't really want to make but, once I'd come to it, it felt right and I couldn't shake it.

There had always been something off about Hunter for me. I'd always been ever so less comfortable around him. Been slightly wary of the things I said or did around him because of how he might react. I guess it was this… Beckett had called it an obsession and I couldn't see anything about me that would make two guys 'obsessed' with me – even thinking the possibility was ridiculous to me – but I'd also learnt that Beckett didn't lie, and he very rarely exaggerated. If he'd seen obsession in Hunter, then it was quite likely it was there.

When I was done, Mum sighed. "God, where to start?"

"I know. I'm sorry."

She shook her head. "Don't be sorry. Although, I'm rethinking our policy. God, I want to say I'm not surprised, Edie. But Hunter's always given me the heebie jeebies. I'm more surprised about Beckett, to be honest."

I looked down. "Yeah. Me, too."

"You really like him?"

I wrinkled my nose while I thought about the best way to put it. "Yeah. Given time and room for…whatever this is to grow, I think it's real. He…he's not the guy I would have chosen, but I do want to see where it goes."

"Hm," Mum said, and I looked back up at her. "I'm not thrilled you're hanging out with Beckett Maxwell. He is the *epitome* of everything that's wrong with this place. But I trust you to make good decisions and be sensible. So maybe there's more to Beckett than the rest of us see."

I wasn't going to say it out loud, but I hoped so, too. I hoped more now after hearing not only Sam but Mum suggest it. Only time would tell, I guess.

"Okay," Mum said, shaking off the morbidity of the last hour or so. "I want to know everything, of course. But Sam has been going out of his tiny mind over you disappearing."

"To be fair, my phone died."

"To be fair, Jaeger's 'Beckett has her. She's safe', was less reassuring than I hope he wanted it to be."

I nodded. "Okay. That is fair."

She looked me over like she wanted to chastise me for the last three days, but also like she remembered what it was to be young once. "Just promise me, you were…sensible," she said.

When I looked down this time, it was to hide the heat in my cheeks. "Yeah. I was sensible."

"Good. Text Sam. Get him to come over. I may have panic bought enough ice cream to fill the freezer."

I snorted as she got up and went to the kitchen. That was no mean feat, we had a pretty big freezer.

**E-denQ**

We need to talk.

**Samwise Kap-gee**

Oh, so you're finally talking to me?

Where the hell have you been?

We've all be worried sick.

Was the sex at least AMAZING?

**E-denQ**

I'll explain it all. In sordid detail.

Promise.

Can you come to Mum's?

**Samwise Kap-gee**

I suppose so.

Of course. I love you.

Be there in ten.

Sam naturally forgave me once I explained everything. He figured he really couldn't not after he'd bailed on me and *that* had happened. But I refused to let him feel bad about it because it was hardly his fault.

"Maybe not," he said for the umpteenth time that night. "But I should have been a little wary after he was the one who told me Tyler was looking for me and I found Gunner there instead. It seemed too good to be true."

I didn't want to dwell on just how premeditated it might have all been, so I changed the subject and we got on with our lives and the last week of April holidays without Hunter.

No one had seen him since I'd got back. Not that Sam or I were

310

really missing him all that much.

We wouldn't have thought about Hunter's absence usually; it had been holidays so maybe he'd gone home. Except, he'd told us he was staying at school that holidays. Numerous times. He'd made a great big show of it which made his subsequent absence weird and mysterious.

The state of Beckett's knuckles when I'd seen him the day after we got back had also been weird and mysterious, but I doubted it was coincidental. Beckett didn't say anything to me about it of his own volition, and he was more than happy to distract me anytime I looked like I was going to bring it up. Not that I was complaining when his brand of distraction was to see how many orgasms he could give me in the shortest timeframe.

When Beckett and I weren't in his room, I was with Mum, or Sam and Abby. Beckett wasn't overly happy that I didn't drop everything for him the moment he wanted something, and he had a lot of choice words to say about that, but his actions spoke volumes. Or rather, his lack of action, in that he didn't try to stop me, told me he wasn't going to stop me doing anything that made me happy.

Abby had filled in the Hunter-sized space quite easily and it was soon like it had always been Abby and Sam and me. I tried not to compare her with Hunter too often, but it was hard to argue that I didn't feel instantly more relaxed than I had around Hunter.

She also went a long way to bridging the gap between my friends and the Royals. Jaeger was clearly eager to spend time with her as well as Sam and, with half of the inner sanctum spending time with me, Sam and Abby, half the next gen had little choice but to join in, too. Phoenix would probably always make me overly wary, but I could see there was actually quite a lot to like about Regina, if she actually gave anyone the chance.

A week later, the next term started, like it always did, but nothing felt the same.

Beckett had spent the better part of two weeks, for lack of a better word, wooing me. And I was royally wooed. I felt light and floaty and spent more time smiling than any sane person should. Which wasn't to say I wasn't feeling a little nervous about what was going to happen once the larger student populace was back.

Same, Abby and I were on our way out of the dining hall at lunch on that first Tuesday back when we were practically steamrolled by someone I'd never seen before.

She had hair so black it had to be dyed. She carried herself like she was expecting an attack from any direction at any moment. She looked like the chip on her shoulder was chippier than any of the Royals. Thick eyeliner smudged under her eyes, her tie was as wayward as Jaeger's, and her skirt was shorter than short. As she passed, it flicked up and I saw she had a tattoo on her leg. The only kids who had tattoos at Rivermont were Royals. The only ones – I'd thought – who could find a way to circumvent the age restrictions in this country. I guess I'd been wrong.

"Who's that?" I asked Sam and Abby as we watched her scurry away.

"If you weren't busy being seduced for the last week, you would have noticed that there's been a disruption to the Royals' usual composure," Sam teased.

I frowned. "What?"

"That is Bianca Michaels," Abby said by way of explanation.

"Soon to be Bianca *Finch*-Michaels," Sam added.

My frown deepened. The only Finch I knew at Rivermont was Rowan. "She's marrying Rowan?"

They both shook their heads.

Abby leant towards me. "Her mum's marrying Rowan's dad."

"Sold to. Married to. Much of a muchness in the grand scheme," Sam added.

I blinked. "Sorry. What?"

He shrugged. "That's the rumour anyway. I don't know if it's true."

I smirked, guessing where he'd heard that rumour and how few clothes he had on when he heard it. "She was *sold* to Rowan's dad, though?"

"Something about a debt. Very *Beauty and the Beast* if you ask me."

I snorted. "First, you think Beckett and I are bastardising Austen, now you think Rowan – Rowan *Finch* of all people – is going to go Disney?" I scoffed.

"Not Disney," Sam clarified. "OG fairy tale. Dark as shit."

I nodded. "Uh huh. Let me know how that goes, will you?"

He nodded as well. "Thank you. I will."

# CHAPTER TWENTY-THREE

I knew he was trying. That was the frustrating thing. I could see Beckett fighting his conditioning, his upbringing, every moment of every day for that whole week.

Me or his crown?

I wasn't sure he could have both.

He was going to try anyway.

But was it going to be enough for us?

As much as he was trying, the whole week felt like push-pull. One step forward, one step back. Like he'd said only days earlier, other people complicated things. They demanded his time. They looked at us like we were something taboo. Jaeger was the only Royal who'd hang out with me and my friends, and he was likewise the only Royal my friends would ever really tolerate hanging out with. Not that I wanted to suddenly be in the 'in' crowd, nor did I blame my friends.

But I was sick of it. The uncertainty. I needed to know where we stood and what Beckett's expectations for this thing was, because his actions seemed terrifyingly indecisive. Half the time, it felt like we were a romance for the ages. The other half, it felt like we were fighting way too hard for something that should have been so easy.

In my free on Friday morning, I thought he wasn't going to turn up. I laughed at myself, as I sat at my desk, alone for the first time in months and wondering when I'd started looking forward to sitting across from him. He'd even started bringing his own work with him, so we could study together like we were playing at a real relationship.

I wasn't sure why, that morning, I started doubting everything again. That feeling, that something big was coming and I wasn't going to be able to stop it, hit me again.

Then, Beckett strode out of the library stacks, but I still felt weird. He bent down to kiss my cheek, and I knew he'd noticed it.

"Eden?" he asked, a note of concern in his voice as he looked me over.

I nodded. "Beckett."

He put a hand on my arm. "What's wrong, baby girl?"

I shook my head. "I don't know. *Is* there anything wrong?"

He sat in his usual chair opposite me. "Why would you ask that? What's running through your head?"

I sighed. "I just… I don't know, Beckett. I don't know."

"If this is about the incident–"

I laughed, but it was humourless. "The incident? That's what you're calling it."

He huffed and scrubbed a hand over his face. "I wasn't choosing…" He growled in frustration. "I am Rivermont's King, Eden. As such, there are certain…responsibilities placed on my shoulders. Responsibilities that, if not dealt with, could turn into another Fox debacle."

I blinked. I hadn't realised the extent of his reasons. "You stood me up to avoid another coup?" I asked incredulously. "For your fucking crown?"

"Eden…"

I shook my head. "I thought…" I sighed.

"What?"

"I thought we were going to war together, Beckett."

He looked me over uncertainly. "We are."

"Then it can't be this difficult. It can't be me *or* your crown."

"Baby, it was *one* time."

"It's not the number of times, Beckett. It's what it represents."

"I don't know what you're talking about. Are you saying I have to choose between you or my place as Rivermont's King? It's you or my life?"

"I..."

No. That's not really what I was trying to say. As far as I could tell, Fox was done with his coup and no one had stepped up to really give it another shot. It wasn't about me versus Beckett's crown anymore. It was about him choosing to want us despite the obstacles, and I wasn't really convinced yet that he could put aside the man his father had made him in order to do that. It felt like he still had one foot out the door, ready to discard everything that was between us if anyone questioned his place in his world.

And I got it, it was the only world he knew. It was his world. But was it so wrong of me to want to be at least as important to him? To want him to find a place for me in his world, even if the prospect was kind of terrifying. To want to know that he loved me more than he feared what loving me would do to his reputation.

So, this was about *my* fear. My insecurity. And my inability to know how to voice it properly. I chewed on my lip as I thought about it, and he did me the courtesy of waiting to hear what I had to say.

"Do you know what you want?" I asked him softly. "Because I do. I want you, Beckett. I want us. I've tried not to. I've told myself it's futile and stupid and not actually ever going to happen. That the rest of the world will just keep getting in the way until we're both broken by it. But I can't stop."

"What are you saying, Eden?" he whispered, his voice hoarse, almost choked.

"I'm saying, ball's in your court, Beckett. I'm not asking you to choose *between* me and your crown. But I am asking you to choose me, that I'm actually a choice you consciously make, no matter what might complicate it. It's either us or it's nothing."

Emotions warred in his eyes. Emotions that couldn't make a dent in the porcelain perfection of his stony face. He wanted to say yes. He wanted to say it was us. His heart was in it. His head just needed to catch up.

Maybe it would. Maybe it wouldn't. If he couldn't let go of his fear, then there'd never be an us.

"I'll wait for you, Beckett. But I won't wait forever," I told him before I picked myself and my books up, and walked away.

This time, he didn't call after me. This time, he didn't try exerting the tour de force of his personality to get the way he was so used to getting. He just let me walk away.

I could have seen it as an omen. I could have thought that was his way of telling me he couldn't go all in, he never would. But I wouldn't give up hope yet. He still had time to make the first right choice he'd ever make.

While we all sat at lunch, hundreds of notification tones went off all around the room. Even mine, Sam's and Abby's phones went off with the rest of them.

We all looked at each other in surprise as we pulled our phones out. I was just opening my Rivermont app when Sam smacked my phone out of my hand and snatched it off the table. Even the look of shock on his face, like the action itself had surprised him, didn't assuage me.

"What?" I asked him, annoyed.

"You do *not* want to know," he told me softly.

I frowned. "What do you mean, I don't want to know?"

"Exactly what it sounds like."

My frown deepened. "Abby, let me see your phone?" I asked.

She took a deep breath and she and Sam played a game of 'eyeball whispers', but she turned her phone screen to face me. Sam obviously disagreed and I could see why when I saw the picture on the student message board.

My stomach dropped out of me, and I felt all the blood in my body try to follow.

"What?" I whispered.

Because there was me. Waist up. Flushed. Smiling like an idiot. In nothing but my bra with my hair all messed across someone's pillows so everyone would know – or take a very educated guess – about what I'd just been doing. Across the picture were the words 'the face of a delusional pleb' and then the devil horn emoji followed by a crown. It didn't say who'd posted it, but it was clear by the caption that they wanted you to think a Royal had sent it, intimating that a Royal had just had me and had just been playing me.

The funny thing was that I knew who'd posted that.

At least, I knew which Royal had just had me before that picture was taken. I knew which of them had made me feel that giddy and satisfied. And that picture had been on his phone.

It also didn't take a genius to know that the rest of the school would probably know who it was as well.

Everything in me crumbled and I felt Abby take my hand.

Was this why he hadn't answered me when I gave him the ultimatum?

Was *this* his answer?

And why did I look so damn happy?

My face in that picture gave so much away.

It was the face of the ridiculously infatuated.

Well, I was feeling ever so slightly less infatuated than I had been previously.

I looked at the Royals' table, but he wasn't there. Was it coincidence or was there a part of him who didn't want to face me with his answer? And, if it was the latter, did I take comfort from that, or did it just mean I was beneath his notice. He didn't need to see me crushed because all that mattered was that I was.

As I dropped my eyes again, they roved over Fox. His face told me everything I needed to know about what had just happened; I'd been put in my place and there I would remain. I was sure his smirk also heavily suggested that, had I chosen him, this wouldn't have happened. I didn't believe it for a second. All the Royals were the same. I knew that, even if I'd temporarily let myself forget.

A sentiment that was strongly echoed on Regina's and Phoenix's faces, but without any of the sympathy.

"Edie?" Sam said slowly and I shook my head and finally pulled my eyes from the Royals' table and Fox's victory.

"Hm?"

Everyone in the dining hall was looking at us. They were all talking about the picture, and they weren't really all that concerned with the volume of their voices. But I'd pretend they weren't. I'd been mostly invisible before Fox and Beckett started their pissing match over me, it would only be a matter of time before I was invisible again.

What was that quote? It's better to have loved and lost than never loved at all?

I wasn't so sure about that. But there was a part of me that didn't regret Beckett for a second. I might have loved hating him, but I hadn't hated loving him. And, in the privacy of my own head, I was happy to admit that I'd fallen in love with Beckett. Despite everything. I'd known it couldn't last, I'd known it was going to end sometime. Logically, there couldn't have been any other ending than an end. And him being not only *a* Royal but the *King*, I think I'd always expected something like this. No matter what we both thought or felt when it was just the two of us.

It didn't feel like a surprise.

If anything, it felt like a confirmation of the fact he'd fallen for me, too. Not that that was any consolation really.

"Edie?" Sam said again, with a hand on my arm, and I shook my head and finally pulled my eyes from the Royals' table and Fox's victory.

"Hm?"

"Are you okay?" Abby asked.

I took a deep breath.

Weirdly, I was. The whole thing had been so much like a surreal dream that it only now felt like reality had righted and all was right with the world. I was disappointed and I could feel anger threatening, but I was okay. I would be okay.

I nodded and gave them a small smile. "Yeah. Yeah. I mean... Yes."

Abby and Sam shared a glance.

"Are you sure?" Abby asked as Sam took my hand.

I nodded again. "Never let them see you cry, right?" I said.

Sam leant into me. "Shall we run away and have a cry?" he asked.

I managed a weak laugh. "No. Everyone in here will report back to him. I won't give him the satisfaction of walking out. He– They can't think they got to me."

"Okay."

So, we sat and ate lunch and pretended that I wasn't the talk at every table in there. I put on my bravest face, careful not to look too chipper to ruin the façade, and told myself I really shouldn't have expected anything else.

I wasn't planning to let Beckett get away with it, but my method of interrogation was yet to come to me. I thought about texting him, but I wanted to see his face when I accused him. I thought about going to find him, but I didn't think my heart could handle seeing him in person.

Fate decided for me in the end. I ran into Beckett on my way back from the bathroom in the next lesson.

"Eden," he said, his voice stilted and cold, even for him. It was the kind of voice you use when you would otherwise completely ignore a person but past situations made that somewhat impossible.

I felt white-hot anger. "Did you leak the photo?" just popped out of me.

His face hardened and I was sure he was about to walk away. He made to take a step and I followed him.

"I'm only going to ask you once more, Beckett. Did you leak that photo?"

He gave nothing away. Visually. "Consider it a reminder of what happens when you deal with Royals."

It wasn't a yes, but it was definitely not a no. "Why? After…everything. Why would you do that?" I could guess, but I wanted to know if he'd admit it.

He stepped up to me, baring down on me with all the intimidation and callousness he could. "I will not be seen as weak, Eden. I will not lose my crown to some upstart idiot who thinks Beckett Maxwell has a shred of *softness* in him. I get what I want and crush anything in my path to get it."

Yep. That's what I'd thought.

I wouldn't be intimidated by him. Not now. He could walk through school, life, whatever, browbeating everyone else into believing he was superior, but I saw it for the act it was. I always had. I just wasn't falling for it anymore. I'd spent enough time falling for Beckett Maxwell. If there was any part of him that could ever choose me over his lofty throne, then it was going to have to fall too. And there was such a damn long way to go, there was every chance that, if it finally did, it could get lost along the way.

I looked him over, feeling tears pricking my eyes. I wasn't embarrassed. I wasn't angry anymore. I wasn't hurt he was throwing me away. I was sad that all that potential – his potential – had just been erased as easily as that. I was sad that he was so scared of being anything other than what his world had made him – that he didn't know how to be anything else – that he had to lash out and push away anyone at risk of getting so close to jeopardise that.

*'I would die before I let any harm come to you.'*

Yep, he'd crush anything in his path to get what he wanted. Even himself.

"Did you think you were special?" he continued when I didn't say anything. "Did you really think you could mean anything more to me than a means to an end? A pawn in the game of Kings? You're not even a pleb, Eden. You're nothing." His voice was ice, and it shattered my heart into a thousand pieces.

"I'm not nothing, Beckett," I told him, embarrassed now but only by the weakness of my voice. "You might have the rest of the school fooled, but the fact you're even doing this tells me I'm not nothing. And even if you weren't, I was someone before you decided I was yours. I'm still someone now you're over it."

Beckett snarled, but said nothing.

"Funny. You told me you'd never be over it. You told me we were forever inextricably linked." I gave a pathetic little shrug. "And here I thought you never lied."

"You are still mine, Eden," he said gruffly. "You will always be mine."

I nodded, thinking that sounded about right; the Royals getting everything they wanted while no one else got anything. "So, I'm yours but I mean nothing to you?"

He took a second long to retort than I'd expected. "I own the bitch, but she need mean nothing more to me than the next litter of pups I can sell to the highest bidder."

I knew why he'd picked the analogy, though it amused me to think that the Maxwells were into something as mundane as dog breeding. And part of me was flattered that he was implying any child I gave him would be highly sought as a means to their father's wealth, power, and status. But both of us knew any bitch could give him that.

"Then you can hardly be surprised when she turns around and bites the hand that feeds her," I told him, hoping my return analogy made any sense and packed any punch.

The disdain in his eyes as he looked me over rivalled that which had only ever been given to me once before; by his father. The tiny spark of hope in me wanted to think he hated himself for doing this, but I wasn't sure he was capable of separating his instincts of self-preservation from any impact it might have on me.

Because Beckett had made his choice, and he'd chosen his crown.

I wasn't going to take it personally. Beckett's baggage would have filled an entire passenger plane manifest's allocation, and then some. I wasn't going to beat myself up for not being able to change him. It wasn't my job. He had to change. No, not change. I loved him as the person he was. But he had to change his thinking. His knee-jerk reactions. And if he didn't want to change those so we could work, then he wasn't worth it.

And maybe it if I told myself enough, I'd believe it.

Beckett didn't say anything more so, before I did anything quite so tragic as crying in front of him, I started backing away.

"I hope this gets you what you need, Beckett," I told him, sincerely, as my voice cracked. "But you've given me my answer. We're done. I'm not waiting any longer for a man who'll never choose me."

I wasn't sure if he was going to surge forward and hit me or kiss me. Everything told me, even now, that Beckett would never raise a hand to me. And if he kissed me now, I'd lose all strength to ever walk away from him.

I took another step backwards, then wrapped my arms around myself and hurried off.

Tear were hot in my eyes and heavy in my throat. I swallowed past the lump and took a deep breath. I wasn't going to cry over Beckett Maxwell. He wasn't worth it, and I was worth more than that.

Still, I must have looked forlorn enough when Mum opened her front door and found me on the front steps of the townhouse.

"Edie, you should be in–" A pause as she saw my face. "What did he do?" she asked, and I guessed she'd felt the disappointment of the end of a relationship at least once. Stood to reason that she could recognise it.

"Turns out there wasn't more to Beckett than you thought."

Mum nodded and bundled me into her arms. "I'm sorry, sweetie."

I buried my face in the comfort of her shoulder and shrugged. "I think I knew it. Deep down. I'm not even sure it was nice while it lasted, but I don't think I regret it."

"Some of our biggest mistakes are the best times of our lives,"

Mum said, giving me a squeeze before she put me to arm's length.

I sniffed a watery laugh and managed a smile. "They really are."

"Ice cream and movie binge?" she asked, and I nodded.

"Yes, please."

I spent the night at Mum's, pretending I was fine. For the most part, I was.

The whole thing was disappointing, but still not a shock to me. Like I'd wished for more, but not truly believed it was possible. I hadn't had faith, but I'd had hope that I'd be enough for Beckett to choose me. I could only hope that, one day, someone came along who was enough so he didn't have to go through the rest of this life so alone. Or, worse, end up like his father.

The next morning, I woke up to the smell of Mum's famous omelette. I looked at the clock and was sure she should be at practice, so I hurried downstairs and found her in the kitchen still in her pyjamas and definitely not showered.

"What are you still doing here?" I asked her and she grinned at me.

"The Quin ladies are having a Saturday to themselves for once. I told Coach Clint he'd have to front practice this morning, and told Coach Andrews that you couldn't make the game this afternoon. We have the whole day to ourselves. I actually slept in, for the first time in about thirty years. This whole heartbreak thing might be good for us."

I smirked, but my reply was interrupted by a banging on Mum's front door, accompanied by a, "Coach! Eden?" in Jaeger's recognisable voice. "Quincy!"

Mum threw me a look and I shrugged. I followed her to the door and watched as she opened it. The minute it was unlocked, Jaeger was forcing himself through the door, yelling my name and throwing his head around in panic until his eyes landed on me. He looked white as a sheet.

"What in the hell, Richards?" Mum said.

He looked from me, to Mum, to me, to Mum, back to me. "I thought you were dead!" he accused.

"Drama much?" I scoffed. "What is with you Royals and thinking I'm dead?"

"Your mum's never missed practice. You've been missing. Beckett's… I'm not even going to get started on him. But you're okay?" he panted, taking a step towards me and holding my arms like he couldn't be sure I was actually real.

I nodded. "I'm fine. I'm spending the weekend with my mum. That's not illegal," I reminded him, pushing him off me and stepping back.

"She's entitled to some privacy after what you lot have put her through," Mum said pointedly, and Jaeger had the decency to look chastened. "How could you, Jaeger? How could he?"

He shook his head. "I don't know. I don't know what happened. Beckett won't talk to me. He took what was left over from the ANZAC bash into his room and locked the door. I figured he was safe enough in there. For now. And if he cuts himself on whatever he's smashed, he probably deserves it."

I shook my head. "I don't care, Jaeger."

"Please, Quincy," he begged. "Please care."

"He…" I looked at Mum, who suddenly pretended she wasn't listening and bustled to the kitchen, mumbling something incoherent. I turned back to Jaeger. "That photo was… It meant something. He knows that. And now the whole damned school knows that."

Jaeger huffed. "I don't know what happened with the picture. I don't know anything about it. He didn't say anything to me."

"That really doesn't change the fact he sent it to the whole school."

Jaeger looked like his mind was whirring at a dizzying speed. "Did he?"

I shrugged. "Who else would have? I told you before, it's not my fault he doesn't know how to deal with his feelings for me. But I'm done, Jaeger. It's one too many pushes. It's reached the point it's too hard. I deserve more than this."

Jaeger put his hand on the still open door. "I know," he said. He breathed out heavily and hung his head. "I know. Fuck. Fine." He took a breath in and stood up again. "I'll let you guys get back to it. Have a lovely weekend with your mum, Quincy."

Had his eyes not mirrored the sincerity in his tone, I'd have said that Jaeger Richards was full of shit. As it was, I knew he was full of shit, but I'd also learned these last few months that he was also a weirdly approachable and actually likable guy who seemed to legitimately care about me for some reason.

I could only nod and say, "I will, thanks."

He gave me a nod in return, patted the door, and jog back down the path. I watched him go. He shoved his hands in his pockets and looked like he was utterly conflicted about the whole thing. He reminded me of that guy from *Love, Actually* after he leaves the girl in his studio and he can't decide if he should go back or not. Jaeger had the same kind of nervous, uncertain energy.

But it wasn't my problem. Whatever the Royals were going through, it had been made painfully clear that I was on the out again. Which is exactly where I'd once wished they'd left me. So I wasn't going to waste my precious energy on worrying about it.

Instead, I closed the door and texted Abby and Sam to invite them over to hang out with me and Mum in our pyjamas all day.

# CHAPTER TWENTY-FOUR

The week after the photo leak and Beckett's denouncement, life seemed to almost go back to the way it was the year before.

Almost.

Beckett was back to pretending I didn't exist again.

I was still in a constant state of half-hoping that he'd just look at me once, even if it was a total accident, and even if I totally regretted it moments later.

Sam and I were still teased and bullied and belittled for just walking down a corridor.

The things that had changed were that now Abby was subject to Sam's and my torment, Hunter was spared it in his continued absence, and it wasn't just Royals who were dishing it out.

It seemed every Tom, Dick and Harry in the damned school had decided that I was fair game now that the King was done with me. Every one but Fox.

I was used to enduring my (un)fair share of people making rude comments, or pushing me as they walked past, or looking at me and whispering or laughing at me.

What I wasn't used to was the physical aspect. Fox and Beckett had been all about getting in my physical space, but Beckett hadn't been unwelcome and Fox had been short-lived if intense.

The next week wasn't.

Guys took a pass at me. They dared to touch me. Crowd me. And I didn't know how to deal with it. Jaeger was getting damned sick of it, but he didn't hover nearly as much as he used to.

So it was just damned luck when one of the guys who dared touch me was a swimmer, and he so dared after a swim meet at Rivermont late that week.

The guy pushed me up against the wall. "I hear you're first come, first served now," he said in my ear.

Before I could do anything in response, Jaeger was there and pulling him off me.

"Jaeger," Preston said from a good few steps away, firmly but with that quiet authority.

Jaeger stood between me and Preston and Rowan. He looked at Preston, and Preston shook his head. He looked at Rowan and I almost laughed at the idea that Jaeger was looking to Rowan to back up protecting a little pleb nobody like me.

"She's not our problem anymore," Rowan said and there was a tinge of something almost regretful to his sadistic glee.

It was enough to make my heart twitch uncomfortably, make me wonder for the briefest of nanoseconds if maybe I did have the power to make a dent on not just their King but all the Royals. But I pushed the feeling away, knowing it was ridiculous.

"How can you bastards just walk away?" Jaeger asked them. "Just sit back and let her be—"

"Like you did?" Rowan said evenly.

Jaeger took a step towards him, full of fury. "You know that wasn't my choice."

"No one's going to do her as badly as the little heir." Was that a tiny hint of reassurance in Preston's tone?

"So, you're just doing to stand back and–"

"Just leave it, Jaeger!" I snapped, shoving him hard. "Just leave me."

"Quincy, I just want to make sure you're okay."

I huffed. "You lost that right the day you made the bet with Fox."

"Quincy…" he breathed, like that had been the worst insult I could give.

I shook my head. "Give it up, Jaeger. None of you ever cared about me and it does us all a disservice to pretend otherwise."

"I care, Eden," he said. "Beckett–"

"Beckett made his choice," I said, the ice in my voice giving Beckett a run for its money.

Jaeger visibly quailed.

"I will not be a pawn," I told him. "I fight my own battles. Follow Rowan and Preston's lead. I'm not your problem anymore."

I walked away from them all and pretended I didn't hear the echoes of Rowan's empty slow clap follow me out.

The next time someone pushed me against a wall or got in my face, or just plain implied I was up for grabs by the general populace now, I was ready.

The next guy to insinuate he was going to get first dibs on the King's sloppy seconds got himself shoved none too gently, and also none too threateningly.

I improved quickly after that.

The next idiot got himself bitch slapped.

The next one got a knee to the crotch and went down like a satisfying sack of potatoes.

The one after than got a punch in the face, lost a tooth, and I fractured two knuckles doing it.

People were a little more wary about me after that. They looked at me in a similar manner they'd watch Regina or Phoenix pass. There was an awed caution like they knew just looking at me would get them stamped into the ground. Even with my hand in a splint, I knew I gave off an aura of 'mess with me and I'll mess with you worse'.

Which wasn't to say there weren't still people willing to try to break the Royals' sloppy seconds. But over the next few weeks, I went from physically standing up for myself to one look and no one even touched me. I didn't need to resort to hitting back. I took it graciously. I tried not to remember my conversation with Jaeger about how leaders walk away, that they used nothing but words and their own sense of superiority.

But that's what I did. And that's what I used.

Because I'd meant it when I'd told Jaeger that I would be no one's pawn. I wouldn't put up with the bullies anymore. I was done thinking that ignoring them would make them go away. Someone had to stand up and say it wasn't good enough.

And three weeks after Beckett's betrayal, I took my biggest shot yet. I didn't give a single shit that I was about to confront Rowan-goddamned-Finch and his terrifyingly cold almost-inhumanness. That was the level of arrogance and unbothered I'd risen to.

He had Bianca crowded against a locker and she was looking mighty daunted. So I stormed right over there and just grabbed his arm. He turned to me with utter fury on his face.

"Back off, Rowan," I told him.

Rowan looked me over. "I don't answer to you."

I drew myself up, in no way coming anywhere near his height or intimidation. "And yet, here I am, telling you to back the fuck off."

Bianca just looked at me like she was angry with me somehow.

"Leave me out of your power struggles, thanks," she huffed and

Rowan actually smirked like he'd won.

I frowned at him, totally unimpressed and dangerously lacking any fear of him or what he could do. Some days, it felt like I was numb. That was the only way I could explain how above it all I felt now. I had to be numb. Because I vividly remembered Fox scaring the shit out of me even when I was more scared of Rowan. And, now, Rowan didn't scare me at all. The cynic in me wondered if I'd decided that I'd been burnt too badly already; whatever the Royals threw at me next could hardly compare, so what did I care?

It was a dangerous attitude, but I was going to use it to my advantage.

I stepped up to Rowan. "I don't give a shit what your parents did to you when you were little, Finch," I said, my tone dead. "But I'm not giving you a free pass anymore."

He sniffed, almost bored, then bared down on me. "You think I give a fuck about your passes, pleb?" he hissed.

I actually felt myself smile at him. "You don't scare me, little rose."

Yeah, I knew how to work Google, and I'd discovered that a rowan tree was actually in the genus of the rose family. It didn't matter whether he understood the insult. I did, and I could feel superior in my knowledge it was a good burn.

We stared into each other's eyes for the space of a very tense few heart beats. I didn't understand or care what I saw in his, but I didn't feel any immediate danger to my person.

"It's almost a shame," he purred.

"All right," I said with a nod. "I'll rise to the bait. What's a shame?"

"That you waited until now to *really* make him suffer."

My heart stuttered, but I hid it well. "Then, he's the only one suffering now."

Amusement flashed in his eyes and he huffed what could almost be considered a laugh. "Well done," he said with an incline of his head. "Very few people surprise me. Even fewer manage not to disappoint me."

"You're labouring under the misapprehension that I care what you think of me," I reminded him.

He shook his head. "And yet, here I am, thinking it anyway." He looked at Bianca. "We'll finish this later."

"You–" I stared, but he interrupted.

"*You* are done flexing your authority for today, Miss Quin." He inclined his head again and stalked away.

I breathed out heavily once he was a fair distance away and turned a look of sympathetic relief on Bianca. It seemed she didn't feel the same way.

"I didn't ask for you 'help'," she snapped. "And I certainly don't want it."

I blinked. "But, I–"

"Thanks, but no thanks. Keep your revolution to yourself."

"They'll keep getting away with this unless we stand up to them!" I said vehemently.

She rolled her eyes. "Yeah. And we all saw what happened to you when you 'stood up to them'. Just keep me out of it."

"This is the problem–"

"No," she hissed. "It's your problem. I've got like a year until I'm eighteen and our of their lives for good, and I plan to keep it that way. The only way I'm going to do that is to stay off their radar. If that means taking their bullshit, fine."

"But, we don't have to. They're the minority. We can change things here."

"Says the person who has the luxury to stand up for what she believes. Some of us don't have that. Some of us have people relying on us whose lives depend on us not ruffling the shitty feathers of the likes of the Royals." She stepped up to me. "So, why don't *you* back the fuck off, Eden?"

She adjusted her backpack on her shoulder, then ducked away. The way she looked around, it was like she was expecting an attack or judgement or unwanted attention, or something, to come from any direction.

Everything in me itched to go after her. She looked so damned alone. But then, I'd already made a new friend that year – and lost one – I wasn't sure I was quite ready to shake things up in the group any further.

I went back to Sam and Abby.

"Did you just take on Rowan?" Abby whispered and I forgot about Bianca in the face of her amazement.

"Why, yes. I did. Someone had to."

"Who even are you?" Sam asked me, massive awe and pride in his voice.

"I don't even know anymore," I answered honestly, and I didn't completely hate it.

"Multiverse," he whispered conspiratorially.

"Multiverse," Abby echoed.

I laughed. "Sure. Multiverse."

But, as much as I laughed it off, I knew I was different now. The last four months had changed me more than any of the years before them. I would not go quietly into that good night. I was going to rage. Fucking rage.

# CHAPTER TWENTY-FIVE

Four weeks after Beckett's ultimate betrayal, a body crashed through my dorm door, and I looked up to see Jaeger uncharacteristically out of breath.

"He needs you," he panted. I didn't have to ask who he was talking about.

"Good for him," I said as I went back to my homework.

"No, Quincy," Jaeger said. "I mean, he needs you."

"Well, he had his chance and he fucked it."

"Eden." His voice was firm, unshakable but not raised.

I looked back to Jaeger and saw there was a hardness to him. It was like the hardness that Beckett always carried, but it was, unbelievably, darker. There was something going on that was honestly worrying Jaeger Richards.

"What?" I asked, my voice pathetically weak especially in comparison to Jaeger's.

"He's about to do something incredibly stupid. I need you to stop him." I could see – hear – the evidence of the years Jaeger and Beckett had spent side-by-side. Jaeger's voice was quiet in its power. It was stern and sent a shiver down my spine. It was the first time that Jaeger had the potential to scare me. I could certainly see how easily he could scare grown men.

"Then I'm calling in my favour, Jaeger," I told him. "The one you gave me for not telling Beckett you made an *IT Crowd* reference. I'm calling it. Leave me out of it."

He shook his head. "Quincy, I would give you any favour – I would kill for you if only you commanded it and consider it a good day out – but I won't give you this one. Ask anything else of me and it's yours. Favour or not. Let me owe you ten in return, but you need to do this. Only you can do this. You need to stop him."

"How could I stop him doing anything?" I scoffed, not wanting to acknowledge that it sounded important; stupid was never a word associated with Beckett.

"Because you have a power over him no one else does. You're the only one who can stop him killing his father!" Jaeger's voice was strangled in desperation and reality crashed around me.

There are those times when you know you're barely strong enough to save yourself. Then there are times when, despite that, you manage to find the strength to save someone else. I didn't know where that kind of strength came from. Most days, I couldn't fathom being able to find it for anyone. At that moment, regardless of where Beckett and I stood or what he'd done, that strength was there.

There was no other option. Literally. There was no question of whether I could be there for Beckett when he wasn't going to be there for himself. No option of what would happen – to Beckett, to me, to us – if I told Jaeger he could deal with it.

Just because Beckett had chosen his bed, didn't mean I had to lie in it, too. I was a decent human being, damn it. I prided myself on trying to be kind and thoughtful, of being there for my fellow beings.

"You honestly think he'd kill his own father?" I asked Jaeger.

"He'd kill himself if he were stronger."

I searched Jaeger's face.

There was no sign of his usual teasing. No hint of the jester. He had dark circles under his eyes like he hadn't been sleeping. His hair had slightly less structure to it than usual, like it would fall under the simplest pressure. As though it were mirroring his mental state.

I'd joked about how well anyone knew the real Becket Maxwell. Most days, it wasn't even a joke. But Jaeger knew murder and he knew Beckett. If he was honestly worried enough to come to me for help after what had happened, then the threat was real.

I was pulling on a jacket before I realised what I was doing.

"You'll come?" Jaeger breathed, his voice heavy with relief.

Of course, I would. I hated Beckett, but that didn't mean I didn't love him.

I nodded. "It doesn't mean I forgive him."

"No. I didn't expect it would." Jaeger ushered me out of the dorm and to his waiting car. Except, it wasn't his car. It was Beckett's.

As he tore out of the quad, the gravel kicking up behind us, I was glad he kept talking. It kept my mind off the possibility of imminent death.

"I've never seen him like this," Jaeger said.

"What? Drunk?" I doubted that.

Jaeger shook his silver head. "Ranting and railing about love not being weakness. Wanker brought my family into it. It was a whole mess."

"What's your family got to do with it?" I asked, not for the first time wondering why Beckett deferred to Jaeger in matters of the heart.

Jaeger shot me the ghost of a smile through the concern eating at him. "The Richards firmly believe that love is sacred. Love is to be cherished and protected at all costs. True love. None of this lusty obsession. We believe true love makes you stronger. A partner through life? How could that possibly make you weaker?" He scoffed. "It's the only thing I'm aware of that our old men disagree about. Murder. Money. Power. All good. Love? Pfft. Old Beckett Maxwell the third thinks women are only useful as punching bags and for childbearing."

Jaeger had gone and confirmed much of what I'd guessed the night I first met Beckett's father.

"He sounds as delightful as he looks. Am I meant to feel sorry for Beckett now?"

Jaeger threw me a look as he expertly drifted around a corner. "Are you telling me you don't?"

"Did you go to driving class as well as assassin class?" I asked, intending for it to be a joke.

"Driving course, yes. Assassin class isn't 'til next semester."

We sat in silence for a while, and I wondered how much of that last statement was true.

Finally, Jaeger spoke again. "None of us have it easy, Eden," he said softly. "Our parents put massive expectations on us. We grow up in hostile environments. We're taught to survive in an unforgiving world that is darker than any of us want you to know."

"Is this your character development? You realise your growth areas and work on becoming a better man?"

He laughed. "No. When it's my time, I'll fuck it up worse than Beckett has."

"Then what's the use in telling me? What's the point of hinting at motives for whatever's going on inside your heads? What is even the point of your discretion, Jaeger?"

"Because maybe that's what this story needs."

"Story? Like we're in the pages of some book. On the big screen? Shall I get some popcorn and re-watch my life implode?"

"Everyone has a story," he told me as we were waved through a giant set of gates. "You and Beckett, yours is in the same book, for want of another analogy."

He pulled up in front of a massive mini mansion that looked like the little castles you could find in Crafers.

Jaeger turned off the car and looked at me. "Some stories are easier than others," he said, like that explained it.

I looked up at the foreboding front doors. This wasn't the country house.

"And some," I said quietly as I followed him inside, "hurt more than others."

Jaeger touched a hand to my arm as he guided me inside. "See?" he asked gently. "You get it."

"Do I?" I asked as I heard the sound of something breaking, followed by muffled yelling.

As we got closer, I heard Beckett's angry voice through the door. "No. You will heed me–"

"Heed you?" I heard his father scoffed, and Jaeger threw me a look. "I've done nothing but heed you as you've pined away for that worthless girl. It is time to grow up, Beckett. Be a man."

"Eden is worth ten times our family fortune!" Beckett cried and Jaeger smiled at me encouragingly. I frowned at him.

"Don't let the other Royals hear you talking so, son. Their tolerance for weakness is only second to mine."

"Emotion isn't weakness," I heard Beckett say, but I wasn't sure how much he believed it.

Jaeger pushed open the door and we found Beckett holding one of the swords that probably usually lived in pride of place on the wall as he faced off with his father. I wasn't sure what he was planning to do with it but, if that was the method of patricide he'd chosen, I suspected Beckett Senior wasn't making it into the Headless Horsemen.

The father who was leaning against his desk and sipping a scotch as he scoffed, "Do not confuse love with lust, Beckett. You were raised better than that."

"I never mentioned love," was Beckett's too-fast response.

"What are you doing?" finally burst out of me as I finished taking the whole ridiculous scene in.

Beckett swayed and looked in our direction. He looked plastered. Like, I wasn't sure how he was still standing plastered. His clothes were crinkled and askew like he'd been in them for days. His jaw was covered in what counted more like a full beard than stubble. And his hair was sticking up all over the place like he kept running his hands through it in frustration. Which is exactly what he did as he saw me.

"Jaeger, what is this?" Beckett's father asked. The disdain in Beckett's voice had nothing on the disdain his father was capable of.

Jaeger looked between Beckett Senior and Junior like he wasn't sure what or how much to give away. "We're here to take you home, boss," Jaeger told Beckett.

"Before you do," Mr Maxwell said smoothly. "What perfect timing. Now she's here, what was it you were saying, Beckett?"

Beckett swallowed. "What?"

Mr Maxwell smirked, his eyes full of a dead sort of glee. "You want to put me in my place? Show me. Prove to me how *strong* you are."

"Why is she here?" Beckett asked Jaeger, his words slurred.

"Excuse me?" I spat. "What am I–? You ungrateful piece of shit!"

"You're so weak, you'd let this *girl* speak to you like that?" Mr Maxwell huffed.

"And you!" I turned to him and almost quailed under his stony gaze but held my own. Sort of. "Sir… You can shut up, sir. Please. This is between me and your son."

"You walk into my house uninvited, dare to interrupt a private conversation, and then command me to be quiet?" Mr Maxwell asked, his face like thunder.

"Yes. I do," I said, shakily. "I'm only here because, according to some people," I shot an accusing look at Jaeger, "I'm the only one who could stop your son doing something idiotic. But the only idiot here apparently is me."

Mr Maxwell nodded. "Finally, something we can agree on."

My eyes narrowed at him. "You are a horrible person and a worse parent."

"You've got a backbone on you, at least." There was something new and predatory in the way Mr Maxwell was suddenly looking at me and I didn't like it.

"What have you done, J?" Beckett asked Jaeger as he dropped onto the couch like his legs were done for the night.

"I'm saving your fucking arse, B," Jaeger answered, but whether Beckett heard him or not remained to be seen.

"And I'm obviously wasting my time," I said, turning to leave.

Mr Maxwell was clearly happy with that. "Good. People like you don't belong–" he started saying, but I turned back and held up a hand.

Yup. I held up a hand to Beckett Maxwell the third and shushed him.

"I'm sorry, sir, but no offence…" I paused. "Actually, whatever. If you take offence, whatever. But I could literally not care a single shit *less* about your money, your infamy, or your lifestyle. All of this?" I motioned the house. "This isn't attractive to me. In case it escaped your notice, I'm a girl. A woman. As such, to choose this –

to choose your son," the son I wouldn't look at, "would be choosing a life of being talked down to, belittled, questioned, ordered around, and locked up under the guise of protection." I took a breath, but no one cut in, so I continued. "I'm well aware I'd be expected to be nothing but a pretty accessory designed to flaunt power and wealth, and I don't know if you've noticed, but I'm kinda lacking the required equipment."

Here, I indicated to not just my face, but my whole person. It was a good time to be making the point because I was in my rattiest hoody, my old jeans, and scuffed Chucks. My hair was grimy with chlorine and pulled back in a messy bun. I looked not one bit like any sort of future Mrs Maxwell the fourth that their world expected, and I didn't care.

"Were I," I finished, "in a position to choose your son… Firstly, you needn't worry, because he would never be interested in the very little that I have to offer people like you. And secondly, if he was and I accepted that, you can damn well believe that I'd know exactly what you think about people like me and would give absolutely zero shits. Furthermore, if I, for one second, lost all common sense and thought there was a chance in hell that I loved your son, you can best believe I'd do it no matter what you thought about it!"

*Jesus Christ. We are doing Austen...*

Mr Maxwell looked me over for a short moment. Finally, his eyes slid to Jaeger, and he gave one single nod.

Jaeger returned the nod. "Thank you, sir."

"Dismissed?" I muttered, understanding the men's exchange for what it was. "Brilliant. No thanks for your time, *sir*." I waved my hand at him in a mockery of a salute, gave him a single nod of my own and stalked out.

Jaeger was hot on my heels, dragging a very drunk Beckett along with him.

"Did you see that?" Jaeger breathed.

"Did I see the mighty lion be not a single whit bothered by the tiniest thorn in its paw?" I asked sarcastically. "Why, yes. I did."

"No," he said. "You got approval from Daddy Maxwell."

I scoffed. "Ya-huh. No. Of course, I did. Because Eden Quin, what? Impressed a middle-aged, obscenely rich man who has no reason to care at all what a nobody like me has to say?"

"He's got one reason," Jaeger said, getting a better hold on Beckett, who had basically passed out at this point.

I waved my hand pitifully in Beckett's direction. "Yeah. I choose the time he wouldn't remember as the time to show my spine."

"He knows you've got a spine, Eden."

"Sure, he does."

"Why do you think he fell for you in the first place?"

"Because I was the first person in his existence who said no?"

Jaeger snorted a rough laugh. "May have been the second reason."

I helped Jaeger get Beckett into the back seat, then we were tearing out of the Maxwell grounds and heading back to school.

"Beckett knows who you are," Jaeger continued. "That's why he loves you."

I told myself my heart wasn't breaking.

I wanted to say that was great. I wanted to say I'd stay with Beckett until he was sober, then we could talk and put all this behind us. But I wasn't going to be weak about him anymore. I couldn't. Beckett had made his choice and getting drunk and informing his father that I was worth ten times their family's fortune wasn't going to change what he'd said.

"If Beckett's got something to tell me, then he can tell me

himself," I told Jaeger. "No more middlemen or guard dogs or mess makers doing his dirty work for him."

"There are a few broken bones that prove Beckett's willing to get his hands dirty for you, Eden," he reminded me, and I guessed he was talking about Hunter.

"Breaking bones is easy. For you lot at least." I sighed. "If Beckett really wants to claim me, then he's got to do more than flex his dominance and beat his chest. He threw me away, Jaeger. In front of the whole school. Everyone else in his life might let him get away with that shit, but I won't. I stopped caring about how he treated other people because of the way he was starting to treat me. Then he broke my heart. I don't think I'm worth ten times the Maxwell fortune, Jaeger, but I am worth more than that."

"I'm taking notes," Jaeger said.

"Does it matter?" I sighed.

Jaeger nodded. "It matters. I'll pass on the message."

I wanted to be as positive as he was about it. Now that the threat of Beckett killing his dad had passed, it seemed Jaeger was returning to his usual self. It wasn't a complete comfort, but it did make me feel a little better about the absolute shit my life had suddenly become.

# CHAPTER TWENTY-SIX

Sam had spent hours telling me I'd done the right thing.

Abby had spent hours telling me I'd done the right thing.

Jaeger had even assured me I'd done the right thing.

So why in the hell did it feel like I'd done the wrong thing?

I wasn't even sure what the thing was that had been wrong.

Going to Beckett in the first place?

Not staying with him until he sobered up?

I think I'd managed about two hours of sleep the night before. And I was feeling it. So I was not prepared for what was waiting for me.

As I walked into the dining room for breakfast the next morning, my progress was halted because suddenly a bruised and broken Fox Maddox was thrown at my feet by Beckett, blood streaming down his face. I'd have called it a big romantic gesture, had the King of Rivermont's face not suggested he could have been doing something so mundane as merely watching Jaeger effortlessly win yet *another* swim meet.

The rest of Beckett looked worse for wear. I didn't doubt the hangover was real after the night before. His stubble was still thicker than usual, his hair was dishevelled, his clothes looked more like Jaeger's. He looked tired and annoyed and probably had a headache. It didn't stop him being utterly lickable and fiendishly delicious. Annoyingly.

"Apologise," Beckett growled at Fox, and I noticed that his knuckles looked worse than they had the day before. Not that I'd been keeping tabs on the state of his hands. Because that would be sad.

Fox looked up at me and I was sure there was venom in his eyes. "I'm sorry, Eden."

I frowned, wondering what, of all the things Fox had done to me, he was supposed to be apologising for now. "What for?"

Beckett hauled Fox off the floor none too gently. "Properly."

Fox sighed. "I stole that photo off Beckett's phone and leaked it to the school. Please accept my apology. I'm sorry it hurt you and I'm sorry you thought Beckett did it."

My eyes darted to Beckett, but his face was unreadable. It wasn't just the fact that the photo had come from Beckett's phone that had made me think he did it.

"Thank you, Fox. I'll take your apology under advisement."

Beckett threw Fox to the side and the younger boy scurried away, clearly not willing to risk Beckett turning around and making him apologise some more. "Well?" Beckett asked me.

I believed Fox totally capable of such a stunt. I less believed that Beckett's phone was hackable by the likes of Fox Maddox. This could easily have been some plot on Beckett's behalf. String me along some more by making Fox take the fall and then just throw me away again later. Then again, if he wanted to make amends, nothing less than a very public grovel was going to even compete after the very public denouncement. Either way, I wasn't going to let him get away with either option so easily.

"Well, what?" I replied, keenly aware that the better part of the whole school had eyes on us, and the rest were no doubt being kept in the loop.

"Fox was the one who leaked the photo."

I shrugged. "So he says."

Beckett looked like he was about to lose his patience. "So?"

"So, what?"

"It wasn't me."

I nodded. "Okay."

He took a step towards me, a frown marring his features. "Eden…" he said quietly. It was a warning, a threat. It was the tone he used when suggesting there would be dire consequences for disobeying him, and he would really rather be spared the bother.

Would he ever learn? "If you think that changes anything, Beckett, you're a bigger idiot than I thought you were."

And I turned on my heel and walked back out again. I walked away from Beckett-fucking-Maxwell in front of practically everyone in the school. I recognised a smattering of applause start to trickle slowly through the room behind me and I felt a smile tugging on my lips, even if I was feeling a little sore in my heart.

"Eden!" Beckett yelled after me.

Actually yelled, then the applause was drowned out by surprised gasps and suddenly, a hand wrapped around my arm and Beckett was turning me to face him. Beckett-fucking-Maxwell had run after me. The King of Rivermont Academy had chased me. In front of most everyone at the school. I was feeling far more confused in my heart, but still wary.

"Eden," he pled. "Don't do this."

"Don't do what?" I challenged him.

"Don't walk away from me." In a first for Beckett, his usual bark of order was marred by pleading. Like he knew he couldn't demand anything from me, but his natural persona couldn't help it.

"Or what?" I asked sarcastically. "You'll make my life a living hell? You'll ignore me and pretend I don't exist? You'll have your cronies tease and bully me every waking moment of the day? Newsflash, Beckett, you've done that to me since my first day at Rivermont."

"I…" He paused. "I don't know how to deal with my feelings for you, Eden," he said, his voice full of meaning. I remembered the conversation and I was trying not to be impressed that he was voicing aloud his foibles, even if he was quoting me.

"So, what? You thought if you even just looked at me once in the last four years that you'd be overcome by passion and desire and not be able to control yourself?"

"Yes," was not the answer I was expecting.

I blinked. "What?"

He sighed. "Jaeger told me what you said to my father."

Oh, shit. "I didn't–"

He shook his head and took a step towards me. Warmth and tenderness flooded his eyes and I tried to school my heart against it. He touched his hand to my cheek. "I didn't think anything could make me love you more than I already did."

I was floored. Actually floored.

So were the people who were passing us.

Beckett had made a lot of noise about who I belonged to. He'd danced around his feelings for me with some pretty – and some not so pretty – words. But not once had he outright said he loved me. Not without a bunch of insinuation and interpreting required on my part.

"You love me?"

"Of course, I love you," he said, as though the alternative just wasn't a possibility. "How do you not know that?"

I glared at him. "Seriously?" I asked, taking a step away from him. "After everything, you actually think it's a given? You're going to act like *I'm* the idiot for not knowing?"

"Eden–"

"You don't just get to 'Eden' me and think that actually says anything. I'm going to ask you again, Beckett, do you know what you want?"

"I want you."

"That's not news. You've spent the better part of four months telling anyone who'll listen that I'm yours. Better question: can you let go of your fear to let there be a real us?"

He blinked like he hadn't been expecting that.

"Don't pretend you don't know what I'm talking about," I told him sternly. "Your crown. Your position. Your reputation. It's all meant more to you than me. Can you tell me honestly that you can put all that aside for me, for us?"

"I'm Beckett-fucking-Maxwell. I get what I want, and I'm having it all."

I scoffed. "You certainly haven't thought so before now. What's changed?"

"Nothing."

"What?"

His jaw clenched. "I let you think it was me," he said stiltedly. "I thought it was better for you. I thought I wasn't strong enough to protect you from our world and the best thing for you was to let you go. If you went back to hating me, it would make it all that much easier. Once again, I made a glaring error in the calculation of my life."

"Oh, really," I said sarcastically. "And what was that?"

"You."

I rolled my eyes. "Again. How original."

"I didn't count on you, Eden. I refused to see that you were – are – strong enough to survive our world. You don't need my protection.

349

You have all the protection I can grant you, but you stood up to my father and walked away with his respect. Respect he doesn't even afford his own son and heir.

"You might not need me, but I need you. I don't want or need to be a better man, but I do want to be the man I am when I'm with you. You let me have it all, Eden, and I want to give you everything in return."

"Everything is an awful lot to promise, Beckett. Are you including the bad in with the good?"

He nodded. "That's how it works. Or so Jaeger tells me."

"You're taking advice on love from Jaeger?" was the first thing that came out of my mouth.

Beckett shrugged. "I don't know anyone who knows love like the Richardses."

I looked him over. I so badly wanted to believe him. Wanted to believe that he was all in now. It might not have been a choice between me and his crown anymore, but I was a choice and he'd made it. Finally.

"How do I know you're not just going to turn around and act like a dick again the next time you don't know how to deal with your feelings for me?"

"I have Jaeger's promise to beat me into the ground if I do."

"You shouldn't need someone else to keep you honest, Beckett. Not if you really love me."

Beckett swallowed hard. I saw it. But he didn't look around nervously or seem to need to think about what to say. "This is new to me, Eden. All my life, I've been taught that love is weakness. Emotions are weakness. I would be cut or bruised, broken or locked up every time I showed one. It was quite painfully beaten out of me. I know people say I'm quite literally heartless, but you make my heart beat. You make a lifetime's worth of conditioning mean absolutely nothing. It doesn't mean I'm not going to fuck it up while I find my feet, while the conditioning fights back, and I'm man enough to ask for help when I know I need it. I will do right by you, Eden. One way or another."

"I can't just… forgive and forget everything," I said, and he nodded.

"I don't expect you to. Not straight away, and maybe not ever."

"Then what do you want? What are you asking?"

"I'm asking for the chance to show you what you mean to me. Really show you. Give me the time to learn to not fuck it up. *Help* me learn. Please."

I looked him over like I needed a second to think about it.

But I didn't need any time to think about it. I could have told him that he could go off and do the hard work, and come back to me when he was ready and done. Logically, it wasn't my job to make him dateable. But I didn't want to wait until he'd fulfilled his potential, I wanted to watch him grow into it. I *wanted* to help him, to be with him and see him putting in the effort.

He was already one step towards proving he was trying to do this right. He was giving me a choice. He was asking, with hope but without the expectation that I'd just do as I was told.

So, my answer could only be one thing.

"I'll give you the time, Beckett," I told him sternly. "The chance. I'm not saying 'one more fuck up and it's done', but I also can't promise you more than one chance. You might be fighting to prove yourself to me until the day you die."

"Gladly."

"I expect monogamy. I expect the words 'girlfriend' and 'boyfriend' to apply to us more than once and despite any teasing they might bring. I expect you to take criticism if it's offered. And I expect you to own up and face the consequences if you do fuck up again."

He nodded. "Done."

"I also expect the same of me in return–"

"You have nothing to prove, Eden."

"Relationships are give and take, Beckett. We grow together or not at all."

He nodded. "Then we grow together."

I gave him a smile. "Okay, then."

"If I asked you to sit with me, what would you say?"

"Why don't you ask and find out?"

A bright glow of humour lit his eyes. "Will you sit with me?"

I started to nod my head, then shook it. "No. I'm not a Royal."

"You still not making things easy for me, huh?"

"Always."

He inclined his head. "Can I sit with you, then?"

"Will the rest of the Royals join us?"

"No more than Jaeger, Preston and Rowan."

I pretended to think about it, then held my hand for his. "Yeah. I think that we can make that work."

Ignoring my hand, Beckett dragged me into his arms and kissed me. I melted against him. God, how I'd missed him. His touch. His presence. The safety he made me feel. Only after he'd given me a kiss to remind me exactly what this thing between us was, did he pull away and take my hand.

"All hail the Queen of Rivermont," Jaeger crowed as we walked back into the dining hall, and the room answered, "Long live the Queen," like it wasn't actually a joke.

I threw him an annoyed look as Beckett put his arm around me.

"You'll have to get used to it, baby," he said quietly.

"We don't make the rules," Jaeger added as he fell into step with us.

"You literally make the rules," I reminded him.

He shrugged. "Not this one. You're the king's lady, ergo you're the queen."

I rolled my eyes. "Being Beckett's girlfriend does not a queen make. Look at me. Am I really queen material? I don't want to be your queen, Jaeger."

He shrugged. "All right, then." Then crowed, "All hail the Un-Queen," to the room at large with a mischievously cocky wink.

"Long live the Un-Queen," was the chorus that followed as Preston and Rowan stepped into place behind us, and I knew any further protests on my part would go ignored.

I wasn't going to condone their behaviour. I'd fight it and use my position to do so. The only way this institution had any chance of toppling was from the inside. And if it wasn't me, then I'd have to make sure it was the next generation.

"So, do you guys sit here now?" Sam asked as we all sat down, sharing a cheeky smirk with Jaeger.

"Where she goes, I go," was Jaeger's response.

# CHAPTER TWENTY-SEVEN

The next week after Beckett's grand declaration, things looked a little dicey, but he stuck by me just like he said he would.

After hearing him be so emotional, there were those in the school who tried their luck with him. But he proved that he could love me unconditionally and still rule Rivermont with a fist of iron and a heart of ice-cold stone. Beckett hadn't changed for loving me, but I knew he did love me.

I had the guy who picked me up and swung me around in the middle of the dining hall on those rare occasions we didn't walk in together. But, I also had the guy who effortlessly cast people to their knees if he thought they needed a reminder of where they belonged.

Fox wasn't one of those. He bowed his deference from the moment Jaeger declared me the Un-Queen. Which, annoyingly, was apparently my new title. Or nickname. Jaeger took pleasure in using it as both.

My rise to the previously unattainable status of Queen of Rivermont Academy had made that month of me defending myself and standing up for the little guy somewhat futile. The system was the epitome of broken. Everyone acted like my defiance was proof that I belonged at the top of the hierarchy. That everyone had been wrong about my place being the bottom or that I was fair game. They said I was worthy of the crown, of the King, of everything that would bring me.

It annoyed me.

It also amused me.

The lengths these people went to in order to justify their existence.

The further lengths they went to in order to please those they followed.

In reality, they all knew I didn't really belong. They all whispered about me behind my back. Behind Beckett's back. But to our faces, it was all smiles and supplication.

To say Mum was hesitant about the whole thing was an understatement. As faculty, she was privy to more knowledge and rumours than I would have liked. But, as always, she tried to put the majority of them aside until and when I was ready to talk about them.

And my version of talking about them was taking Beckett over to her townhouse for dinner that next week.

"So, it's officially official, then?" Mum asked us as we sat down to eat.

Beckett nodded. "It is."

"And the Fox thing?"

"Done."

She nodded. "Okay. But," she pointed her fork at him, "you hurt her again and I don't care what your family does for money. You hear me?"

Beckett tried to hide his smile. "I hear you, Coach Quin."

Mum rolled her eyes like she was telling herself she was making the right call. "Call me Everly," she said before picking up her wine glass and draining it.

He inclined his head. "Everly."

"How advisable is it for me to ask you what you plan to do when you leave school, Beckett?" Mum asked.

"Depends how much stock you hold in plausible deniability."

"At least you're honest."

"This isn't going to work without a certain level of honesty," Beckett admitted.

"No, I suppose not." She blew out heavily as she looked between us. "Edie, you're dating a mobster," she chuckled like we all had to address the elephant in the room, as she sat back.

I nodded. "Uh. Yeah. Yeah, I guess I am."

"Is that going to be a problem, Everly?" Beckett asked.

"Jesus," Mum breathed. "What a question. Just promise me that you'll keep her safe."

"Always," he promised. "Your daughter is my priority now."

I saw it in Mum's eyes. That was the exact moment that she warmed up to him. To the idea that there was a chance that, one day, he might be her son-in-law. "And also promise you'll keep yourself safe. I don't need you dying on us, okay?"

Beckett did smile now. "I'll do my best. Jaeger and Rowan are exceptionally good at their jobs already. They'll only get better with time."

"And does Edie get her own bodyguard?" Mum joked, pouring herself more wine.

"Do you want her to have one?" Beckett asked.

"I don't need a bodyguard," I said quickly.

"*Can* she have one, though?" Mum asked.

Beckett looked at me and I gave him a look like he'd better not dare. I knew it was yet another futile protest.

"It will be arranged," Beckett told my mum.

Something in her relaxed visibly and I thought that, at least on paper, maybe it wasn't a bad idea. I still wasn't sure exactly how much danger Beckett's world possessed. I hadn't really seen all that much of it. I guessed I'd know sooner or later.

****

So, dinner with my parent had gone down a freaking treat. Dinner, as it were, with Beckett's still loomed large. And what did Beckett Maxwell Senior decide for the official meet and greet as Beckett's girlfriend?

Rowan's dad's wedding. Yep. Mr Maxwell was so goddamned busy and important that he couldn't spare a single cup of tea to sit down with me. Instead, I had to kill two birds with one stone and be Beckett's date to what promised to be an epic social event in their calendar. It was gearing up to be so epic both Rowan and Bianca had been pulled from school in the week leading up to it.

Which is why Beckett and I were dressed to the proverbial nines and sitting in the back of one of the fancy Maxwell limousines.

"Are you ready?" Beckett asked me, and I know I visibly quailed.

I took a deep breath and looked out the window of the limo. "Not really. I feel…naked."

"I wish you were."

I looked back to him. "I'm serious, Beckett. This is hands-down the most terrifying thing I've ever done. And I said no to you!"

He pulled me into his lap and held me tightly. "You are mine, Eden Quin," he said, but it wasn't an order now, it was a reminder. "I will always keep you safe. You belong at my side. Let no one tell you otherwise." His words were stern, but the rest of him was relaxed and soft around me.

357

"That's easy for you to say. You've been superior your whole life."

Beckett ran his fingers up my naked back and brushed his lips over my jaw as he said, "And I will spend the rest of yours ensuring you know you are."

Flutters exploded in my chest, and I saw the warmth in the depths of his brown eyes. "The rest of my life?" I challenged.

He nodded, the motion making his nose trail over mine. "The rest of your life," he said against my lips. "You will be mine and I will be yours."

I fought a smile. "Do weddings make you mushy, Beckett?" I teased.

I saw the humour light in his eyes. "You make me mushy, Eden." He sounded like he wasn't pleased about that, but also couldn't help being very pleased indeed.

"Should I be wary of catching the bouquet?" I smirked.

I felt his lips tip in that sexy half-smirk. "Do what you like. You will wear my ring either way."

"Is this you proposing?"

"Would you say yes if I was?"

*Yes!* I mean, "Why don't you ask and find out?"

He opened his mouth and I was sure he was going to say his usual line, but then he closed it, smiled, and said, "No, but it is me assuring you that I will."

My whole body vibrated. I was torn between feeling like I wanted him to do it right then and also never. "When?" I tried to act nonchalant and failed spectacularly.

"When you're ready."

"What about when *you're* ready?"

"Then this would be me proposing."

A thrill ran through me, and I quickly tallied up the pros and cons of having a quickie before we got out of the limo. But with my dress, it would be less a quickie and more just an awkie.

"You want me to marry you?" I asked him.

"I want to marry you. When you're ready."

"What if I'm never ready?" I joked, trying – and a little failing – to remind myself I wasn't actually ready now.

"You'll be ready," he told me, in the same sort of voice he'd first started trying to order me around in. "No one says no to me."

I bit my lip before I replied coquettishly, "I do."

I was very proud of myself, because it worked on so many levels. And I was even more proud when Beckett broke out in a wide grin.

"Pleased with that one, are you?" he asked.

I could feel my eyes shining with humour and happiness as I saw it mirrored in his. "Very."

He wrapped his arms around me. "You will pay for that sass later," he promised in a dark voice, and my clit throbbed.

"I look forward to it," I told him.

He crushed his lips to mine, and it was beyond me how I'd managed to resist him for so long. I still wasn't entirely decided that loving him was a good idea, but I was powerless to it. Time would tell if Beckett Maxwell proved himself unquestionably worth of me, but I would give him a fighting chance to do so. And, two weeks in, he was doing his damnedest.

This Beckett would have assured his crown the moment he first felt me up in the library. This Beckett made my heart melt, and my head imagine white dresses. This Beckett made me absolutely sure than love could blossom between us, because it already had. This Beckett even had me thinking our relationship could be built on trust and laughter as well as raw sexual energy.

Beckett finally pulled away from me, and I was more than a little disappointed. "You're the one who doesn't want to ruin your look," he reminded me with a cocky smirk.

"It'd take you about five seconds to fix your suit and wipe off any rogue lipstick. Once I'm mussed, that is it."

He inclined his head. "I wouldn't dare disagree with you, darling."

I shook my head and tried not to smile at his cheek. "Don't sass *me*, Beckett."

"Of course, my queen."

Goddamn but he was sexy when he got all arrogant and cheeky. And it was all done with the same level of passion he did anything. Which was only one of the reasons I loved him.

The car finally pulled into an estate somewhat like the Maxwell's manor, but it was surrounded by more fields and scrub and gardens. I could see where the wedding had been set up to the side of the house and cars were lining the driveway up and down while people milled around further down.

The butterflies set in again. Not just at the thought of meeting Beckett's dad as his actual, no-arguments girlfriend, but also because I'd be getting a glimpse of Rowan's dad. Who, if Beckett Senior was a harder and scarier version of Beckett, I assumed would be ten times worse than his son. Who was terrifying enough.

Beckett took my hand and kissed the back of it absently. My heart settled somewhat and I felt the nerves were also excitement, as well as trepidation. This would be my first proper 'society' do and I was looking forward to seeing how these people did things.

Beckett helped me out of the car and tucked my arm in his as we walked around to where the rest of the guests were assembling.

Staff weaved around with trays of drinks and food, but Beckett was on a mission to get this over with, and I didn't blame him.

"This one again?" Mr Maxwell said when he saw us, as though bored by the notion alone.

I felt Beckett stiffen his back. "*This one*," he said pointedly, "might well be the mother of your grandchildren one day, and I expect you to give her the respect she deserves."

Mr Maxwell looked me over and I saw that note of predatory lingering I'd seen the night Beckett had been drunk. It sent a shiver running down me and memories of Hunter pushing me up against the wall crashing into me. But I would not be cowed by the likes of Mr Maxwell.

"Still giving zero shits?" he asked me.

I held my own. "Yes."

He inclined his head. "Well." He sounded almost resigned. "You sold yourself short, Miss Quin."

"Oh?"

"You make a very pretty…accessory."

"I'm not sure if that's a compliment or an insult, Mr Maxwell."

"I was under the impression you didn't care what I thought?"

I swallowed hard. "I don't, but clarity is hardly concern."

"Well said." Mr Maxwell looked at his son. "She will do, but I would advise you to keep her under check." He breathed in. "I will see you both after the ceremony." As he left, he spared me one more of those uncomfortable lingering glances. "It was a compliment, by the way." Then he was gone.

A rush of breath left me, and I sank into Beckett.

"You're fucking amazing," he said, holding me tight. "Are you sure I can't convince you to find a quiet corner?"

I smirked and turned in his arms. "Is this the power I hold over the King of Rivermont Academy?" I teased. "That he just can't keep his hands off me."

He pressed the side of his head to mine, whispering into my ear, "It's not just my hands that are eager to feel you." Those very hands toyed with the skirt of my dress like he was about to drag it up around my waist and have me right there.

I shivered with excited anticipation. "What a power to have."

"The power of a queen," he purred and I felt it in my clit.

"Un-Queen, please," I teased.

He wrapped an arm around me possessively. "You've taken to the nickname."

I nodded. "I think it suits me. I feel very Alice down the rabbit hole."

"You've certainly turned my world upside down."

I shifted slightly and my hip brushed his erection. He wasn't the only one quite eager to…feel. "Tell you what," I said slowly, taking the lobe of his ear in my teeth. "You can have me if you promise no one's going to notice."

"I'm not against giving a show, baby, but not at my friend's father's wedding."

I smirked. "That's not what I meant."

I felt him nod. Then he took my hand and led me inside. If anyone guessed what he was dragging me upstairs for, they didn't show it.

"Where are we going?" I hissed.

"Rowan's room," Beckett answered as we got upstairs, and he made for a door.

"Boss?" Rowan asked as he turned from the mirror.

He was wearing nothing but his suit trousers and shoes. I saw the tattoos and the scars all over his body. There was a veritable map on there. A terrible and painful story I was dying to know. But now was not the time.

"Bathroom," Beckett said by way of explanation as he dragged me through.

Rowan looked at me, his eyebrow quirked. I gave him a dicky little wave and a smile before Beckett pulled me into the bathroom and used me to close the door behind us. Beckett looked down at me with that feral dark heat in his eyes and, God, but I loved it.

"Like he's not going to know what's about to happen in here," I sassed.

Beckett shrugged. "He'll pretend not to hear."

"Oh, you think it'll be that good?"

The dark heat got a rueful tint as he spun me and pushed my front against the vanity cupboard. We caught each other's eye in the mirror, both of us issuing a challenge the other was more than happy to meet.

Beckett shoved my dress up, bunching it at my waist. He kicked my legs apart as his fingers trailed between my legs. This was no foreplay. This was quick and dirty. Beckett made me cum in minutes, then he lifted my knee onto the vanity cupboard and was driving into me.

He gripped my hips hard. I felt the top edge of the cupboard digging into my knee, but I didn't care. I didn't even care that, for a moment, I thought I wasn't going to cum again. The whole thing was hot and I didn't need multiple orgasms every time. But then Beckett groaned my name, his head pressing into mine, his fingers on my clit again, and we came together.

Breathing hard, we caught each other's eye in the mirror again and I smiled at him. He returned the smile and I saw it mirrored deep in his eyes. He kissed my shoulder gently as he pulled out and helped my knee off the cupboard.

"Good thinking," I said. "With the bathroom."

His eyebrow rose in question.

"Easy clean up," I explained and he nodded.

"Not something I thought about when we stopped using condoms."

I pressed a kiss to his lips and couldn't help my smile.

After that first weekend at his cabin, we'd never gone back. It made some things – showers, baths, hot tubs, pools – easier. But I also now knew what Lily Allen was talking about when she sang about wet patches.

By the time we were cleaned up, Rowan wasn't in his room, so we made straight for the party. We had enough time to do a bit of mingling, but Beckett never made it as far as Rowan and I saw the looks of concern Beckett kept throwing his way.

It made me more sure that, as fucked up as Rowan was, he and Beckett were friends and, when it came down to it, they cared about each other. As much as their upbringings let them anyway.

The ceremony started and everyone took their places.

Rowan looked the most uncomfortable I'd ever seen him in his suit trousers and vest. They were dark blue, with a white shirt that was open at the collar with the sleeves rolled up. Tattoos swirled at his chest and his hair was cropped short as ever.

He wasn't the only one who looked uncomfortable.

The bride and bridesmaid looked not just uncomfortable, but just a little bit terrified.

In a soft green, Bianca looked totally different than she did at school. I had to wonder if her thick black eyeliner and her stud belts and hair in her face was a kind of armour, a mask. Because, without it, she looked small and fragile and so much less sure of herself than I'd seen her so far.

I watched her eyes flit to Rowan. Likewise, Rowan's flitted to her, and I wondered what was going on between the two of them. Knowing Rowan the way I did, I suspected he was just messing with her.

If Rowan had ever looked like he was about to bathe the whole world in blood, then this outstripped that by a long shot. He looked ready to murder every single one of us if it got him out of this heinous nonsense. I sure hoped Beckett wasn't planning on asking Rowan to be part of the bridal party.

Not that I was thinking about marrying him anytime soon.

# CHAPTER TWENTY-EIGHT

The next holidays, Beckett did take me back to his cabin. As promised, 'we' were more organised. There were extra jumpers and jackets that fit me perfectly. As well as anything else I might need, like packing a bag was beneath us.

Not that we had much cause to use them. It was even colder than it had been in April and we spent most of the week inside. Just not necessarily in bed.

A lot of time was spent in the kitchen, which I was learning was a place Beckett didn't have to force his dominance through sheer will alone. He enjoyed it there. He enjoyed cooking for me – and with me – as a more intimate and personal way of providing for someone he loved.

We watched movies and binged TV shows, sharing old favourites and finding new ones. I even convinced him to do a *Frozen* double feature. In return, I was persuaded to sit through an *IT* double feature. I accused Beckett of just wanting me glued to his side by fear, and he didn't deny it.

Jaeger brought Abby and Sam up for a couple of days, and the rest of the Royals, even Fox and Gunner, trailed for one night. Considering we were eleven teenagers with a house to ourselves, we were actually quite restrained. Which was not to say that there wasn't drinking, debauchery and shenanigans, it was just surprisingly sophisticated.

But it wasn't all playing domestication because, those holidays, Beckett also took me to meet his mum. He drove us to the country house where his father had held the Easter Ball. Although, thankfully, no one else but staff seemed to be there. We found her pottering among the veggies, smiling to herself as a well-suited guy watched over her.

"Mum?" Beckett said, and she looked up.

"Bekkie," she said, and I heard the love and warmth in her voice.

"There's someone I want you to meet, Mum," he said, as he went to help her up.

I had to look at him because his voice was totally foreign. It was soft and calm and gentle. The kind of voice you use on a small, terrified child or a wounded animal. It was reassuring and settling, and I hated to think what she'd endured for him to need to use such a tone with her.

"What day is it?" she asked him, drinking him in like she never got enough of looking at him.

"Wednesday."

Now she frowned. "You should be at school, Bekkie. Did your father make you skip?"

He smiled gently. "No. It's holidays. I brought someone to meet you."

Finally, Mrs Maxwell looked at me and I saw the emotions cross her face; question, confusion, interest, knowing.

"That's a girl, Bekkie," she whispered conspiratorially.

He fought the grin. "Yes, she is. She's my girlfriend."

She looked at him with wonder in her eyes. "A girlfriend?"

Beckett nodded and I saw the half-amused, half-annoyed

resignation in his eyes. "A girlfriend. The 'going steady', 'dating', 'one and only' kind."

"It's a pleasure to meet you, Mrs Maxwell," I said, taking a few steps towards her. "I'm Eden."

She waved her hand at me. "Call me Stella, dear. Ms. Harper if you must." She came over and took my hands in her gardening gloves. "But please, Stella."

She looked me over and I felt the absolute opposite to how Beckett Senior managed to make me feel. I felt welcome and already so loved, and for quite possibly nothing more than being with her son and – hopefully – making him happy.

"Shall we have a cup of tea? Something stronger?"

Beckett huffed a rough laugh and nodded. "Sounds good, Mum."

She prattled about her garden as we went in and waited in the sitting room for drinks. She seemed so carefree and relaxed. But then, so did Beckett and I realised this was the difference between his father's absence and presence.

A little later, Stella looked at me warmly, but with some sadness in her eyes. "I *am* sorry I missed your wedding, dear. But I…" She seemed vaugue and like she'd forgotten something. "I wasn't well."

Beckett smiled at me as he took his mum's hand. "It wasn't our wedding," he reminded her gently.

She nodded, a slight frown creasing her forehead. "No. No, of course, it wasn't." Then her eyes cleared and she looked him dead in the eye. "You'd better not have too much of your father in you to do right by this girl."

"I'm working on it."

"Well, what's holding you back?"

Beckett's smile grew. "She is."

She looked at me in pleasant surprise. "You are? Dear, you're not worried, are you?"

"About what?" I asked her.

Stella looked at Beckett, then back to me. "You don't need to. Loving Maxwell men only breaks you when they don't love you back. And, you wouldn't be here if Bekkie didn't love you."

I nodded, appreciating her openness. "I didn't say no. Just, not yet."

She looked at Beckett and pride shone in her eyes. "She's good for you, Bekkie."

He caught my eye and I saw the love in there. The love that was getting easier and easier as the days went by. "Yes, she is."

We spent the rest of the afternoon chatting and walking the grounds with Stella. She told me stories of Beckett growing up, maed sure I told her plenty in return. It was all good things and I saw that, even if their world was shadow and danger, there were good things as well. There was space for good things, and that was going make everything else worth it.

Stella convinced us to stay for dinner and, a few too many drinks later, we were staying the night. This time, I was the one who let my mum and Sam know where we were.

****

By the time term three started, nothing would ever be the same again but, this time, it wasn't a bad thing. There were still external strains on our relationship, but Beckett made sure I was still a choice. Every time. And it didn't feel hard to be together anymore.

Hunter was back after those winter holidays as well. His nose was crooked like it had been broken, and he was obviously still healing.

Even as he cut quite the tragic figure, there was no warm reception waiting for him.

But neither did he receive any more punishment. Clearly, the Royals believed that missing over two months of school after whatever beating Beckett had given him was punishment enough for his crimes. Sam wasn't quite as convinced when he and I ran into Hunter in first lesson Maths on the first day back.

"Sam. Eden." Hunter nodded carefully.

Sam looked him over. "You're back."

"Yeah," he replied slowly. "I'm back."

"Bold of you to show your face after what you did."

Hunter had the decency to look apologetic. "It was…unforgivable. I'm in counselling."

That was all very well, but I didn't really want to talk to him any longer than necessary. Just seeing him again was giving me this feeling of fight or flight and I didn't like it.

Until I heard someone clear their throat and I turned to see Jaeger posted up against the wall across from the classroom door. Security flooded me, even though I knew Jaeger was only there to look pretty, and intimidating; he wasn't actually going to do anything.

Weirdly, Fox was beside him.

As Sam and I gave Hunter a cordial nod goodbye and walked away, Jaeger and Fox fell into step with us.

"What's this?" Sam joked. "Apprenticeship?"

"You could call it that," Jaeger said evenly.

I stopped and the boys all stopped to look at me. "But Fox is the heir, not a…bodyguard."

"Who better to guard our king's queen than the heir," Jaeger said.

"Queen Regent, more like," Fox said and there was the smallest hint of warmth in his eyes, like he was okay with the idea he might not get the crown after all.

"What?" I huffed. "Because I'll rule in Beckett's stead?" The idea was honestly laughable.

"I don't see why not." Clearly Fox didn't agree.

"Is this you making amends, then?" I asked him, not sure I trusted him at all.

Fox inclined his head. "It's me trying."

I nodded. "Well, I guess I can let you try," I said.

After all, we were all still kids really. Prone to making heinously poor decisions. Maybe Fox could still have his redemption, too.

And that was when it hit me.

Is Fox had the potential for redemption, then maybe he wasn't the only one. There was no way I could redeem them all in the eighteen months I had left at school. Four of them were graduating in like five months anway. So, if I couldn't bring down the institution in my time at Rivermont, and I wasn't yet sure that I could rely on the next generation to help me, then I was going to have to extend my time at Rivermont.

Which left me with one option.

Teaching.

I was going to do teaching at uni.

Someone had to try to break down the system that was the Royals, and the only teachers the school hired were Rivermont alum, unless you were Olympic-level good at something. And I was very decidedly not Olympic-level good at anything. Unless you included the ability to bring kings like Beckett to their knees.

But I would be Rivermont alumni and I, for one, wouldn't stand for the Royals' bullshit. Which, actually, made me excited for university applications for the first time in my life. Even if they were a year away, I was looking forward to it.

It was a plan, and I wouldn't forget the end goal, but I still have eighteen months left of school to enjoy while I tried to break down over a century of tradition.

I wanted to believe it said a lot about Beckett's control over the school that him wearing a waistcoat and tie to match my dress to the formal had the rest of the Royals following suit instead of tormenting us for being juvenile. And I was sure it did. But I was also under no delusions that the Royals accepted their new Un-Queen on more than face value.

But none of them were stepping out of line anymore and they kept all their snide comments as criticisms amongst themselves. So, I guess step one was complete? Not that I really cared about being accepted by those idiots. I did, though, care that my relationship with Beckett wasn't made even harder than it had to be.

Which it wasn't, especially when it was just the two of us alone. And he made sure it was just the two of us alone as often as possible.

After all, we had our whole lives to work out how to live in the real world together. Side by side in both his world and mine. But it was getting easier every day.

**The King's cleaner. The good girl playing bad girl. And a price not usually paid between stepsiblings.**

Rowan's up next, and this one gets DARK. A stepsibling, enemies-to-lovers story where two broken souls have the chance to learn that love doesn't just exist but is possible for people like them.

Get it here: https://books2read.com/u/meKQLR

# THE RIVERMONT ROYALS

If you liked *Reign*, share the love and let me know! While Beckett and Eden's story is a standalone, there are seven more stories to tell. All the Royals and the Quintet are getting their own HEA.

You can also get fill-in novellas from Jaeger's POV – the Rivermont Royals Reveals, starting with the prequel, *Obsess*, that covers Jaeger's opinion of the first time Beckett sees Eden, and the four-year obsession that ignites.

# LITTLE NYMPH

If you liked *Reign*, you might also enjoy *Little Nymph*. A New Adult darker, enemies-to-lovers, mafia romance, perfet for fans of *365 Days*. Get it here: https://books2read.com/u/bW0GdW

*From Elizabeth Stevens, writing as E.J. Knox, comes…*

**Forbidden lust, a marriage pact, and the dangerous secret that could ruin it all.**

My job is simple; protect Olive. Whatever she needs. Including spending the summer with the family of her intended fiancé.

Mav Vitali is anything but simple. Olive's future husband. Heir to his father's crime empire, he's as deadly as he is gorgeous.

I have one job. One. Goddamned. Job. My life is hers. So, of course I fall head over heels into lust at first sight with Mav.

I could have resisted – he's an arsehole, after all – if the feeling hadn't been mutual. And it takes just one inadvisable kiss for him to decide I will be his at any cost. Luckily, Olive's had more spark with a wet towel but, when a stalker comes after her, we've all got other things on our minds.

To save her, I'll have to team up with the man I love to hate. As the stalker grows closer, so do we. But what price will we pay to be together?

# GODS & ANGELS

If you liked *Reign*, you might also enjoy *Gods & Angels*. A New Adult darker, high school, bully romance. Book 3 is coming soon! Get it here: https://books2read.com/u/38yaGw

*From Elizabeth Stevens, writing as E.J. Knox, comes…*

**A ruthless god. A sinful angel. And the princess between them.**

My life is perfect. My life is planned. My life isn't mine.
Promised to a man I love. A man I hate. Not even a man. A god.
Apollo Callahan is that and much more.

My life is broken. My life is fractured. My life isn't free.
Craving a man I hate. A man I need. Not even a man. An angel.
Valen Kincaid is nothing I could ever want.

Though the Saints rule the hallowed halls of Saint Benedict's College, they're anything but saintly. Behind closed doors, they call themselves the Sinners. Sex. Fast Cars. Drugs. Money. The odd assassination or two. Nothing is beneath them, except the next in a long line of women. Can one little princess, searching to break free from her prison tower, bring these mighty lords crashing to their knees?

The stunning first book in the Sinners of Saint Benedicts series.

# PRINCE OF THORNS

If you liked *Reign*, you might also enjoy *Prince of Thorns*. A New Adult darker, enemies-to-lovers, academy, gang romance. Get it here: https://books2read.com/u/bryaD7

*From Elizabeth Stevens, writing as E.J. Knox, comes…*

**The bad boy willing to risk everything – even his life – to get the girl.**

People call them the V.I.C.E.S. because they'll wring you for everything you are and leave you ruined. They are the Princes of Rosewood Hall, and no one says no to them. Until now.

Vaughn Saint. The racer. He dubbed the Prince of Thorns. Pretty as a rose, but one touch and he'll leave you bleeding.

He chases death on two wheels at least twice a week. Used to controlling powerful things between his thighs, nothing is more powerful than the lure of the pleasures he promises.

And he wants to give them all to me. Only problem? I'm the daughter of the leader of the Blood Roses. His leader. I'm off-limits. Dad wants me to walk away from all that, not get dragged down deeper into their hell, but Vaughn Saint threatens to take me to the very depths and still have me begging for more. Loving me will kill him.

Not loving me will destroy the both of us..

Thank you so much for reading this story! Word of mouth is super valuable to authors. So, if you have a few moments to rate/review Beckett and Eden's story – or, even just pass it on to a friend – I would be really appreciative.

Have you looked for my books in store, or at your local or school library and can't find them? Just let your friendly staff member or librarian know that they can order copies directly from LightningSource/Ingram.

If you want to keep up to date with my new releases, rambles and writing progress, sign up to my newsletter at https://landing.mailerlite.com/webforms/landing/y1n6q2.

You can find the playlist for *the Rivermont Royals* on Spotify:
I also have a generic writing playlist you can check out ☺

Follow me:

# THANKS

This book was only about three years in the making, lol. This was my first ever fully-formed bully romance idea and I have Beckett to thank for setting me on this path of utter decadence and shenanigans. I absolutely love writing these stories and I really feel invigorated to write again, which is so lovely after the last couple of years.

First and foremost thanks go to Kaity, who is always ready for the next chapter, and whose brainstorming is not only invaluable but also responsible for the Rivermont Royal Reveals and a lot of the goodness in these books.

Thanks, too, go to Charny for letting me blather about every new idea I have, and who champions me every step of the way, even when she's moving interstate. Miss you 3000, babes.

Thank you to my parents and in-laws for the child-minding so I could get back to work, even with the never-ending infection making me so damned slow.

A massive thank you to my husband, as always, just for being you even if you didn't really have a specific impact on this particular book other than existing and being awesome.

# MY BOOKS

E.J.'s list is firing up. While you wait for the next release, you can find where to buy all my books in print and eBook at the website; www.elizabethstevens.com.au/ej-knox.

# ABOUT THE AUTHOR

E.J. Knox is the Darker/Bully Romance penname of Elizabeth Stevens. E.J. is the name to read if you want darker/bully romance in the Mature YA/NA crossover space. Think high school, college, and academy. E.J. brings my usual wit, banter, and repartee in good old enemies-to-lovers showdowns between alpha males and the sassy heroines strong enough to knock them down a peg or two. There'll be fake-dating, love triangles, kidnapping and danger, second chances, and more.

Writer. Reader. Perpetual student. Nerd.

Born in New Zealand to a Brit and an Australian, I am a writer with a passion for all things storytelling. I love reading, writing, TV and movies, gaming, and spending time with family and friends. I am an avid fan of British comedy, superheroes, and SuperWhoLock. I have too many favourite books, but I fell in love with reading after Isobelle Carmody's *Obernewtyn*. I am obsessed with all things mythological – my current focus being old-style Irish faeries. I live in Adelaide (South Australia) with my long-suffering husband, delirious dog, mad cat, two chickens, and a lazy turtle.

<u>Contact me:</u>
*Email:* ejknox@elizabethstevens.com.au
*Website*: www.elizabethstevens.com.au/ej-knox
*Twitter*: www.twitter.com/writer_iz
*Instagram:* www.instagram.com/writeriz
*Facebook*: https://www.facebook.com/elizabethstevens88/

www.ingramcontent.com/pod-product-compliance
Lightning Source LLC
Chambersburg PA
CBHW010547170726
48285CB00011B/2786

9 781925 928273